Burden of Memory

Also by Vicki Delany
Scare the Light Away

Burden of Memory

Vicki Delany

Poisoned Pen Press

Poisoned Pen Press
6962 E. First Ave., Ste. 103
Scottsdale, AZ 85251
www.poisonedpenpress.com
info@poisonedpenpress.com

Printed in the United States of America

mys
Delany.v.

To my father, John Hartley Cargo.
Who put on his pajamas.

Acknowledgments

Thanks to Carol Lem, Julia Vryheid, Jan Toms, Karen Mitchell, and Gail Cargo for their help, advice, and enthusiasm.

And to Pat and Roy Ashforth for welcoming me many times to their own slice of Muskoka heaven, and for boat tours of Millionaires' Row.

Prologue

September 1939

It had been a mistake, a bad one, telling the old man. Better to have kept it between the young one and herself. Her mother would be cursing her, if she could, screaming and turning all red in the face, pulling at her hair, pacing in front of the fire, the latest howling baby clenched in her scrawny arms.

But her mother hadn't lived, had she? The last one had killed her. Killed her and himself as well, the fool. Her mother cursed God and His mother as she died. Amy was the oldest, it was up to her to clean up the mess and call Father O'Malley—who did come, right away, to the girls' surprise. And offered genuine sorrow at the deaths. He was a great comfort to her sisters, but not to her, Amy, the eldest. What comfort could anyone find in such a death?

Her father, however, remained in his usual seat at the King Street bar, even after she stopped there with the news, drinking until his eyeballs fairly floated. Spending what little was left of his thin pay packet on all who gathered to drink to his wife's death. Amy and her sisters would clean up, they assured him. They were good girls, and isn't that what good practical girls were for?

She shook her head: enough remembering. Think on the here and now. She had never been a "good" girl, but she always prided herself on being a practical one. This was an excellent position: The food plentiful and good—meat, milk and eggs, fresh bread, crisp vegetables, not the half rotted ones the staff had been served at her last situation—the bed warm and soft, the mistress not too harsh. The younger girls were spoiled and rude and difficult. But she had lived with much worse. Too bad that the oldest daughter wasn't with the family more. She was kind.

Stupid thoughts. She had only herself to blame. Too practical this time. Everything ruined by foolish ambition. If she had told the young one, and him alone, things would be all right, wouldn't they? He would take care of it all. He had piles of money, what else mattered?

She pulled the curtains aside and peeked out. Not that there was anything to see. The drapes had been pulled down from the nursery at the big house years ago, when the children started to grow and wanted something more grownup. So her room received the curtains adorned with the yellow dolls with the blue hair, who played in the wildflower meadow in pretty frocks with flowing ribbons and smiling faces. But the drapes were thick and blocked the light and the worst of the cold, so who was she to care what childish fantasy the fabric mocked?

She loved her little room. She had it all to herself—the family were short staffed this year and had no need for nannies any more. A poor servant girl, daughter of rough Irish immigrants, she had never had a room all to herself before. The luxury was incomparable. Her only regret was that there was no view of the lake from her window. That would be truly wonderful—to watch the play of light on the water from her own bedroom.

She had never been to Ireland, she had never seen the open, storm tossed, angry sea. But she still wanted to. She had sat enraptured as her mother spun words as she spun the cloth beneath her fingers. Her thick accent relating the long tales of her childhood: tales of the dark sea and the cursed, pagan creatures that lived there. And the beauty that was the soft green land beyond.

She would be happy here, if only she had been able to see the open waters of the lake. But her tiny window looked out on the dark forest. The foreboding, enclosing, primitive Canadian forest. She hated it and always would.

She had never been to Ireland. Never touched what her mother called *the sacred soil.* But she had promised her mother that she would make the trip one day. Alone among the numerous siblings, she had absorbed her mother's wild tales of the Emerald Isle and dreamt of the day that she would return. Drenched in diamonds and fine silks she would sweep upon the condescending charity school and the arrogant church that had between them conspired to destroy her mother's soul and, full of pride and arrogance, she would announce her name and the name of her mother. She would tease them with alms and offers of donations and then withdraw the offer at the last moment. They would crawl in the dust (was there dust in Ireland? Probably not. Her mother spoke only of rain upon endless rain and lush green fields). They would crawl in the mud and she would laugh and offer a few scraps of her benevolence. Leaving them hopeful that she would return another day.

Once again, she cursed her wandering, dreaming mind (a gift, that was sometimes a blight, from her mother, weaver of words) and forced her thoughts back to her immediate concern. How could she have made such a mistake? Daring to confront the old man? How could she have been so proud, so vain and foolishly unafraid? Her mother had told her many stories of the landlords back in Ireland, the evil English men. And as she related the tales, old and new, the bitter, hot, salty tears fell on top of her daughter's red head.

But all was for naught and her daughter had forgotten.

It was near dark. Night came late at this time of year, this far north. But not as far north as the Emerald Isle her mother spoke of every day of her life.

The family in the big house they called a cottage had finally settled down, to read or write letters or play cards. Dinner over, the cook and her helpers collapsed by the scarred table with thick chipped mugs of sweet tea. And at last she had been free to escape to her own little room. Finished for another day.

She let the curtains drop and walked to the table where she kept her few belongings. She unscrewed the top on a bottle of cologne he had bought her, touched the open end to her index finger and dabbed the moisture behind her ears and at the throbbing pulse in her throat.

This was the only present he had ever given her. He didn't want anyone to wonder how she could afford anything too "nice."

Footsteps on the path. Kicking last year's dead leaves out of the way. The dog was with him, chasing squirrels and chipmunks through the woods.

It would be war soon they said. Even after the horrors of the last one, the men's eyes glowed with the excitement of it. The women, young and old, rich and poor, loved or not, those with and those without, knew that the men were all fools.

It was time. The footsteps had stopped. She stood tall, braced her thin shoulders and placed one hand over her belly with a memory of the prayer she had abandoned as her mother died.

Chapter One

A chipmunk dashed out from the shelter of the undergrowth directly into Elaine's path. From high above, an enormous dark bird swooped silently over the roadway on wide, serrated wings, and snatched the animal in its heavy talons. The pert little mouth stretched into a death scream. The hawk watched Elaine where she sat, shocked, in the illusionary safety of her red BMW. The hawk grinned at the prospect of the meal to come, and perhaps in enjoyment of the crushing of a life in its powerful claws.

In the days to come Elaine would replay the scene in her mind. Over and over.

The hawk and its prey disappeared behind a line of naked trees without a sound.

Unsure of where she was going, Elaine had been driving so cautiously that a gentle nudge of the pedal sufficed to slow the car down. She pulled over to the side of the dusty road and took a deep breath.

As her heartbeat returned to normal, she checked the scribbled directions one more time. After several false turns, at long last this looked as if it might actually be the place she wanted. A handcrafted sign had been nailed to an old pine tree on the other side of the road with the single word *Madison* written on it in flowery green script.

A narrow driveway ran under the tree, and beside it sat a hand-made wooden garbage bin freshly painted gray with a cheerful green trim—the sign and box that she had been told would be her signposts.

She switched the CD player off in mid-song—leaving Springsteen dancing in the dark no longer—shifted into gear and pulled into the lane. It was narrow, but paved and in good condition.

Once she left the main road the forest closed like a cape around her. Primitive, untamed northern forest that had never seen a chainsaw or shovel. Large boulders mottled ancient white and gray littered the landscape, some of them cut into pieces under the unrelenting, ruthless work of time, water and ice—nature showing off her power. Trees stretched high overhead where they tried to link arms. Branches reached out and scratched a warning on the sides of the car; long grasses stroked the undercarriage with a seductive whisper. Elaine cringed at the thought of her paint job, but the red car handled the steep hill and sharp curves with ease. It was much more car than she could afford, but in one all-out show of bravado she had sunk a good portion of her divorce settlement into the purchase. The car purred as it crested a sharp rise, and she patted the dash with affection.

The lane was long, very long. But at its end the driveway burst out of the shadows and returned to the warmth of the sun, widening to create enough space for a convoy of cars. A rusty old pick-up truck sat beside a shiny green van with handicap plates. A gust of wind blew a snowfall of brown and yellow leaves across the open yard. They swirled to a stop against the garage door, joining the season's residue already piled in the nooks and crannies of the outbuildings and against rocks and massive tree trunks.

Elaine stepped out of the car and breathed in both the air and the view. She pushed the image of tiny black rodent eyes open wide in shock to the back of her mind.

She only caught the briefest glimpse of a wide gray building the color of a northern lake on a cool, cloudy summer's day, trimmed with dark forest green, empty terracotta pots, abandoned for the season, and a flash of sunlight on blue water, before the door flew open and a short, stout woman bustled out.

"For heaven's sake, Mrs. Benson, don't stand there gaping. You're late enough as it is," Ruth Czarnecki scolded, her voice tinged with panic, truly felt. "Leave your bags. Someone will get them. I told you she doesn't like to be kept waiting. Didn't you listen?" She virtually shooed Elaine into the cottage.

"Miss Madison expects punctuality above all things," Ruth huffed, leading the way. The door led through what had no doubt been a mudroom in the years when the cottage overflowed with children and weekend guests. It had since been demoted to the storage of a collection of old coats, gumboots, and umbrellas.

Ruth led the way down a long corridor, walking at a brisk clip. The passageway was dark, in the style of grand old hotels. The floors were hardwood, ancient and worn. A very old, very threadbare, and probably very expensive oriental rug ran down the center of the hallway. Elaine resisted the urge to drop to her knees and run her fingers across the fine wood and inspect the quality of the carpet. The walls were also wood, stained dark. In the middle of the day it was necessary to have lights lit in the wall sconces scattered along the hallway.

A collection of small oil paintings dotted the walls. The style of several of the paintings was familiar and she was sure that if she had a minute, and better light, she could identify them. Ruth stopped so abruptly that Elaine, entranced by the pictures, almost tripped over her. The housekeeper straightened her shoulders and tugged at the sides of her immaculate black dress. Taking a deep breath she raised one hand and knocked firmly. Without waiting for an answer, she pushed the heavy wooden door open and gestured to Elaine to precede her.

"You're late," the old woman seated in the wheelchair said. Her voice cracked with age but it was still deep and powerful. A voice that expected to be listened to.

"By," Elaine said as she examined her watch with great care, "ten minutes. Not bad considering that there was an accident on the 400 and the highway was closed for a good few hours."

Behind her she felt more than heard Ruth pull in her breath.

Miss Moira Madison laughed. "But late none the less. Not acceptable when I was young. My grandfather would have dismissed you out of hand. But things have changed, and most of them for the better, I believe. Come, sit over here and we can talk. Ruth, you can leave us. Ask Lizzie to have tea ready in half an hour."

"But Miss Madison…."

"Thank you, Ruth." Also a voice that tolerated no "buts." The door shut firmly.

"I like you already, Mrs. Benson," the old lady said. "Sit down and tell me why I should let you into my life."

Elaine sat. Moira Madison was tiny. She couldn't be much over five feet, and probably weighed less than a supermodel after a bout of stomach flu. The hands that rested on the armrests of her wheelchair were gnarled with arthritis, resembling claws more than strong human hands, the fingers looking as if they would snap as easily as matchsticks. The proud face was deeply lined and dotted with liver spots and the gray hair was sparse, almost bald in patches. But her deep brown eyes blazed with intelligence, and Elaine told herself not to underestimate this woman simply because she was old. Incongruously Miss Madison was dressed in khaki cargo pants and a beige T-shirt that proclaimed the purchaser had planted a tree in Africa (or at least donated towards one).

"I have read your books," Miss Madison said, nodding to the little pile stacked on the desk in front of her. "And I enjoyed them a great deal."

Goldrush was on top with *Into the Bush* peeking out from underneath.

"Thank you."

"But they are old, are they not? Not as old as I might be, but old for the publishing world?"

"Indeed," Elaine said, uncomfortable defending her work. "I haven't had anything published for a while. But they're still in print," she hurried to add. "And *Goldrush* is being considered for use as a high school history book. Or so I've been told."

"In Hollywood they say that you are only as good as your last picture. Is that true in publishing as well?"

"What do you want me to say, Miss Madison?" Elaine bristled. "Those two biographies were great successes, I'm proud of them. But I turned my attentions elsewhere and didn't receive similar recognition. That's all."

The old lady chuckled. "Fame is fleeting indeed. Tell me what you turned your attentions to then?"

"My husband is…was…a screenwriter. He…we…believed that there was a good deal more to be gained by writing popular movies than biographies of pioneer Canadian women. The last few years I concentrated on doing research and editing his screenplays."

"So why are you here, then? Without your husband? At my little cottage on Lake Muskoka, instead of delighting in the glamorous life in Hollywood?"

"Are you aware, Miss Madison, that it is against the law to enquire of a prospective employee any details of her personal life? We are veering close to that line. I've applied for the job of assisting you with your memoirs. You've seen my resume and read my work. If that isn't enough, then perhaps I should take my leave sooner rather than later, and save us both some time."

The old lady laughed a deep rich belly laugh that had her shaking in her chair. Her chest heaved and she patted it rapidly with one frail, vein-lined hand.

Elaine rose to her feet, wondering if she should rush for help. She didn't want Miss Madison to collapse right in the midst of dismissing her. But she waved a thin hand in the air, indicating that Elaine should sit, and gradually collected her composure.

"Oh, my dear. That is so good. Of course you are right to remind me of my legal obligations. Sit down, sit down."

Elaine sat.

"I went for a job interview once, when I was first looking for a position as a nurse, and the hospital administrator, a male of course, actually asked me if I had ever had intimate relations with a man. I was young then, so young, and times were so different. When I was a child I had to help feed my brother, I told him, when his arm was in a cast. The result of falling out of the apple tree."

Elaine laughed.

"Oh, you can laugh, young woman," Miss Madison said, smiling. "But I had no idea what the lecherous old fool was asking. And that is why I want to get it all on paper, before it's too late. You may find it funny, but I honestly didn't understand why that man wanted me to take off my blouse in order to continue with the interview. Although I did know quite enough to decide that it was time to leave. I had plenty of money, of course, and all the arrogance that came with it, but I have wondered since what a frightened young woman, with few prospects and desperate for a job, would have found herself coerced into doing.

"Anyway, my dear, I obtained another position and then at the start of the war joined the Canadian Army Nursing Sisters and I learned soon enough what intimate relations are. And thus I would like you to help me write it all down."

Elaine smiled at her. "Do you mean that I have the job, Miss Madison?"

"Indeed, you do. But only if you refuse to call me Miss Madison. I do wish that everyone who lives here would call me Moira. It is my name, after all. You may not believe it, but there are still people who remain firmly stuck in the old social structure, and not all of them are the employers."

"Moira, it is, then."

A subtle knock and the door opened to admit Ruth pushing a small trolley bearing an enormous silver tray, complete with matching teapot and milk and sugar bowls. They were accompanied by three sets of antique cups and saucers, painted the most delicate blue with a rim of soft yellow flowers. Small sandwiches, tiny pastries, and what appeared to be real homemade scones with clotted cream occupied a matching three-tiered cake tray.

Elaine struggled to contain her excitement. The traditional English ritual of afternoon tea was her idea of heaven.

Ruth placed the tray on the table beside Moira and arranged the food on the antique desk closer to Elaine. She backed up to a chair, tucked her dress under her ample bottom, and lowered herself as if to sit.

Moira coughed. "We are not quite finished with this interview, Ruth. Perhaps today you can take tea with Lizzie."

Ruth flushed to the roots of her over-dyed black hair and stumbled awkwardly to her feet. Mumbling hideously contrived apologies, she hurried from the room.

Moira smiled at Elaine. "Would you please pour, dear? I am afraid that my hands find it to be a bit of a chore these days."

A trembling Elaine poured the tea into the delicate cups. She had an extensive collection of teacups herself, and she was knowledgeable enough to recognize the quality that she held in her hands. At a nod from her hostess she added a splash of milk. Moira declined sandwiches, scones, or cakes.

Elaine served herself and sighed happily. She lifted her teacup up to admire it. "This is a beautiful set."

"My grandmother on my mother's side brought the service over from Ireland when she came to Canada to be married."

Elaine almost dropped her cup in terror. Then she gripped it so tightly it was in danger of shattering.

Moira swallowed a secret grin. "If you appreciate the history of my family things, my dear, I have a feeling that you will appreciate the history of my family and me. I trust you can stay." It was not a question.

"I would be delighted to."

"Good. We'll begin tomorrow. Ruth will discuss terms of payment with you and you can sign a bit of a contract. If you're uncomfortable living here, you are certainly welcome to seek accommodation elsewhere, but there isn't anything close at hand."

"I am sure I'll be happy here." Elaine helped herself to a scone and topped it with a dab of cream.

"Good." Moira smiled. Her teeth were badly stained and fitted poorly in her large mouth. A surprise, considering the kind of money this family had. "The first thing you'll want to do is to have a look at the boxes in the old guesthouse. Alan will show you where they are. I have saved practically every letter I ever received. You will doubtless even find a few dressmakers' bills, as well. And a great many letters that I wrote but never sent. I was a terrible one for writing all my feelings down in a frenzy of emotion. But come the cold light of day, I would recover my wits and could never get around to posting the silly things."

She sipped her tea and smiled at the memory of her younger self.

Elaine shivered with biographer's delight and selected a salmon sandwich, the bread cut so thin it was almost transparent.

Tea finished, Ruth was summoned by a press of a bell to show Elaine to her room.

"Just one more thing," Moira said as Elaine got to her feet. "Can you swim?"

"Can I swim?" What an extraordinary question. "Quite well, actually. I was on the swim team at University. Breaststroke mainly. I won some medals. Why do you ask?"

"No reason. I'll see you at dinner."

"When I originally applied for this position, I was rejected," Elaine said, as a tight-lipped Ruth showed her to her room at the end of the second floor corridor. "You wrote and told me that someone else had been hired. What happened to her?"

Ruth shrugged. "Does it matter?"

"It matters if she quit because she felt that she couldn't do the job expected of her."

"That wasn't the case. She died."

"She died!"

"Drowned in the lake her first week on the job. Dinner is at seven. Be on time."

◇◇◇

Elaine was given an enormous bedroom at the front of the cottage, overlooking the expanse of lake and the fiery display of the gentle, rolling hills beyond. The room had been decorated in typical Canadian cottage rustic: good wooden furniture, colorful area rugs, a bright handmade quilt on the huge bed, a bookcase bulging with well-handled old classics and crisp modern biographies. Television, VCR, phone, and a computer complete with printer and permanent high-speed Internet connection seemed quite out of place, but welcome nonetheless.

Elaine sank onto the bed and bounced a few times to test the springs. She could scarcely believe her luck. Although her luck, according to Ruth, had come at a high cost to someone else. But no matter—she was here now. This place was called a cottage, but to any normal person it would pass as a mansion. It was old, probably as old as any other place on the Muskoka Lakes. A remnant of the days when wealthy Torontonians and New Yorkers, with full retinues of children, relatives, and assorted hangers-on, would come north on the train, preceded by an entire network of servants who traveled ahead to ensure that all was in order when the family arrived. In those days, before a network of roads and driveways linked every property to the community, they would catch a lake steamer and be deposited, each group, right at the foot of their own dock. Wives and children, the occasional mistress and all the servants, would spend the summer here, from June through to September, and the "head of the family" would enjoy his bachelorhood back in the city and travel up on weekends to join them.

The bed found to be more than satisfactory, Elaine unpacked in haste, unable to control her impatience to explore more of the old home and property. She stopped in front of her wide window and drank in the panorama. Tough working conditions. Thick storm clouds the color and consistency of steel wool were gathering behind the hills across the lake and moving fast in the wake of heavy winds, and the lake tossed tiny whitecaps in agitation. The tree-covered hills beyond were wrapped in a frenzy of color. Orange, yellow, and auburn, as well as all the shades of green so beloved of nature and the limitless possibilities of red-to-black.

Elaine slipped into her hiking boots, anxious to explore a bit of the property before the fury of the storm crashed down upon them.

The house was multi-storied. A wide flight of stairs in the center led down to the main hall. A device for transporting Moira's wheelchair was attached to the staircase. Stern and forbidding Madison ancestors eyed Elaine as she made her way down the stairs. She could feel their disapproval. She was an interloper, an outsider. She didn't belong here, the pictures told her, not in the family wing. If she had any place at all, it was with the servants.

One portrait spoke to her so forcefully that she half expected to see the painted lips move. She stopped at the bottom step and faced him. He was dressed in a severe woolen suit, tie knotted tightly enough to cause the ample flesh on the neck to bulge around it. Tiny black eyes, bulbous red nose and perpendicular ears were almost caricatures. Almost but not quite. Without knowing how she could be so sure, Elaine knew that the artist had hated the subject, hated him with a passion. But he needed the commission. And so proud was this Madison ancestor that he was either not aware of the animosity or considered it to be of no consequence.

"That's Mr. Augustus Madison, the man who built this place." Elaine started at the voice. Ruth stood at the bottom of the steps, also staring at the portrait, her eyes unfocused and distant. "Long before my time, of course. He was Miss Moira Madison's grandfather. A pillar of North American industry. A true visionary."

"Really? How nice."

Deep circles the color and consistency of used tea bags underlined Ruth's eyes, and time had carved sharp crevices into the delicate skin of her throat and around her mouth. The harsh black hair and the glimmer of dislike in her small shrewd eyes accented every crease. She stood firm, arms crossed, blocking the steps, her expression indicating that she had swallowed something exceptionally unpleasant.

Ruth said nothing, but neither did she step aside. She filled the wide staircase simply by her refusal to move. Elaine sucked in her stomach and slithered against the polished wood of the banister. "Going for a walk," she explained where no explanation was needed. "Get a bit of air. Feels like a storm's about to settle in."

Ruth's hostile eyes followed Elaine as she walked down the hall and out the front door.

The instant she saw the view, Elaine was in love. A wide deck wrapped itself around the front of the building. In contrast to the aged stone and wood cottage, the deck was of modern style and materials: stained wooden floor, Plexiglas fronting tucked inside a blond wood frame. The deck was bare and empty, deserted in preparation for the long winter ahead. But in her mind's eye Elaine could see it coming alive with sun umbrellas the color of tropical parrots, matching cushions on comfortable lounge chairs, terracotta pots overflowing with radiant blooms of petunias and impatiens, small tables holding bowls of black olives and mixed nuts. And relaxed, sun-kissed bodies, toweling off warm lake water, laughing and reaching for cocktails.

She looked over the edge of the deck. Wooden steps were braced against the solid rock of the Canadian Shield to lead down the hill to a flagstone path, which meandered casually along the water's edge, as if it had nowhere in particular to go. Beside the steps an electric wheelchair ramp cast a discordant modern note into the ancient beauty of stone and wood, trees and water. A wide dock extended a good distance out over the water, and to the right of the dock there were two enormous boathouses, painted the same gray and green as the house, both closed tight against the encroaching cold. Lonely empty window boxes, green to match the trim, snoozed in the wide windows waiting for the renewing touch of spring sun. A staircase curved up the side of the largest of the boathouses, leading to a second story and the flat roof above. Everything was in immaculate condition. Not a fleck of loose paint, chipped wood, or misplaced weed could be seen.

Beyond the boathouses, across a narrow strait, sat a tiny island. A thick barrier of pine and hemlock flowed down to the boulders at the water's edge. It boasted no signs of a dock or cottage, even of a clearing, but two rowboats were pulled up onto a bare outcropping of rock and a single column of smoke curled up from under the trees to blend into the storm-cloud gray.

The path running along the water's edge ended at a clump of old white pine and undergrowth so thick that it blocked any view of what lay beyond. Elaine walked forward, narrowing her eyes in an attempt to peer through the curtain of foliage.

The air, heavy with moisture, swirled before her eyes. She blinked. A strange smell rose around her. Perfume. Cheap perfume. Applied with much too heavy a hand.

Through the mist and beyond the trees she saw a cabin. A neat, freshly painted cabin, nestled in the thick woods. Small but clean. Someone's home. She saw a young, red-headed woman absent-mindedly stroking her flat belly and pacing in front of the window and Elaine sensed that the young woman was consumed with worry that she had made a mistake, a terrible mistake.

One drop of rain landed on Elaine's nose. Her eyes flew open. The cabin, the pacing woman, the scent of perfume were gone. Leaving only the trees.

A standing-up dream. How amazing was that?

Enough exploring for today. She pushed the strange image out of her mind and dashed for shelter.

Chapter Two

Moira Madison watched Elaine Benson stroll along the path beside the lakefront. The young woman stopped and held her arms out to her sides and took several deep breaths. Moira smiled to herself. The land was working its charm.

As with the first woman she'd hired as her biographer, the one who had come to such a tragic end not more than a few yards from where Elaine was now standing, Moira wondered how much to reveal. All she wanted from her biography was an account of the war years and after and what life was like for a nurse in those days. But any biographer worth her salt would expect more than a dull recitation of facts and dates; she would want to get at the feelings and emotions lying just out of sight, the ones too private to be freely committed to paper. Moira had initially rejected Elaine Benson's application, and instead hired Donna Smithton, because she feared that she would find herself revealing more than she wanted to the woman who had written *Goldrush* with such passion for her subjects. Donna seemed so much safer—more academic.

But Donna's sudden, tragic death seemed like a rebuke to Moira, and so she had returned to her first choice.

Outside, Elaine picked up a small rock and tossed it into the lake, probably just to hear the sound of it hitting the water. Moira closed her eyes and remembered.

◇◇◇

"I will not be sick. I will not be sick. I am a Madison and I refuse to disgrace myself." The nursing sister clung to the rails of the rusty old ship and with the force of her not inconsiderable will calmed the heaving in her stomach. She hadn't eaten a thing since they'd left Halifax three days earlier, and she was starting to fear that she would never eat again. Through the deep gloom of the North Atlantic she could only vaguely make out the shifting shapes of their escorts. Keeping pace with the defenseless old ship, one destroyer on either side watched over them. The rest of the convoy was strung out ahead. No lights marked their passing. Merely a displacement of the darkness, an unusual ripple in the timeless rolling pattern of the waves.

It was full, impenetrable dark. The all-encompassing dark, which the sailors liked the best, a cloud cover so thick there was not a glimmer of moon or stars. Three days out of Halifax and to the nurse it felt more like three months. Ten more days to go. If only she could live that long. The convoy zigzagged across the North Atlantic headed for Liverpool. They were an old ship, bound for England and the war, but so far the only casualties were soldiers and nurses hurling up their innards and cursing the power of the sea with every feeble breath. They slept in their clothes with life jacket and essentials constantly at hand in case of attack by enemy submarines.

Despite her misery, she managed a weak smile at the memory of her new-found friend Susan, a plain, plump girl from Saskatoon, Saskatchewan, who, the first night at sea, had demurely slipped into a frothy nightgown all ready for a good night's sleep in the hard, narrow bunk. The nightgown was fabulously expensive, although Susan didn't appear to have money. It must have been a gift, a farewell to a beloved daughter or niece leaving for war. A dream of cream satin brimming with pure white lace and pale yellow bows. How Matron had carried on at the sight of it. Hadn't they been told they would have one minute to get up on deck for the lifeboats in case the ship was hit? And if so how did she expect to survive in the North Atlantic in that garment?

At least they were part of a convoy. It was rumored that the first ships had set out unescorted.

After the passage of several lifetimes on a shifting, watery world, they docked in Liverpool. The Nursing Sisters staggered off the ship, some of the girls as gray as the winter's snows on a cloudy Toronto day, others down ten or more pounds from the start of their ordeal. Moira had never thought that the solid earth could feel so good. With scarcely time to think, much less notice their surroundings, they were loaded onto a train heading for London. She had assumed that they would have comfortable coach seats at the very least, even private compartments if they were terribly lucky. A relaxing train journey with well prepared, nourishing food would go a long way to help them recover from the sea voyage.

Instead the train was a madhouse. It was bad enough on the platform, crowds pushing and shoving. Soldiers and sailors in British uniforms were clinging to sobbing wives or girlfriends. Many of them with crowds of confused children clutching at their knees. Those from other countries, Canadians, Australians, South Africans, New Zealanders, as well as a myriad of uniforms she didn't recognize, milled about in confusion. The air rang with a biblical cacophony of languages and indecipherable accents. The Nursing Sisters followed Matron in a neat line, their traditional crisp white veil a sharp contrast to the sea of Army khaki, Navy and Air Force blue, and traveler's gray.

Bad as the train station was, the train itself was a nightmare. Every available place, and a great many not available, was taken. Soldiers sat on the floor or leaned up against the doors, their rifles and kit at their feet if they couldn't find room in the overflowing luggage bins. Red Cross workers passed through the cars—how they actually managed to move she couldn't quite figure out—with dry sandwiches and over-strong, over-sweetened tea. She nibbled cautiously at the edges of a sandwich. The filling was an odd sort of pale gray, and she didn't dare investigate any further. But her stomach didn't revolt at the first taste of the food, so she gobbled it up in record time, pushing aside memories of salmon and cress sandwiches served on the lawn by nameless, unspeaking maids in starched white aprons and black dresses.

The Sisters and many of the foreign soldiers crowded around the windows to catch a first glimpse of the fabled city, in those days still the Center of the World, as their train pulled past suburbs and industrial estates.

It was June 1940, and Nursing Sister Moira Madison had arrived in England.

Chapter Three

Elaine stood in front of the open closet in her lovely new bedroom, trapped in an agony of indecision over what she should wear to dinner. Moira herself seemed modern and casual but Ruth would have fitted comfortably into Mr. Darcy's staff. She hadn't met any of the other residents and didn't know what to expect. Perhaps Moira would dress to the nines for dinner and expect her guests to appear the same way.

In early summer, Ruth had interviewed Elaine for the job of helping the formidable Miss Moira Madison with the writing of her memoirs. Even Elaine, who tried hard not to pay the slightest bit of attention to the business or social news, had heard of the Madison family. Fingers in every pie from airlines to discount grocery-and-drug store chains to gas stations; it was hard to avoid them. And now the Matriarch herself wanted to write her memoirs. It was difficult for her to travel, so Ruth came in her place, to check out Elaine and ensure that she was at least moderately presentable.

Which apparently she hadn't been as she was rejected in favor of another candidate. She had forgotten all about the Madisons, and was still trying to figure out what to do with her life, when Ruth called to tell her that the job was again vacant and did she want it. With the understanding that Miss Madison would have the final say.

Always the optimist, Elaine sublet her apartment in Toronto, loaded a season's worth of clothes into the BMW, and put the rest of her belongings into storage. If this job didn't pan out, she intended to simply keep on driving. And decide at the intersection of the highway whether to turn left or right.

But she was here, for now.

She looked at herself in the wood-framed mirror over her dressing table and cocked her head to one side. Should she wear her gold earrings or keep the silver hoops she'd worn all day? Like all those well bred but impoverished governesses so beloved of Gothic fiction, she struggled to understand where she fitted into the household. She was not a servant, but she was here as an employee. Would her PhD in Canadian History rank her as equivalent to a guest?

Better to keep the gold for a more formal occasion, if one should arise.

Her reflection frowned and chided her for trying to squeeze herself into the social hierarchy. Writing the memoirs or cleaning the toilet, it was all work. She chose a denim skirt, and paired it with a brightly patterned Navajo blouse, a gift from Elaine's late mother, who before her death had spent her winters in the dry sun of the American Southwest. She added a set of clattering gold bangles, and jaunty costume earrings, and set out for dinner.

No one had told her where to find the dining room, but this was, after all, a cottage. It shouldn't be too hard to locate. Elaine nodded to Augustus on her way down the stairs. Scarcely noticed on her previous trip, a matching portrait of a woman adorned his upper side. The same painter, beyond a doubt, for the technique and style were identical. But this time the artist had a kinder eye for his subject. The woman was not attractive, and never had been, with a large nose much too prominent for her face and a chin too small. But the slight grin at the corner of the thin lips, the wisps of gray hair escaping the severe bun and the brown eyes, looking to be constantly on the verge of a wink, offered clues to a gentle, loving personality. The eyes were identical to those that had earlier greeted Elaine across the antique wooden desk.

She tiptoed down the silent hallway, listening for the sounds of people gathering for dinner. The light was poor, but the beauty of the art collection broke through the gloom. She recognized several of the paintings—Tom Thomson and the Group of Seven, the most famous school of Canadian art.

Somewhere in the distance a door opened, ushering in the sounds of frantic barking. Two enormous German shepherds bounded down the hall and took positions on either side of her. Their lips curled back to display rows of no-nonsense teeth. Pointed ears stretched flat against their heads and thin tails stood tall, flicking ever so slowly, back and forth, back and forth, full of warning and menace.

Art forgotten, Elaine sucked in her breath. "Nice doggy? Nice doggy?" She stretched out one hand, palm upward. She loved dogs, always had. One of the greatest bones of contention in her divorce had been, of all things, the custody of the beloved border collie. Elaine sacrificed a lot to keep her. Only weeks after the papers were finalized, a car hit her pet while they were visiting friends in the suburbs. Two thousand dollars' worth of vet's bills had not been able to save the dog.

These two growled in unison, a sound beginning deep in their throats and edging past the bared teeth and curled lips. Elaine drew her hand back. "Nice doggy?" Her eyes darted around, checking out possible escape routes.

"Hamlet, Ophelia, down. Down!"

She looked up from the dogs to see a man descending upon them. He was in his early forties, with plain but even features, a tousled mane of curly black hair liberally streaked with gray, cheeks ruddy from the cold, and eyes, an unusual shade of olive green, sharp with stern authority as he stared down the dogs. Dressed in a brown-checked flannel jacket, practical jeans, and heavy work boots, he looked as to be as much a part of the forest outside as the trees themselves. "Leave the lady alone. Now!"

The dogs, Hamlet and Ophelia presumably, paid him not the slightest bit of attention. The larger, and if possible the meaner, moved a bit closer and growled a bit louder.

Involuntarily, Elaine stepped back. Show no fear, let them know who's boss, wasn't that what you were supposed to do? Easier said than done. She pressed her back up against the wall. Nowhere else to go.

The man grabbed the dogs' collars and jerked them back. They snarled. Wait until next time, they seemed to say before allowing themselves to be tugged into a sitting position.

"Sorry about that," he said. "I'm Alan Manners, and I guess you'd be Elaine, who's come to help Moira write her memoirs." He didn't wait for acknowledgment. "I'd shake hands but they're kinda busy right now." He nodded at the two dogs sitting by his feet, still held by their collars and bristling with resentment.

"Nice to meet you," Elaine mumbled.

"Don't mind these two," Alan said. His voice was soft and pleasant, a nice contradiction to the rough country exterior.

"They don't seem too friendly."

"They'll do you no harm. They like to look tough, that's the extent of it. Over-bred like crazy and way too indulged, if you ask me. Never quite sure if they're supposed to be frolicking family pets or ferocious guard dogs. Messes up their already dimwitted heads." His tone wasn't entirely joking. "I'll take them back into the kitchen for their dinner. Cook shot a deer this morning. That should keep them happy for a few hours."

Elaine tried to smile.

"Just kidding. They eat nothing stronger than Purina. See you at dinner. It's the second door on the right, if you're looking." He grinned once more and dragged the dogs down the hall.

Elaine blushed. She wasn't sure why.

But she pulled open the second door on the right, to find a formal dining room laid for dinner. No one else had arrived yet. She'd been careful of the time and was, even after studying the paintings and the encounter with the dogs, a good five minutes early. If punctuality was prized here, Elaine Benson would be punctual.

There were five places set at the long table, each marked by sterling sliver flatware, dishes that at a glance appeared to be Royal Doulton (she would have had no compunction in lifting one up and examining the bottom but for the potential embarrassment of discovery), heavy crystal wineglasses, one for red, one for white, and a matching water glass. An ornate silver candelabrum, filled with tall, fresh white candles, unlit, occupied the center of the table. A huge old oak sideboard, scarred and stained by years of heavy use, empty except for a glass bowl of tired pink roses, filled one side of the room: the other was taken up by a wide expanse of glass. The thick curtains were pulled back, so that the room showed off the breathtaking view of the dark lake and the black outline of gently rolling hills beyond. A set of French doors led out to the deck.

It was heavy dusk and the storm had passed. The long limbs of trees swished in the dim glow cast by the house lights. Through the darkness of night and weather, a touch of flame as if from a campfire flashed up, then fell back to earth and disappeared. It came from the scrap of an island, but although Elaine watched for a while, the fire did not show itself again.

The dining room door opened and Moira's wheelchair, pushed by Ruth, came in.

"Settled in nicely?" Elaine's new employer asked, with a bright welcoming smile.

"Very nicely, thank you. My room is a delight. I could admire the view forever."

Moira beamed, genuinely pleased. "As could I. I am happy that you like my home." Ruth placed her at the head of the table, where there was no chair, and slipped into a seat of her own.

"Sit down, please. Dinner will be here shortly. We usually eat in the kitchen, but for your first night I thought something more formal would be nice." Moira smiled. She hadn't changed clothes, except to loop a set of brightly colored beads around and around her thin neck. They matched the African tree-planting shirt in color and in theme.

Elaine was about to comment on the necklace when a heavy-set young woman bustled in, her eyes sparkling above a giant tureen from which rose the most superb odor. Alan, keeper of the dogs, followed, carrying a wooden platter of rough-cut brown bread, several types of yellow and blue cheeses, and a colorful assortment of fruit.

The platters having been plunked down without ceremony, the chubby woman smiled at the newcomer and extended one hand. "Hi and welcome, I'm Lizzie, better known as the Cook."

"Pleased to meet you, Lizzie. Elaine."

Lizzie pulled up a chair and unfolded her napkin. Alan lit the candles, dimmed the lights and disappeared. He was back with an uncorked bottle of Australian Shiraz in one hand and five glasses dangling, in an apparent feat of anti-gravity, between the fingers of the other.

Through the closed door they could hear the whining dogs, begging to be allowed to join the festivities.

While Alan poured and the women accepted, Lizzie dished up steaming bowls of thick red lentil soup and passed them around. The platter of bread and cheese and the tray of apple slices and red and green grapes adorned with a sprinkling of cashews had been placed in the center of the table.

"Welcome to our little household." Moira extended her wineglass towards Elaine. The candlelight caught the liquid and reflected back the richest shades of ruby and scarlet.

"I'm happy to be here." Elaine lifted her glass in response. The others at the table smiled broadly.

With one notable exception. Ruth scowled into her drink and mumbled the tightest of greetings.

Moira made the introductions. The platters were not passed to her, but instead Ruth sliced a bit of bread and placed it, with a piece of cheese the size of a thimble and a scattering of grapes, onto her plate. "Alan is our gardener and handyman. Absolutely essential for keeping the place running. Unfortunately the gardens don't look like much at this time of year, but they are a joy come spring and summer."

Alan smiled shyly at the compliment.

"Dear Lizzie here is my cook. And the best I have ever had. At last, no more thick, grossly-overdone steaks with béarnaise sauce, tough roast of beef, boiled vegetables, and enough greasy bacon and fried eggs to sink a battleship."

"Here, here," said Alan.

"Well this soup is great," Elaine said. "Not what I was expecting, after that lovely tea." This whole house, from the people to the décor to the food, was a fascinating contradiction of the old and the new.

"Let me guess," Lizzie chuckled, "you were expecting roast beef."

"Actually, yes."

"I rather like roast beef," Ruth mumbled, her mouth set in a tight line.

"Lizzie cooks Italian food as well as any Italian. I have always loved real Italian food. Can we have pasta tomorrow?" Moira asked.

"Of course."

Elaine cut herself a sliver of the blue cheese and popped it into her mouth. Stilton. Real English Stilton. Comfortable at this table already, feeling like she didn't have to be unnaturally polite, she served herself a much larger slice. "Do you live here all year, Moira?"

"Yes, I do." The old woman picked up a grape in her crooked fingers and lifted it to her mouth with great care. "I love it here and I'm quite comfortable. If I went back to Toronto, I'd only end up boarding with one of my sisters like a charity case, but here I can have my own household."

"Does your family come up much?"

"On occasion. My sisters' grandchildren like to spend a good deal of their summers at the cottage, as I did when I was a girl. And they are welcome indeed. It's wonderful to have children underfoot; they do bring the old place back to life. The family can usually be expected for holidays. They were all here Labor Day weekend. When…." Moira coughed.

Elaine looked around the table. Alan made patterns of wine in his glass, Lizzie ate her soup with great concentration, and Ruth watched Elaine.

"When…" she prompted.

Moira took a deep breath. "When, sadly, Donna died. I should warn you: They will all be here for Thanksgiving. Bit of a chore, really. But I can't tell them to stay away, even if I wanted to. Under the terms of my father's will, my two sisters and I own the cottage jointly. Fortunately for my peace of mind they don't like to be far from the city lights for long. In that way, as in so much else, they haven't changed a bit from when they were girls."

"If I can put up with them, Moira, so can you," said Lizzie, with a stiff laugh, clearly relieved that the conversation had moved on.

"You'll earn your wages this year, with that crowd expecting a Thanksgiving feast," Alan said, the green eyes twinkling with mischief.

Lizzie tossed her head. She was young and quite pretty, shining blond hair tied back in a bouncy ponytail, perfect teeth set into a wide and generous mouth, large brown eyes and the lingering traces of a summer's tan. Only her excess weight threw her out of the modern definition of beautiful. "Like I don't every other day of the year, looking after you bunch."

Moira chuckled. It was a delightful laugh, the tinkling of fine chimes in a warm wind. She had a bowl of soup in front of her, but didn't lift her spoon once. She nibbled at the edges of the piece of cheese, and ate a couple of grapes. Her lips touched the rim of her wineglass after their toast, but the level didn't go down, and the glass wasn't picked up again.

Conversation swirled around the table, light and friendly, after the brief awkward pause at the mention of death. Lizzie slipped out to the kitchen to refill the soup tureen and fetch more bread and cheese, and Alan brought in another bottle of the excellent wine. Even Ruth relaxed and smiled and joined the conversation in brief spurts. The dogs continued to scratch and howl in the background but no one else seemed to be terribly bothered by the racket. Talk was mostly about the neighbors—who was still here and who had closed up for the season—and chores that were waiting to be done in preparation for winter. Alan mentioned that he wanted to cut down a couple of big branches that had died over the summer and were threatening the driveway. Lizzie told everyone that she had received a letter from her cousin, traveling through Europe, and that the girl was having an absolutely wonderful time.

Moira said little, and slowly her head drooped and her crepe-paper eyes fluttered closed.

"Ready to go upstairs, Miss Madison?" Ruth asked.

The old woman started. "Yes, I believe I am. Thank you for the lovely dinner, Lizzie. What time would you like to start in the mornings, Elaine? I am up early, but whatever suits you."

"Early is good. I'd like to go for a run first thing, if that's all right? Could we start about eight?"

"A runner are you? Good for you. It would do Lizzie some good to get out running as well. Perhaps you can take her with you one day."

Not at all pleased with the comment, the cook grimaced into her bowl.

"Eight in my study, then. Breakfast will be ready in the kitchen shortly before. I am greatly looking forward to starting work. No need to get up. Finish your wine. I'm sure Lizzie has made something wonderful for dessert."

Lizzie held the door to allow Ruth to steer the chair out of the dining room, and Alan slipped out to let the dogs out of the kitchen. They yelped with the sheer joy of freedom and scampered down the hallway after the two women.

Lizzie collected the dirty dishes and Alan resumed his seat. "Hamlet and Ophelia go up with Moira at bedtime," he explained. "She fusses over them and they stay with her while Ruth gets her ready for bed and then brings them back down."

"They spend the night in the kitchen. Horrid things," Lizzie said, pushing the swinging door open with her ample bottom while she maneuvered the stacked tray. "I love living here, and I love Moira to bits, but if I ever quit it will be because those beasts have driven me away."

Alan rolled his eyes and held up the bottle.

"That was more than enough for me, thank you," Elaine answered the unspoken question.

A breeze blew in through the open door and the candles flickered. They cast a warm golden glow onto the old oak table and caused sparks to fly off the silver flatware and sparkling glasses. Alan tipped his glass from side to side and watched the red liquid swirling around the bottom.

Lizzie returned with a warm apple pie straight from the oven and a carton of good vanilla ice cream.

"That was a great dinner," Elaine said, accepting a plate piled high with pastry, soft sugary-cinnamon apples and melting ice cream. "But Moira hardly ate a thing. Is that normal?"

"Oh, yes," Lizzie said. "She had her dinner upstairs, before coming down, like she always does. Her hands are so bad, she can't eat anything more difficult to manage than a piece of toast or a thin slice of fruit with any degree of manners. Poor thing. Appearances are so important to her. Ruth helps feed her and Moira would prefer to keep that private. Old age, ugh." The girl shivered.

"She seems in good spirits, though."

"Usually she is. But she has her bad days. And then we all run for cover. I'm looking forward to reading her book. I bet it'll be great. She has had a real interesting life. Did you know she was a nurse in World War Two?"

"Oh, yes. Before I agreed to work with her, I needed to have an idea of what she wants to say. You'd be surprised at the number of people who've never stepped foot outside of their own dust bowl of a home town but think that the world is waiting with bated breath for them to commit their life story to paper."

Alan chuckled. "I can imagine."

"And as long as she doesn't think that it'll necessarily find a publisher, I'm happy to work with her."

"It won't be published?" Lizzie said, her voice overflowing with disappointment.

"Unlikely," Elaine replied, as she attempted to scoop up the last dribbles of ice cream with the tines of her fork. "Although when I see what we have I'll decide how to continue. But even if a publishing house doesn't pick it up, Moira understands about self-publishing and she only wants to get her life down on paper for the enjoyment of her family and friends and any academics who might be interested."

"I guess that's all right." Lizzie nodded towards Elaine's plate, scraped down to the flowered pattern. "More pie?"

"I really shouldn't," she mumbled the time-honored words, passing her plate across at the same time. "Ruth seems a bit out of place here, if you don't mind my saying so. More formal than the rest of you. A bit old worldly, I thought."

"Ruth's mother was the housekeeper for old Mrs. Madison, Moira's mother, for years and years, back when God was a choirboy," Alan said, leaning back in his chair and patting his slim belly. "Great pie, Lizzie. Ruth was raised with the family. She spent her summers here when she was young. Mrs. Madison was quite a tyrant, I understand. Although I didn't know her, that was long before my time. There was a true division of classes in the household in those days, and Ruth would have been raised among the Madison children, but much apart. Kept in her place."

Lizzie laughed. "Like me, the poor lowly cook."

"Yeah, right. Anyway Ruth got married and left home. Her marriage broke up around the time her mother died, and Moira's arthritis was getting so bad that she needed full-time personal help, so Ruth stayed on after the funeral."

"She's a funny old broad," Lizzie added. "Not much of a sense of humor. She still refuses to call Moira anything but 'Miss Madison.' Yes, Miss Madison. No, Miss Madison. Three bags full, Miss Madison." Her voice was tinged with spite and her pretty eyes metamorphosed into ugly slits.

Elaine was startled out of her comfort zone. She had thought of this bunch as one somewhat unusual but happy family.

Relaxed, comfortable and content in their circle. Apparently she was wrong. She changed the subject, looking for neutral ground. "Do the Madisons own the patch of land behind the boathouses, at the end of the path and through a thick stand of pine?"

"Yes, it's part of the property. Why do you ask?" Both Alan and Lizzie were staring at her.

"I had the strangest sensation earlier. Like I'd wandered into a dream or something. There was this cabin and a woman wearing way too much perfume."

She was enjoying the last bite of apple pie, and almost missed it. A warning look flashed between Lizzie and Alan. Elaine swallowed a piece of sugared apple without tasting it and when she looked again the glance was gone.

Lizzie clambered to her feet and gathered up the dessert dishes. "There are three things we don't talk about around here: how much we hate the dogs, what goes on out on the island, and most of all…."

"Speaking of the dogs, watch your footing when walking outside, Elaine," Alan interrupted. Lizzie disappeared with unseemly haste through the swinging door. "They run wherever they want. I try my best to tidy up after them, but they think the whole outdoors is their private toilet. Good night, see you tomorrow. Nice meeting you." And he was gone. Elaine blew out the spluttering candles and found her own way to bed.

Crooning in soft tones, Moira tossed bits of dog cookies to Hamlet and Ophelia. Her grandfather had always insisted on keeping German shepherds. The best guard dogs, he would say, in the voice that tolerated no argument. And her father would never, ever, contradict anything Grandfather said. The young Moira would have loved to have had a little dog to play with, a spaniel perhaps or a poodle, a soft, fluffy white poodle like her friend Rosalind owned. But they could only have German shepherds who frightened the few children that were allowed to come and visit. All the years of her growing up, Moira promised herself that she would have a little dog, lots of little dogs, a whole kennel full of lively, yapping little dogs. Dogs that were allowed on the furniture and the beds and dogs that you could give treats to without fear of spoiling them. But she had traveled too much to keep a pet, and when the day came that she could travel no longer and it was time to come home, even though her father and her grandfather were long gone and no one had to do what they said any more, Moira went to the breeder and bought two German shepherds. She named them in memory of a long line of Macbeths and Ladies and Horatios and Gertrudes, and even a Puck and a Tatiana.

For what was home without them?

Hamlet jumped up on the bed and wiggled in delight against the warm, thin line of Moira's old legs. He dug his cold nose into her side and his tail flapped like a flag coming loose in a hurricane as he eyed the paper bag on the bedside table.

"Nothing more for you, you greedy thing," she giggled. "Down now. Time for bed." If she did have shepherds she would at least let them be pets. As she did every night, Moira smiled at the thought of Grandfather's reaction if ever he could see dogs on the beds.

Paying no attention to her words, Hamlet lunged at the treat bag. Unwittingly he placed the full force of his substantial weight on Moira's right leg. She screamed in pain.

The huge dog flew off the bed as if he had sprouted wings and skidded across the floor to hide under the massive dressing table. Ophelia followed, somewhat unsure of why she should, but deciding it was probably a good idea.

Ruth dropped the container of medication she was handling and scurried across the room. "Miss Madison, Miss Madison. Are you all right?"

"Of course I'm not all right, you fool," Moira hissed. "The dog jumped on my leg."

Ruth moved to shoo the dogs out of the room.

"Leave them alone," Moira ordered. "It's not his fault that he doesn't know I'm a useless old woman with useless old legs and useless old hands."

"Now, now, that's no way to talk." Ruth bent to pick up the medicine bottle.

"How else should I talk? Like all is perfectly lovely and I will wake up in the morning right as rain, as my sainted mother used to say?" She seized the bag of dog treats from the bedside table and hurled them across the room.

It wasn't much of a hurl, more like a plonk. The cookies spilled across the carpet and the two dogs crept cautiously out from under the dresser, noses first.

"There, there," Ruth mumbled. "No need to be upset."

"Well I am upset. My leg hurts."

"Shall I take the dogs away?"

Moira sighed. She liked to throw the ball for them after they had their snacks, but tonight she was too tired.

Too tired to play with a couple of dogs. Once she could work all day and then dance all night, snatch a couple of hours sleep and be bright and alert, the first back on the wards for morning rounds. But then she was young and it was necessary. After days spent in the crowded hospital wards, or even worse, canvas surgical tents or heaving ships, she had to get out, to dance the night away. To flirt and party with all the handsome young men, handsome and whole. How else could one forget those that would never be handsome, or whole or even sane, again?

"Yes, take them away. That girl has worn me out. What do you think of her, Ruth?"

"Nothing to think," Ruth replied. She dragged Hamlet across the room by his collar and Ophelia followed. She shoved the dogs into the corridor and slammed the door after them. Someone would find them wandering around, eventually.

"Nothing? You must have some opinion."

"You know what I think, Miss Madison." Ruth returned to counting out the pills. "The same as I thought when the other one came: it'll do you no good to be working on these memoirs. It'll tire you, that's all. And for nothing. No one cares what happened in the war anymore."

"And what else would you suggest that I do with my time, pray tell?" Moira's voice cracked as she fought back the tears. "Will it keep me from perfecting my tennis game, or detract from swim practice?"

Ruth placed the collection of multi-colored tablets into her employer's open mouth and offered her a glass of water. "You're old, Miss Madison, old and arthritic and no one cares what happened in the war anymore."

Moira swallowed the pills in a gulp. Her eyes brimmed but she would not allow the tears to flow.

Chapter Four

The Canadian Army General Hospital Number 15 was assigned to the site of a brand-new British Army hospital in Bramshott, Surrey. The hospital, in fact, was so brand-new that it wasn't actually finished. The nurses stepped over gaps in the partially-laid flooring as they moved through the wards in their working uniform of white shoulder length wimple—a memory of the days when nurses were also nuns—white apron over a plain dark dress with a double row of buttons, stiff white collar and cuffs. The sound of hammering and sawing accompanied them on their rounds.

At first the hospital was rather a pleasant place. The work was not hard. There were a few casualties from training incidents, but most of the patients were either ill or accident victims. There were a disproportionate number of accident victims. The enthusiastic Canadian boys were having a great deal of trouble managing their army motorcycles on the narrow English lanes, particularly at night under blackout conditions.

But all in all, it was not much different than the nursing Moira had done in Canada. The accommodation was surprisingly nice, close to the hospital, only two women to a room (tiny and damp though it might be), meals served in their own mess. And the social life was beyond compare. Women surrounded by a sea of men, they were constantly being invited to parties and events held either in the town or any one of the many nearby military bases of numerous nationalities.

Unlike a good many sons and daughters of privileged families, Moira had always known that she was gifted only through an accident of birth. And that the attention her youthful self received at dances and parties back home had much less to do with her own wit and charm than her family's influence and wealth. But here, where no one knew who her grandfather was, or that her father could seal a million dollar contract on a handshake, it was lovely to watch the other girls, from the working class suburbs of Montreal and Winnipeg or the farms of the Prairies or the fishing villages of the Maritimes, delighting in the attention. And it was nice also, she admitted to herself, to be asked to dance because some fellow liked her rather than because of how much money or influence her grandfather and father might have.

The only thing about which the women had to complain, and most of that was good-natured, was the quite dreadful food. Plentiful but dull in the extreme. Meals were identical from one day to the next, a tiny quantity of tough meat, lots of potatoes, boiled to the point of dissolution, and limp vegetables. Not much in the way of fresh vegetables (fresh fruit even rarer), dairy products, or eggs.

Moira Madison thought that for every morning of her life she had been served an egg. Sometimes the eggs were soft-boiled and presented in a beautiful china cup, alongside slim fingers of toast or fluffy scones and pots of homemade preserves, taken in the morning room which overlooked the roses of her mother's prize winning garden. Or they might be fried to the consistency of rubber and served with burnt bacon and toast that had been sitting in the kitchen for ages before being brought to table, as they were in her rooms at Nursing College. If she had been asked, at home in Canada, if she would miss her morning egg, she would have laughed until her thin shoulders shook and her eyes teared with humor.

After only a few weeks at Bramshott, Moira Madison thought that she might well kill for a simple boiled egg.

But the work was light and the Sisters had plenty of free time. Time to write long letters home, travel into the nearest village, or explore the countryside.

The bell hanging over the door sounded feeble indeed as she entered the village shop. The man behind the counter looked up from his ledger and grinned. The smile split his face in two and for the first time she understood the saying "from ear to ear." He was well past middle aged, almost old, heavily wrinkled, back stooped, a few thin strands of greasy gray hair stretched across his shiny head. His eyes were red and watery but nothing could hide the sparkle of delight that lit up his face at the sight of her.

"Welcome, welcome," he beamed. "Ladies, we are so happy to see you here. Betty, Betty. Come see who's here."

Moira looked over her shoulder to see who might have followed her in, but it was only Jean, who had tagged along, uninvited.

An elderly woman bustled out of the back of the shop, wiping her hands on a faded apron. She also broke into a huge smile at the sight of the customers and nodded with enthusiasm.

"I'm Bert, and this is my wife Betty," the man said. "What can we do for you lovely ladies today?"

"Nothing in particular," Moira said, almost lost for words under the force of the welcome. "We thought we would see if you have a few candies—sweets—for sale. We're from the Canadian Army Hospital, you see."

"Of course, of course," Burt said. "And more than welcome all you Canadians are."

At last Moira understood. It was neither she nor Jean that the old couple were so happy to see, but Canadians. Any Canadians, and probably any foreigners, would do.

Someone had made an attempt to make the shelves look full, although they didn't have much to work with and hadn't had a great deal of success. What Bert and Betty offered for sale were mostly dry goods and tins, and precious few of those. But Burt smiled a sly smile and reached under the counter to come up with a bag of humbugs. Plump and brown with white stripes.

"For my Canadian friends." He held up the bag as if it were an offering to the god of peace.

"But shush." Betty touched her lips with one finger. They were suffering from no shortage of lipstick: Betty's mouth carved a dark red slash across her face. The edges of the stick had missed the outline of her lips by a wide margin. Thick pale face powder accented the crevices in her face and the deep lines around her mouth. Moira chastised herself for being nasty and tried to pay attention and smile at the woman.

"We mustn't let the word out that we have such delights."

"Indeed not," said Burt. "Or they'll be banging down the doors. Now, is there anything else I can get for you lovely young ladies?"

"Cigarettes?" Jean said, to Moira's surprise. She had never seen the bold, friendly Sister smoke. The only American among their group, Jean, with the flat tones and hearty manner of a Wisconsin native, had come to Canada to join the effort almost as soon as war broke out in Europe. Her family, so she told them all, had been simply horrified. But Jean knew that she had to go—she was a nurse, and the Army needed nurses.

"Only for you, my sweet," Burt beamed, displaying two rows of rotten and missing teeth. He disappeared under the counter once again.

A girl bustled into the shop through the back door. She was in her early teens, horribly plain but with enormous, delicate eyes an unusual shade of green. They were the color of an olive dropped into a crystal clear martini, and went a long way to soften the effect of her sharp face, thin lips, and much too long nose. Those pretty eyes and a ripening figure scarcely contained beneath her stiff print dress.

"And here's our beauty." Burt beamed, grabbing the girl in a hug that her posture indicated was not at all welcome. "This is our daughter, Catherine."

Betty smiled as proudly as her husband. The menopausal offspring of an ageing couple. A blessing for the parents. A curse at times for the child.

Catherine shrugged her father's arms aside. "I'm off to Millie's, Dad."

"Be back in time for tea," Betty trilled as the girl slammed the door of the shop on her way out.

"A lovely town you have here," Moira said, not meaning it.

"Why thank you, dear. We like it," Betty replied as Burt reappeared with the precious cigarettes. "But not quite as exciting as Montreal, I expect."

"Actually, I'm from Toronto."

"Toronto! What luck. My brother Eddie emigrated to Toronto, must be twenty or more years ago. Perhaps you know him, Eddie Burton?"

"No. I'm afraid not."

"Oh well, too bad. But Toronto's a big place, I gather."

"Indeed. Well, we must be off. Thank you for the humbugs, and the cigarettes."

The couple stood at the door, waving enthusiastically until Moira and Jean had crested the hill and disappeared from sight.

Moira let out a huge sigh. "A bit overwhelming, I would say. What do you want with cigarettes, anyway? You don't smoke."

"Better than money," Jean replied with a sly smile. "Much, much better than money."

Shortly after their arrival, Moira invested in part-ownership of the most precious of all commodities—a bicycle. Throughout the summer and autumn of 1940 she toured the length and breadth of the peaceful Surrey countryside.

Moira's original roommate, Marie, a shy woman from Montreal, had taken seriously ill not long after their arrival, and was shipped home, drowning in tears.

Jean was re-assigned to Marie's bed. She moved in happily, complaining about her previous roommate as she arrived. "If I had to spend the last few months of this war with her I would simply die," she declared, dumping her suitcase on the cot.

"I thought she seems rather nice."

"Perhaps. Until you have to room with her. An absolute horror, she never shuts up from morning to night. Even when I'm trying to sleep."

"Do you think the war will be over soon?"

"Of course. Nothing's happening. They'll all shake hands and say how sorry they are and that'll be the end of it. Maybe when I get home, Freddie will appreciate me a bit more."

"Who's Freddie?"

"I had the most frightful crush on him, all the time we were in school. But he never paid me any attention. When I was home on leave last time, he came around to my house and declared his undying love for me."

"Really?"

"Can you believe it? He finally realized what he might lose. Okay if I put some of my things here?" Without waiting for an answer, Jean swept Moira's few possessions into a corner of their shared dresser and laid out hairbrushes, bottles of cologne, and pots of makeup.

"What did you say? To Freddy?"

"That he'd have to wait for me, of course. I have a duty to perform."

Moira lunged for her family portrait, about to be knocked off the edge of the dresser. It was a nice photo of the siblings. Terribly formal. It had been taken at home in the autumn of 1939, the last time they were all together. Megan and Maeve and Moira sitting primly in the front, hands crossed on their laps, Ralph splendid in his uniform, standing tall and proud behind the row of chairs. Moira's mother had insisted that she put on a pretty dress rather than wear the severe Nursing Sister's uniform for the portrait. At first Moira refused. She was as proud of her uniform as Ralph was of his, but Mother had dissolved into tears, fled to her room and refused to come down, and Grandmother had suggested to Moira, in her quiet, gentle but firm way, that she grant her mother this one request.

"And what did he say to that?" Moira asked.

"He's real keen for America to join the war. He says he'll enlist the first day, but he won't fight for a foreign country. Probably be too late, though. Everything'll be over." Jean sighed luxuriously.

Moira doubted that Freddy was pining away for Jean, but it would do no harm to humor the girl. After all they would be living together for the foreseeable future. "How romantic."

Not much more of this war. Moira remembered the conversation as she tried to force herself to fall sleep. Not easy, as Jean had a snore that would embarrass a drunken sailor. *Not much more of this war.* Then they would all be on their way home. She would be dipping her toes into Lake Muskoka by springtime.

Chapter Five

Elaine crawled out of bed and slipped on jogging shoes and an old tracksuit as the first rays of sun touched her pillow. The first night in a strange room never led to a restful sleep. The nighttime temperature was set to accommodate a thin, elderly woman: a degree Elaine found nothing short of sweltering. The storm had returned, and lightning flashed and thunder echoed throughout most of the long night. Enormous ancient trees grew close to the cottage and the winds had them scratching rhythmically against her window.

Now the house was silent. Augustus Madison watched her, his dark beady eyes brimming with hostility, as she tiptoed down the stairs. Childishly, she stuck her tongue out at him.

Her foot touched the bottom step and the dogs, shut in the kitchen for the night, howled. Elaine dashed down the hall, struggled to unlock the sliding glass doors leading to the deck and plunged outside, jerking the door shut behind her. For the first time, her heart was racing before she had even begun to run.

Because she didn't know where she was going, Elaine decided that the best idea would be to simply run for thirty minutes in one direction, then turn around and jog back. Simple. She rounded the house and headed up the driveway. The trees sloughed off the remainder of the night's storm and the air was fresh and clear with a hearty autumn bite.

A snake lay in the center of the driveway, flattened right across the midsection, clearly by the wheels of a car. Which might even have been hers. The snake wasn't big, and no doubt perfectly harmless in life. But in death it filled the lane and her imagination. Elaine cringed and clung to the sides of the road, almost walking through the trees in order to pass the elongated corpse. The image was fixed firmly in her mind throughout her run, enough that she scarcely noticed her surroundings. On her return trip she was alert for the dead creature miles before she reached it.

Eyes to one side, breathing deeply, and not only from the exercise, Elaine trotted up to the parking area. Her car remained where she had parked it, covered in a sparse blanket of colored leaves. She plucked the dead vegetation off the windows and roof and gave the car a good pat.

Alan walked around the side of the building, Hamlet and Ophelia at his heels. The dogs bristled at the sight of her, and she was sure that they were measuring her for size and weight. Alan growled deep in his throat and they sat, their sleek haunches twitching.

"Sorry," he said with a not-at-all-sorry grin. "They'll take some time to get to know you."

She didn't acknowledge him, merely lifted her head and followed the flagstone steps around the cottage.

The sun rose behind the building and this early in the morning long shadows stretched out over the water. Instead of heading inside to get ready for her first day on the job Elaine strolled down to the dock.

The air was heavy with the scent of decaying foliage and woodsmoke but was, at the same time, light and fresh, free of the odor of car exhaust, overworked factories and too many people confined into far, far too small a space.

The flowerbeds were neatly raked and tidied, the lawn mowed one last time. The flagstone path wound its way down from the deck to the boathouses and the dock. And there it ended. Abruptly, unexpectedly.

A line of white pine rose up, blocking the way, the dense forest closing in behind. Elaine loved nature, in all of its costumes, but she didn't like the feeling of these trees. They crowded her, closed in on her, although she was standing several feet away. Her breath struggled in her throat, the airways fought to stay open. The well-maintained lawns and gardens of the family estate lay behind her.

Safe.

Secure.

But she wanted to step off the path. To see what lay behind the tall white pines.

She pulled air into her lungs and stepped forward. One hesitant step and then another, and another.

No one had been here for a long time. The path simply ended where it touched the woods. Nothing but moss and weeds and saplings sprouted between the trees. If the trail had once continued on through here, no trace of it remained.

There was nothing unusual here, except for the smell. Not pine nor wood nor wet, decaying leaf mulch as she would have expected, but a hint of...perfume? Far too sweet and coy in this setting. Not at all pleasant, like cheap toilet water. A bit of effluent flowing through these beautiful woods? These days anything was possible.

It was cold; the temperature dropped dramatically once she left the path. So cold that she could see her breath forming in gentle puffs in the air in front of her face. A gust of wind picked dead leaves off the forest floor and swirled them around her feet. Through the barrier of untrimmed trees and undergrowth run wild, she imagined that she could see a building. A cabin, standing alone in the dark woods, its outline the same as she had seen in yesterday's wide-awake dream.

A children's playhouse, or guest cottage? Surely it would be visited, enjoyed, loved? Not abandoned to fall into ruin and decay at the end of an overgrown, untrammeled path.

Elaine placed one running shoe-clad foot in front of the other with great care. Because of the heavy rain during the night, the non-existent path was damp, the carpet of leaves and pine needles soaked with moisture.

Behind her, one of the dogs barked. Only once, short and sharp, a sound brimming with alarm. The air between two of the larger trees seemed almost to move. It shimmered in space, as if it were struggling to take form. She stepped forward; she couldn't quite see. She wanted to see more.

Squelch. Elaine looked down at her feet. One of her top-of-the-line shoes was sinking into a puddle of glutinous, ugly, black mud. She pulled it out with a curse and walked out of the woods.

◇◇◇

Elaine found the kitchen by the simple act of following her own nose. The fragrance of freshly ground and brewed coffee flowed down the hallway, carrying with it the aroma of breakfast.

The kitchen was all wood, stone, and rock. A massive fire-place, rows of logs stacked in neat formation beside it, filled one wall. An antique rocking chair, looking as if it were waiting for a wizened grandmother with a pile of pink and blue knitting, took pride of place in front of the hearth. Elaine settled herself to the big table, and a smiling Lizzie served up a virtual feast: coffee first, then spicy Italian sausages, toast with jam, eggs any way she wanted, crisp home fries. Elaine happily dug in to a meal the like of which she hadn't dared touch in years.

"Have you worked here for long?" she asked, through a mouthful of runny fried egg on whole-wheat toast thickly coated with slabs of creamy butter.

"Coming up to two years. It's easy and comfortable and pays well and so...here I am." Lizzie poured herself a fresh cup of coffee and pulled a chair up to the timeworn wooden table.

"What made you want to be a cook?"

Lizzie watched the liquid swirling in her cup. "My father was a chef, a good one. My parents owned a restaurant for years. Enormously successful it was too. My mother managed the business end of it, my dad cooked. I'm an only child and they raised me rolling pastry and dodging pots of boiling water and temperamental sous-chefs. My parents always intended that

I come into the business with them. Dad had great plans for opening another restaurant and putting me in charge."

"But you didn't want to?"

"They were killed in a car accident. On one of their rare vacations. They closed the restaurant for a few days and drove down to Florida to visit my grandparents. They never made it home."

"I'm so sorry."

"I couldn't imagine trying to run the restaurant without them. I didn't want to be a chef anyway. I love to cook, but a restaurant is such hard work, absolutely killer hours, stress beyond belief. I was afraid of how to tell them I didn't want it. Then I didn't have to."

A pot hissed and Lizzie moved to attend to it. "Everything happened so suddenly. I had no idea of what to do. A friend of my dad has a place near here. He knew that the Madison cook had quit and told me about the position."

"You were lucky."

"If luck had anything to do with it, my parents wouldn't have died. But I know what you mean. I needed time to decide what I want to do with my life, to sort my mind out. That's the absolute worst thing about sudden death; the survivors are left so totally lost."

Elaine considered herself to be a survivor of a different sort. Survivor of a broken heart perhaps, a ruined life. There were times when, in the dark recesses of her mind, she wished that Ian had been struck dead, perhaps in a car crash like that which took the lives of Lizzie's parents. But no such luck. They never die when you want them to.

"Will you stay here?" she asked, rather than contemplate that which hadn't worked out. In more ways than one.

"As long as it suits me. And it suits me now."

"Moira seems nice." Elaine dipped a segment of sausage into a red puddle of tomato ketchup.

"She has her moments." Crisis taken care of, Lizzie sat back down and added a generous splash of cream to her coffee.

"Meaning?"

"Meaning nothing. She's a rich old lady. She's great, but she's used to having her way. She pays better than anyone else in the area, although I'd be happy to work here for much less. But don't tell her I said that."

"Pardon me, Lizzie, if I seem a bit unsure. I've never been part of a household before. It's all a bit strange."

Lizzie smiled. "Not much different from living at home, with Grandma and Mom and older brother. Actually it's a lot nicer than living in some people's homes. But wait until the family arrives. Then there'll be more than enough to do. Those tight-assed old ladies don't approve of me and they won't ever let me forget my place."

The relaxed, chatty mood shattered. While Elaine finished her breakfast in silence, Lizzie gathered up the cooking equipment and piled it into the sink.

"I can understand that no one wants to talk about it, but I really want to know what happened to the first woman hired to write Moira's memoirs."

"She drowned."

"So I heard. But how?"

Lizzie sighed and squirted dishwashing liquid into the frying pan. "We don't really know. I guess that's why we're so afraid to discuss it. She'd only been here a few days, when Alan found her floating in the lake at the end of the dock one morning. It was very early, everyone else still in bed. Alan often gets up before the rest of us—he likes the morning light, he says. And there she was, fully dressed, floating in the lake."

Elaine shuddered. "How awful."

"The police looked into it, of course. The coroner said it was an accident, no signs of foul play or anything like that; apparently the body had been there all night. When her family came to collect her, her father told Moira that she couldn't swim, not one stroke. So it was assumed that she'd walked out to the edge of the dock and somehow fell in. Although the coroner said that she hadn't had a heart attack or anything like that. It's very deep at the end and a good distance to the rocks and the ladder out of the water. Next summer, Moira's going to have a ladder put in at the end of the dock. The coroner recommended it. Bad things happen, that's all. Why did some redneck drunk kill my parents?"

Lizzie scrubbed furiously at a bit of grime stuck to the bottom of the pan. "Anyway, Donna's death had nothing to do with you, so why worry about it?"

Chapter Six

September 1940. The peaceful serenity ended, and the Battle of Britain began. The soldiers and Nursing Sisters of Hospital Number 15 sat alongside the people of Southeast England in grandstand seats to the spectacle, cheering on R.A.F. Spitfires in their aerial dogfights against Luftwaffe fighters escorting the waves of bombers to their targets and standing with hearts in their mouths as a tiny aircraft would plunge downward, spiraling back to the arms of mother earth, trailing long plumes of fire and smoke.

At night the eastern sky glowed red, telling the tale of another heavy raid on the city. The nurses lay awake in their hard, narrow cots, listening to the sound of planes overhead. German bombers flying to or from their targets, English fighters in urgent pursuit.

One perfect, crisp day in early autumn Moira took her bicycle out to get some exercise. It had been a hard duty shift. A young soldier, famous around the camp for his easy laugh and sense of fun, fell off the roof of the barracks during a childish prank and rather than foolishly breaking a leg or two, had fallen onto an iron spike lying abandoned in the long grass. The spike pierced his chest and he died on the operating table. It was a horrible, foolish, tragic waste, and Moira had been brought to tears.

She cycled through a small path cut around the farmers' fields. The sun shone bright overhead; the crops were lush and full.

She stopped pedaling to wave enthusiastically to the Land Girls bringing in the harvest. She was still waving when the whine of an airplane engine in distress sounded directly overhead. It was a German bomber, no doubt about it; they had all been trained to recognize the distinctive appearance of enemy aircraft. Smoke billowed from under the wings and, as she watched, minuscule figures leapt from the undercarriage and drifted on billowing clouds to the outstretched arms of a welcoming green earth. There was nothing for her to do: excited Land Girls and angry farmers armed with pitchforks descended on the fluffy parachutes. Moira watched as the aircraft spun out of control and crashed into a far distant field, exploding in a ball of flame. It was too far for her to reach, across the farmers' ploughed fields, on her ancient bicycle, in time to offer aid. If indeed aid should be required. Heavy of heart, she turned and headed back to the barracks. There was nothing she could do, she was too far away, and help (if needed) was on its way, but for many years after, she berated herself for her selfishness, because she did not want to see the face of the enemy.

Chapter Seven

At eight o'clock sharp, Elaine tapped on the study door and edged it open. Moira's chair was pulled up to the ornate antique desk, and Ruth, dressed in a different dress than yesterday but still proper servant's black, stood stiffly beside her.

"Good morning, dear. Did you sleep well?" Moira asked. Today's T-shirt proclaimed support for kidney research. Ruth nodded once in greeting.

"Very well, thank you," Elaine lied. "And I've already been out jogging and had a lovely breakfast. So I'm more than ready to get to work."

"Sit down then and let's do just that."

Elaine sat in the straight-backed chair pulled up beside the desk. Nothing in the room would put one in mind of the early 1900s except for Moira's desk. Carved out of solid oak, it was coated with a patina of decades of love and care and attention. The rest of the furnishings and the room itself could have substituted for a spread in this month's issue of *Modern Home*. Sofa and chairs, piled high with white cushions, were upholstered in a fresh shade of blue. The walls were painted white, decorated with large, colorful pieces of modern art, and one heartbreakingly beautiful painting of the lake outside the study window, but as it must appear in deep winter—a lone moose crossing the endless white expanse of ice and snow in search of enough food to see his massive body through to the plentiful days of spring. The carpet was a thick soft cream with a touch of blue edging. Navy blue horizontal blinds had been pulled back to let the morning light stream through two bay windows. Pillows were piled invitingly on the window seats in the bays. Luscious philodendrons sat in white wicker pots on either side of the windows, drinking in the morning sun.

"This is a beautiful room, Moira," Elaine said. "Different from the rest of the cottage."

Moira looked around her, admiring the surroundings with an air of long established comfort. "This is my study so I've done it up to suit to my taste. The cottage itself belongs to the Madison family, of course, thus I have chosen to keep the rest of it in the style as chosen by my grandmother and mother." Her brown eyes twinkled. "Saves family arguments that way."

Pleasantries over, the old woman clapped her hands. "Now to work. Where do we start?"

Elaine pulled a tiny tape recorder out of her sweater pocket. "With your permission, I'd like to tape all of our conversations. Simply because I have a hideously bad memory and it's easier than writing everything down."

Moira nodded.

"Before I begin going through your correspondence, if you could give me a general idea of how you want the memoirs to be constructed, who your audience is to be, what you hope to achieve? That sort of thing." Elaine pressed the record button and whispered the date. She placed the machine on the desk between them and pulled a small notebook for jotting down comments to herself out of the other pocket. Ruth slipped across the room and took a seat in the bay window.

"This is to be a book about me, not about my family. We are a prominent family indeed, but my father and grandfather and my brothers-in-law can be accessed in any moderately competent history of Canadian business. Am I speaking loudly enough?"

"Yes."

"I want this to be the story of the life of one Canadian woman. I won't pretend false modesty and call myself ordinary; these surroundings would make a mockery of that word. But I do hope that my life has something to say to women today. It is so hard to get women's stories told and once told, heard. Stories of who they really are, not as appendages to their husbands' careers. Do you know what Maryon Pearson said when asked about her husband's success?"

Of course Elaine did. Maryon Pearson was the wife of the late Lester B. (called Mike), a much-loved former Prime Minister of Canada. But she knew better than to interrupt the flow of narrative.

"She said that 'behind every successful man stands a surprised woman.' I always liked that line." Moira chuckled with a warmth that made her appear decades younger.

"I decided that as I have the money and leisure to tell my story the way I want it to be told, I would do so. Is that all right with you, young woman?"

"Perfectly all right. A great idea."

"Of course, I can't forget about my family entirely. I'll tell you about the early years, how wonderful it was growing up in this place, having everything a young girl could possibly want, and then some. But most of all I want to tell you about the war years. Those wonderful, terrible years in London and Italy, and all the people I knew back then. And my years in Central Europe with the Red Cross and after that my work for Médecins Sans Frontières."

Elaine looked up. "You were with Doctors Without Borders? How absolutely fantastic. But you didn't mention that in your letter."

"No, I didn't. I thought it would be a nice surprise. I went to Zaire with them, in 1978." She coughed lightly, then with more strength, until a fit of choking had Ruth rushing over from her seat by the window with a glass of water. She placed one hand on the back of Moira's head and helped the old woman to take a sip.

"You're too tired for any more of this," Ruth said, sounding more nanny than assistant. "Let Elaine get into the storage room and read what she wants in the boxes. You need your rest."

Moira lifted her right hand and hit the glass with enough strength to knock it flying out of Ruth's hand. It struck the sharp edge of the desk and shards of glass and droplets of water flew through the air.

"Don't you tell me what to do," Moira shrieked. "I'm not a baby, do you hear me? Do you? I don't need to rest five minutes after I've started. Go and clean up that mess and then leave us alone. I'm sure you can find something useful to do, if you put your mind to it."

Ruth burst into tears and fled from the room. Elaine scrambled to her knees to pick up the sharp pieces of glass, more to hide her embarrassment than from any desire to be useful.

"Leave that," Moira snapped. "Ruth will do it. I don't know why I put up with her. Incompetent fool."

Ruth chose that moment to slip back into the room, bearing pail and cleaning cloth. She gathered the bits of debris and mopped up the spilled water silently and efficiently. Her hands trembled.

"Where were we? Oh, yes." Moira settled back into her chair. "I had scarcely begun talking to Donna, what with the arrival of my sisters and their families for the Labor Day weekend. So I am starting this from scratch. Tell me if I get too boring. I don't have many letters saved from when I was a girl. Simply because there weren't many. I lived with my mother and father. They sent my brother Ralph away to boarding school, but we girls stayed at home. There were four children. Ralph was the oldest, and my mother's favorite. She absolutely adored that boy. Even all these years later I can remember how jealous I was at the fuss and attention Ralph got when he came home for school holidays. To my father and grandfather, he represented the future of the company and the family. Ralph would be trained to follow in their footsteps every step of the way."

"Did you resent him?"

"No, I didn't. Does that surprise you? I should have, but instead I idolized him. Everyone loved Ralph. He died in the war. So sad, such a tragic waste. My grandfather died the day after they got the news, and my mother was never quite the same again." She breathed deeply and stared into another space and time. Elaine did not interrupt, but made a quick note to find out more about the doomed Ralph. Paragons were rarely quite what they seemed. Ruth finished tidying up and left the room. Moira missed her resentful glare, but Elaine didn't. It would seem that she had made an enemy, through no actions of her own.

"And then there were the three girls. I came first. Moira, the willful one, my mother called me. Maeve arrived right after me, the attractive one. She was quite pretty, but never the stunning creature my family pretended. Of course, with our money, if they said a donkey was a great beauty everyone would have bayed in agreement.

"And Megan, the baby. The talented one. She played the piano. Quite well, actually. If she wasn't so spoiled she might have achieved something in the world of music. Do you notice anything about our names?"

"They all begin with M. A coincidence?"

"Not at all. My mother thought of herself as a poet. She wrote quite a bit, although she never showed anyone her work. She burned everything not long before she died. I often think about the significance of that. That huge body of work, never seen by another soul. Tragic, don't you think?"

"Yes."

"She loved alliterations. I suspect she only married my father for his last name. She certainly didn't love him. And she didn't need to marry him for his money. Her family had quite enough of their own, thank you very much. Her name was Mary Margaret. But her last name was boring old Brown. After their marriage, she wrote or embroidered 'MMM' on absolutely everything—towels, stationery, linens. She would have loved to have lived to see the year 2000."

"Why?"

"MM, of course. Roman numerals for 2000. Her family was of Irish ancestry. She liked the old Irish names. I can well imagine that my father had to put his foot down to avoid a son named Liam or Sean. But he didn't have much interest in the girls, so she named us as she liked.

"I never remember a time when I got on well with my mother. My father, as suited our class and times, was a distant, almost mythical figure. What could I be but difficult? Sandwiched between Ralph, the sacred male child, and the beauty and the artiste."

A frisson of excitement crawled up Elaine's spine. She had taken this job for the chance to start a new life, get away from the city and the memories and the familiar haunts. Her career that once blazed with such promise had flat-lined, leaving behind it not the faintest signs of a pulse. She'd hoped that helping a rich old woman write her boring memoirs would give her a chance to breathe new air and come to some decisions. But maybe there would be a story here, after all.

Moira switched tracks so quickly Elaine almost fell off. "I can't tell you how wonderful it was to be growing up between the wars. In the fabulous twenties. The strong, healthy child of a rich family. Only years later did I come to understand that not everyone lived like us. Or even like our servants, whom I did think of as part of the family, in my patronizing little way."

Elaine thought of the difference between how Moira talked to Ruth and to Lizzie and herself, and that perhaps some things hadn't really changed at all.

"Those years were simply absolutely, fabulously magical. Despite all the usual childhood fights and tantrums and bickering. We came up here every summer, immediately after Ralph arrived home from school, and we stayed until Labor Day. I was born in 1914, so I was a girl and then a young woman, what today they call a teenager, through the twenties. The best of all times, I often think. The twenties I mean, not my youth.

"Then came the crash of '29. It scarcely made a ripple in our lives. We were all right. The family industries were diversified enough that we escaped the worst of the Depression. But all over the lake places were sold or closed up and neighbors and good friends never seen again. I had a dear friend, Lorraine Hamilton.

The summer of 1929 we were all of fifteen. Surely the most perfect and innocent of ages. At least it was in our time, although I suspect it is no longer. We swore our undying friendship to each other, like Anne and Diana. We had simply devoured the Anne of Green Gables books that wonderful summer. When I wrote to her at Christmas she never answered and come the next season, their cottage was boarded up so tightly a cockroach couldn't have found a way in. I never saw or heard of Lorraine again."

She paused for a breath and looked around her in some confusion. "I seem to have misplaced my water glass, dear. And I am getting quite parched, all this talking. Could you call Lizzie and ask for a cup of tea. Push that button here and someone should answer."

Elaine did as instructed and in the time it took a kettle to boil, Lizzie was kicking the door open, laden tray in her arms.

The cook poured. This time tea was served in thick mugs, one of which was a souvenir of Niagara Falls, and the other a testament to the World's Greatest Aunt.

Lizzie noticed Elaine reading her mug with a disappointed frown. "Good cups and silver are for afternoon tea. This is morning tea. No ceremony."

Moira gripped her mug as she thanked Lizzie. The tips of her fingers turned white and her arthritic hands shook, but she raised the quarter-filled cup to her lips and took a tiny sip.

"I can't tell you, dear, how horrible it is to grow old. Helpless as a blind kitten is bad enough, but it is knowing that things will only get worse that is hardest."

Elaine swallowed. "My mother always said that getting old is hard, but the alternative is worse."

Moira threw back her head and laughed. Elaine was so startled she leapt to her feet and failed to catch her hostess' mug before it hit the floor. The thick carpet absorbed the impact and the cup bounced away, unharmed. A bare dribble of tea seeped into the fibers.

"Oh, that is so true. I will remember that. When things are the hardest. Please pour me more tea, dear, I seem to have lost what bit I had." She wiped her eyes with a scrap of tissue tucked into the sleeve of her T-shirt, but the smile died too soon. "There are times I wonder if the alternative might actually be better. That is why I want to work on these memoirs. So it is not forgotten when I'm gone. Just a touch, thank you."

Elaine checked the tape. "You were telling me about when you were young."

"Indeed I was. The parties, the dances, the picnics, the boat races, games on the lawn. The summers passed in an endless haze of fun and irresponsibility. My grandmother loved her garden with a passion and the property blazed with flowers all season long. We had a full-time grounds staff of three, here at the cottage, and that's apart from the staff at the house. Can you imagine?"

Elaine couldn't imagine. Her idea of a garden was two tomato plants stuck into plastic pots, struggling to survive out on the balcony.

"Ralph was always inviting school pals up for a weekend, or boys from other places on the lake. We had the grandest parties, and the boys absolutely swamped us, Ralph's sisters, with attention. At the time, of course, I assumed the force of my sparkling personality attracted them. Now I know that being the oldest daughter of Frederick Madison was more than enough.

"You must see some of the wonderful photographs of those days. I'm sure they can explain it all better than I. Would you like to use our pictures in the book?"

"With your permission, it would add a great deal."

"Take whatever you find, as long as you return it."

"I will."

"My father would come up for the weekends sometimes, and my grandfather a good bit more as he got older, but usually it was only we children with my mother and grandmother. Better that way."

"Why?"

Moira looked startled. "What do you mean why? It just was."

"If you want this to be an honest account, you have to tell me everything."

"And you think there is something to tell?"

"Of course there is. Most children would welcome their father's company, particularly when it was sporadic. When they don't, I have to ask why."

Moira sighed. She turned her head and looked out the window. A minute passed in total silence. Then the old woman took a deep breath, as if she was coming to some sort of a decision. "Because he was a bully and a tyrant. Because my mother hated him and did everything she could to stay out of his way. Because when he was here she spent the days locked in her room with a headache and a bottle of gin and the maids tiptoed around the place as if the smallest sound would bring it all crashing down around them. We lost at least one maid and one groundskeeper every summer. They would do something my father didn't like, or be in the wrong place when he wanted to be there, and they would be sacked on the spot.

"It was easier the rest of the year, when we were at home in Toronto. The house was bigger, we had school, and Father didn't normally come home until long after the children were in bed. We weren't as close to the servants in the city, even if they were the same people. Things were different. If a maid was gone one morning, no one cared, another would be in her place by the afternoon."

"Did he abuse you?"

"What an amazing question. Are all you young people so blunt?"

"I am not young, Moira, as I'm sure you noticed. And we are writing your memoirs after all."

"Oh, I understand that it is quite the thing these days to display all your family's dirty laundry for a good airing. But please remember I was a nurse, and in the army. Quite out of place for my class, I was. I do know the more sordid facts of life. But my father did not abuse me in any way, physically, mentally, or sexually. In fact, my father didn't even know I was there. He must have sometimes wondered why the dining room chair was speaking. I was not a boy, nor was I pretty or talented. Ergo, of no consequence."

"But you went on to do wonderful things. To get out in the world, and to make something of your life."

"I did, didn't I? And how shocked they were when I told them I had decided to study for a nurse. My mother once again locked herself in her bedroom with her beloved gin and my father forbade me to even mention it again. I suspect that he had already lined up a junior partner to be my husband. My great-aunt died in 1935. She never married and had no children, and so she left us three girls a bit of money of our own. A wise woman, my aunt.

"I was twenty-one years young. Old to go for a nurse in those days, but at last I had my own money, and all the wonderful freedom and independence it represented."

Elaine scribbled notes as fast as she could. The tape recorder whirled away. This was great. Better material than she had dared hope for. "Tell me about your grandparents, on your father's side. I've seen their portraits in the stairway. Impressive."

"They are. My grandmother was a powerful influence on my life. My mother was somewhat…shall we say, uninvolved…in her children. She was happy to leave us to a succession of nurse-maids and nannies. But Grandmother Elizabeth would step in and act as mother. Particularly over the summer when we were here, at the cottage. We weren't quite as close when we were all in the city. We had our own house. Maeve lives there now. Megan and her husband have Augustus and Elizabeth's home.

"Grandmother Elizabeth was the only truly caring and loving adult I had in my childhood, other than a stream of nannies. I loved her dearly. She died when I was still in Europe, after the war."

Outside, Alan the gardener strolled past the big bay windows. A streak of mud ran down one side of his face and dead brown leaves were tangled in his hair. He carried a rake and shifted it to his left hand to wave cheerfully at the watching women.

The voice drifted off. Elaine looked up, another question poised on her lips. Moira's eyes were closed and her head bobbed. A touch of drool slipped out of the corner of her mouth. Elaine cleared her throat. She could see Alan clearing out dead brush from a flowerbed, his slim hips swaying lazily as he worked. Hamlet and Ophelia danced eagerly at his heels.

Moira didn't move and Elaine coughed again, trying to be discreet. The old woman started and shook her head, blinking her eyes back into consciousness.

"I have more than enough for this morning," Elaine said. "I'd like to start into your correspondence, if that's okay?"

"Oh, yes. Let me call Ruth. She'll show you where we keep everything." Moira pushed a button on the intercom. "I would come with you myself, if I could." She shrugged and indicated the wheelchair. The gesture was tinged with so much hopelessness that Elaine felt tears prickling behind her eyes.

"Bring anything down that you want to talk about. I'd love to see some of the old letters and pictures again. It's been so long. But be warned. Nothing has been sorted. My mother merely stuffed correspondence into a pile and then tied everything up with a ribbon."

"I've been through worse. Believe me."

Chapter Eight

The winter of 1940-41 was harsh. Not harsh compared to February on the Prairies, or even a cold day in Toronto, but the nurses' accommodations were, simply, freezing. Try as they might, women used to central heating or roaring fireplaces and thick clothing couldn't get warm. Moira's spirits fell with the thermometer and she wrote home, complaining of the cold and the damp. As fast as the mail could travel, her mother wrote back beseeching her to give up this foolishness and come home. For once, her father penned a sentence at the bottom of the letter, echoing his wife's sentiments.

Of course, nothing could make Moira more determined, and she managed to survive the winter with a minor revival of her spirits.

Some of the Canadian women had a hard time managing in the blackout. It didn't bother Moira, accustomed as she was to wandering the back roads of Muskoka late into the night. But for women who had spent their entire lives in cities or towns, night outside without a glimmer of light made a fearful place.

Off duty hours passed in a social whirl. The nursing sisters were outnumbered by soldiers hundreds to one, and they were invited by every unit stationed anywhere nearby to dances in the Officers' messes or out to the pubs. Matron watched over her girls like a jailhouse warden and few of the nurses had the social skills or the nerve to venture out on their own, anyway.

Jean loved every second of the attention and enjoyed a steady parade of admirers. Invitations were constantly forthcoming. She traded her carefully hoarded supply of cigarettes for any luxury that might come her way, a fresh egg, a pot of rouge, even a pair of silk stockings that had the other nurses groaning with envy as they prepared for an excursion to the English Officers' Mess.

Poor Freddie. A Wisconsin farm boy would have an impossible time trying to compete with all of this.

Shy Susan from Saskatoon made up the last member of Moira's trio. It was hard to imagine two women more opposite than Jean and Susan. The one bold and forward, always on the lookout for the possibility of a good time, delighting in being the exotic American, the other so shy she practically disappeared in the company of men. But they clung together like the women far from home for the first time that they were.

Bramshott was located close to London, and the women reveled in the opportunity to tour the great city on their leaves.

Moira, Jean, and Susan went to the cinema, as the English called it, to see the wildly popular George Formby in *Spare a Copper*, a film about Nazi spies. They were enjoying the movie enormously, such a treat, when the screen went black and the words *Air Raid On* appeared. The three disappointed nurses filed out and made their way into the tube to await the all clear.

The subway platform was crowded. Lines of bunk beds had been stacked against the walls: whole families spent their nights down here. Makeshift beds were set up on the platform between the bunks and the train tracks. Generally people managed to keep their spirits up and chattered quietly amongst themselves. Groups would spontaneously break into song or ribald laughter. An elderly man with thick glasses and an immaculate suit held a book so close to his face it almost touched his nose. *A History of the Hundred Years' War*. Some things never do change.

The three nursing sisters stepped in, unasked, to take charge of a restless brood belonging to a sobbing young woman. She had four children under the age of four and was trying to nurse her baby while at the same time keep the older children, including a set of redheaded, freckle-faced twins whose very appearance screamed mischief, sitting still.

The woman was burping her baby, and trying to smile through tear-reddened eyes at her rescuers, when the all clear sounded. They emerged into a sea of destruction. The row houses on one side of the street were gone, nothing remaining but piles of smoldering rubble, while on the other homes stood strong and secure. Emergency personnel were already sifting through the wreckage and the scream of ambulances sounded in the distance.

The young mother settled her baby into the pram, sitting unscathed at the tube entrance, and ordered the other three to grip the handles. "Thank you for your kindness," she said. "We'll manage now." She herded her family down the road. The sisters watched her go, and sighed with relief as she turned left, into the untouched row, and guided her children through the door of a house, still in one piece.

Others weren't so lucky and emerged from the shelter to face the destruction of everything they owned.

The man with the book strolled on down the road, stepping over rubble and around vehicles and people, the *History of the Hundred Years' War* still pressed to his nose.

"Perhaps next week we can come back and see the ending of the film," Jean said. "I want to find out how it turns out." Buildings on either side of the movie theatre had been demolished. The theatre was untouched.

Chapter Nine

The next couple of weeks passed in a swirl of work and reminiscences. Elaine met with Moira every morning in the light-filled white-and-blue study. Moira talked about her childhood and her years as a nurse in the Royal Canadian Army Medical Corps during World War II. Elaine's notebook filled up and she had to drive into Bracebridge, the nearest town, to stock up on more tapes.

"We were talking the other day about your grandmother, Elizabeth," she asked as the autumn rain fell in an unceasing stream outside the bay windows. "But you didn't say much about your grandfather. Can you tell me more?"

"Augustus. I didn't know him as well as I did her. Like my father he was always caught up in the terribly mysterious goings on of business. He was a forceful personality. We children were terrified of him, even Ralph. Grandfather was a good deal harder on Ralph than on the girls. He expected so much of him, you see—the solitary boy, The Heir, in capital letters. The only time I ever saw Ralph cry was when Grandfather laughed at him. I don't remember what had happened. But he called Ralph Missie and told him to go and play with the other girls.

She stopped her narrative and stared at Elaine. The sharp brown eyes burned with remembered anger. "I saw that in the war a great deal. Fools whose idea of a finely toned insult was to suggest that a man was more like a woman. Ha! He should be so lucky. Women have come a long way in my lifetime, my dear, and this is a good part of what I want my story to be about. But you will only know you have indeed achieved equality when to tell a man he is acting feminine will be offered and accepted as a compliment.

"I agree with you there."

"But, back to the story," Moira said. "It's always been somewhat of a wonder to me that poor Ralph turned out to be a semi-functioning human being at all. With all the pressures he had on him. The only son, the only grandson. But we can discuss Ralph another day.

"For you were asking about Grandfather. The force of his anger would put a tropical hurricane to shame. He bullied my father quite terribly. And that was when he, my father, was an adult, with a wife and children of his own. I can only imagine what it must have been like when he was a child. I'm no psychologist, but it doesn't take a degree to see why my father grew up to take delight in picking on those weaker than himself. Those were the only times I ever saw my grandmother as powerless. When Grandfather was having a go at Father, she would get up and leave the room, or sink her head into her embroidery or the letter she was writing."

Moira sighed, and her deep brown eyes clouded over. Elaine checked that the wheels on her tape recorder were still whirling.

"My father learned to be a cold, uncaring man from his own father, the master indeed. Strangely enough, or perhaps not, my grandfather could actually be rather fun and kind with the granddaughters. He wouldn't play with us often, but when he did we had a grand time. I can remember one occasion when he actually got down on all fours to play horsie and gave us rides around the playroom. As we got older Grandfather would even remember to ask us how were doing with our studies or if we'd had a good time at a party. But Ralph always failed him in some regard.

"But, as I have said, we didn't see him, Grandfather, a great deal. My grandmother, Elizabeth, visited often, and spent most summers here, at the cottage. It was the pattern for many families in those days you know, to send wives and children out of the way all season. The occasional visit to pat the offspring on the heads and make sure the wife behaved herself, and then back to more important matters in the city. But for women such as Mother and Grandmother, it was somewhat of a blessing."

"Do you know that for sure? That they felt that way, I mean?"

Moira sighed heavily and rubbed her forehead, her eyes closed.

"If you'd rather continue later...." Elaine worried that she had overstressed the old woman.

"No, it's quite all right. I slept badly last night. I usually do, these days. Do I know for sure what my mother and grand-mother thought? Of course not. But I was an inquisitive child, into everything, always hiding behind the bookshelves or under the table. I heard a great deal, and I know that my mother in particular was a very, very unhappy woman. Things would have been so much easier for her had she been able to be friends with her mother-in-law. But there was little or no room for female alliances in such a male-dominated household and they were never allowed to forget their positions: family matriarch and interloping daughter-in-law. They both suffered in silence."

It had become their working habit: when the old woman tired and her voice broke and her eyes drooped, Ruth would pack her off for a nap and Elaine would return to the loft above the storage rooms to examine the boxes of letters, notes and photographs. Then after lunch eaten in the kitchen with Lizzie and Alan and an afternoon spent among the family papers, Elaine and Moira would meet again for luxurious afternoon tea and Moira would resume talking of her life or they would discuss the work Elaine had accomplished.

Nights drew colder and darkness settled in earlier and earlier .although the days stayed sunny and warm. Colored leaves fell from the trees and the forest canopy got thinner and thinner. The woods were frantic with activity as squirrels rushed about in a last minute panic to gather as much as they could of acorns, nuts, and seeds.

The first week of October, the week before Canadian Thanksgiving, saw Ruth, Lizzie, and Alan erupt into a whirl of activity. Silver was dragged out of storage to be polished, pies and casseroles baked, groceries brought in by the truck load, the lawn cut one last time, leaves raked, flowerbeds and vegetable plots turned over. Unused rooms were aired, linen shaken out of mothballs and new sheets and towels purchased. Two women arrived from town to give the place a cleaning from the top of the kitchen fireplace to the bottom of the deck steps.

On the Friday morning, Elaine hesitantly brought up the subject on her mind. "With all your family here and Thanksgiving preparations underway and all, should I be planning on spending the weekend alone, Moira? I have plenty of work to do. Going through the tapes, typing up my notes, a bit of research on the Internet." Elaine had no reason to think much about her predecessor, Donna. And what had become of her on the previous holiday weekend. But the thought occasionally chewed at the recesses of her mind. "I can stay well out of everyone's way, if you don't want to continue working. And if you need my room, I'll take myself to a hotel."

Moira snorted. "What ever gave you that idea, young woman? I have no intention of letting my overbearing sisters and their horrid children and stuffy husband—there is only one left and as little said about that the better—interfere with the task at hand. I intend to keep on working with as few interruptions as possible." She peered over the rim of her glasses. "Unless you have Thanksgiving plans, of course."

"No plans. Nothing at all."

"Someday you can explain to me why a lovely young thing such as yourself has no family and no friends with whom to spend the holiday. But as you so forcefully reminded me, as your employer that is none of my concern. Let me tell you about Matron. She was the most amazing woman; she ruled us with an iron fist and we were in absolute awe of her...."

On Friday evening the extended Madison family arrived in a small convoy of luxury cars and SUVs. Elaine watched from the kitchen window as people and luggage poured out of the vehicles and flowed into the cottage. All day a cloud of depression had been hanging over her, just barely out of reach, too far for her to push it away, but close enough to leap forward at any time. Out of nowhere, it had snuck up on her when she'd been discussing plans for the holiday weekend with Moira. Elaine had realized with a shock as sharp as if she had thrown herself into the cold lake that she really didn't have anyone to spend the holiday with. Her parents were dead, her brothers didn't write often, she'd lost her family of in-laws when she lost her marriage, friends hadn't extended invitations. She didn't even have a dog.

"As long as you're standing there, not doing anything, would you get six or seven apples out of the bin and peel them?" Lizzie was up to her elbows in flour as white and fluffy as fresh snow. Elaine turned away from her self-pity and went in search of the apples.

◇◇◇

Elaine dressed in a blue business suit, put on the gold earrings, and snapped her best (and only) string of pearls around her neck. She dabbed on the faintest touch of blush and lipstick and fluffed her short blond curls, which were, in Elaine's opinion, her best feature. She took a deep breath and went out to face a room full of strangers.

Drinks, she had been told, would be served in the drawing room. Even after living here for a few weeks, she had absolutely no idea of what constituted the drawing room.

It turned out to be the front room she'd been into many times, the one with wide French doors and a wall of glass overlooking the deck and the panorama of lake and sky and hills beyond. The sounds of livid dogs shut outside, braying their dismay at being banished from the party, followed her as she walked down the hall. She followed the flow of voices and there they all were.

Huge logs crackled and spat, bright yellow flame danced, and red embers glowed in the enormous stone fireplace. The mantle was decorated with a cornucopia of sugar pumpkins, colorful ears of Indian corn, and tiny orange, yellow, and green gourds. Votive candles in crystal holders had been tucked around the vegetables. The rich voice of John Lee Hooker filled the room, emanating from a CD player placed discreetly out of sight.

Lizzie had piled her hair into a severe bun on top of her head and put on a demure black dress covered with a stiffly-ironed white apron. She winked at Elaine as the older woman paused at the entrance into the room, hesitant and self-conscious. Alan, dressed with equal formality, manned the bar set up in front of the French doors. He looked quite the part in black suit, starched white shirt, and cheerful red bow tie with matching cummerbund. Only his tumbling mop of curly salt and pepper hair contradicted the image of the picture-perfect butler.

Spotting Elaine, Moira pulled away from the group in front of the windows. No wheelchair today: the elderly Miss Madison gripped a pair of steel arm braces and staggered across the room bravely. She looked spectacular in an evening gown of pale yellow wool, plain and unadorned, which fell in gentle folds over her skeletal frame to float around her ankles. Her only jewelry was a pair of glistening diamond earrings that reflected white and yellow light from the array of candles scattered around the room like a star going supernova.

"Do shut your mouth, my dear," Moira chuckled. "You look rather like a fish wondering how she came to be in this particular aquarium. I can manage to get around. Although with a bit of effort. But Ruth is nearby, as always, to ensure that I don't fall, or otherwise disgrace myself. Let me introduce you."

Moira led the way, her twin crutches balancing the frail body. Ruth, dressed as an extra playing the part of a maid in the movie version of a Jane Austen novel (although the skirt was a touch shorter), hovered within reach.

If she'd passed them on the street in a blinding snow storm Elaine would have recognized the two elderly women standing by the makeshift bar as Moira's sisters. The same tiny frame, the same awful teeth, the same striking brown eyes. But where Moira exuded confidence and authority whether in wheelchair or arm braces, these two blended perfectly into the background.

"My sisters, Maeve and Megan," Moira made the introductions. "My biographer, Elaine Benson."

Elaine stepped forward, hand outstretched in greeting. The sisters each took it with as much enthusiasm as if they had been asked to hold a fish plucked fresh out of the lake. Maeve's hair was dyed a youthful red and rolled into tight curls. She might be Moira's younger sister, but her face was so tired and lined that she looked ten years older. Megan had chosen to go blonde. Elaine vowed right there and then that when the time came she would let nature have her own cruel way. Megan's perfume was Chanel Number 5, which Elaine's mother had always worn, but Megan had applied it with far too heavy a hand.

"I hope that you're not digging up any of our family skeletons," Megan said, waggling one painted claw at Elaine. "This family does have a reputation to protect." She stretched her wineglass out behind her, and without a word Alan filled it with a soft, golden liquid. Moira and Maeve scowled matching expressions of disapproval.

"I intend to tell the truth," Elaine said.

"However you find it, I am sure," Megan replied. She took a gargantuan gulp of her wine and turned to her older sister. "I really don't approve, my dear, of the modern fashion of letting it all hang out."

Elaine stifled a grin. "Letting it all hang out." She hadn't heard that expression since her university days, and that was more than a few years ago.

"Some things are best kept private," Megan continued, "I have always maintained. Didn't I say that to the previous girl…what was her name…? Dianne? No, Donna."

Unasked, Alan handed Elaine a red wine. The glass was huge, handcrafted to crystal perfection, dwarfing the drops of scarlet liquid that filled the bottom. She nodded her thanks and sipped the drink gratefully. She looked up from her glass to see Alan smiling at her. When he smiled he could be almost handsome. She felt herself blushing and looked quickly away.

An elderly gentleman approached their group. He nodded to Moira and smiled at Elaine. "You must be the writer of whom we have heard so much. I am Charles Stoughton, and am delighted to meet you. I quite desperately wanted to be a writer myself in my younger days. But, alas, it was not to be."

Elaine extended her hand, expecting to receive a polite shake. Instead Charles lifted it to his lips and kissed it. She was enchanted. He was well into his eighties and so emaciated that the bones of his aristocratic face protruded as if they were a finely crafted sculpture of stone or marble covered by a paper-thin layer of skin. The candlelight reflected off an almost bald scalp with a few wisps of white hair high above a pencil-thin gray moustache. His jacket was brown tweed in a herringbone pattern, with leather patches at the elbows. A cheerful red cravat accented the long patrician neck. "If you're in need of any assistance with the war years, I would be more than happy to help in any small way that I can."

"Charles is a true war hero," Megan piped up, her voice high with excitement. "He was decorated many times over. In particular the Army chose to honor Charles with the George Cross."

Elaine smiled. "I would be delighted," she said, with total honesty. She could listen for hours to old-timers telling their war stories. It wasn't her period—she had much more interest in the pioneer women and men who opened up the expanses of North America—but there weren't many pioneers left for her to talk to. "Perhaps we can find an opportunity to get together over the weekend."

Charles Stoughton preened. It had been a long time since someone had wanted him to talk about his youth.

"Later, later." Moira drew Elaine away from the circle of the elderly, by the force of her personality if nothing else. She was visibly tiring on the braces.

A gaggle of teenagers leaned up against the far wall, looking even more out of place than Elaine herself in this elegant setting. At Moira's arrival the group fell silent.

"My great-nieces and nephews," she told Elaine.

They were two girls and a boy. All with shiny hair and rows of straight white teeth.

"Welcome to the Castle of Darkness. I'm Phoebe. These two know-nothings are Amber and Brad," said a dark-haired girl whose makeup had been applied with an extremely heavy hand. Thick black circles rimmed her eyes; dark brown eye shadow, pale foundation and lipstick a deep plum all gave her a look approaching macabre. But her teeth shone, and the sparkle in the dark eyes struggled with her vampiric image. In honor of the season, she wore a jeweled turkey on her left shoulder, the brown and orange of the brooch the only color in a head to toe expanse of black.

"Castle of Darkness, an interesting name." Out of the corner of her eye Elaine saw Ruth helping Moira to a comfortable leather chair before the gigantic fire.

The young people turned away to giggle at a shared joke, which left Elaine feeling quite self-conscious amongst this group of relatives. She sought out the company of people more her own age. An attractive couple stood by the French doors, talking to Charles. The woman was thin and delicate in an oatmeal linen jacket over a deep blue raw silk blouse and beige slacks. The man wore a country sweater colored with the flavor of autumn woods.

The talk was about the stock exchange, the economy, and the fortunes (apparently bleak) of the Canadian dollar. Elaine clutched her glass and forced a smile.

"Such a boring conversation. But they do insist on talking about the same things every time we get together." The woman detached herself from the group and smiled at Elaine. "I'm Alison. I noticed that you've already met my mother, Maeve. And this is my husband, Elliot."

The man's gaze passed over her and dismissed her instantly. He returned to what Charles was saying.

Screw you, too, buddy.

"I must tell you that most of my family aren't at all happy about Auntie Moira recording our history for all the busybodies in the neighborhood to enjoy. But I think it's quite wonderful." Alison fingered the toothpick that skewered an olive securely in her cocktail. "I spoke to Donna briefly about it. I'm so sorry that I didn't have a chance to get to know her better."

"With all due respect, Moira, I must insist that you do something about those people." Charles Stoughton's deep baritone rose above the polite chatter of cocktail party conversation, John Lee Hooker, and irritated dogs. "The place is turning into a hippie camping ground. You're here practically by yourself all week, you can't have these…people…hanging around."

"I thank you for your concern, Charles." Moira's voice was as sharp as steel. "But I don't think that it's any of your business, now is it?"

All conversation ceased as the gathering turned to watch. Charles had abandoned Elliot to loom over a tiny Moira sitting proudly erect in the best chair. "It is very much my business. I am after all the head of this family…."

Moira snorted. "I never could understand quite what makes you think that, Mr. Stoughton."

He grimaced but held his ground. "This property belongs to my wife as much as to you, and the occupation of the island is of considerable concern to her."

"Then she may speak to me of it at another time. Not that I'll do anything, of course. They're my guests and welcome here as long as I say so."

"You tell him, Auntie." Phoebe grinned broadly. "Poor old Grandpa never could stand up to Auntie Moira," she whispered, "but he keeps on trying."

"What are they arguing about?" Elaine asked.

"In reality, they're arguing over the pecking order in this family. As the eldest surviving male, although only by marriage, Grandpa thinks he is the head of the family. As the oldest surviving child of the Madisons, Auntie Moira knows that she is.

But tonight, they're fighting about the people Auntie is letting camp over on the island."

"You must see sense, Moira," Charles said, his sculpted face erupting into undignified red splotches. "This can't continue." He held up one arm and jabbed a finger in the air to make his point. The old woman calmly raised her brace and smacked him on the side of his hand.

"That is quite enough." Maeve, the redheaded sister, pushed her way between them. "We do not discuss our family differences in front of outsiders."

Phoebe giggled. "That means you," she said to Elaine. "The servants don't matter."

"Dinner is served," Lizzie announced from the doorway, her voice resounding with the spirit of centuries of staff speaking those same words. But she couldn't quite pull it off and she sounded more like a bad actor in a third rate amateur production of an English farce.

Lizzie's words had broken the tension and the company filed out for dinner. "Let me help you, Auntie." Phoebe rushed to help Moira to her feet. Ruth brought the wheelchair and Phoebe guided her great-aunt into it.

"Do walk with us, Elaine," Moira said, summoning her with a wave of one frail hand. "Have you met Phoebe? Good. You may take me in, dear."

Extensions had been placed in the table so that it ran the length of the dining room. An impressive array of starched white linen, sparkling silverware, fine leaded crystal, pale blue and white china, and silver chargers glowed under the light of candles resting in highly polished silver candelabra.

But it was the pictures that attracted Elaine every time she came into this room. The wall above the heavy antique sideboard was covered with a mass of photographs of the family throughout the years. There were pictures of swimmers in one-shouldered men's bathing suits or gruesome ruffled caps. Of boating parties, dressed in tweed jackets and ties, or corseted dresses and ornate hats. Of serious-faced picnickers sitting on blankets, the men wearing cloth caps and in shirt sleeves, but still sporting the ubiquitous dark tie, the women in stiff summer dresses and stiffer hair and hideously ugly, clunky black shoes. Picture after picture of somber elders and laughing children.

While everyone took their places at the table, Elaine stepped closer to admire one sepia photograph of a large group just disembarked from the lake steamer. She recognized the location of the dock and the lake beyond, but the people were from another world. The men were dressed in suits and hats, ties knotted tightly, many sporting enormous black moustaches. The women's dresses, ornately festooned in flurries of ribbons and bows, skimmed their ankles, and their heads were topped by straw hats the size of umbrellas. Even the children wore either miniature suit and tie or frilly dress. A massive pile of luggage was assembled on the dock, and in the background the steamer pulled away. Two maids in black dresses and stiffly starched white aprons and caps struggled under the weight of suitcases and hat bags, frozen permanently in time as they stared uncomfortably at the camera. A large man, enormous cigar stuffed into his mouth, waistcoat stretching over ample stomach, filled the foreground. It was Augustus Madison, whose portrait also overflowed the limited space of the staircase.

"I've invited the Josephesons for dinner tomorrow," Moira said after the wine was poured and the soup served. "I do hope that is all right with you, Charles, dear." Her smile was provocative.

The old man glowered at her.

"Grandpa, don't be glum," Phoebe said lightly. "You know you like old Mr. J. You've always said how much you do."

Charles shrugged, but the edges of his mouth cracked under the thin moustache. His granddaughter knew him well. "He's not a bad sort. Knew him in the war, he was a good lad, then."

Tension broken, the conversation swirled around. Only the endless barking of the dogs spoiled the lovely evening.

"Why does everyone put up with those dogs?" Elaine whispered to Phoebe. "Don't they ever stop barking?"

"As soon as Lizzie has the main course on the table, Alan will bring them in to be fed. That should quiet them down a bit. Aunt Moira loves them desperately, so what can we say? If you notice, Grandpa has turned his hearing aid down a bit, and Grandma can hardly hear a thing at the best of times. And the rest of us would never be quite brave enough to drum up the courage to say a word against them."

A woman had been hired to serve as maid. She wore a black dress with white collar and cuffs tucked under a neatly ironed white apron. The dress stretched across the expanse of her ample hips and stomach to the very edges of its seams. Elaine leaned back to allow her to collect the soup plate.

"I do hope you're not going to let any of our family secrets into that book of yours, Moira," Megan said, her thin voice rising above the chatter of dinner table conversation. "Don't you let her, uh, uh...?"

"Elaine," Phoebe said, loudly.

"Don't you let Elaine air our dirty laundry."

"Oh, do we have dirty laundry, Aunt Megan?" Amber laughed.

"Tell all, please do," Brad said.

"I intend to tell this young woman the story of my life," Moira said. "As I lived it. If some people don't like what I say, then that's their problem."

"Yeah." The boy raised one thumb.

"What's that? What did she say?" Charles fumbled with his hearing aid. "Something about her memoirs?"

"Aunt Moira said that she'll tell the truth and that's that," Alison said, pronouncing each word with precision.

The maid carried in the platter of roast beef and the table fell silent.

Chapter Ten

On her day off, exploring the countryside on her bicycle, Moira happened upon a traffic incident. A Canadian soldier riding a motorcycle had taken a corner much, much too fast. He couldn't see around the hedge, but apparently didn't consider that to be a problem. Fortunately he saw the young girl walking dreamily down the center of the lane at the last possible moment. Instead of killing her, the impact merely dislocated a few bones. On the girl. The soldier spent several months in the hospital regretting his love of speed. Moira jumped off her bicycle to attend to them while a passing farm hand ran for help. The girl was Catherine, the daughter of Burt and Betty the shop owners, and their effusive gratitude was beyond embarrassing.

Moira's older brother, Ralph, was also stationed in England. She'd heard little from him, the news mostly passed through their mother or grandmother. But at last, in the early spring of 1942, they managed to organize leave at the same time. Moira took the morning train up to London.

The devastation took her breath away. They knew, of course, of what was happening in London and the other great cities of England. They heard the bombers overhead and watched the sky turning red night after night during the blitz. Bert and Betty had each lost a sibling in the rubble of the East End. Moira had seen some of it for herself that night at the movie theater, but she had not been back to London since. That day she realized that her imagination had scarcely understood the depth of the destruction. Their train wound through rows and rows of burned out homes and factories. Entire streets were reduced to piles of rubble, while the next road would stand in the sunlight, whole and untouched. Children played and women pushed prams through the ruins. A few pots of early geraniums filled window boxes as if to hold a defiant fist up to the enemy planes flying high above. The blitz had ended, although bombing raids could, and still did, plague the cities.

This train, like the one that had brought them from Liverpool, was jammed well past capacity with civilians, mostly women, and troops of any and all nationalities, including a group of dark, hard faced men in uniforms of traditional British khaki topped by full beards and turbans. Fascinated, Moira watched them out of the corner of her eye.

The journey from Surrey to London didn't normally take long, but they came to a sudden, unexpected halt and sat in the middle of a farmer's field for a long time. Cows on the track, tracks bombed out, an accident up ahead. The car swirled with rumor and speculation, everyone growing restless and bad tempered.

The hospital cook had packed her a picnic lunch consisting of two dry cheese sandwiches, thick slices of currant cake, and a thermos of overly sweet tea.

Moira had foolishly neglected to bring a book, so for lack of anything else to do she offered to share her sparse meal with a chubby, pasty-faced young woman of her own age sitting across from her. Delighted at the unexpected treat, the girl proudly told Moira that she was going to London to take a factory job. She was dressed in a heavily-mended, but clean and crisply ironed dress of pale blue, with a jaunty navy beret, which looked as if it had been bought specially for this journey. Her teeth were small and badly stained but she smiled brightly and chatted with enthusiasm while they waited. She didn't want to stay on the farm, she told Moira, although she was valuable there, what with all the ignorant city girls being sent to replace the farm boys gone to the army. But her cousin, Nancy, had a job in a factory in London and had secured a place for her. This was her chance to escape from the stifling confines of her family, and she was determined to make the most of it. Rose was her name, and she consumed most of the sandwiches and drank almost the entire contents of the thermos. But Moira didn't mind, and she insisted that her new friend finish off the last slice of cake. She found it fascinating to listen to the harsh country accent as it told of a life she couldn't imagine.

"You don't have a boyfriend, then? A young man, I mean?" Moira asked as they watched nothing much happening in the cool green countryside.

"Well, there's Davy Blake from the next farm over. He's been thinking that we'll be married ever since we were children playing in the haystacks together." She chuckled and touched her index finger to the last currant hiding in the folds of the wax paper wrapping. "Least his mother has been thinking that. No knowing what Davy thinks. He's not much for talking."

"Where is he now?"

"Still on the farm. Essential worker. He's plenty glad to be told he has to stay there. Poor Davy never had much of a wish to travel."

"But you do?"

"Course, I do. Imagine, trapped in that old farmhouse for the rest of my life, fetching tea and crumpets for old Mrs. Blake. Mr. Blake is long gone, and Mrs. Blake has been old as long as I can remember. For all that she isn't any older than me own mum."

"Well, good for you," Moira said, with feeling, "for wanting to see what else is out there before you have to settle down."

They talked for a long time, about men and boys they had known, families and school and dreams. Moira toned her life story down considerably, declining to share information on the family's Muskoka cottage, her private girls' school, her mother's army of servants, and the dinner parties attended by bank presidents and cabinet ministers. Instead she talked about meeting her brother in London and how her mother continued to beg her to come back home.

"Mothers," Rose said.

The companionship made the delay fly past and soon they were underway again and the gentle fields were turning into grimy factories and long lines of bleak row houses. "Almost there," Moira said, her excitement rising as she spoke.

"Almost there," Rose echoed, her voice etched with apprehension.

Soldiers in the aisle gathered up their kit, eagerly stretching cramped legs. Women folded their knitting into voluminous cloth bags and packed away children's books and tinker toys. The dark faced soldiers with the turbans rose to their feet like a soft, liquid mountain. One of them caught Moira staring at him and winked broadly. No longer ferocious, he was now just human. Human and handsome. She blushed deeply and turned back to her window.

"Sikhs, from India," Rose whispered, her washed out blue eyes flashing with excitement. "Come all this way to help us win the war, I've heard. Great soldiers, my dad says. And it certainly don't hurt that they're so handsome. He's watching you, that big one." She gave the soldier a coy smile and cocked her head flirtatiously to one side. Moira cringed in embarrassment and stared at the city passing outside her window.

The station was a pandemonium of churning bodies, thrashing suitcases and handbags, crying children, shouting soldiers and dangerous trolleys overloaded with luggage and boxes. Rose clung to Moira's arm. "Where are you off to?" Moira asked, attempting to disengage the fingers digging into her arm like a limpet. "It's been wonderful to meet you. Let's keep in touch, shall we?"

Rose twisted a scrap of paper in her hands. "Me mother's cousin, Maureen, Nancy's mum. I have the directions right here."

"You don't have to wait with me, if you have to be on your way. I'm sure my brother will be along in a moment." Moira was sure of no such thing. Their train was so late arriving that she expected that he would have given up the wait and abandoned her. Ralph, her older brother, handsome, smart, charming, the family favorite as well as her own idol, was a man now, a lieutenant in the Royal Canadian Army. But she suspected that he could still be as irresponsible as that skinny boy playing on the dock off Lake Muskoka. The one who threw his school friend into the water and walked away before checking if the lad could swim. (He couldn't and fortunately for all concerned the head gardener, weeding the flowerbeds that butted up against the flagstone path, could.) She would wait until the crowd had thinned and if her dear brother still didn't appear, well, she had the address of the hotel he'd booked her into. (Pray he had managed that at least.)

"I couldn't possibly leave you here all alone," Rose said, trying to smile. "I'll wait with you."

At that moment Moira caught sight of the flaming cloud of hair passing above the horde. As if they knew he was a Madison, the crowd seemed to step aside to clear the way for her brother. He was taller than everyone around him and his crown of red hair shone like the Holy Grail against the grime and smoke of the station. He was even handsomer than she remembered, strong and confident in his plain army uniform. He'd lost a good deal of weight and built up muscle in its place. It suited him.

His face lit up at the sight of her and he rushed forward, hands outstretched. They fell into each other's embrace and hugged until ribs were on the verge of breaking.

"You look so wonderful," Moira gasped, stepping back.

"And so do you, M., so do you. All grown up. Imagine. That is surely the ugliest uniform on the face of the earth. They must have designed it to strike terror into the hearts of lonely young men. But if anyone can do it justice, that someone is you."

Moira was extraordinarily proud of her plain brown uniform with the flat hat, double row of buttons, leather belt, and jacket with sharp white cuffs and collar. To her it spoke of history and pride, dignity, service, and sacrifice. But she was so happy to see her brother that she allowed his remarks to roll off her shoulders.

There was gentle coughing behind Ralph and a smiling young man stepped forward and held out one hand. He was exceedingly thin and his uniform, identical to her brother's, hung on him as if it had been made for another, much larger, person. "Miss Madison. So thrilled to meet you at long last."

Ralph laughed. "I see that I am forced to introduce this vagabond to my sister. Charlie Stoughton. My sister, Moira. And hands off all around."

Charlie actually kissed Moira's hand.

A gentle nudge at her back and Moira remembered her manners. "I'm so sorry," she gasped. "I have a friend as well. This is Rose—uh—Rose?"

"Robinson."

"Rose Robinson. We met on the train. Rose's got a job doing war work in London."

"Lots of that, I hear," Ralph said. His dark eyes scarcely flickered as he glanced at Rose and turned back to his sister. "I have booked one of the best hotels in all London. Time for a bit of a wash and a nap and the town is ours. Let's see if we can find a cab, shall we?"

Moira cringed in embarrassment. Her brother had summed up her new friend in one glance that lasted less than a second and dismissed her as not worth his while.

"Let me carry your bag, Miss Madison." Rose already forgotten, Charlie picked up Moira's suitcase. He was no doubt a nice young man, but Ralph would have selected him as a friend mostly because he would be trusted to follow Ralph's lead.

She loved her brother dearly. Who didn't love Ralph? But he could be such a spoiled brat sometimes. "Actually I promised Rose tea at the hotel and then a cab ride to her cousin's home. I'm sure we can all fit into a cab, don't you think?" she smiled brightly. "Come along everyone. We're going to have such fun."

Moira linked her arm through Rose's and pulled the open mouthed young woman after her. Lieutenant Charlie Stoughton relieved the English girl of her cheap cardboard suitcase and followed them across the crowded platform.

Chapter Eleven

Elaine blew yet another cobweb out of her face as she bent to examine yet another box. This dark, damp, cluttered, moldy, and spider-infested loft was an historian's dream. Decades of the family's mementos and cast-offs were stored in the upper level of what had once been a guesthouse. The cabin was situated only a few yards to the left of the main building. It consisted of one open room, once a seating area, now used to store gardening paraphernalia, handyman's tools, summer furniture, lounge chair cushions, water sports equipment, even a shiny wooden canoe. Steep stairs led up to what had formerly been a sleeping loft. Which was where Elaine sat, happily surrounded by boxes and more boxes of correspondence, social invitations, announcements, newspaper cuttings, household accounts, photographs, and assorted memorabilia.

They filled her head with the sweet scent of forgotten stacks of moldy old papers and legions of memories. She had carried her portable CD player up the stairs and the Indigo Girls sang to her while she worked. The loft was poorly insulated, so she had also brought up a small electric heater.

Why, oh why, she asked herself, did she abandon all this to write screenplays of all things? She'd earned her PhD in Canadian history and set out to pursue an academic career. Jobs at universities teaching Canadian history were pitifully thin, and when she did, finally, secure the long dreamed for position, she hated it. Dull, unenthusiastic students, full professors sound asleep under layers of dust, inadequate funding, and university politics drove her screaming from the field.

Instead she took advantage of a tiny inheritance from her grandmother and spent an astonishing two years researching and writing *Goldrush*, the story of the women who followed, accompanied, or preceded the men up the perilous Chilkoot trail leading from Alaska across the mountains to the goldfields of the Yukon—the promised land. For a history, *Goldrush* was a huge success, and it catapulted Elaine into the top rank of Canadian non-fiction writers. *Into the Bush* followed soon after, the story of women and their families struggling to carve a home out of the early 19th century wilderness. The title was a risk: a direct reference to Susanna Moodie's famous *Roughing It in the Bush*. Unlike Elaine's scholarly perspective, Susanna lived that which she wrote. But the modern work was received with critical and popular enthusiasm, accompanied by unprecedented sales, and Elaine was on a roll.

A roll that she abandoned for love.

She had been easily persuaded (far, far too easily, she would later reflect bitterly) to give up her own blossoming career and help Ian with his screenplays. He dangled visions of Hollywood and million-dollar contracts in front of her love struck eyes. They lived off the profits of *Goldrush* and *Into the Bush* until Ian started selling a few dramas to Canadian television. But the big break always remained out of reach and Elaine grew exceedingly tired of the tedious, mind numbing movie plots they were churning out. Loyally, she continued churning and said nothing.

Finally the great day came: Ian sold the options to his screenplay to a major Hollywood studio. And promptly abandoned Elaine for a more Hollywood-friendly emaciated blond bimbo in her early twenties.

This was what Elaine loved—what she held in her hands here and now. The scent of mildew on old papers, the crackle of photographs exposed to the light of day for the first time in decades, the excitement of reading just one more letter. Musty, abandoned rooms and sealed tea chests.

A commemorative plate, the type designed to hang in pride of place on a 19th century drawing room wall, lay on top of the first box she'd cracked open. It bore the images of two rather stuffy old men, dressed in stiff military uniforms with matching moustaches, and the slogan in flowing gold script: *Conquer or Die.*

Elaine had to have it. She hoped she could persuade Moira to give it to her. After all, it wasn't doing anyone any good in this box.

"Thanks for giving me a hand," Elaine said to the woman working beside her. "It's nice of you to sacrifice your holiday weekend."

Phoebe had enthusiastically stepped in to help wipe dust and mouse droppings off the boxes and drag them into a long line waiting for inspection. She rubbed a cobweb off the end of her nose, and managed to wipe a good sprinkling of dust across it at the same time. "It's no problem. My cousins are going into Port Carling to shop and I'd do about anything to avoid that. The other choice is cards in the drawing room with Auntie Maeve and Grandma and Aunt Alison." She rolled her eyes. "Can you imagine anything worse?"

Elaine laughed, "I can't imagine it at all. We didn't have a drawing room when I was growing up."

"Meanwhile Uncle Elliot and Grandpa are prowling the grounds looking for something to complain about. Perhaps Alan will let the dogs loose on them." Phoebe chuckled, and blew another cobweb out of her way. "Don't you think he's quite a babe?"

Elaine pretended to misunderstand. "Your grandpa? Definitely, in an older, sort of classic movie way. He reminds me a bit of Clark Gable. If I were but forty, fifty years older I could quite happily set my cap for him."

"No silly, Alan. He'd be perfect for you. I assume you're not married."

"We have work to do here. It won't get done by itself." Elaine pulled a stack of letters out of a shoebox tucked into a tea chest. The letters were tied up in a fragile ribbon that only remembered once being blue. A quick flick through them showed that they were from Ralph, the war-dead son, and all from England, dated 1941-1943. She carefully put the letters aside for later, thoughtful reading.

At the bottom of the box she found a picture. An amazingly handsome young man, in World War Two Royal Canadian Army uniform, standing under the wing of an aircraft. In her ever-present notebook, Elaine made a note to look up the type of plane. Behind him she could see smaller, faded figures dashing about, but the young man stood alone, one hand resting possessively on the metal skin of the aircraft. She imagined that she could see a hit of a grin at the edges of his mouth, the eyes crinkled upwards in laughter. He wore his uniform like he was born to it.

"What have you got there?" Phoebe crawled over on her hands and knees to peer at the picture in Elaine's hand. It was creased badly around the edges from damp. There were other pictures of him, among the family photos in the dining room and on the stairs with Elizabeth and Augustus. But this one, it was amazing.

"Who's this?" Elaine asked, although she didn't have to.

"I'm pretty sure it's Ralph Madison. Auntie Moira and Aunt Maeve and Grandma's older brother. He died in World War Two. He was in the army or something. They say his death killed my great-grandfather."

Elaine tucked the picture under the blue ribbon, to keep company with his letters. The rest of the day, as she dug through boxes, deciphered household accounts, read records of parties given and attended, handled letters fading to dust, and examined silver cup awards from regattas and horse jumping competitions long past, her eyes returned again and again to the cracked and faded picture.

"How did he die?" Elaine asked Phoebe as the light coming through the windows faded, and they gathered up the day's haul for Elaine to take to her room to catalogue and read into the night.

"Who?"

"Ralph."

"I don't know, only that it was in the war. Ask Aunt Moira. She knows everything about the family."

Elaine was sitting by the window at the back of the loft. She heard the sound of a car engine and looked up idly to see an Ontario Provincial Police cruiser pull up. An officer and a man in civilian clothes got out and walked towards the cottage door. They disappeared from her view.

"The police are here," Elaine said. "What do you suppose they want?"

"More questions about Donna, I'd imagine," Phoebe sighed.

"What sort of questions?"

"No one's said anything, but I'm convinced that they aren't entirely satisfied that her death was an accident. Even though that was the coroner's conclusion."

"Not an accident? What does that mean?"

"She was a young woman, in good health. She went for a walk down on the dock after dark and fell into the lake. No one noticed she was missing, and the body wasn't discovered until the next morning. She didn't have a heart attack, there are no loose boards or anything to trip over. Even if it happened after everyone had gone to bed and the house lights had been turned out, there was a bright moon that night, no clouds."

"Were you here?"

"Yup. It was my mom's fiftieth birthday, so practically the whole family came up for the party and the long weekend."

"What do you think happened?"

"Me? I think she tripped over her own feet. Heck, I've done it myself more than once. Unfortunately she fell in the lake and couldn't swim, and either the party was going hard or it was over and we'd all gone to bed, so no one heard her calling for help. The cops up here don't have much to do other than chase drinkers on boats or break up bar fights so they'd love to get their hands on a nice juicy murder investigation. But why would anyone kill Donna? Other than Auntie Moira and Ruth, not one of us had laid eyes on her until the day before she died."

◇◇◇

As was becoming their custom, Elaine met with Moira in her study before dinner.

"I'd like you to tell me more about your brother, Ralph, if you could," she said, switching on her tape recorder.

"Why?" Moira was tired and almost as faded as the picture of her brother, the skin on her face as thin as a single layer of Japanese rice paper. The invasion of relatives wasn't doing her any good.

"If you're tired, we can talk tomorrow."

"I'm not tired," Moira snapped. Ruth rushed over to wrap a blanket more securely around the old woman's shoulders. Moira pushed her off with as much strength as she could muster.

"Why does everyone keep fussing over me? I have trouble walking but I'm not a total incompetent, not yet. For heaven's sake, Ruth. Haven't you got anything better to do? Go and ask Lizzie what time the Josephesons are due."

The study door closed with a bang.

"You're awfully rude to Ruth." Elaine had been told more than once that her straightforward honesty wasn't one of her better features.

The brown eyes looked at her. "Am I? And what would you know of being rude, young woman? Of being confined to this cursed chair all day. Of not being able to enjoy a bowl of Lizzie's fabulous pasta e fagoli without the majority of it dripping down the front of your favorite Merino wool sweater. Of needing help to get to your feet, or into bed, or even attending to your most private functions. What would you know of all of that?"

"Nothing," said Elaine. "Absolutely nothing. But I do know about rudeness and taking people for granted."

Moira snorted and changed the subject. "The Josephesons are coming for dinner tonight. They're old friends of the family."

"Tell me about your brother, Ralph." Elaine also could change the subject if she had a mind to.

"What do you want to know?"

"We talked about his childhood, but I'd like to hear more about him. I found some of his letters. I'll start reading them tonight. It would be helpful if I could have your impression first."

"Why?"

Elaine sighed. Did this woman have to argue about everything? "These are supposed to be your memoirs, Moira. So we will see everyone through your eyes, won't we? Tell me about Ralph."

"Ralph, indeed, what to say? My dear brother Ralph. The golden boy. Everyone said he was fabulously handsome. But I never noticed it. Sisters don't, I suppose. He was away at school most of the time, and when he came home or up to the cottage it was usually with a crowd of boys. All of them dressed alike, and clamoring for his attention. He chose his friends carefully, boys who would hang on to his every word. I remember that last summer, in '39. All the talk among the men was the tensions in Europe and that upstart Hitler, as they called him. They stopped talking the minute one of the women or girls entered the room. Didn't want to upset us. As if we wouldn't find out soon enough, and be a good deal more than upset. I was quite wonderful at hiding behind doors or under staircases in my younger days, so I usually caught a bit of what went on.

"But as for Ralph, the golden Ralph. He couldn't wait to rush off to war, to teach Mr. Hitler a lesson, he said. I always thought he was a bit too eager, Ralph. What did he know, or care, about Hitler and the oppressed peoples of Europe. I often wondered...."

The door opened so suddenly that Elaine almost jumped out of her chair. Hamlet and Ophelia rushed across the room, baying every step of the way. They ignored Elaine, for which she thanked her lucky stars, and danced in front of Moira, begging for attention and anything else that might come their way. They smelled of mud and lake water. Elaine pushed her mind away from wondering what else they had picked up.

"Gee, sorry, Aunt Moira," Brad said from the doorway. His trousers were so big you could comfortably fit at least one other person into them, two if they were small. "They wanted in here, so I let them."

Moira scratched behind Hamlet's ear and rubbed Ophelia's chin at the same time. "That's all right, Brad. I'm happy to see them. They love to see their mommy. Don't you, my snookums?" She babbled like a baby and made kissy noises. The dogs wiggled all over and rubbed their ample rumps on the floor and whined in an ever-increasing pitch of excitement. Moira pulled her chair closer to the desk and found a bag of dog treats. The animals sat instantly to attention, their ears and the tips of their tails quivering with anticipation.

Elaine knew when she was beaten. She slipped quietly behind Brad and out of the room. There would be no further discussion of the late Ralph Madison today.

Instead she went for a walk. Something to clear her head, get rid of the dust and the cobwebs of the loft and the noise and smell of those awful dogs. She wasn't looking forward to another formal dinner (probably nothing too fancy once again). It had been great fun the first time. All the silverware and the wonderful crystal, the expensive wine, the great food. But enough was enough and Elaine wanted to sit in her room with a tuna sandwich, an apple, and a glass of milk, and do some serious research on the Internet. Instead she feared offending Moira, who she guessed would accept any personal criticism given face-to-face but would never excuse hospitality refused. She decided to go for a walk, explore the property a bit, before dinner.

In the morning she liked to have a run, but in the later afternoon or evening, a thoughtful slow walk offered her the time to enjoy the woods and appreciate the so-quick changing of the seasons. Every day she'd walked along the waterfront, or up the driveway to the main road.

But Elaine never stepped foot on the dock, fearing, for some reason she didn't understand, to walk out to the point from which where her predecessor had never returned.

Sometimes she stopped to peer into the woods beyond the flagstone path, where the wet forest floor had halted her previous attempt at exploration. The neat, well-groomed path ended where the forest began. The end of civilization and the beginning of nature. She was about to turn, to retrace her steps and perhaps sit on the rocks for a while, hoping to see the blue heron that lived on a patch of hydro right-of-way at the end of the Madison property. A flicker of dappled brown and white, and a startled Elaine came face-to-face with an equally startled doe. They watched each other for the eternity of a heartbeat, neither knowing the etiquette of such situations. The doe blinked her enormous liquid brown eyes once, decided she had the most to lose from a confrontation, and fled into the forest with a flick of a tiny white tail and a flash of brown rump.

Elaine followed. Maybe the doe would have babies, fawns. Her knowledge of the lives of deer was limited to Bambi, and wasn't Bambi born in the spring and nearly grown by the fall? But it wouldn't hurt to have a look.

She stepped off the stone path and pushed aside a curtain of branches. The rich scent of decay filled the air and seeped into her clothes. Lush and primal and intense, the autumn woods were alive with the essence of life and death.

Her nerve endings twitched, but she wasn't sure if she felt a ghost of the memory of her strange unease the last time she'd ventured past the white pines or a fairy-tale fear of dark, deserted woods.

Elaine kicked piles of brown and russet leaves aside with every step. Their crunch echoed under the weight of her hiking boots. Overhead, trees blazed with the brilliance of the colored leaves that remained. Yellow, shades of yellow beyond counting, red so dark it approached black and red as bright as a child's Valentine's Day heart, fading green and myriad shades of orange, most of which seemed more likely to be locked inside the frantic imaginations of the wildest artist than part of nature herself. Through the trees, she caught brief glimpses of the lake, shining blue and reflecting the late afternoon glow of the autumn sun.

From the copse to the right a swift rustle announced the departure of a surprised mouse or squirrel, maybe even the doe. Elaine stopped in her tracks, strained her eyes and ears, but nothing could be seen and the sounds did not come again.

She picked her way through the encroaching woods, the path fading to nothing behind her. She pushed the grappling branches aside and stepped lightly over moss-covered rocks. In the distance the two dogs barked fruitlessly at imagined invaders. Normally, she loved dogs, but these two....

As she headed up the hill, away from the lake, the undergrowth closed in around her. She pushed through thick bramble and branches that reached greedily at her clothes and limbs. For a moment her heart caught in her throat and she considered making a run for it. But a cooler head prevailed. This patch of forest might look like it was on the way to the end of the world, but it was not far to the asphalt road, the flowerpot-lined path along the waterfront, or the manicured lawn leading down to the freshly painted boathouses.

The trees were smaller here than most of the others on the property, and the undergrowth thicker, indicating that this had once been a clearing. Past a stand of jack pine she could see a small building. Surprised to see it here, deep in the woods and far from the rest of the compound, Elaine walked towards it.

The sun disappeared behind a cloud and a wind blew up from the lake, its sharp bite full of the taste of the approaching winter. Elaine buttoned her cable-knit sweater to the chin and looked up in time to avoid a rogue branch swinging dangerously at eye level.

The cabin stood alone in the remains of a clearing, the woods encroaching on it from all sides. Paint, no telling what color it had once been, was peeling off pieces of lumber in chips minuscule and large. The roof sagged, badly. Let one more leaf fall onto it and the whole structure might well collapse. The windows were boarded up as tight as a vampire's lair, without so much as a single crack to admit a sliver of light. A carpet of thick green moss and weeds crept up the crumbling steps and reached greedy tendrils into gaping cracks in the mortar.

The cabin was so out of place in this perfectly maintained property that Elaine glanced behind her, wondering if she had wandered off, like a modern day Rip van Winkle, only to emerge in another place or time. But she could still see the twinkle of sunlight dancing on lake waters, the clouds that seemed to be over her head only, and hear the barking of the dogs.

As she stepped out of the shelter of the trees an unexpected gust of wind forced her backward. Her foot hooked a gnarled old root; only by grabbing a low branch did she manage to save herself from an ignoble tumble onto the rough ground. The icy wind pushed eagerly through the openings in her sweater to dig frozen fingers through the thin cotton of her T-shirt. The branch cracked under her weight and Elaine fell onto her knees.

Cursing, she struggled to her feet and was inspecting her jeans for damage when a low moan echoed around the cabin. It spoke of cold and loneliness and pain and was alive with a force unlike any wind Elaine had ever experienced. Goosebumps rose along her arms under the layers of warm wool and caused the short hairs at the back of her neck to stand upright. She was reminded of the dogs the first time they saw her, every wiry, black hair along their backs twitching with scarcely contained tension.

The wind lifted the piles of dead leaves that had fallen into a mess on the front porch into the air, higher and higher. Reaching knee height, they circled, faster and ever faster, into a maelstrom of rust-yellow, black, and brown. The whirlpool churned. Individual leaves broke away and flew across the clearing, while those lying further away were sucked relentlessly in. A piece of paper joined them, a disconcerting flash of human-bleached white, pure and clean against the complex colors of nature's death. She caught the whiff of cheap, stale perfume, borne on the wind, the kind a pre-teen girl would buy, counting out her meager allowance at the cosmetic counter in a drug store.

The moan sounded again, if anything softer and more oppressive than the first time. It came directly from the void that was the churning middle of the tiny storm.

Heedless of dirty jeans, sore knees, and scraped knuckles, heart pounding and limbs shaking, Elaine turned and fled.

Chapter Twelve

Acting quite unlike her normal self, Moira chatted cheerfully on the short cab ride to the hotel. The men smiled politely and said little; Rose stared in wide-eyed wonder out the windows of the car. She had scarcely closed her mouth since Moira announced that they were to have tea.

The great city of London was alive with activity. They passed government buildings surrounded by mountains of sandbags, bombed out homes, and shops that were not much more than piles of rubble. The streets were crowded with soldiers, sailors, and airmen in every possible combination of uniform and nationality. Bicycles were everywhere, weaving in and out of traffic with reckless abandon.

Huge posters and billboards covered the city, on the sides of fences and buildings, calling on people to register for war duties: "Don't leave it to others." To save food, to save for Victory. They issued instructions on how to behave in an air shelter, reminded people to carry their gas masks, to eat carrots (supposedly to help one see better in the blackout), and of numerous other tasks and responsibilities, both large and small.

"I suppose London has changed considerably since your last visit, Miss Robinson," Ralph said when Moira stopped to take a breath.

Innocent that she was, Rose fell into the trap. "I've never been to London, sir," she said. "I mean Ralph. Lieutenant Madison." She giggled and her pale face turned a blotchy red.

"Really," he said dryly. "I never would have guessed."

"That's all right, Miss Robinson," Charlie spoke up, the words stumbling awkwardly over themselves in an effort to find their way out of his mouth. "This is my first time in London too. I'm hoping to go to the National Portrait Gallery tomorrow. Perhaps you'd like to join me? If you have nothing planned, I mean."

Rose lowered her head, shyly. "That would be lovely," she mumbled.

Moira smiled her gratitude at Charlie, while Ralph tried to cut him with a glare. There was hope for the friend, yet. Perhaps he wasn't quite the sycophant she had imagined him to be.

Even the piles of sandbags stacked outside couldn't disguise the timeless elegance of the hotel. An elderly man dressed in stiff livery, too old for war work, hurried curbside to help the cabbie with their scraps of luggage.

Moira's shoelace was unraveling. She bent over to tie it and straightened up as Ralph paid off the cab driver. She had no idea what the fare might be and no interest, but she caught a glimpse of Rose's stunned face as the English farm girl saw the size of the tip and the driver's toothy grin of appreciation.

A chill touched Moira's spine. Now that it was too late she feared that she might have made a mistake inviting this awkward girl into their circle.

But what's done is done, and they followed Charlie up the steps to the hotel. The endless sea of khaki and blue-gray of the streets broke as they reached the lobby. Carefully made-up women wore bright dresses with colored hats, real nylon stockings and shoes with high, sharp heels. Most of the men were older, in neat suits and thin black ties. Only a few wore a uniform.

Ralph marched up to the desk. Moira hung back. Nothing for her to do; everything would be taken care of. Trained to recognize money, the bellhop scrambled to help with their bags. He was fairly young—strange to see him out of uniform. But his hip was badly twisted, and he walked with an awkward, loping gate.

Tossing the room keys casually in one hand, Ralph herded the group to the elevator. Moira reminded herself to call it the lift.

"Downstairs in half an hour?" Ralph called to her as the bellhop showed Moira into her room.

"Beat you to it," she laughed in echo of a childhood memory. He smiled the wide comfortable smile she remembered so well and, as usual, she forgave him everything.

Rose stood in the middle of the huge, lovely room drinking in the details.

"Sorry to drag you off like that," Moira said, pressing a tip into the bellhop's hand. He closed the door silently on his way out. "But my brother can be so domineering, I simply wanted to be on our way." She opened her suitcase and rummaged around for her toiletries. "You're welcome to have tea with us, and I'll see that you get a cab to your cousin's house. But I'm sure she's wondering where you are. So if you would like to be on your way?"

"No. This is lovely." Rose sat on the bed and bounced tentatively, up and down. "Even me mum and dad don't have a bed this big," she said in awe. "Your brother must be so rich! And he's dishy, too. He looks like he could be in pictures. Clark Gable or someone."

"No," Moira said, gratefully tugging off her tie. How she hated wearing a tie. If there was one thing that threatened to drive her out of the Army Nursing Sisters it was being confined in a tie: that medieval instrument of torture. She sometimes fantasized about the delight she would have, ripping the thing off in front of Matron and the doctors and running from the room screaming. "My brother isn't rich. He likes to spread his money around. More fool him."

"Still," Rose sighed. "This is such a beautiful room. I can't wait to tell Mum and Dad all about it."

"I'm going to wash and get changed," Moira said. "Help yourself to anything at all. Then we'll go down for tea."

Rose strolled over to the windows and pulled the thick blackout curtains aside. "Do you think that perhaps your brother could help me find a job? If the factory don't work out, I mean?"

"No!" Moira almost shouted. Looking at Rose's startled white face, she felt sorry immediately. "Please, don't ask Ralph for anything. He's my brother and I love him…but he's not terribly nice. Really."

"Well, I think he's nice," Rose said, dreamily watching the city moving below. "His friend Mr. Stoughton is nice too, don't you think?"

"I'll have that wash now. See you in a minute."

The two women were ready and waiting in the lobby when Ralph and his friend arrived. Moira had changed into her best dress, a soft blue color that flared from the tight fitting waist to billow in gentle clouds around her knees. She had been about to slip on a precious pair of silk stockings sent by her mother when, catching sight of Rose, staring lonely and lost at the blackout curtained window, she returned them to her case. They would keep for another day. She would venture out barelegged—too bad about the legs shockingly pale from a long English winter.

Moira loved every detail of the English custom of afternoon tea. And unlike her sisters, she had never tried to hide her ferocious love of eating. But the war's long tentacles stretched even as far as the kitchens of this hotel. The sandwiches were liver paste rather than salmon, the watercress well past its best date, the clotted cream thin and runny, and the pastries even tougher than the currant cake prepared in the kitchens at Bramshott. But the ritual was what mattered, and as long as the china was paper thin, the waitress dressed in crisp black and white, and the tea served hot and fresh in a silver pot, nothing else would concern her.

Moira and Ralph talked throughout the meal, mostly news of home, gossip about their comrades and complaints about the severity of the work and the hardships of war. Rose and Charlie said almost nothing. They seemed happy to listen to the siblings babble.

When the tiny plates were cleared away, the men settled back and lit up cigarettes. Charlie extended a pack to Rose and the English girl accepted with such gratitude that once again Moira felt a twinge of guilt.

"That was so lovely," Moira sighed, patting her stomach. She must have consumed three quarters of the tea all by herself. She didn't care for tea all that much, unless it was as sweet as treacle, and the wartime sugar bowl was shockingly low, but she loved drinking the hot liquid out of the bone china cup with the delicate blue flowers. "Your cousin will be dreadfully concerned by now, Rose. We must get you off to her."

"I didn't give them a time," Rose said. She also was sated into contentment by the luxury of her surroundings, the wonderful sandwiches (on bread so thin, with the crusts cut off!) and cakes, and the marvelous Canadian officers who sat across the table.

"Well, if you must go," Ralph said lazily, exhaling a stream of smoke as he eyed a flashy blonde in a low cut red dress and the highest of heels, who had entered the room and stood in a display of obvious confusion, apparently looking for her companions.

"Miss Robinson," Charlie said formally, the color rising in his thin face. "Allow me to call you a taxi."

Rose giggled and glanced hopefully towards Ralph. He wasn't even looking at her. Without a word he pushed away from the table and strode across the room to the blonde. She reached into her purse for a cigarette. Ralph arrived in time to flick open his silver lighter.

"That's nice of you, Mr. Stoughton. Thank you," Moira said, trying to draw everyone's eyes to her. "We've kept you long enough, Rose. I hope we'll get together again soon."

Charlie leapt to his feet. Rose had carried her suitcase down to the tearoom and he lunged for it. "I'm sure we will. The National Gallery tomorrow, remember, Miss Robinson."

"Please, call me Rose." The English girl smiled broadly at Moira and the small, stained teeth didn't seem to matter. "Thank you so much for your hospitality."

"And thank you for your company," Moira said, meaning it.

Charlie walked to the road with Rose to help her hail a cab. Ralph and the blonde settled at a table in a dark corner and he was ordering something more substantial than tea. Moira took herself back to her room. It had been a long day and she was dead tired and would love a bit of a nap. She wondered if Ralph would extradite himself from his new companion in time to take her to the theatre and then to supper, as was their plan.

An exhausted Moira crawled into bed wearing only her thick army-issue underwear. Being spring, it was still full daylight outside; fortunately the blackout curtains blocked the sunlight.

Her last conscious thoughts were of Rose Robinson. Moira rather liked her: shy and awkward but so excited to experience different surroundings. She doubted that she would see Rose again.

Ralph failed to arrive at the expected time. Instead an embarrassed Charlie Stoughton stood at Moira's door, clutching a bunch of wilted purple flowers bought from a street vendor.

Moira laughed and gathered him into her room. "I've been stood up by Ralph Madison before, more than once. I do hope he didn't have to pay you too much to take me out."

"He didn't pay me a single penny," Charlie insisted indignantly. Moira believed him. Charlie wouldn't need to be paid. He had the air of a fortune hunter, she could smell them a mile off.

Guessing that Charlie might not have the money to spend on the sort of evening Ralph would have planned, Moira made a suggestion. "Some of the girls were all excited about the Maple Leaf Club on Moreton Street. It's near Victoria Station they said, so we can take the tube. All the Canadians on leave go there, they said, and it's lots of fun. Shall we try it, Charlie?"

Charlie agreed, with something like relief, and they had a wonderful evening, meeting men and women from all over Canada. By general agreement, no one talked about the war. The soldiers and airmen were on leave, enjoying a few days to pretend—despite the blackout curtains on the windows, air raid sirens overhead, ample but unimaginative food, and crowded accommodations—that they were back home in Winnipeg or Moose Jaw or Halifax or an unnamed stretch of the vast Canadian bush. Canadian and English Red Cross workers, women, worked hard to make the men feel welcome. Moira enjoyed the evening far more than she would have out on the town with Ralph.

In all it was a wonderful leave. Ralph arrived the next morning full of lame excuses and apologies and Moira forgave him, as she always did. They toured the wonders of London during the day and dined and danced as the sun set. They didn't see Charlie Stoughton again, nor did she hear from Rose, for which she was guiltily pleased. This was her time to be with her beloved brother and to forget the horrors of the job and the war all around them. She didn't want to be bothered with an awkward English farm girl with bad teeth and worse social skills.

Chapter Thirteen

"I noticed a cabin, back through the woods, above the boathouse, out walking this afternoon." Elaine accepted the bowl of peas.

She looked up to see the family staring at her. Even Phoebe sat open mouthed and gaping.

"You went to that ghastly old cabin," Amber said. "Whatever for?"

"Well, it was there."

"We don't go there," Moira said. Her voice placed a firm period at the end of the next sentence. "Nor should you. More wine, Desmond?"

"Thank you, my dear." Alan slipped silently behind to pour. Elaine wanted to talk about the cabin, ask why it was boarded up and deserted. Why it hadn't been torn down in favor of a more modern out-building for guests and their friends to bunk in. Why the foliage gave silent testimony to scarcely a human visit in years. And why the wind moaned and the leaves gathered and the scent of cheap perfume permeated the air and she knew that she had to run for her very life.

Tonight they had been joined by the Josephesons. A family from a neighboring cottage, friends of the family for many years. Mr. Josepheson walked with the help of a cane and was dressed in a gray business suit, white shirt, and silk tie with alternating thin red and gray stripes. Mrs. Josepheson had cut her gray hair exceedingly short, almost to the scalp, and wore a plain black dress with a single string of pearls, which gave her an air of quiet dignity. The effect, however, was somewhat ruined by the orange reflective necklace, a favor handed out by a large fast food chain one past Halloween, that encircled her neck. Mrs. Josepheson might be physically in their presence, but mentally she appeared to be absent most of the time.

They were accompanied by their son, Greg. Handsome in that sort of heart-stopping, breath-clutching way that drew the gaze of every woman in the room regardless of her age. If there had been a baby girl at dinner, she would doubtless have been equally smitten. His short hair and neatly trimmed moustache were dark; tiny laugh lines crinkled the edges of his sea-blue eyes and generous mouth. He smiled at Elaine over the dancing flames of the silver candelabra and she forgot all about the strange cabin and the wind that had a mind of its own.

"You absolutely must ask Desmond about the war years," Maeve had said to Elaine, the moment the guests arrived. "He and Charles were great friends."

"True," Moira interrupted, steering Elaine off to a far corner of the drawing room to converse with the younger generation of Madisons. She huffed. "If that reactionary bunch had their way, my memoirs would be about how great my brother and all his friends were. And oh, yes, he did have a rather unattractive little sister, whatever was her name?"

Elaine touched the thin arm and bent to look the old woman balancing precariously on her two walking sticks straight in the eye. "But that is why you hired me, if you remember. Because I know that the saving of lives was as important as the taking of them. And that we built a nation on sharing and caring. Am I right?"

Moira threw back her gray head and laughed so much her tiny frame shook like an earthquake rollicking under the San Andreas Fault. "Indeed. Otherwise, why should we bother to continue?"

"Why indeed?" And they had gone into dinner.

As much as she liked Charles, Elaine detested his friend Desmond Josepheson from the minute she met him. The man loved to talk about nothing other than himself, his fabulously successful business ventures, his great wartime glory, and his successful family. On and on he prattled. "I'd be delighted, my dear," Mr. Josepheson said, his deep voice rising above the general hum of conversation, "to let you interview me about the war years. Charles and Ralph and I served together in England. That's where I met the boys. I was devastated when I heard the news about the death of Ralph. A tragic, tragic loss indeed."

"That was when Charles won the George Cross," Megan piped up.

"If you knew Moira over in England, then I would like to talk to you," Elaine said. "The war years will be the focus, but not the entirety, of the book."

"I didn't actually meet Moira until after the war, when my father bought a piece of property up here on the lake. He was searching for a holiday home and I remembered Ralph talking about his family place. Turned out to be a great investment, eh? The old man would be fighting to get out of his grave if he knew what property goes for on Lake Muskoka today."

"That paints a charming picture," Phoebe mumbled around her spoon.

Elaine almost choked on a mouthful of soup and had to pretend a coughing fit, held discreetly behind a crisp linen napkin.

The conversation took off: all to do with land values, and property taxes, and the prices people were paying for good water frontage.

"What would a property like this fetch these days?" Brad asked.

Mr. Josepheson named a sum well beyond Elaine's wildest imaginings.

"And to someone who would truly appreciate the quality of the main house and the out-buildings, probably a whole lot more," Elliot added.

"Did you hear that they tore down the McDonald place?" Megan said. "That wonderful old cottage. It was built in the true Muskoka tradition, every plank, every beam an original. The new buyers, some sort of dot com millionaires, whatever that might be I have no idea, thought the cottage too old and dark and tore it down right down to the foundations. Tragic."

"Have to go with the times, my dear," Mr. Josepheson said, leaning back to allow the maid-for-hire to clear his plate. "Modern people don't want these old places. Have to go with the times."

"Well, I agree with Mrs. Stoughton," Greg said, smiling at the old woman. Beneath the excessive layers of peach blush, Megan colored like a schoolgirl. "There's still land up here for people with money. Let's leave the historic cottages for those who truly appreciate them."

"Like this place," said Elaine. "It's absolutely irreplaceable. The quality of the wood, of the stone, not to mention the patina of age and respect that covers everything. I would hate to see it torn down to be replaced by some modern monstrosity of steel and glass."

"If you like the older cottages, then you must come and see ours," said Greg, taking a slow sip of wine. His lovely blue eyes smiled at her over the rim of the glass, reminding her of a week's holiday in the Caribbean. "It's of much the same age as this one. My mother has gone to considerable trouble decorating it."

Mrs. Josepheson beamed broadly but her husband snorted. Always the academic, Elaine noticed that Greg's words weren't exactly a compliment, merely a statement of fact.

"You'd talk out of the other side of your mouth, boy," Mr. Josepheson said, "if you had the chance to sell it. If it wasn't tied up between you and your sister, you'd have your signature on the page before I was cold in my grave."

As his father talked, Greg's eyes narrowed to dark slits and his mouth set in an angry line. Before he could reply, Moira interrupted. "Plenty of time to discuss your legacy in the years to come, Desmond."

Lizzie and the maid carried in the main course and conversation ended. But as she picked up her fork, Elaine saw Greg and his father exchange looks that would freeze the lake solid.

Liquors were served in the drawing room. The dogs were, at last, silent, and the fire blazed cheerfully. The blinds had been pulled back and outside the moon cast enough light on the deck to bleach the pale wood a strange shade of ghostly white.

Alan winked at Elaine as he passed her a cut-glass snifter shimmering with brandy.

Was Alan flirting with her? Elaine studied the glass as her heart pounded furiously in her chest. She scolded herself for the thought. He was just trying to be friendly, after they had gotten off on such a bad footing—what with the dogs and all. But maybe not—she prepared what she considered a charming smile and looked up. But he had turned away to talk to Alison.

Furious with herself, Elaine turned her attention back to the general conversation.

Mrs. Josepheson chattered to herself in the corner and they all politely pretended not to notice.

"Well, I for one am greatly looking forward to reading Aunt Moira's memoirs," Alison said once everyone had been served drinks. "She won't let any of us help with them. It's all quite secret and terribly hush hush."

Elaine laughed. "That isn't the intention, Alison. It's easier to work without an audience."

"Perhaps I do have my secrets," Moira said. She sat in pride of place beside the fireplace. Despite the heat, she'd asked Ruth to place a wool throw over her thin shoulders. "Don't assume you all know me so well."

"Oh, Auntie," Phoebe laughed, helping herself to a miniature chocolate from a sliver tray. "I don't think any of us take you for granted."

"Skeletons in the closet," Brad said, trying without success to make his voice deep and mysterious. "Maybe a family scandal."

Amber stood by the bar, in four-inch platform shoes and a tight, short skirt that barely covered her pert bottom. "Maybe Great-great-grandpa was a pirate and all our money is the product of his ill-gotten gains. The Scourge of the Muskokas they called him." She tossed her long blond hair, peered out from beneath her eyelashes and smiled seductively at Alan as she held her glass out for another sweet liqueur. He managed to scowl without being rude. A difficult feat.

"Really," Maeve said, her voice tinged with disapproval. "Our family has never been anything but perfectly respectable. Anyway, I don't think there were any pirates on Lake Muskoka, were there?"

Alan stirred the embers and placed another log onto the fire. He winked at Elaine, and she struggled to keep her face straight.

The young people, however, didn't have her self-control. They erupted into gales of laughter.

"Bluebeard," Amber shouted. "They called him that because his beard matched the color of the lake."

"He traveled the lakes in a canoe, a giant skull-and-cross-bones painted on the bow." Brad scooped a handful of the tiny chocolates up and popped them into his mouth, all at once.

"No, no," said Phoebe. "He couldn't fit any henchmen into a canoe. It would have to have been a rowboat. Or maybe after he earned some money, he graduated to terrorizing the lakes in a wooden power boat."

"I don't think that's at all respectful of your great-grandfather," Maeve said. Her voice was small and timid but puffed with indignation. No one heard her except Elaine and Moira.

"That is quite enough of that," Moira said, realizing that things had gone too far and her sister was highly offended. Her voice cut through the laughter.

Elaine held her glass up to indicate to Alan that she would love another brandy. The golden liquid had slid down her throat like nectar.

"I'm sure that your aunt has no family secrets to impart," Greg said, in a feeble attempt at calming troubled waters. He tossed a lopsided what-can-you-do? smile towards Elaine.

Without asking permission Desmond Josepheson lit up an enormous cigar. Judging by the look on Moira's face, permission would have been refused. Alan discreetly pulled a silver ashtray out of the recesses of a cabinet.

"Isn't that right, Moira, my dear?" Desmond puffed happily. "What secrets could a respectable lady such as yourself possibly possess?"

The brown eyes looked at him without blinking. "Respectable was never a goal for which I aimed, Desmond. I have always believed that the supposed value of a woman's reputation has never been anything other than a weapon used by society to keep her under control. And as a woman of means, respectability never mattered to me one whit. Money always beat out reputation. Still does, I am sure. Why I could have been the Whore of Babylon...."

Maeve gasped, Charles harrumphed, Amber twittered, and Brad actually blushed.

"...but it wouldn't have mattered in the least to all the prospective young men lined up at my father's door. As for secrets...I have many more than these young people would believe, Desmond. As you and Charles well know."

"Moira, I must insist that you not continue with this foolishness," Megan said, the color rising in her face. "I may not have mentioned my objections before, but...."

"You have mentioned them, dear," Moira said, "more than once. But this project is important to me, and I can assure you that...."

"Pirates," Mrs. Josepheson announced from her chair off in the darkest corner of the room, her voice clear and strong. "I was a pirate at a Halloween party once. I had a black patch over my eye and a stuffed parrot standing on my shoulder. It was so much fun. But the parrot fell into the punch bowl. Desmond said it was embarrassing."

A log crashed into the fire amidst a shower of flames. Brad helped himself to the last of the chocolates.

Chapter Fourteen

Her leave ended, as all good things must. Ralph and Charlie returned to their unit and Moira caught the Monday morning train south.

Heading out of the city, the train was a good deal less crowded. Moira spent the journey in uncomfortable silence seated opposite a fat old woman who said not a word but cried constantly into a sodden cotton handkerchief. At Ralph's request, the hotel had prepared her a good boxed lunch, but she was too self-conscious in the face of the woman's misery to open the packet and examine it. She decided to save it to share with her roommates back at the barracks.

Being in London again had brought the reality of the war so much closer. She had seen the destruction first hand and was nothing but amazed at how well the Londoners were faring. She often thought of the crying young woman with the four unruly children, and a husband presumably off at war, if not already dead. She could only imagine how people with family and children (despite the evacuations, there were still children running happily through the London streets and playing in the mounds of rubble) to worry about managed to go on. Yet they did, and more often than not with a smile firmly in place and a quick joke whenever the conversation got too serious.

But for the women at Canadian Army General Hospital Number 15 the war remained a distant threat. They had plenty of work: sickness, accidents, training incidents, men recovering sheepishly from their own foolishness.

August of 1942 and everything changed.

Moira had thought the work hard when she was in training. And then as a junior sister at Toronto General Hospital. The daughter of a privileged family, until then she had never known what it was like to really work. She tried hard at her schoolwork, and played a wonderful game of tennis, although her mother told her not to play quite so well. The young men didn't like it, she said, if a lady beat them. Moira thought that if the young men wanted so much to win then perhaps they should learn how to play properly. She told her mother so, and was banned from the annual family Labor Day picnic for her honesty.

Not much of a sacrifice. Instead of spending the day eating soggy sandwiches and pretending to be charmed by elderly uncles and obnoxious sons of the prominent lake families, all of whom seemed to be in search of a respectable (read wealthy) wife (she preferred the uncles), she spent the day catching up on the stack of medical journals hidden under her bed. She didn't understand a good deal in them, but in those days it was enough to read the words and dream.

Nothing in Moira's life had prepared her for the days after Dieppe.

Canadian General Hospital Number 15, Bramshott received the worst of the Canadian wounded from that vain, ill planned, heroic, and foolish raid. Moira had wished for some excitement in the daily hospital routine, and now she bitterly regretted that wish. The nurses and doctors worked around the clock, snatching what bits of sleep they could when they could no longer keep exhausted eyes focused at the task at hand.

There was one young man in particular, from *Les Fusiliers Mont-Royal*, whom Moira remembered for a long time. His accent was French Canadian but his last name and soft red hair spoke of an Irish ancestor who had landed long ago upon the shores of Old Quebec. He had lost both legs and his right arm. Claude was his name, and Moira sat by his bedside longer than necessary after changing his bandages, whispering sweet words of encouragement into his ear. He looked to be all of eighteen years old.

"Maman," he cried out one night. He had taken a turn for the worse and raged with fever. *"Écrivez à ma maman, s'il vous plaît."*

Moira's high school French was barely up to the task, but she was desperately afraid that Claude wouldn't live until morning. Fortunately she found a sister who had a French grandmother, and the two women sat long into the night copying a letter to Claude's mother.

He was still alive in the morning, and as the days passed Claude got stronger and stronger. Before she would have believed it possible he was being wheeled about the wards in his makeshift wheelchair, and doing what he could to cheer up the other patients, many much less seriously wounded than he.

As soon as the doctors considered him to be ready for travel, Claude, and the other seriously wounded and maimed, were packed off to a ship heading home to Canada. As he was being pushed out of the ward by a man with half his face wrapped in bandages, Claude gestured for a stop before Moira, standing by the door with the rest of the duty nurses to wish the men a good trip.

"Merci," he said.

Many years later Moira enjoyed a rare holiday in Montreal, touring the narrow streets of the old city on a brilliant summer's day. She caught a glimpse of a man in a wheelchair, enjoying a pastis at a sun filled sidewalk terrace, close to the Nelson monument. His knees were wrapped in blankets, one sleeve pinned across his rough woolen sweater. She hesitated, wanting to go forward, but afraid to intrude. As she stood in the square in the warm sunshine a young woman, perhaps eighteen or nineteen, the very age Claude himself had been when Moira knew him, walked out of the building and resumed her seat. A glass of white wine waited for her. A granddaughter?

Moira bought a posy of purple violets from a street vendor and sniffed deeply as she continued her walk down to the water's edge.

Chapter Fifteen

Early Sunday morning, the day before Thanksgiving, a couple of leaky rowboats carrying a group of modern day hippies invaded the cottage. Elaine was returning from her run as the boats pulled up to the dock.

Six people clambered out: three women, two men and one tiny girl, carefully helped over the gunwales of the rowboat. The women wore colorful knee- or ankle-length cotton dresses, and wool sweaters, and the men were dressed in an assortment of tattered pants and rough jackets. Male and female alike, most of them wore their hair long, either in a mass of thick dreadlocks or thin and straight, but covering all the colors of the human spectrum. One of the young men was black: the soft, beautiful color of the lake at midnight when clouds obscured moon and stars, the shade of rich velvet in a fabulously expensive evening gown.

They saw Elaine watching from the path at the bottom of the deck and raised their hands in greeting. She waited while the group clambered up the path.

"Hi." The woman leading the child reached Elaine first and held out a hand, clean but work-worn with ragged cuticles and nails cut to the quick. "You must be Elaine, come to write the memoirs. Good for you, women's history needs to be told."

One of the men, the white one, and the only one of them with short hair, rolled his eyes behind the woman's back.

"Rich or poor," the woman continued. "The females of any family have to fight to have their voices heard."

"Uh, can I help you?"

"I'm Rachel, and this is Dave and Jessica and Kyle and Karen. The girl is Willow. Say hello, Willow."

The child mumbled and stuck her hand into her mouth. She wore a rather odd arrangement of overlarge wool sweater, tattered jeans and brand-name children's running shoes. But everything, from her clothes to her face and hair so pale it approached white, was clean and sparkling.

"We've come to wish Moira a happy Thanksgiving," Kyle, the black man, said.

"Isn't it a touch early for a social call?"

The women's light laughter was as delightful as ceramic chimes swinging in a strong wind. "We're sure that Moira has been up for absolutely ages," Rachel said. "In fact, if truth be told, we thought this might be a good time to avoid running into her stuffy relatives."

"Stuffy, stuffy," the child chanted. She spied a chipmunk searching for an overlooked acorn amongst the piles of leaves blown onto the path, and set after it, leaning eagerly forward, her tiny, quivering body balancing on the edges of her toes.

The group climbed the stairs up to the deck. Elaine could only follow. The white boy, Dave, gave her a wide smile, but one that didn't reach his eyes.

"I'll see if she's able to receive visitors." Elaine pushed her way through the crowd.

Chipmunk forgotten, Willow clambered up the steps to join them. Finger back in her mouth, she followed Elaine through the deck doors and Elaine didn't quite know how to stop her.

In fact, she didn't know how to stop any of them, and the somewhat disreputable bunch followed her into the drawing room.

"Nice place this," said Kyle, sinking into a huge brown leather chair, as soft as butter left out on the kitchen counter on a hot summer's day. "I've always thought so." He ran his hand over the fine leather, worn and cracked with age.

There was no need for Elaine to fetch Moira or anyone else. The voices of their visitors had carried and the Madison

Matriarch emerged from her study in her wheelchair. In the absence of Ruth, the chair was being propelled by its motor. Moira approached her guests with a broad smile and outstretched arms. Willow flew into their embrace.

"My dear friends. To what do I owe the honor of this visit?" Moira patted her lap to encourage Willow to clamber onto the wheelchair for a ride.

"Only to wish you a happy Thanksgiving, dearest." One by one they lined up in a neat row to kiss Moira on her wrinkled old cheek. She beamed from ear to ear, delight consuming the dignified old lady. Only Dave stood apart, arms crossed, gazing out the window.

"Sit, sit," she said, waving at empty chairs. "And we can visit for a bit. Elaine, please go down to the kitchen and ask Lizzie if she would be so kind as to provide coffee and sweet rolls and anything else she can rustle up."

Elaine did as she was bid. No doubt these were the people camping out on the island, about whom Moira and Charles had argued so vehemently.

The scent of fresh coffee announced that Lizzie was hard at work. It was Thanksgiving Sunday and the cook, like cooks everywhere, be they paid help or loving mothers, had a heavy day ahead of her. The largest turkey Elaine had ever seen sat on the table. Breadcrumbs, celery, onions, sage, apple slices, butter, piles of walnuts, and a single egg waited to be magically transformed into fragrant stuffing.

"We seem to have a sudden influx of visitors. A strange looking group have arrived in rowboats, and Moira's invited them all to breakfast."

Lizzie sighed. "As if I don't have anything else to do. Now breakfast on the fly. I was hoping to get the stuffing mixed and the vegetables peeled before the family stumbles down demanding to be fed." Grumbling, she pulled packages out of the freezer and juice from the fridge. "At least the coffee's ready. Help yourself."

"Who are they?" Elaine asked, pouring herself a cup. "Can I help?"

"We'll need a tray set up with coffee things, glasses for the juice, toast in the toaster and jam and marmalade on the tray. There's a larger coffee maker on the top shelf to the left. We'd better get it started.

"Heaven knows," Lizzie said, finally, in answer to the first question. She pulled a honeydew melon from the bottom of the fridge and set about cutting it into thick chunks. "They arrived in the summer. Said they were looking for a place to stay for a while. Moira happened to be in town, on one of her rare shopping outings, spoke to them, and ended up offering them the use of the island for as long as they'd like. You'd think she, of all people, would show better sense."

"I've seen their fire."

"I'm convinced she did it just to get up Charles' nose." Lizzie threw back her ponytail and began laying cinnamon rolls out on a baking sheet. Elaine wondered from where they had been conjured up. Intended for the family's breakfast, perhaps? "And it seems to have worked, hasn't it? But it's still only early October. What they'll do when winter settles in, I can't imagine."

"I didn't see a cottage over there," Elaine said, searching through the well-stocked cupboards for juice glasses.

"That's because there isn't one. They're camping, that's all."

"But they have a child with them!"

Amber stumbled into the kitchen, rubbing sleep out of her eyes and looking quite fetching with her hair all tossed from the pillow, wearing a yellow silk bathrobe thrown open over a pair of shortie Mickey Mouse pajamas.

"You're up early," Lizzie said.

"I forgot to pull my curtains closed last night so the light woke me and then I heard voices. Do we have visitors? Um, smells nice. Coffee?"

"Do you think I should offer scrambled eggs?" Lizzie waved one hand towards the coffee pot, deep in thought. "Start the coffee in the big urn, will you, Elaine? Beans are in the freezer. We have plenty. I guess I will." She pulled eggs out of the fridge and began cracking them into a white ceramic bowl.

"So the rest of the family isn't too happy about these interlopers?" Elaine asked, doing as she was told.

"Not half," Lizzie laughed. "Charles and Megan and Maeve don't have a charitable bone in their collective bodies. Moira isn't charging these people rent, so what good are they?"

"What people?" Amber asked, adding one spoonful of sugar after another to her coffee. "Are you talking about the people camping out on the island? Are they here?"

Lizzie checked the sweet rolls in the oven. The air in the kitchen overflowed with the aroma of cinnamon and warm butter, fresh yeast and the best coffee. It smelled so wonderful that Elaine wished she could crawl inside it and remain there, enveloped forever in a scented heaven. Crashing back to Earth, she helped Lizzie fill a utilitarian wooden tray with glasses and plates, knives and forks and serving spoons, butter and pots of jam and marmalade.

"But what are they going to do, come winter?" Elaine asked, hoisting the tray. "Surely they can't camp out there much longer?"

"That's for them and Moira to decide." Lizzie placed the smaller coffee pot onto a second tray, already occupied by an assortment of mugs. It would do while the bigger pot got going. "God help me if she invites them all to stay here. Although it wouldn't surprise me one bit. Amber, you can help Elaine. Take that other tray."

"But I'm not dressed."

"Well, get dressed, quickly. These are breakfast visitors. Don't worry about hair and makeup, just put on a pair of jeans or a track suit and you'll look fine."

Elaine carried the first of the trays into the drawing room, Lizzie going first to open doors. Moira was laughing at a joke, while Willow snuggled into the old woman's lap.

"I never wanted to marry," Moira said, rubbing the tousled head, "and I have no regrets about that. But I do believe I have missed much by not having grandchildren."

"I'll be your granddaughter, Moira," Willow said, her thin voice brimming with sincerity. "My real grandma lives in Victoria. That's really, really far away."

"They do her the world of good, I'll say that for them," Lizzie whispered. "You start serving coffee and juice. I'll be right back with the food." She cleared the tray with practiced efficiency and scooted out of the room.

"This is so kind of you, Moira," Karen said, helping Elaine distribute the mugs of coffee and glasses of orange juice. "We really did come over only to wish you a happy Thanksgiving."

"I know you did, dear. But my grandmother taught us that one had to feed and water one's visitors. Sort of like plants, she said. If you want friendship to grow it needs generous doses of hospitality."

The young man with the short hair stopped in the act of adding countless brimming spoons of sugar to his coffee and again rolled his eyes.

Elaine held out her hand to take back the mug. "You don't have to drink that. If you're not comfortable with Miss Madison's hospitality, I'm sure you can wait outside and enjoy the weather."

Only Kyle and Rachel were close enough to hear. Kyle threw back his handsome head and roared with laughter. Dave gave Elaine a sly grin over the rim of his cup. "Nice coffee this." He walked to a far corner of the room to admire the artwork.

"Sorry about that," Rachel said. She was strikingly beautiful, tall and thin. Her red hair was tied into dreadlocks swept behind her head and caught in a bright blue scarf shot with gold threads. Her complexion was flawless and her cheeks glowed pink, either a residue of the chill outside or the warmth of the drawing room. Green eyes trimmed with long black eyelashes brimmed with intelligence and sensitivity. She dropped her voice and whispered to Elaine, "Dave can be a mite touchy, but he means no harm, I assure you."

A wave of delicious scent heralded the arrival of warm cinnamon buns, scrambled eggs, and more coffee carried in by Lizzie and a hastily dressed Amber.

Rachel rushed to clear a space for the tray. "Really, Lizzie, you needn't have gone to all this trouble."

"No trouble at all," the cook said. She snatched a cinnamon roll off the plate for herself before the others had a chance to decimate them.

The guests dug into plates of cinnamon buns dripping with white icing, fluffy scrambled eggs, and whole-wheat toast accompanied by homemade jam, chunky with fruit. Willow hopped down from Moira's lap to politely take her place in the line-up. Lizzie collapsed in a heap in a chair with a cup of coffee and her roll. Elaine took that as a sign that she could also help herself.

Dave turned from the painting on the wall to look at the food. He caught Amber watching him and grinned like a tiger first catching the scent. She smiled softly and did not turn away.

"Are you all quite comfortable, out there on the island?" Moira asked. "It will be getting cold soon."

"It's great." Karen licked cinnamon sugar off her fingers. "The best time of year to be outdoors."

"Don't worry about us, Moira," Kyle said, throwing her a huge smile. "We're more than comfortable. That island beats a crummy apartment in Toronto."

"I'll have a piece of toast," Moira said to Willow as soon as the girl finished her own breakfast. "Will you fetch it for me please, dear? And I need some help with cutting it up, can you do that?"

Willow rushed to do as she was asked.

"What on earth is going on here?" The drawing room doors flew open and Charles stood there, large, formidable, and in charge, his timid wife, and a sheepish Ruth, cowering behind. "Hardly a time for social calls, I would think." He wore a dressing gown, an elaborate Noel Coward affair of red satin and trimmed collar.

"Oh, do sit down, Charles," Moira sighed. "Coffee is ready."

"I don't want coffee, Moira. I want to know what these people are doing here. Ruth came and woke us, to say that these people were bothering you."

Ruth cowered behind Charles, trying to appear insignificant.

"No bother, Charles. There are my friends. Ruth rather over-reacted, as she sometimes does, didn't you Ruth?"

Willow cut a sliver of toast, added a touch of jam and offered it to Moira. The old woman accepted it in her gnarled hands and gently nibbled off a corner.

"Regardless, we have a busy day ahead. Lizzie in particular." Charles glared at the cook. "Should be attending to her own duties."

Lizzie glared back, but rose to her feet lazily. "On me way, gov'," she said in a parody of an English accent. "Time to black the stove and wring the turkey's neck. 'ope the fool thing's dead this year, 'ad a 'orrible time last year, wot with chasing it all over the yard with me 'atchet."

She stopped in front of Moira. "I'll clear the dishes when everyone's finished," she said in her normal voice, and left the room. For a large woman she moved with incredible grace.

Dave tore his eyes away from Amber. "Isn't Moira the owner of this property?" he said, trying to look as if he wasn't at all aware that he was stirring up trouble. "Free to invite guests as she wants?"

Charles sputtered. Kyle put his hand onto Dave's arm. "Let's finish our breakfast, eh?" He whispered something that Elaine couldn't hear and pushed Dave backwards. It was gentle shove but it threw the other man off balance.

"Time to be going," Rachel trilled in a cheerful voice as false as a politician at an all-candidates debate. "Thank you so much for the wonderful breakfast, Moira. I'm pleased to see you looking so well."

The group moved as one toward the French doors leading onto the deck. Willow was confused at the sudden change of atmosphere, but she bobbed along behind.

"Please come visit again, Willow," Moira said. "How about dinner tomorrow night? We'll have lots of leftovers because all my family will be gone." She grinned at Charles, the edges of her sharp brown eyes turned up like those of a particularly malicious cat.

"Okay, that'll be great. I love turkey." Karen grabbed Willow's arm and yanked the child out the door.

Dave followed, his eyes locked with Amber's until he was forced to turn away to concentrate on keeping his footing.

"Really, Moira," Charles said at last, when the footsteps had descended the wooden stairs and faded from earshot. "Why on earth are you encouraging those people?"

"I like those people," Moira said. "Elaine, please go to the kitchen and thank Lizzie for making such an excellent effort with absolutely no notice."

Elaine rose to her feet. Moira sat in her wheelchair, head high and chin defiant; Charles glowered at her from his impressive height.

"They're not to be trusted," he said. "Look at their hair and the way they're dressed. Why, that white boy was quite insolent."

"Hardly. He merely made a statement of fact."

Megan and Ruth flattened themselves against the wall as Elaine passed. The sound of two strong voices arguing followed her down the hall.

◇◇◇

Elaine stood in front of her bedroom mirror, watching herself as she slipped on her one pair of precious gold earrings. This was the night to dress to the nines in her clinging black cocktail dress, stockings, and dangerously high stilettos. The party clothes were clingy and highly uncomfortable after months spent in the freedom of nothing but jeans, running shoes, T-shirts, and loose sweaters. She tugged at her pantyhose in disgust. She also hated wearing the high heels, but she did feel wonderfully sexy in them.

Nothing was going right. The post of the left earring fell out of her clumsy fingers and hit the floor, forcing her to her knees (mindful of the fragile pantyhose) to scramble for the lost object amongst the grain of aged wood. Finding it, she struggled back to her feet and faced herself, once again, in the mirror.

She tried not to think about last Thanksgiving. But trying not to think is a Herculean task, far beyond the capabilities of mere mortals. She remembered being told as a child that one could not think of nothing, and, determined to prove them wrong, she lay flat on her back in her neat bed beside her massive collection of stuffed animals, trying hard to think of nothing.

This was exactly the same. An exercise doomed before it began.

They had gone to Ian's parents, as usual. Her husband's parents lived in a beautiful old home in Rosedale, the best part of Toronto. The turkey was overcooked, as usual, the stuffing as dry as dust, the gravy the consistency of colored water. As usual, Mr. Benson was three sheets to the wind before his guests even rapped the copper knocker that graced the old oak door. All that was missing was the face of Jacob Marley on the knocker itself.

She suffered through the horrible meal, the boring conversation of traditionalist males, and the empty, vicious gossip of their wives. Elaine smiled and tried to be friendly, daring to offer the weakest, slightest, most hesitant political disagreement in a charming manner.

Mr. Benson (she could never bring herself to call him "dad" as he always insisted, in his drunken, leering, drooling-all-over the-both-of-them manner) finally drove everyone out the door, as usual, while Mrs. Benson pressed aluminum foil-wrapped leftovers on her daughters-in-law.

"God, how perfectly awful," Elaine said, kicking off her shoes the minute they stepped through the door of their condo. The dog ran to greet them, restless after an evening spent alone. Elaine ruffled the black and white fur in a heartfelt greeting and walked straight into the kitchen to toss the aluminum packets into the trash.

Ian stood in the doorway, watching her. "I don't think it's proper to waste good food that way."

Elaine laughed, blissfully unaware of the abyss into which she was about to step. Ian hated his mother's cooking even more than she did. "Good food, yea. But this ain't it."

She looked up, smiling. His face was tight and closed. They had been married for almost fifteen years and Elaine still loved him with something close to the passion she'd felt in those first heady years. If she saw him walking down the street, unaware that he was being observed, the look on his face and tightness of his body could still make her pulse speed up and her heart skip a beat.

Her body yearned for him. Perhaps not quite as much as in those intoxicating days when they were first together, but he could still switch her to a slow burn with just a look.

Lately his touch had been cool and regulated, as if he did the duty only because it was expected. For Elaine the last few months had passed in a daze of terror. Knowing that something was wrong, fearing the worst, afraid that if she confronted it, she would, like a character in a fairytale, somehow cause her nightmares to come true.

He looked into the fridge. "Wine?" He pulled out a half-emptied bottle of Bordeaux.

"No, thanks," she said, the words dry in her throat, desperate to escape to the safety of her bed.

But he said the dreaded words.

"We have to talk, Elaine."

And so it ended.

The bottle of Bordeaux was followed by an excellent Cabernet Sauvignon, one that they had been saving for a special occasion. There would be no special occasion. Ian told her that he was leaving for Los Angeles; an offer had come through on his screenplay.

"This isn't a good time for you to leave your work." He buried his face into a dime-store glass brimming with expensive wine. "Didn't McMaster say he would be in touch with you soon?"

"Actually," she said, standing at the window and watching the traffic move on the street below, "he said 'don't call us, we'll call you.' Or words to that effect."

A taxi pulled up to the building opposite and an elderly man climbed out, bent almost double over his walker. It was raining heavily, and the streets had a dangerous, slick look under the yellow glow of the streetlights. The taxi driver hustled out of his seat and offered a strong arm to assist the old man into his building.

"Things are pretty uncertain, down in L.A. I'll go on ahead and check it out. Find a place to live, that sort of thing." He babbled, a man not knowing how to come right out and tell his wife he didn't want her any more. Their border collie, a beautiful, hugely intelligent dog named, not terribly originally, Lassie, crawled under the kitchen table. Not at all pleased at the tone of voices filling the room.

"You do that." Elaine turned away from the window and tossed a full glass of wine down the sink. "I'll sit right here, waiting by the phone for your call."

"Elaine."

"Yes, Ian. Are you about to change your mind and tell me that we'll all go together? You and me and Lassie. Because that's the only thing I want to hear."

"No. I can't say that."

"Then don't say anything. Please. But tell me one thing. Who are you going with? There has to be someone."

His face still held a touch of memory of the hot summer sun. It was late, and a day's worth of stubble added to his dusky good looks. He had the grace to appear embarrassed, which contributed to the charming, boyish look. Elaine almost cried at her thoughts. She should be screaming and yelling and hating him, not thinking how wonderfully attractive he was.

"I'm sorry, Elaine. It isn't anyone you know. I met her over the summer. She's a scriptwriter. She's done some good stuff and she has contacts in L.A. She'll be a great help to me."

"Oh, I'm sure she will. Be gone in the morning, okay?"

A year later and Ian was long gone, the condo sold, fifteen years of possessions divided up, and the dog dead. Ian's movie deal had fallen apart; his young girlfriend returned to Toronto in disappointment.

Elaine had surprised herself by the viciousness of her delight when a friend eagerly told her the news.

Chapter Sixteen

Moira continued to explore the countryside on her half-owned bicycle. The autumn of 1942 found her sailing between the hedgerows like a ship in full sail. Another winter of rationing and hard work, cold beds and colder baths approached; she was determined to enjoy the gentle sunshine and the soft cries of birds venturing off to warmer climes for as long as she could.

He came around the corner, from behind a thick hedge, going in the opposite direction, but his speed and absent-mindedness matched hers exactly.

They met at the bend in the road with a screech of inefficient brakes and cries of indignation. A flock of sheep watched the confrontation with idle interest.

She hit the ground, spiraling forward with enough force to knock the breath out of her. Her right knee caught the worst of it, and her body collapsed at the unexpected lack of support. Face first, Moira ploughed into the roadway.

"Good heavens. I'm so dreadfully sorry. Didn't see you coming." He dropped beside her prone body on one knee. "Can you move? I don't quite know what I should be doing here."

Moira laughed, surprising even herself. She rolled over and did a quick mental inventory of body parts. "Just a scrape, I hope. No need to call for assistance." Unfortunately the knee was torn right out of her favorite pair of slacks. Couldn't be helped. She tried to sit. The world swam before her eyes.

"I'm so dreadfully sorry," he said again, slipping one arm under her back to offer a bit of support.

"You all right there?" Two Land Army girls leaned over a farmer's fence. One of them carried a sharp pitchfork. Their overalls were caked in farm dirt, dust lined their eyes and their hair was trapped behind severe, plain scarves. Several sheep also gathered to offer moral support.

"We're fine." The young man waved one arm. "Just a bit of a bicycle collision, I fear."

The girls nodded and returned to their work. The sheep kept watching. Moira smiled up at the young man.

He helped her to her feet, apologizing some more.

"It was my fault, perhaps more than yours," she said. "I was so enjoying the beauty of the countryside that I wasn't really watching where I was going."

"Canadian," he said, pointing an index finger.

Moira was about to reply that it wasn't really such a great guess, their being in the vicinity of the Canadian Army Hospital, when he continued. "Ontario, I would say, probably Toronto. A comfortable childhood and some higher education. But an Irish mother for sure."

She stared at him. "My mother has never been to Ireland."

His face fell so much that she felt sorry for him, so she hastened to add, "But my grandmother was Irish, very genteel, and she raised me almost as much as my own mother did. So that was quite a good guess."

He held out one hand. "Grant Summersland. I don't mean to appear pompous, but it was no guess. Before the war I studied the language and dialect of the English peoples and I do rather feel the need to practice now and again."

She shook his hand. "Moira Madison. I studied nursing before the war, and I have absolutely no need to keep practicing any more. In fact, I sometimes wish I could stop practicing."

He wasn't good looking. What with an overly long nose, and huge ears, he looked rather like a basset hound left outside for too long in bad weather. But he was close to six feet tall and extremely brawny. A huge basset hound. His cropped hair was so blond as to be almost white and his eyes were the color of blue cotton left too long out on the wash line, forgotten and faded. His well-patched tweed jacket and brown pants were much too snug on his bulky frame. Intelligence and sensitivity shone behind his eyes and Moira melted.

She also felt a trickle of warm moisture running down her cheek. She lifted one hand and touched tender skin. Blood dotted her fingers.

He pulled a handkerchief out of his pocket and handed it to her. "Please, take mine."

It was clean, although badly wrinkled, and Moira scrubbed delicately at her aching face.

"Much better," he said. "Keep the handkerchief, please. You may need it later."

"I'll wash it for you."

"Let me help you get your bicycle back upright. It seems to be none the worse for the experience."

"True. But I fear the same can't be said for yours, Mr. Summersland." Moira stuffed the bloody handkerchief into her pocket. "Your machine is a bit of a mess."

He kicked the fallen contraption. The front tire had burst free of its moorings and lay at a strange angle.

Moira laughed. "We aren't far from Bramshott. I'm sure that between us we can manage to carry your craft to some sort of repair shop."

"I hope so." His face was the very picture of despair, the basset hound imagery all the more striking. "I'm not terribly good at fixing things."

"Well, I know someone in town who is. Come along, Mr. Summersland."

Moira walked her bicycle down the country road while Grant Summersland dragged his. Her knee stung badly, but they walked slowly. The Land Girls and the sheep watched them leave. The girl with the pitchfork lifted one hand in greeting and turned to her companions with a word. They broke out in gales of laughter. Neither the sheep nor Moira understood the joke.

As they walked, they talked. Grant Summersland was a pilot in the RAF. He said it as if it were something to be ashamed of, instead of making him one of "the few" in the wonderful words of Mr. Churchill.

"I'm really more interested in linguistics. I was doing some incredibly interesting work with Professor Langley at Oxford. Do you know him?"

"Uh, I don't believe so."

"You see, my father was quite the fanatic about aircraft, long before anyone else saw the possibilities it offered. He built one of the first airplane factories in the world. I learned to fly not long after I finished drinking my mother's milk." He stopped abruptly and colored red. "I'm so sorry, Miss Madison. Please excuse me, that was quite indelicate."

"I'm a nurse. I know what mother's milk is for." Moira smiled on the outside but inside she cringed. Not Grant Summersland's fault, but why, she wondered, not for the first time, were women expected to give bloody birth, tend the dying aged and the hideously wounded young but at the same time know nothing about the facts of life?

"Therefore because I could fly already the Royal Air Force was dreadfully eager to take me on. It's quite exciting, actually. But I think I'd be of more use cracking codes and the like. Don't you agree, Miss Madison?"

"Moira, please. But if you and your fellows hadn't stopped the Nazis last year and the year before that, would anything else you could have done matter?"

"Perhaps not." He kicked at a rock in the roadway, his long thin face lined with seriousness. "Sometimes I wish I had been born in a time when one was allowed a life of indulgent study."

Moira laughed so hard she had to stop walking. She liked this man whom she had met a less than an hour ago, very much indeed. "Do you think that Archimedes or Plato or Galileo lived a life of indulgent study?"

He chuckled. "No, they certainly didn't. But I would like to live in a world in which one is allowed such a life."

Moira smiled. "So would I."

"But as we live on the planet Earth in the Year of Our Lord 1942, we have to take that which we are given. True?"

"Sad. But true."

"And Hitler waits to be defeated, regardless of the movement of the planets or the progress of linguistics. So perhaps my father, who lived only to build aircraft, was right after all."

"I think I would like your father. What is he doing these days?"

Grant's face clouded over and Moira knew the answer before it was voiced.

"1938. A routine flight. Good weather, a first class aircraft, nothing too experimental. Pure bad luck. You have nothing, if you don't have luck."

"How true."

"Particularly for a pilot."

The edges of town and the Canadian Army General Hospital came into view. They stopped walking.

"I like talking to you, Lieutenant Nursing Sister Moira Madison," he said, the very picture of embarrassment.

"And I to you," she replied, also caught in the grip of mortification. What should she do, what to say? Would he ask to see her again? Oh, she hoped so. Would he invite her to a church supper to meet his sainted wife and aged mother? Let the earth open up under her feet.

But he only stood in the roadway and smiled awkwardly.

"Moira, there you are." A group of her fellow nursing sisters descended on her out of the long shadows of the approaching evening. They were gaily dressed in their best civilian dresses and hats, hair combed and curled, perhaps a bit of lipstick carefully applied. Jean stepped forward; she had appointed herself the head of their group.

"We've been looking for you everywhere. We're off to town. There's to be a dance and Matron said that we can all go. She'll be there, of course, in full battle armor. We can only hope she'll be taken desperately ill and rushed off for immediate surgery. But who is this young man you have here?"

A man on the loose. Jean smiled with all the warmth of a shark. The rest of the women either giggled and held their hands in front of twittering mouths or tossed their hair at Grant.

He visibly cringed under the force of their attention.

"I've had a bit of a mishap," Moira said. "And I really would like to go for a nice wash and maybe a nap. You won't miss me for a moment, will you?"

The women exchanged glances. "I guess not," said Jean. "Perhaps you could come on later."

"Perhaps I will."

Moira and Grant continued pushing their bicycles down the road. They came to the edge of the camp and Moira mounted her bicycle.

"Thank you for walking me back. There's a shop as you come onto the main street where I'm sure they can fix your bike. It's a bit late so they may be closed, but no doubt you can leave it in the yard and they'll know what is needed."

"Will do. Thanks again. Moira. That's a beautiful name."

"My mother loved all things Irish," she said as an explanation.

It was getting late, the sun reluctantly falling into a carrot sky.

Moira sighed, deeply. Grant watched her, shy and afraid. She knew she had to make the next move.

"This is where I live. I had better go on in. I'm late and it sounds as if they have been missing me. But please do come and visit one day, soon."

He grinned from one flapping ear to the other. "I would love to. Thank you."

"Good day."

"Good evening."

He wrote to her the next day. A simple note, explaining that he had enjoyed meeting her and that the mechanic in town, retired from Grant's father's aircraft factory, was sure he could have the bicycle back into shape in no time. His leave had been cancelled and he had to return to his unit. He would write again.

And he did. He wrote regularly, long letters in his cramped, nearly impossible to understand handwriting. Nothing about the war or news of his fellow pilots but full of his hopes and dreams, and before long she could read his handwriting as easily as that of her own mother. Several times a week, she wrote back. The Battle of Britain was over, but even so he had a dangerous job, and she tried not to worry.

Moira threw herself into her work. She thought of Grant Summersland often, and every time the memory of his awkward, smiling face popped up she made the effort to push him out of her realm of consciousness. And every time she failed. She kept his letters hidden at the bottom of her dresser, folded neatly under her rough underwear.

Chapter Seventeen

"You look tired today, Moira," Elaine said. The old woman had a bright silk scarf, patterned in the most delightfully exotic shades of turquoise and ocean blue, wrapped around her neck. But the beauty of the fabric could do nothing to countermand the paleness of her complexion or the dark shadows under her ancient eyes.

On Monday, Thanksgiving Day, recovering from the enormous dinner, the plentiful drinks, and games late into the night, Elaine had slept in and missed her run as well as breakfast. She scrambled out of bed with barely enough time for a fast shower and a quick rub of her hair with a towel, before dashing down the stairs to meet with Moira, only to find the old woman setting into her study, and Ruth fastening the top buttons on her crisp white blouse. Full of apologies for being late, Lizzie scurried in with coffeepot and mugs.

"A bit too much making merry, as Mr. Dickens would say," Moira chuckled. Her brown eyes were thick with fatigue and the delicate skin encircling them was even more cavernous than usual, if that were possible.

"I have plenty that I can do, what with going through the boxes and all, if you'd like to have a rest day."

Moira nodded. "I am rather weary. Yesterday was quite exhausting. If you don't mind, I'd like to spend my morning reading. Reading always relaxes the body as it stimulates the mind, wouldn't you agree?"

"I certainly would."

"At my age, I'm grateful that I still have my eyesight. Although not as excellent as it once was. I was famous for my eyesight in my youth. I'll tell you about it one day. Ruth, where is my book?"

"Here you go, Miss Madison." Ruth passed the latest mystery bestseller, a special edition in large print.

"That's a great book," Elaine said.

"I always read English police procedurals. I've only been back to England once since the war and that a long time ago. And now, sadly, it's too late for me to do any more traveling. But these books tell me that it has changed greatly, and yet in many ways not much at all.

"Ruth, would you please be sure and ask Alison to spare me some time before she leaves this afternoon. I have some things to discuss with her." Moira adjusted her reading glasses and bent her gray head over the book. Patches of pink scalp were visible through the thin hair.

Dismissed, Elaine and Ruth left the room.

Elaine took the opportunity she'd been waiting for to examine the paintings and photographs in the main areas of the building in greater detail. Her interest wasn't merely casual; she carried her notebook with her and made rough notes on which pictures she would like to have photographed for inclusion in the book and appropriate captions. It wasn't possible, but she would love to use every single one of them. Material for another book perhaps? She filed the idea away for future reference.

She stopped before the portrait of Moira's grandfather, Augustus, the one that had so captivated her the first time she saw it. She paused almost every day to look at it. She debated including his likeness in Moira's memoirs. She didn't want anything to distract from Moira; it was, after all, her story. But the force of this man's personality had affected his family and everyone around him. She jotted a note in her book.

"Quite the collection, eh?" Her hand jerked and dragged an ugly scratch of ink across the page. Dave and Kyle stood behind her. She had been so engrossed in thoughts of the intimidating

Mr. Augustus Madison that she didn't hear them coming down the hall.

"He's quite the ugly bugger," Dave said, nodding at the painting. "Imagine wearing a tie so tight you can't hardly breathe. No thanks."

"What are you doing here?" Elaine asked. They had frightened her, and she was embarrassed at the sharpness of her tone.

"Not going to steal the family silver, if that's your worry," Dave said. His lips turned up as he were making a joke, but the amusement didn't reach his eyes.

Kyle smiled at her. "Never mind my pal here." The look he gave his companion wasn't entirely friendly. "He takes offence at almost everything." Kyle rubbed a hand through his hair. It hung in thick dreadlocks past his shoulders and was pulled off his face by a cheerful yellow bandana. A tiny silver hoop sparked in each earlobe, making an amazingly attractive look, like Johnny Depp in *Pirates of the Caribbean*. "I'm sorry we startled you. We've come over to help Alan cut down a couple of dead trees and chop them up to dry for firewood. Lizzie's making us a snack and I wanted to look at the paintings."

"They are quite good, aren't they," Elaine replied. "This is an A. Y. Jackson." Trying to be friendly she pointed out a tiny oil trapped in a frame much too large and overpowering. "A member of the Group of Seven. They're the most famous of Canadian painters."

"I've actually been to an art gallery once or twice," Dave interrupted. "And I didn't mistake the door of the men's bathroom for a painting. Ain't that fuckin' amazing?" He turned on his heel and marched off toward the kitchen.

"I'm so sorry," Elaine said as they watched Dave leave, his shoulders set in a stiff, angry line. "That was incredibly patronizing. Should I go after him and apologize, do you think?"

"I doubt it would do any good." Kyle smiled down at her, his teeth brilliantly white against the black skin. She was tall, but he was much taller, lean and hard muscled.

"And before we go any further," he chuckled, "perhaps I should mention that I also can recognize a Group of Seven masterpiece when I see one."

"I'm sorry." Elaine stumbled over the words. "I spoke…I thought…without…."

"No matter. Which one do you like the best?" he asked, placing one large paw gently under her elbow. Without applying any pressure at all he guided her to where he wanted her to stand. "This is my favorite, over here. But you have to get back a bit to truly appreciate it." He pulled her across the passageway, to stand with her back almost flush against the wall. "This painting only comes to life from a distance, don't you think? This hall is much too dark and narrow for a proper display. A couple more feet and the color of the trees would practically jump out at you. These paintings are wasted here. Not only the famous ones, but that picture over there." He pointed out a more modern painting, a delicate watercolor depiction of flowers growing in spring sunlight and a woman's straw hat, lying forgotten in the fresh, yellow-green grass. It was a beautiful picture in itself, but it spoke volumes about loneliness and abandonment. "That picture should be in a public gallery, so the artist can get the recognition he or she deserves."

"The artist must be the same person who did the picture of the moose in winter in Moira's study. The signature is the same, and the styles are similar. Have you seen it?"

"No. I've never been into the study. Can you sneak me in one day?"

Elaine laughed. "All you have to do is ask Moira. You know she likes you."

"Kyle, are you coming to eat or what?" Alan bellowed from the end of the hall. "Let's go, man."

"I do odd jobs for Alan and Moira," Kyle said, "so I can spend some time in the house. Dave wants the money, but I need the art. Talk to you later." His deep voice rose. "Keep your shirt on, Al. That wood isn't going to get up and walk away if we're a few minutes late."

After Kyle had gone, Elaine studied the sun speckled painting for a long time. Kyle was right: it was dreadfully out of place in this dark hall filled with a mixture of Canadian masters and ancient family photographs. She promised herself to try to find out more about the artist.

In the early afternoon, Lizzie climbed the stairs to the loft with a tray of turkey and cranberry sandwiches, iced tea, and homemade cookies. Phoebe had provided the music today. Something loud and modern that Elaine tried, unsuccessfully, to ignore. They were crouched over another basket of letters. These appeared to have been written by Moira's mother, Mrs. Mary Margaret Madison, to her husband, Frederick (she never called him Fred or Freddy), during the war years. Fortuitously, Mr. Madison had saved them all and returned them to his wife at some date. He'd spent the better part of the war traveling between Ottawa and Washington, negotiating defense contracts and arranging the shipment of war supplies. How Elaine would have loved to have letters from him, full of the minutia of wheeling and dealing in the instruments of death. But he didn't write to his wife often, and the few that she had saved said not a word concerning business. Her letters to him were mostly family and household news, monotonous in their mind-dulling trivia. The maid who had quit after putting on a good deal of weight, all of it around the abdomen. The ineffectual, aged man pressed into service after the head gardener and all his staff departed to join the war effort (*the best roses I have ever had, so perfectly fabulous this year, I fear what is to become of them without due attention. Let us pray this nasty war ends soon*). Elaine set Phoebe to the task of scouring through the household accounts and minor gossip (*It has been noticed that since Bradford Connaught left to join His Majesty's service, his younger brother, Jeremy, has been paying a great deal of attention to the lovely young Mrs. Connaught*) searching for a useful scrap of news of Moira or the family's perspective on the progress of the war.

Judging by Phoebe's chuckles and groans, the girl was enjoying the job enormously. It would be great if a future historian were being inspired right before Elaine's eyes.

"She seems such a dimwit," Phoebe said at one point, lifting a letter, crackling with age, to read aloud. "Mary Margaret, I mean. But then, listen to this: 'My dearest friend and neighbor, Roberta Armstrong, I am sure you remember her, received news today that her only child, Richard, has been killed in a training incident in Halifax. Can one begin to understand her grief? The dear boy hadn't even left the safe shores of Canada. Roberta is devastated beyond belief. We are blessed with four healthy children; what can it be like, I wonder, to have only one precious child and then to lose him, so young and full of promise unfulfilled? I rushed over to offer her what consolation I could. Precious little, I fear. By the time I arrived that hopeless gaggle of sisters of hers had descended, dragging along that perfectly hideous Reverend McLeod and they were all carping on about God's will and in a better place. Such Tommyrot. I made fast work of them, I must say. As I pushed them out the door, I dared to ask Mr. McLeod that if death is so to be welcomed, then why don't we all rush to embrace it the moment we can stand straight enough to wield a kitchen knife'."

Elaine laughed out loud. "It's well worth it, poring over all the household records and accounts of endless tea parties, to come across a gem like that. Beneath the almost-impenetrable façade of respectability, we finally have a rare glimpse of Mary Margaret as she was."

They worked on for a few more hours, until Elaine's knees were complaining fiercely and Phoebe was sneezing non-stop.

"Enough for today," Elaine said, rising to her full height, joints protesting every inch of the way.

"But this box is so interesting," the girl protested, stifling another enormous sneeze. "Mrs. Madison, my great-grandma, really wanted to do something for the war effort. But all they'd give her was the job of knitting endless piles of socks. She keeps asking Frederick what's happening in Ottawa, so I think that he's not bothering to write to her much. I wonder if he was having a bit of fun on the side."

Elaine shook her finger. "Don't speculate without the facts, Phoebe. Never, never. And even if we found proof of paternal hanky-panky, it would have had no impact on Moira, so far away. Keep focused, that's my first rule. If you get distracted by everyone's story, you'll never end up with one worth telling."

Elaine picked up the letters that she'd put aside as ones to read in more detail. Phoebe switched off the CD player and unplugged the electric heater.

"What time are you leaving?" Elaine asked, pulling the guesthouse door shut behind them. "It's close to three o'clock."

"Not until tomorrow," Phoebe replied. "I was supposed to be going back today, with Uncle Elliot, Aunt Alison, and Brad, but they changed it to tomorrow, something about the traffic. Suits me. I've enjoyed helping you. Can I come back up next weekend, and do a bit more?"

"I need all the help I can get. I had no idea when I agreed to start this project that there would be so many letters to plough through. But I'll provide the background music from now on, okay?"

Phoebe only grinned.

They parted at the bottom of the steps: Phoebe to put in a bit of time on an assignment—she had mentioned in a voice brimming with lack of enthusiasm that she was studying psychology at university—and Elaine to go for a walk in an attempt to clear some of the cobwebs out of her head.

She pulled on her coat and gloves and, full of familiar, welcome thoughts, walked out onto the deck. There was nothing Elaine loved more than to spend a day going through boxes of old letters. In the mounds of chaff there was usually a grain of wheat waiting to be found. A phrase or a word or an unguarded thought that provided insight into the true soul of the writer. She thought of herself as a prospector, sifting through tons of ore to find the speck of gold inside.

Thankfully she was a historian today, while there were still letters to read. What the scholars of the future would have to work with, studying a people who jotted only their most instant, superficial thoughts onto a computer and then deleted even that the moment it was read, she hated to contemplate.

The sky was a robin's egg blue, the color matching the pristine waters of the lake. The month of October was passing. Most of the trees had lost the best of their glory; only a few scarlet or golden leaves still clung bravely to nearly bare branches. She breathed in deeply, drinking the heady aroma of crisp, clean air, decaying vegetation, and lingering traces of last night's wood fire.

She walked up the driveway towards the road. In the distance Hamlet and Ophelia were barking their stupid heads off. Cornered a stray tennis ball, no doubt. Elaine sucked in the fresh autumn air and felt the crunch of leaves underfoot. Someone, probably Alan, had long ago removed the snake corpse from the driveway. Elaine pulled a thin, broken branch off an overhanging pine tree and broke it into sections as she walked, enjoying the crisp snap of the dead wood as it broke under her fingers.

Eventually she turned and reluctantly headed back to the cottage. The sun that had been so warm a few short minutes ago disappeared behind a bank of heavy, black storm clouds. The probing touch of an icy wind crept under the collar of her coat. Under a patch of ancient white pine, a dark shape shifted and tried to form substance, like black smoke an instant before breaking into flame. It hovered in the crisp autumn air, as indistinct as fog rolling over the lake in the early morning, or sunlight shining through falling snow. Elaine slowed to a stop, her head moving to the right of its own accord, her heart accelerating to a rapid pounding in a fraction of a second. Her skin prickled with that sixth sense of knowing that someone was surreptitiously observing her. She watched in return, tightening her heart and her fists in preparation for flight.

Before she could move, either to run backward screaming for help or forward yelling in defiance, she hadn't yet decided which, the shape dissolved into nothing. Behind the spot where it had been, a red squirrel dashed down the oldest of the trees, a precious nut clenched in its tiny jaws. Elaine heaved in relief, cursed herself for her over-active imagination, gripped her coat collar tightly around her neck and ran down the path, while her heart settled back to its normal rhythm. Warm yellow lights were flickering to life in the kitchen, a buttress against the gloom of the evening and the primitive forest.

Chapter Eighteen

Several months, and much correspondence, passed. The nurses were kept busy outside of their regular duties. Day after day, they marched the Suffolk countryside, now awakening to spring. Wearing battle dress of baggy brown trousers and jacket, and carrying their full kit: small pack, large pack, a respirator, a tin helmet, water bottle, suitcase, and purse. The nurses were abuzz at what all this activity could mean. They had been stationed in Bramshott for almost three years and most of the nurses, like the soldiers all around them, were anxious to be on their way. As was Moira only a few short months ago. Now she lived in fear that they would be gone before she saw Grant again.

But they were still marching the neat, hedge-lined roads of southeast England when Moira received a letter with news that had her heart racing. Grant had a few days' leave and invited her to go bicycling with him the following Saturday. She rushed about in a mad flurry to exchange duty rosters. She had never before tried to get out of a shift and was always agreeable to switch with any nurse who asked. It was no trouble finding someone to take on her Saturday workload, and (just in case) she arranged for a Sunday replacement. Of course the first person she asked hurried to relay the news to the others and good-natured speculation flew through the hospital.

It was a beautiful Saturday morning in April of 1943 when Moira pushed her bicycle out of the storage shed. Getting the bike was harder than getting time off duty. Made even more complicated, she was sure, by her co-owners' good-natured desire to watch her squirm. She had had to do some serious negotiating to get the use of the machine for the entire weekend.

Grant Summersland waited for her at the junction in the roads, dressed in a tweed bicycling outfit that would have been fashionable when his father was a boy. His smile at the sight of her lit up his face with the intensity of a searchlight. Several of her fellow nurses had followed her, and watched with open-faced interest as Moira wobbled down the road, cycling with legs that had, for unexplained reasons, turned weak and rubbery.

He smiled at her from a face that had turned the color of a pomegranate like one that she had eaten at a summer party on the lake. So long ago it might have been in another world.

After the initial burst of awkward conversation and exchange of weather and health information, Grant's face returned to its natural color and they traveled in companionable silence. They cycled through the gentle English countryside, the sun warm on their backs. A proper wicker picnic hamper had been tucked into the basket at the front of his bicycle.

All around them the farms were busy. The farmers and their Land Army worked so hard. To put crops into the ground to feed a desperate England through what could only be another bleak winter.

Early in the afternoon they crossed over a rickety old wooden bridge, its planks protesting the weight of their bicycles. A gurgling, rapidly moving brook passed under the bridge. It was so perfectly, traditionally English that Moira almost expected a fairy-tale troll to leap out from the far side and demand they pay the toll.

"This looks like a nice spot for a bit of a rest," Grant said.

"It does."

They dismounted and walked their bicycles to a copse of ancient oak standing back from the roadway. The ground was level and firm and Grant unloaded his picnic basket.

With much fanfare he pulled out a large blue blanket and spread it in the dappled shade under the widest of the trees. He gestured for Moira to sit.

"Let me help," she protested, only because she had been taught to say so.

"My pleasure," he said. "You relax."

"Before I sit, I would like to have a look at that creek. I'll be right back."

She walked down to the water's edge. It was a tiny creek, but moving rapidly. The rocky bottom forced the water to bubble and froth as it came into contact with the stones. The rustle of quickly moving water as it forced its way over unyielding rocks was perhaps Moira's favorite sound in all the world. Well, perhaps her second favorite, after the crunch of feet stepping through the decaying forest floor in a Muskoka autumn. Then again she also loved the impact that new fresh snow made underfoot as one placed the first exploring footsteps onto unplowed city streets or through the black and white Ontario woods.

She pulled off her shoes and stepped tentatively into the tiny brook. It was freezing. She almost pulled back, but decided instead that this was a day to be brave and passed from one slippery stone to another. The water was clear, and she watched her toes swell to strange gray shapes as she placed one foot gingerly before the other. A few tiny fish scattered in the wake of her invasion. She looked over her shoulder to see Grant standing at the water's edge, smiling broadly, a smile so bright that it almost made him handsome. The sun shone behind him and caught in his fair hair, still standing up from the force of the wind and the bicycle ride. A poor man's halo. Moira's breath caught in her throat and she almost fell. Arms swinging wildly, she managed to keep her footing.

The blanket lay on the grass, holding two china plates and two crystal glasses that shimmered in the light.

"Lunch is ready." Grant choked on the words.

Moira picked up the hem of her skirt. In honor of the occasion she had discarded her usual cycling clothes of pants and practical shirt and wore the dress her grandmother had sent for her birthday. Knowing that anything too extravagant would be rejected instantly as out of place and inappropriate, Elizabeth had

sent what she thought of as a simple cotton dress. The simplicity
of which was a threat to the meaning of the word. This was the
first time Moira had worn it, and she had lain awake the previous
night for a long time, wondering if it were suitable. One look at
Grant's face and she knew she had made the right decision. It
was a pale blue, with a pattern of tiny white and yellow daises,
a tidy Peter Pan collar and white belt, falling into a full skirt to
just below the knee. Moira knew she wasn't beautiful, but she
also knew that blue was her best color.

"That all looks quite wonderful." She walked barefoot
through the soft grass, feeling it tickle her toes and tender soles,
and sank to the ground at the edge of the blanket, her skirt
spreading itself out around her.

Grant sat opposite. "My mother went somewhat overboard, I
fear. She hasn't had much to celebrate lately, so she was delighted
to be able to put this together."

"Your mother is very kind."

He pulled out half a roast chicken, one hard-boiled egg
(Moira actually gasped aloud), thick slabs of homemade bread
and fresh butter (another gasp). Green pea pods and a thermos
full of tart lemonade completed the meal.

"Oh," she sighed, chomping on a chicken leg like a woman
possessed. "This is wonderful."

"I told you Mother went to some trouble." He grinned
around his half of the precious egg.

"Well, thank her for me."

He reached into the basket and pulled out a slab of cake, thick
with raisins and currants and even a few nuts and a sprinkling
of bright red cherries. Moira groaned in delight. Her mother
had taught her daughters that a lady always ate delicately when
in the company of a gentleman, and left most of her serving
tucked to one side of her plate. It was not the first time, nor the
last, that Moira ignored her mother's advice.

They talked about matters of little consequence. Grant was
an only child; his mother doted on him, much to his embarrassment. She wasn't finding the war too hard: the men and

women who had been with his father and the aircraft factory from its beginnings made sure she was looked after. Of course the factory had been geared up to operate around the clock. His voice softened as he reflected on how proud his father would be, if he'd lived a few more years. Moira talked about her brother, Ralph, somewhere in England. They discovered that they both adored American jazz, described by Mr. Hitler himself, Grant told her, as "a barbaric and bestial music of the sub-human Negro exploited by Jewish capitalists."

Moira laughed whole-heartedly.

"I do know," she said, sobering, "we are at war for freedom and against tyranny and such. But it is good to remember that we're fighting as much for the right to listen to jazz."

"'ere, 'ere." Grant lifted his glass of lemonade. "And therefore as part of the war effort we must visit a jazz club in London."

She clicked glasses in return. "Done."

"We must, Moira." His basset hound face folded into serious lines. "Let's do that. We must plan a leave together, and go to London. And see the shows and have dinner in a restaurant. Say you will?"

"I would love to, Grant."

He touched her hand lightly and then pulled back, as if afraid that he had overstepped himself, and turned his attention to returning the dirty dishes and naked chicken bones to the basket. There were no leftovers.

Blanket folded, basket re-filled, Moira's shoes on her feet, the picnic site cleared, they made their way to their bicycles, walking slowly, almost but yet not quite touching.

"I was wondering," Grant said, trying not to look at her as he loaded the basket onto his bicycle. "Are you free tomorrow?"

Moira tried to look thoughtful. "As it happens, I am. I don't have to be back on duty until Monday morning."

"Would you like to come for Sunday lunch at my home?" he said. "My mother will be there, of course." His tongue fell all over itself in a hurry to make excuses to permit Moira a graceful escape. "She isn't all that well. The lunch might not be quite what you get in the nurses' mess and all that."

"I'd love to come," she said.

He dropped his bicycle to the ground and took two large steps to gather her into his arms. Unnoticed, her machine also crashed to the earth as she lifted her arms and face to his.

Chapter Nineteen

Dinner that Thanksgiving Monday was Elaine's favorite meal of them all: leftover turkey, with re-heated gravy and all the trimmings. Ever since she was a girl she had loved the day after more than the event itself. Some of the greatest disappointments of her childhood involved having Thanksgiving or Christmas dinner at the home of relatives, with nothing to look forward to the next day.

Lizzie had prepared everything exactly the way Elaine liked it, and she attacked her plate with gusto. Charles turned his patrician nose up, ever so slightly, but Moira murmured happily, "the best meal of them all," as if she were reading Elaine's thoughts. A sliver of white breast, with a teaspoon of cranberry sauce and a single slice of potato, graced the old woman's plate.

Due to the change of the family's plans, Alan had earlier been dispatched by rowboat to the island to regretfully uninvite the islanders to dinner.

Phoebe passed the stuffing bowl to Elaine, who dug as much out of it as possible without appearing to be too much of a pig. "I went for a walk this afternoon," Elaine said, out of nowhere. "It was warm and sunny, but as I passed the stand of old white pine, the ones up from the boathouses a bit, it turned so quickly. Before I could blink, it was dark and cold and somewhat unpleasant." A forkful of mashed potatoes paused half way to her mouth, Elaine looked at the faces around her. Meal forgotten, they were all staring.

"Cool," Amber said, the word almost a sigh.

"A trick of the forest," Moira said, her voice thin and cold and tight. "The wind gets caught in the trees, and cools down. It's always been that way. Pay it no attention."

"More wine, dearest?" Charles asked Megan, signaling Alan to fill up his wife's glass, still more than half full.

"That's so cool," Brad echoed Amber's statement. "I've never seen anything out there, but I've heard…."

"Bradley and Phoebe," Moira interrupted, "aren't you two missing a day of school if you go back tomorrow, rather than today? Can you afford to miss a day?"

Brad sighed mightily. "Yes, Aunt Moira. One day off won't kill me."

"Indeed it won't. But it might kill your results," Charles said.

"We decided to avoid the holiday traffic and go home a day late," Elliot said from behind a mouthful of mashed potatoes.

It was a bit of a surprise to hear Elliot actually speak. He had to be one of the most reticent people Elaine had ever met. She had wondered if he actually possessed the power of speech.

"I'm doing fine, Uncle Charles." Brad scowled and his fingers were white where they gripped the dinner fork.

Phoebe dashed to her cousin's defense. She told them of the importance of the work she was doing to help Elaine. They all spoke with a rhythm that told the newcomer they had had this conversation, or ones very similar, before, a great many times.

It was only many hours later, when she put aside her book and switched out the bedside light, that Elaine realized how neatly the conversation had been turned from her experience in the woods. And it wasn't the first time, either.

Elaine slept badly, disturbed by the vision under the white pines. She couldn't explain it, not to herself. She was no stranger to the wilderness (not that this was what anyone would call the wilderness) and usually the solitude of the forest had been comforting. While researching *Goldrush* in the Yukon, she had taken the opportunity to spend a few gorgeous summer days camping and canoeing on her own. She had experienced no strange apparitions or uncomfortable feelings on the Teslin River, where she was indeed truly, absolutely, delightfully, all alone.

Why would she here, only steps from companionship, luxury, and all that is called civilization?

Elaine tossed and turned under the thick quilt. Almost as upsetting as the feelings experienced in the woods was what appeared to be the family's effort to force the conversation in other directions. But Brad and Amber were interested. Perhaps she'd have a talk with them tomorrow.

She focused her mind on more immediate problems. Moira had to open up more. The old woman talked competently of people she worked with (most of whom she held in the greatest of admiration, some with barely disguised contempt), the deprivations of the war years in England, and the hell on earth that was the Allied push through Italy. But to date she had said nothing of her feelings, her personal hopes and private terrors. Elaine had to get Moira to reveal more of herself, if the memoirs were to have any hope of taking on energy and soul. Passion.

She crawled out of bed, her bare feet recoiling as they came in contact with the chilly hardwood floor. She slipped her dressing gown over her shoulders and her slippers onto her feet and opened the door of her bedroom. The old house lay quiet and still. The only sound the creak of ancient floorboards settling under her weight. One light, kept on all night, stood sentinel over the dark stairway.

Augustus Madison frowned at her, brimming with disapproval, but Elizabeth was on the verge of a wink as Elaine crept down the stairs, a tight grip on the banister. A picture of Ralph also hung in the hallway, but from his portrait she sensed nothing, never had. He was just a not very good painting hanging in a dark stairway. If she were an imaginative woman, she would believe that this house didn't have the pull on him that it did on his grandparents.

Full of false bravado, she stuck her tongue out at Augustus as she passed. Trapped in his gilded frame, the family patriarch could do nothing but glare back.

At end of the hallway Hamlet and Ophelia scratched and whimpered at the kitchen door, alerted to the sounds of an intruder in the house. Once Elaine reached the bottom of the stairs, she could hear more sounds coming from the kitchen, the murmur of low voices and a woman's laugh, cut short. Not in the mood to exchange pleasantries with another nocturnal wanderer, she walked silently down the dark hall, making her way by the dim light over the stairway.

She hadn't been in the library before; the loft was more than enough to occupy her time. But on this restless night, it seemed like a good place for exploration. Elaine pulled open the door next to Moira's study as silently as a ghost moving through the autumn woods.

The single, black, all-seeing eye of a large screen TV occupied pride of place. The books were for the most part modern paperbacks, the kind that could be found in any bookstore. The few legal texts concerning property and estate law would have bored her within seconds.

A disappointed Elaine left the library without venturing any further. The dogs were rising towards a full chorus. Damn fool creatures, she mumbled under her breath. Have the whole household up in a minute. She hissed at them down the length of the hallway, knowing it would accomplish nothing.

Sleep still far away, she decided to go over to the storage cabin, up into the loft, to smell the old papers and mold, perhaps find a letter or two to take up to her room.

She punched the security code into the alarm console by the door, and slipped outside into the velvety night. There was no moon and the Milky Way sparkled like lost diamonds scattered across a cloak of black velvet.

A whiff of smoke crossed the perimeter of her consciousness.

The door to the outbuilding wasn't kept locked and Elaine stepped inside. She flicked on the light.

The smoke was more than a whiff: it caught in her throat. She walked towards the loft stairs, her nose twitching as she went. It was getting stronger. That unmistakable smell of smoke slipping its bounds. There were several fireplaces in the main cottage. One in the kitchen, one in what the family called the drawing room. She didn't know about the bedrooms, and there must be a furnace somewhere, the place was heated well within the bounds of comfortable temperatures. Perhaps the scent had drifted over from there—it wasn't far. Elaine hadn't seen one person smoking, who thus might have left a cigarette burning as they drifted into sleep. Only Mr. Josepheson with his phallic cigar, but that had been two days ago.

Perhaps a bonfire on a neighboring property. She put her foot on the first step.

The odor of smoke was stronger, and above the single light the air was distinct, almost hazy. Elaine rubbed her eyes. It was even thicker, perhaps, at the top of the steps leading up to the loft.

Drawn by nothing but curiosity, not yet worried, she climbed the narrow steps. The smoke was gathering; she could see it in the air. Soft clouds of ethereal white and gray, gentle fingers of smoke swirling before her eyes. Her head popped above the level of the loft floor and she saw a flicker of fire. She watched in horror as the flame stretched towards the ceiling.

Fire! The loft was on fire.

The letters, the documents, the memoirs!

Elaine screamed.

Chapter Twenty

In June of 1943 the 15th Canadian General Hospital left Bramshott and traveled north by train to Scotland. There had been no time for goodbyes. Moira and Jean had become good friends with the shop owners, Bert and Betty, and their daughter. They were so grateful not only for Moira's help at the scene of Catherine's accident, but to all the Canadians, come so far to help fight Hitler. She hoped they would understand.

Arriving in Scotland, they boarded the *Nea Hellas*, and on Dominion Day, July 1st, set sail down the River Clyde. Only once they were on board were the nurses issued lighter, tropical uniforms. Moira continued to write to Grant, but they hadn't been able to arrange time together since the Sunday at his mother's. The lunch had been quite nice. Mrs. Summersland wasn't much of a cook, and didn't have much to work with, but she had tried her best. After a dessert of Mrs. Peaks pudding, she politely excused herself, leaving the nervous young couple to exchange embarrassed smiles across the over furnished sitting room.

From Ralph she had heard nothing in months, but that was so like Ralph that Moira didn't give it much thought. Rose wrote to her regularly, full of the excitement of her job at a factory in London and all the friends she had made there. She alluded to meeting Charlie Stoughton several times but Moira only half-paid attention, enviously wishing that she and Grant were able to organize more time together.

Their convoy moved out to the open sea, like a much needed holiday trip. During the day the exhausted nurses relaxed on the deck in the welcome sunshine. The sun was getting warmer every day. But as night enveloped the open sea all sense of a pleasure cruise ended. No one was allowed on deck after sundown, the women ordered to sleep in full battledress with their kit at hand. Portholes were closed tight, but they could still hear the distant sounds of guns and exploding depth charges.

"Do you think it can get any hotter, Moira?" Jean asked, wiping her brow with a dusty handkerchief. The women were standing at the single cold-water tap that served the entire complement of Nursing Sisters at the sprawling tent hospital in the Algerian desert.

"Reverend McDonald would say it can get a great deal hotter," Moira replied.

"Oh, pooh. Like he knows. I always thought I would love the Mediterranean. I don't."

Susan Kilpatrick laughed as she unbuttoned the top button on her white nurses' uniform to splash cold water down the front of her chest. After three years at war, the nurse from a Saskatchewan wheat farm was plump no longer.

"Nice color, Sue," Jean said. "We could try marketing that, when we get back home. Make our fortunes."

Like her fellow sisters, Susan's face, neck, and bare arms were a strange shade of yellow on top of her newly acquired tan, the result of meticulous application of the anti-malarial cream with which they were all provided.

Number 15 had arrived in the Algerian village of El Arrouch on a baking hot day in July of 1943. The women had thought the day exceptionally hot. They were wrong.

"Oh, God. Is that it?" Jean had groaned as a sea of canvas tents arose out of the remains of a grain field to greet them.

"I'm afraid it must be," Moira sighed, shifting her suitcase from one hand to the other. "Oh, well, you said you wanted a change from Bramshott."

"But I meant a pleasant change."

A community of canvas tents had been set up on a treeless, dry plain. The stubble of fields planted years ago still showed. In the distance a line of hazy purple mountains and green trees beckoned like an oasis.

They remained in North Africa for seven months. The hospital never amounted to anything more than a city of tents on a dusty plain. The weather was never anything but extreme: too hot—even the winds were unbearably hot—and too dry when it was dry. When the torrential rains arrived in November the canvas tents leaked and the ground turned into a sea of churning mud. After Christmas it snowed on the mountains and the winds maliciously carried bitterly cold air onto the plain.

Whenever she had a moment to recover her breath, Moira thought of Grant, and she wrote to him as often as time permitted. He was still in England, still flying, that much she knew, although his letters told her little else. Only that he missed her and dreamed of the day when they could go to that jazz club in London, as they had promised each other.

In February the No. 15 was sea borne again. This time to Italy and Naples. From there they traveled inland to set up a large hospital at the town of Caserta.

The Allies braced for what they hoped would be the final push through Italy. The Nursing Sisters braced for what they knew were horrors still to come.

Chapter Twenty-one

"Will you hush, you'll wake up the whole family." Amber pulled a second bottle of beer from the back of the fridge.

"Hardly. I'd think your family has learned how to sleep through Armageddon, what with all the fuckin' racket those two mutts make." Dave grabbed her around the waist and nuzzled her white neck. "Afraid of getting caught are you, you naughty girl. I'll have to punish you myself." He slapped her thin bottom lightly. "Take that, and that."

She laughed, but quickly smothered the sound. The front of her robe gaped open invitingly and Dave slipped his hand inside. His black eyes narrowed and he breathed deeply through his mouth. "Do you promise never to stop being naughty again?" He ran his fingers in light circles around her nipple, drawing it instantly erect.

"I promise." She stretched onto her toes and kissed him deeply. "If you promise to keep on doing that."

Hamlet and Ophelia had taken excited interest in the arrival of nighttime visitors when Dave and Amber first crept into the kitchen in search of a midnight snack. Immediately satisfied with pieces of turkey, the two dogs crawled under the table. But now they were up again, and eight long legs ran to the door leading into the rest of the house. The animals set up a furious barking.

Amber jumped, and Dave laughed. "What did I tell you, they'll bark at anything."

"Someone's up. I hear footsteps."

"So. Who cares?" He bent his head back down, seeking her mouth.

She pushed him away. "They might be hungry. They might be coming here. Let's go, it might be Uncle Charles." She slipped out of his embrace and tried to push him back outside.

"You think the old man wouldn't be too happy to see the likes of me in his kitchen in the middle of the night, eh?" Dave stood his ground and twisted the top off the beer bottle in his hand. He dropped the cap to the floor. "Are you ashamed to be seen with me?"

"No, of course not. But he'll make a fuss. And if it's Auntie Megan or Grandma it'll be almost as bad. Come on. Please, Dave."

"I feel like a snack. You said you'd make sandwiches. I haven't had my sandwich yet." He opened the fridge door and peered inside. He was dressed only in a pair of shorts, a ragged T-shirt, and scuffed running shoes. Amber had felt terribly brave, sneaking him into the summer rooms above the boathouse on the nights since they had exchanged meaningful glances as the police gathered everyone together to investigate the Labor Day tragedy. They could be alone up there: no one slept over the boathouse in the winter. Amber had made up a nest of duvets and blankets dragged out of storage and warmed the room with an electric heater, candles, and her love. But now she didn't feel quite so brave. She was terrified of her family's reaction if they found Dave in the kitchen.

They were so prejudiced against him, she thought, the taste of bile rising in her throat. Because he was poor and had had a bad childhood.

He'd told her all about his abusive, always out of work father and his frightened, drunken mother. She'd seen the horrible scars, the white puckered flesh, and heard how the little boy had been hurt when his mother, in a drunken daze, had spilled the boiling kettle all over him. How he'd left home for the streets at age fourteen after taking a baseball bat to his dad's head following one too many attacks on his mother. How instead of throwing his father out, the ungrateful bitch kicked Dave out of the house and told him never to come back. So he never had.

Her soft heart wrenched at the injustice of it all. She had so much and he had so little. What right did her aunts and uncle have to throw him back out to the cold of the forest?

He bent further into the refrigerator. "Never can have too much turkey."

A creak of the staircase and an answering bark from Hamlet.

"Please, Dave. Let's go back out to the boathouse. It's cold in here. You can bring that with you. We'll have a picnic. There's so much in there, Lizzie'll never miss it."

He grinned and shut the fridge door with the back of his foot, cuddling packages of wrapped cheese in his arms. "I'd rather take something that'll be missed. That'll set the cat among the pigeons, eh? But if you promise to be really naughty, I'll come."

He got no further than the kitchen door, before Amber reached out an arm to stop him. "What's that noise? Do you hear that?"

"I don't hear anything." With his free hand, Dave jerked the sash from Amber's waist and her dressing gown fell open.

"Stop that," she hissed, clutching at the front of her robe with both hands. "Someone's shouting. We have to go and see what's wrong."

"Come on, Amber. First you're whining that we have to get out of here before Uncle Charles finds out that I've been fucking his precious niece, now you're wanting to troop back into the place. Make up your mind."

"Let go of my arm. You're hurting me. Please. Something's wrong. Look at the dogs." She had made him mad. She didn't want to make Dave mad. He'd had such a hard life. Amber only wanted to him to be happy. But the dogs were agitated as she had never seen them before.

Running footsteps sounded overhead, from the end of the corridor where Lizzie and Alan had their rooms. Someone screamed.

"Please, Dave. I have to see what's wrong."

He shrugged and released her. "Suit yourself. I'll be in the boathouse."

So intent were the dogs on whatever was happening in the cottage that they didn't even notice as Dave threw open the kitchen door with enough force to have it rattling back and forth on its hinges.

Amber almost followed him. She didn't want him to be angry with her.

But the scream was too loud to be ignored. Wrapping the belt of her robe tight she dashed out of the kitchen, practically tripping over Hamlet and Ophelia.

The screaming was coming from outside. Hamlet and Ophelia dashed to the front door and barked to be let out. Alan flew down the stairs, something large and red clutched in his arms. He threw the door open and dashed out into the night, the dogs following.

Traces of smoke drifted around the courtyard, stretching towards Amber like the probing fingers of a ghost. Doors opened above her, accompanied by excited voices and loud screams. Amber took the stairs two at a time.

Chapter Twenty-two

Elaine ran back to the main building, screaming as loud as she could. There was a strong wind, carrying smoke from the roof of the storage building towards the main cottage. And if the smoke could move, the flames would be close behind. She flew up the stairs and ran down the corridor, banging on doors and throwing lights on as she went. "Fire! Fire! The house is on fire!"

Alan arrived first, sprinting down the hall with nothing but a sea-green towel wrapped around his waist, falling low over his hips. Apparently he slept in the nude. Elaine was amazed at herself for noticing. Fortunately, she also noticed, he brought a small fire extinguisher.

All down the second floor corridor, doors opened and heads popped out.

"Where?" Alan shouted.

"The storage building."

He ran down the stairs.

Charles, pulling a satin dressing gown around his shoulders, and Phoebe, clad in T-shirt and sweat pants, rushed after him.

Alan waved them away. "Get everyone out. Phoebe, call 911. Charles, make sure Moira, Megan, and Maeve are looked after. Amber, go with your uncle. Help him with the sisters." Phoebe scurried off to find a phone, and the old man and his niece hurried down the hall.

But Ruth was ahead of them. She burst out of her room and into Moira's next door. She was half-dragging, half-carrying a confused Moira out of her bedroom before Brad pushed her aside and scooped his fragile great-aunt up into his arms. Charles and Amber (who had lost the belt of her dressing gown and was noticeably naked underneath) impatiently hustled the continually-chattering Megan, while at the same time murmuring words of encouragement to a confused Maeve. "The paintings," Maeve sobbed as she started down the stairs. "We have to save the paintings."

Elliot and Alison milled about in the early stages of panic, but finally dashed down the stairs.

The family gathered outside. Red light flickered behind the dormer windows in the loft, and black smoke curled around the open doorway. Elaine couldn't see Alan. She ran into the storage building. Alan stood at the top of the steps leading to the loft, his hand-held fire extinguisher working hard. She ran up the stairs and pulled at his bare arm. Breathing was becoming difficult. "We have to get out of here! That ceiling might collapse in a minute and the whole place will be on fire." She coughed as much as spoke the words.

"Not if I can help it," he muttered.

"Come on, Alan. Let's get the hell out of here before the whole place goes," Elaine shouted.

"But the letters." Rivers of sweat dripped down his cheeks and bits of soot crawled into the lines of his face. How long would a hand-held fire extinguisher last, anyway? "All Moira's letters, her mother's letters. The cottage." Alan again aimed the full force of the extinguisher into the loft.

The distant shriek of a siren pierced through the crackle and pop of flames over their heads.

Burly men in tan bunker gear with orange stripes, oxygen tanks, helmets, and face masks ran into the building. They dragged heavy hoses behind them, and Elaine and Alan were firmly rushed down the stairs and out of the building.

The family had gathered by the back door, dressed in a wild assortment of nightwear, gaping in disbelief. Alan tugged at his towel in embarrassment, and Lizzie slipped off her purple velour dressing gown and draped it over his shoulders.

Hamlet and Ophelia galloped around the yard in frantic circles, nipping at the thick boots of firefighters and howling their terror into the night. Sparks flew through the night air, a gorgeous sight; several landed on the roof of the main building.

"Are we all here?" Moira cried. "Anyone missing?"

The group glanced around. Megan whispered softly to herself and fingered the pearl necklace wrapped around her crepe-paper neck.

"Everyone make it out okay?" The firefighter assigned to watch over the truck and water gages ran over.

"Yes, yes. I think so," Charles answered. "We all seem to be present and accounted for. Thank God."

"Then get out of the way, please, sir. We have work to do. And lock those dogs up."

Brad carried Moira to the fire truck, where, over her protests, he laid her down and wrapped her in a thick blanket. With soft whispers, as if crooning to a baby, Amber led Maeve away; the old woman didn't seem to understand what was going on. Alan called to Phoebe to help him with the dogs and they tried, without much success, to round up the panicked animals.

A second truck arrived, taking out several planters and the overhanging limb of a gorgeous old oak. Hoses were aimed at the roof of the cottage itself, to soak it down and stop the fire from spreading. Debris rained down from the loft window onto the driveway below: bits of furniture, which weren't in very good shape to begin with, shovelfuls of soggy black paper, boxes of documents.

With a cry, Elaine ran forward and fell on her knees before the boxes. A firefighter grabbed her by the arm and dragged her away.

"Keep back, Ma'am. Please." It was a woman. She had pulled off her helmet in search of some fresh air. Her hair was cropped close to her head, all spiky and tipped blond. Her face was unlined, thin and elfin, a contrast to the sweat and soot streaked skin.

Elaine opened her mouth to protest: she had to protect the boxes! All the letters, lifetimes of memories! But one look at the firefighter's steely blue eyes and Elaine's mouth snapped shut. She meekly returned to the truck to stand with Lizzie and Amber. They were all stunned—eyes wide with shock and mouths gaping.

Mr. and Mrs. Josepheson and their son Greg stepped like ghostly apparitions out of the gloom of night and smoke. Greg took one look at the confusion, murmured that he would be right back, and disappeared.

Firefighters staggered out of the building at regular intervals. Oxygen tanks replaced, they returned to the old guesthouse. The fire seemed to be contained, at least as far as the observers could see. Smoke, thick, black, and deadly, billowed from the roof and the loft windows, but it wasn't spreading, and the cottage itself was untouched.

With much effort and a good deal of bad language Alan and Phoebe managed to get the dogs locked into his truck.

Screaming sirens announced another arrival: an ambulance. Moira, protesting in vain, and Maeve, too confused to object, were bustled inside. Ruth leapt aboard as the doors were closing.

At last it was over and firefighters trooped out of the door, dragging their hoses behind them, faces streaked with sweat and smoke and ashes. They pulled off their masks and gratefully sucked in great lungfuls of the fresh night air. A pump had been placed in the lake to provide water; several of the men went down to retrieve it, and pull in the hoses. A curious Brad followed.

Greg reappeared, bearing a bottle of brandy and a grocery bag full of plastic cups. He poured drinks all around. The hot liquid burned all the way down Elaine's throat, as she appreciated every drop.

"You're lucky." The man who'd been watching over the trucks approached them. Firefighters discarded their outer shells, and loaded up equipment. "The blaze was contained to the outbuilding. A good bit of smoke and water damage to the second floor, but my crew say that no one seems to be in residence there. A bunch of papers and old books destroyed…."

Elaine groaned.

"...but not much else."

Greg held a plastic cup out to the man. With a regretful smile, he shook his head.

Charles was the first to ask the question on everyone's mind. "Can we go back inside, Mr. —"

"Johnson. I'm the captain of this crew. Fortunately the main building doesn't appear to have been touched at all. The structure is perfectly sound, so you can go back in. But you have to stay away from that outbuilding, until we give you permission to go inside. An investigating officer will be around in the morning."

"Arson!" Alan picked up the inference. "You're saying this was arson?" Self-consciously he hitched the belt of the purple robe tighter around his waist.

"No, I'm not, sir. I'm only saying someone will be around to look into the cause of the fire. Routine procedure."

"This is awful, absolutely awful." Rachel, Karen, and Kyle broke into the circle.

"We heard a siren," Rachel said, scanning the group, her beautiful face pale and anxious. "So we left Willow with Jessica and rowed over as fast as we could. Is everyone all right? We saw the ambulance leave. Have they taken Moira?"

"Moira's fine," Lizzie assured her. "They took her to the hospital for a bit of a check up. That's all. Maeve as well. She was terribly confused. Ruth's gone with them."

"All's well that ends well, eh?" Dave stepped into the circle. He grinned at Amber. "Nice robe."

"How did you get here? You weren't..." Rachel began, but she was cut off.

"And where were you two, while all this was happening?" Charles stretched himself to his full height, crossed his arms over his chest, and stuck out his chin as he addressed Dave and Kyle.

Dave held out his hands. "We were asleep in our beds, Mr. Stoughton. All nice and peaceful and cozy. Are you implying something else?"

Kyle and Alan stepped forward at the same time. "Nothing said, man. Nothing said." Kyle stretched his arm across Dave's chest. "Right?" He looked at Charles.

"Merely speculating."

"Well, I for one want to put something on that has a bit of decorum," Alan said. "All right with you, Captain?"

"We're ready to leave," the captain said. "The main building is secure, no problem going in."

"I've got to get some clothes on." Amber dashed into the building.

Dave chuckled and Kyle eyed him suspiciously.

"Such a terrible thing." Mrs. Josepheson waved her hands in front of her chest. The paper-thin skin exposed the tiny bones and veins underneath. "You could have all burned to a crisp in your beds." She licked her lips, savoring the horror of it all. "Terrible, simply terrible."

"That's quite enough of that talk, Mother," Greg snapped. He gave Elaine a wry smile as he topped up her cup.

The fire crew was strapped into their seats, pump stowed, hoses rolled up, and equipment secured, ready to be on their way. The woman with the spiked hair raised one hand to Elaine, who nodded in reply.

"We have been lucky," Elliot said.

"Yes, we have," Alison agreed. "But if we stand here much longer we'll die of exposure. I'm simply freezing."

"Terrible, terrible," repeated Mrs. Josepheson with something approaching relish.

"I had better go to the hospital and check on my sisters-in-law," Charles said. "Elliot, you can drive me."

"Coffee," Lizzie announced. "We all need coffee. Then we can decide what we're going to do."

Gratefully, the remaining members of the party trooped into the kitchen.

Alan and Elaine hung behind. Now that it was all over, Elaine was so thunderstruck at the speed and ferocity of events she could barely will her body to put one foot in front of the other.

"I'll drive you to the hospital, Mr. Stoughton," Alan said. "No need for Elliot to go."

"No. You've done enough tonight." Charles coughed. "Thank you. And thank you, Elaine. That fire was far too close to the cottage for comfort. Without your quick reaction, we might well have lost everything."

She smiled, embarrassed at the praise.

"Including our lives. Elliot, hurry up. Get something decent on and meet me by the car." The old man looked down at his pajamas. "Perhaps I should make myself more presentable as well." He stumbled off, back into the cottage.

"A proud man," Alan muttered.

"Indeed."

"I do think that a cup of Lizzie's world famous coffee is in order. Would you not agree, Miss Elaine?"

She smiled at his humorous attempt at formality. "I would indeed, gentle sir."

He held out his arm, bent at the elbow, and Elaine slipped hers through it. "Lead the way." The warmth of his touch felt very nice indeed, and despite the tragedy barely avoided, a soft smile crept across her face.

The stunned survivors were gathered in the kitchen. Kindling roared in the great fireplace and Brad placed a fresh log on top. The ever-efficient Lizzie had coffee and hot cocoa brewing. It was a big kitchen jammed with bodies, everyone talking about the fire and exclaiming over how lucky they all were.

Why are survivors of a catastrophe always described as lucky? Surely, true luck would be if the horrible event had not happened at all? Elaine thought, accepting a cup of rich chocolate.

"Can I give you a hand?" Rachel approached Lizzie as the cook rummaged through the fridge, her more than adequate bottom facing the room.

"I'd swear that I had a whole selection of French cheeses in here. But I can't find them. Did we have cheese with dinner, Elaine?"

"Yes. They were great."

"No matter. Turn on the oven, please, Rachel. I have some frozen pastries. They'll have to do."

Amber and Phoebe came into the kitchen. Phoebe wrapped a long fur coat around her grandmother's shoulders, and Megan buried herself deep in the thick fur. Dave crossed the room and placed one hand firmly on Amber's denim clad butt. She threw him a hard look, but instead of moving away, wiggled slightly to fit herself into the cup provided.

Elaine told herself to mind her own business.

Greg toured the room, offering another round of brandy. He even extended the bottle to Kyle and Rachel.

"How did it start, do you think?" Alison voiced what they were all thinking.

"Lightning?"

"There hasn't been any lightning for days."

"Heater left on?"

"Electrical fault?"

"Until recently, no one's been up into that loft for years. So why did it happen today?" Brad said.

"I didn't leave anything burning up there, if that's what you're suggesting," Phoebe bristled. Scrubbed clean of her excessive black and plum makeup, her complexion glistened with the freshness of comfortable youth and good nutrition. Her short black hair, bare of commercial products, was tousled from sleep and agitation.

"Just mentioning it, that's all."

"Well, don't mention it," Alan said. "The fire investigator will be here tomorrow. They'll tell us what happened. Speculation is futile."

"Resistance is futile," Brad chuckled, echoing his favorite TV show.

"Terrible, terrible. They could all have burned to death in their beds," Mrs. Josepheson muttered to no one in particular, once again.

"Time to take Mother home," Greg suggested to his father.

Mr. Josepheson was puffing happily away at one of his enormous cigars. Lizzie threw him a look that would frighten small children, but with none of the senior members of the family present to back her up, she clamped her lips shut and said nothing.

"Nighty night, then," Dave said, having released Amber's butt. "Leave the bottle will you? There's a good boy."

Kyle crossed the room in two enormous strides and grabbed Dave by the arm. "We've outstayed our welcome. Time for us to go as well." His smile was as strong as his grip. The bare flesh on Dave's white arm stood out in sharp contrast to the deep black of Kyle's hand. "Ladies, as we have only the one boat, I suggest that we all leave together." He practically dragged Dave to the door. Rachel and Karen scurried after them. Lizzie followed with offerings of cookies and half-cooked pastries.

Amber burst into tears and fled the room.

"Horrible people," Megan said. "I'll have another brandy, please, dear. Can't imagine why Moira allows them to stay. She's too kind hearted by half, I've always said."

"Seems quite handy the way they turned up like that," Alison said.

"What's that supposed to mean?" Lizzie turned on her.

"They say that an arsonist always likes to hang around and watch the fire trucks arrive."

"If you're making an accusation, you should be prepared to back it up with something stronger than what 'they' say."

"It's my family that's threatened here. I intend to speculate as much as I want. Aunt Moira is crazy to let those people stay over there. Particularly after what happened Labor Day."

"What's that got to do with anything? Donna's death was an accident, didn't you hear? And Moira isn't crazy in any way. I'll thank you to remember that." Lizzie's hands were placed firmly on her hips, her legs apart.

The phone on the wall beside the back door shrilled like an alien presence, and everyone turned to look at it. Alison was the closest. Her hand shook and she took a deep breath as she picked it up.

"Hello? Okay. Fine. Good. Thank you." She placed the receiver back onto its cradle. "That was Uncle Charles. They're okay, and he and Elliot are on the way home with Aunt Moira and Ruth."

"Just Moira?" Alan asked.

"Mom was apparently quite disoriented when they got there, so the doctors want to keep her in for another night."

"The poor dear," said Megan. "She absolutely hates hospitals. A bit more brandy if you please, young Greg."

Grateful for the interruption, they all pretended to forget about the argument. Alison stared at Lizzie, her eyes throwing daggers, but the cook turned her back to check a tray in the oven.

All the time that family, friends, and staff had been in the kitchen, the dim howling of dogs trying to force their way out of the cab of Alan's pickup truck echoed around the property. Unable to resist any longer, Alan gave in and with a curse he stamped out into the yard to release the beasts.

They immediately found their way into the kitchen in search of offerings.

Brandy bottle and coffee pot were emptied, cookies reduced to crumbs, and pastries nothing but a memory, but no one wanted to take to their beds until the rest of the Madisons returned.

"Amber seemed a bit touchy," Phoebe said, nursing the last grains in her cup. "Not like her."

"Affects us all in a different way," Lizzie said, wondering if she should bring out the sweet rolls she had intended to be tomorrow's breakfast.

Unnoticed, Elaine left the room and crept up the stairs. The walls were tinged with a faint residue of smoke, but the fire itself hadn't reached the old wooden building. Ralph, Augustus, and Elizabeth were, fortunately, quite safe. And, thank goodness, the smoke hadn't reached the precious paintings lining the walls of the main hall.

Not knowing what to expect when offered a chance at the job and summoned north, Elaine had packed a flashlight. She found the heavy instrument in the back of her cupboard, pulled her coat on over her dressing gown, and ventured outside.

In the courtyard she dropped to her haunches and flicked the powerful beam of her flashlight over the desolation. Fortunately the papers still packed into boxes, those they hadn't yet read or put aside until another day, were relatively unscathed, a bit of singeing to the edges of cardboard, but little damage to the precious contents inside. A couple of the boxes had shattered on hitting the ground, and the wind had spread papers around the yard. Elaine did her best to collect all the scraps of paper.

The accounts that Phoebe had been examining when they called it a day had been consumed by the flames and were now regaled to disgusting piles of muck and sludge and ashes.

"Quite a mess, eh?" Phoebe stood behind her.

"Not irretrievable, I hope."

"They're saying it was my fault."

"Who's saying? What's your fault?"

"The fire. That I left the old electric heater on. Which caused the fire. They're all accusing me."

"I didn't hear anyone saying anything of the sort. I heard them wondering how it started, that's all. Did you leave the heater on?"

"Of course not."

"Then the fire investigator will discover so. And that'll be the end of it."

"Do you think?"

"Of course I do," Elaine said with no conviction whatsoever. "Let's see what we have here. This bunch seems to be in good shape. Tomorrow, we'll dry out every scrap of paper that's a bit damp and try to get it all sorted out. Not much seems to be lost. Fortunately, the papers I was studying last, I took into my room to read later."

"You think most of it can be salvaged?" Megan appeared out of the dark, so unexpectedly that both Phoebe and Elaine started and clutched hands to nervous chests.

"I do," said Elaine. A full armory of jewelry weighed Megan down. Strings of pearls, diamond broaches and earrings, and gold bangles sparkled on or dangled over her frothy nightgown. Must make an awful racket when she makes love. Perhaps her husband liked to be reminded of all that money he had married. Elaine scolded herself for being mean: the old woman probably grabbed everything she could on her way out of the burning building. Easier to wear than to carry. "Such a waste of time and effort," Megan said. "Never mind storage space. If it were up to me, I'd get rid of the lot. What's past is past. And best forgotten."

"History is important," Elaine said. "To know where we're going, we have to know from where we've come."

"Modern nonsense," Megan said, taking a sip of her drink. "A woman like you—you'd be better off at home with your husband than chasing my sister's memories." She stepped out of the light and was swallowed up by the darkness. Only the clatter of her jewelry marked where she had gone.

"Weird," Phoebe whispered.

The sky was dark, without a trace of moon or stars, and Elaine feared that rain might accomplish what fire had failed to do. She and Phoebe prevailed upon Alan to help them lug the cartons of papers into the kitchen.

They finished just as a weak sun was wondering whether or not to bother peeking its head up over the horizon. A creature of habit, eventually it did, in time to greet Charles and Elliot returning from the hospital with Moira and Ruth.

"My mother's letters, my papers?" Moira touched the button to roll down the back window and called out before Charles' Lexus had even come to a halt.

"We've saved most of it," Elaine assured her. "I'll have a good look at everything tomorrow, this morning I mean, but I think your mother's letters are safe."

"Thank heavens for that." Moira extended a hand out of the car window. "And no small thanks to you, Charles tells me. Well done, dear."

"No thanks to me at all," Elaine said, squeezing the hand as tightly as she dared. It was icy cold and the fragile bones were tangible beneath the skin. "Alan fought the fire until the truck arrived."

"We must be getting you to bed, Miss Madison," Ruth said, her mouth settled into a tight line.

"Stop fussing, you stupid girl. I don't have to be packed off to bed like a delinquent child."

Ruth recoiled as if she had been struck.

Alan and Greg helped bundle Moira out of the car and into the cottage. Charles shouted to Alan to get a roofing contractor over first thing, and to call him as soon as the fire inspector arrived.

Elaine was much too wired to go back to bed. She wanted only to dive into the boxes and check the damage.

Alison refused to return to the second floor, insisting that she would be safer in the rooms over the boathouse. She sent Alan up to her room to fetch toothbrush, towels, duvet, and pillows.

The rising sun highlighted an ugly jagged wound in the roof above the storage building. Where only hours before there had been a tiny dormer window, exactly like those in illustrated volumes of nursery rhymes, there was now a gaping hole, surrounded by raw blackened beams.

Chapter Twenty-three

"M?"

"Um?"

"Do you miss home?"

"What a silly question. Of course I miss home. Why do you ask?"

"Just wondering."

"Well, stop wondering and enjoy the day. Isn't this heavenly?"

"I guess."

"Oh, for mercy's sake, Ralph. Stop being so melancholy." Moira pushed her dark glasses on top of her hair and peered at her brother, her eyes recoiling from the harsh sunlight. "You're ruining my day."

"Sorry."

"So you should be." She pulled the glasses back down and snuggled deeper into the warm sand. The skin at her throat, face, and arms was still pale yellow. An interesting contrast to the acres of white skin exposed by her borrowed bathing suit. "I'm about ready for another swim. Coming?"

May 1944. The Isle of Capri. Moira had never been anywhere so beautiful. The sun baked their white bodies and the warm sand cradled their war-saturated souls. Ralph and Moira lay on borrowed towels watching the gentle rolling of the azure waters and clouds that moved lazily across a sky almost too blue to behold. Far in the distance, on the rim of the horizon, past the towering limestone rocks reaching up out of the sea like the thumbs of giants, she could see the smoking plume of a ship, heading east through the Mediterranean. A war ship, no doubt. Maybe a troop carrier. En route to God knows where. She shivered in the sun and cast her thoughts to the men it carried, watching until it disappeared over the rim of the world.

She pulled herself to her feet. "Come on. Let's have one last dip. Almost time to be on our way."

"You go without me. I've had enough."

"Ralph." Moira sunk to her haunches beside her brother. "Something is bothering you and I do wish you would talk to me about it."

"Nothing."

"Suit yourself."

She padded across the hot sand and around the rocks and slipped into the water. For a few moments the gentle caress of the soft, warm water on her battledress-roughened skin was enough to make her forget her brother and his unnaturally dismal mood. She flipped onto her back and floated, eyes closed. It was almost possible to believe that she was back home at the family cottage on Lake Muskoka. Taking a quick dip off the end of the dock before supper.

The sharp tang of salt water stung her cracked lips and the image disappeared with a poof, like the end to an insipid amateur magic show.

The beach was not crowded. A few Allied soldiers with their new Italian girlfriends, a handful of local families—only women and children and old men left—several groups of nurses, like Moira herself, on leave at the Number 1 Canadian Nursing Sisters Rest Home at Amalfi. The home was a delight; comfortable, soothing. A wonderful Italian cook lovingly prepared dishes the women had never even heard of, much less eaten; tagliatelli and zabaglioni were Moira's favorites. The rest home was close to Naples and the Isle of Capri so the sisters and their guests took every advantage of the change to have a real holiday.

Moira was absolutely thrilled to see Ralph, for the first time since the weekend in London. So much had happened, and she was a different person than the girl she had been two years ago. It was perfectly wonderful to be grounded in her family again—even if the family representative was only one self-obsessed brother—to be reminded of who she truly was; not always Nursing Sister Madison, but also Moira: daughter, granddaughter, sister. And the woman who loved Grant Summersland.

Ralph had been bad tempered and distracted the entire day. It was unlike him to be moody. Her heart felt like a lead weight in her chest as she watched him sitting despondently on the beach, clutching his knees in his arms and staring out to sea as though he was seeing nothing at all.

Or perhaps he was seeing too much.

"The ferry will be leaving soon." Moira clambered out of the water and picked up her towel and beach accessories. "I'm going up to the hut to change. Coming?"

He shrugged.

"Suit yourself. Be right back."

Reluctantly Moira pulled off her bathing suit, toweled the warm salt water off and struggled into her uniform. She was still on the Isle of Capri but the familiar flat hat, the hated tie, the neatly fitting brown jacket and skirt whisked her back to the war. She would walk in her bare feet for as long as possible before finalizing the uniform and slipping into the thick, practical, ugly shoes.

Ralph was sitting exactly as she had left him. Moira walked up silently; she wasn't meaning to "sneak up," but the sand muffled the sound of her bare footsteps.

"All ready."

He started with as much intensity as if, rather than his sister, a German soldier with a thick accent and thin bayonet had spoken behind him.

"Oh, Ralph." Moira sunk to the sand and grabbed his shoulders in her hands. Tears streamed in a ceaseless river down his cheeks, his chest heaved and he sobbed into Moira's loving embrace.

"You have to talk to me, dearest," she said, when the gasping breathing had stopped and Ralph pulled away, deeply embarrassed. "I refuse to leave until we do. If we have to be sitting here when the rest of the army marches into Berlin, then so be it."

"For God's sake, Moira." He rose to his feet in a single fluid movement, shouting. "You can be such a nag, let's get the hell out of here." Further down the beach and on the stairs leading up to the road, Italian families, Allied soldiers, and Canadian nurses looked their way.

"Sit down, Ralph," she said in her best ward-sister voice. "You're making a scene. People are looking."

Trained by mother and grandmother to respond to the words "making a scene" like Pavlov's dog to a bell, he sat.

She picked up a handful of sand and watched the grains dribble between her fingers.

"I'm so scared, Moira. So scared." His words had the weight of the world behind them. She watched the gentle movement of the sand.

"In Sicily Paul Redmond had his head shot off. God, it was awful. He was right beside me, fell into me and knocked me off my feet. I went down into the mud with Paul on top of me. I yelled at him to get up, but he didn't move. I pushed him off, cursing him for a goddamned fool. Then I saw. Half his head was missing." Ralph buried his own head into his hands and sobbed. "His brains were all over my chest. Everywhere. Gray and lumpy and mixed with thick blood. He came from Winnipeg. Had a wife and two little kids. He talked about those kids all the time. How big and grown up they would be when he got home. He was so proud of them."

Moira gathered him into her arms once again. There was nothing she could say, so she said nothing. She rocked her older brother while the sun fell in the sky. All along the beach, people gathered up the remains of their picnics, collected tired children and, as Moira had done, put their war clothes back on.

"I'm afraid I'm going to die, M.," he said at last. The tears had stopped and his voice sounded strong once again. "But even more, I'm afraid I'm going to be a coward. When I saw what remained of Paul, I ran. I ran. Can you imagine what Father would say to that?"

"Oh, damn Father."

He actually chuckled. "I don't think I've ever heard you swear before, little sister. Father would be shocked."

"Well then damn Father, again. What would he know? Father is safe and sound in Ottawa making lots and lots of lovely money. Doing precisely the same as he did during the first war, I believe. You could have stayed at home, helped him with the business. We both know it. But you didn't. So Father has nothing to say to you. Never again. But never mind Father. Please don't worry about what might happen. Anything can happen, and we will only destroy ourselves if we keep thinking about it. I've seen a great deal as well."

"I know you have."

"And I've learned that people can be amazingly strong. I have also learned that fear is natural and the men who aren't afraid are either lying through their teeth or there is something seriously, dreadfully wrong with them."

He stretched his long legs out on the sand, and snuggled back into Moira's chest. "Thank you, dearest. But M?"

"Yes."

"If I die…."

"You won't die. You're Ralph Madison. Grandfather would never forgive you."

He didn't laugh. "If I die, I want you to know one thing."

She stroked his hair.

"I killed her. And I'm sorry."

Chapter Twenty-four

Moira tossed and turned in her bed. Unable to get a minute's rest she had lain there, watching the sun play on the wallpaper. One would think she would be able to sleep at any time, used as she had been to sleeping in impossible conditions: wartime canvas tents, crowded nursing barracks, tossing hospital ships, hot dusty back rooms behind refugee camp hospitals. An hour snatched here, two precious hours there.

When she was young her father would take Ralph out camping, sometimes for as many as three or four days at a time. Moira begged to be allowed to accompany them (Megan and Maeve cringed in horror at the idea) but it was never permitted. Camping was a manly endeavor, her mother explained (her father never explained anything) and unsuitable for a young lady with good prospects.

She wrote a long, agonized letter to her mother only once. She was working with the International Red Cross. Late in 1968. They were in West Africa, a tiny province called Biafra—an insignificant place no one had previously heard of—which had horrifically, but briefly, burst into the consciousness of the world.

Who today knows, she thought, watching the dust mites play against the morning sun, or cares what had happened there? Probably not a person in a thousand.

Her letter described in great detail the dirt and the heat, the flies crawling through the noses and eyes, thick with mucus, of the starving children, the overpowering odor of unwashed and dying bodies, of desperation, absolute poverty and decay, the closeness of the medical personnel, the lack of facilities for personal hygiene, how her menstrual periods had stopped under the combined forces of bad nutrition and continual stress.

Even now, all these years later, she cringed in embarrassment at the memory.

When she wrote that letter Moira had been spinning in the eye of anger as raw as a hurricane. Not at the poverty and desperation, but at the French doctor who had charmed her effortlessly and made love to her in the tiny tent with the sounds of death and dying all around them, and then returned without a word of farewell to his wife and estates in France. In her rage, she wanted to shock her mother with how absolutely unsuitable she had become. And all she had accomplished was to distress her fragile, cosseted mother into a near breakdown.

Mary Margaret died shortly after receiving that letter, while Moira was still in Africa grieving over her lost love.

And her daughter, Moira, had never forgiven herself.

Moira watched the sun sparkling on specks of dust and she firmly pushed aside thoughts of her mother. Instead she worried about the cottage that made up the beating heart of her family, her mother and grandmother's letters, so carefully preserved all these years, their collection of art, as valuable in sentiment as a good deal of it was in money.

She could tolerate lying here no longer. "Ruth," she shouted, knowing that the humiliating baby monitor was turned on. To her horror the words emerged from her throat as a scarcely recognizable croak. She coughed. "Ruth."

Much better.

A few minutes later, Ruth stumbled into Moira's room, rubbing sleep out of her eyes and clutching her peach negligee around her thin bosom.

"Time to get up. I must go and see what is happening downstairs." Moira struggled to push the heavy covers off. The bed was ridiculously soft and she felt like she was drowning. It took some effort but she managed to get to a sitting position. "Help me to get dressed."

Elaine and Phoebe were hard at work, crouched on the kitchen floor in front of a roaring fire. It was a pleasant day, but the fire had been stoked so high the room was sweltering. They were sorting through the boxes, laying some of the papers out to dry before the fire and drying wetter ones with a handheld hairdryer.

Moira's heart leapt at the sight of them. Working so hard to save her precious papers. "Let me help," she insisted. "I can at least hold that hairdryer for you. My grandmother's letters mean the world to me."

Elaine scratched at her scalp. Her blond hair stood up in a mop of wild curls and she was dressed in an unseasonable outfit of light T-shirt and khaki shorts. Deep circles outlined dark eyes in a pale face. The fine lines around her mouth and eyes, the ones that showed her age, were etched deeper than before. Moira assumed that Elaine had not slept much either. Her biographer touched the fragile papers with reverence as she sifted through the boxes, her long, educated fingers feeling for damp.

Moira thought of Donna, who had been in her employ for less than a week. She couldn't imagine Donna going to so much trouble. Perhaps passion was a good thing after all.

"Don't get too excited, please, Moira," Elaine said. "I'll have no idea what's been lost until we can get back to the storage building and size up the damage. I hadn't even inventoried the boxes, which should have been my first task. I'm sorry, I was so excited to dig into them."

"No matter, I'm sure. Why can't you go in there? The fire's out, isn't it?"

Elaine looked at Alan.

"The fire department won't let us, Moira," he said. "Not until an inspector comes around and declares the place safe."

"How bad is it?"

"Not too bad at all. I've called a roofer to have a look. A good portion of the roof either isn't there anymore or is about to collapse."

"Any damage to the cottage itself?"

"A whiff of smoke, but nothing more."

"The paintings are safe?"

"Everything is fine. The smoke barely touched the main building."

"I meant your work?"

"No damage at all, I'm pleased to say. Not even a touch of smoke."

"I'm glad. But if you need to, call an art restorer. And see to it that you get the best. I'll pay, of course."

"Fortunately, that won't be necessary."

Moira noticed Elaine looking back and forth from herself to the groundskeeper, struggling to understand the threads of conversation.

"I need a cup of tea. Haven't had a drop yet, I'm simply parched. Is Lizzie up?"

"Not yet," he said with a grin, "but I think I can manage to make a pot of tea. Ladies."

The women all watched him cross the room. His tight rear moved under the rough jeans. Moira saw a spark flicker behind Elaine's eyes, and she stored the observation away for further consideration.

"Totally humiliating," she said, once Alan busied himself with the kettle and tea things. "I would have expected you to defend me a bit better, Ruth Czarnecki. Allowing me to be packed into that ambulance like a sack of potatoes. Indeed."

Ruth gaped. "They were only concerned with your best interests, Miss Madison."

"Humph. Those young people. They see an old woman and assume that she belongs in the hospital. That's why I have you, Ruth. To defend me. Don't you know that?"

"I'm sure she does, Moira," Elaine interrupted. "The emergency personnel are highly trained. If they think they saw something amiss, then it was for your own good that they decided to check you over."

Moira harrumphed. Elaine was right, and she knew it. She hated it when other people were right. "I want to see what's in that box. If my grandmother's letters have been destroyed, I will quite simply die. Ruth, pass me the letter at the top. Not that one, the one beside it."

The fire inspector arrived as the family was settling down to lunch and spent what seemed like an eternity tramping about the old guest house. They sat around the dining room table, no one talking, everyone wondering what he would find. Alan and Brad had gone over with him.

Amber excused herself, saying she needed to get some air and would go for a walk. No one broke out of their contemplation of what the inspector would find upstairs long enough to consider her actions odd: Amber had never once been known to walk anywhere, unless it was through a mall.

"The boathouse wasn't cleared out properly at the end of the summer," Alison said, desperate for words to break the solemn silence that had fallen around the table. "There's a bed made up in one of the rooms, or rather not made up. Sheets and blankets scattered all over the place and stacks of dirty dishes. Someone had better see to cleaning it up, or we'll have mice living there in no time."

Lunch served, Lizzie pulled up a chair, uninvited. Charles arched one eyebrow at her, but she stared him down.

Megan peeked between the slices of foccocia on her plate. "Strange bread, this."

"But nice," said Moira, who wasn't having any. Moira had insisted that Ruth take a nap and in her place Phoebe had taken Moira up to her room earlier and helped her to get washed and dressed and have a cup of tea and slice of toast. Moira herself refused to go back to bed until she heard the fire investigator's report.

The door opened and Alan escorted Hal Weiss, the investigator, in. Brad followed.

Charles pushed his chair back. "Why don't you join me in the library, Mr. Weiss. Lizzie will bring some tea."

"Oh, for heaven's sake, Charles," Moira snorted. "I am the head of this household, Mr. Weiss. You may speak to me. Alan, get the man a chair."

Alan pulled two vacant chairs up to the table. Charles resumed his seat, almost admitting defeat. But not entirely. "Perhaps we should excuse the young people, Moira?"

"Whatever for?" she snapped. "They were all here last night. So they have the right to know what is going on. Tea, Mr. Weiss?" She smiled at her guest. He sat down in the chair Alan provided, under no confusion as to who was in charge here.

Moira nodded to Lizzie and the cook slipped out.

He was a huge man, tall and massively overweight. The chest and underarms of his blue uniform shirt were heavily stained with perspiration, old and new. He pulled a handkerchief out of his shirt pocket and wiped off the moisture running in rivers off his glistening bald scalp and down his cheeks and temples.

This fascinating display was scarcely over, the handkerchief returned to its pocket, before Lizzie returned with tea for all, a plate full of cookies, and another pile of fresh sandwiches, one of which she placed beside Weiss' elbow. Brad leaned across the table and helped himself, almost knocking his arm into his mother's face.

"Looks like arson to me," Weiss announced, chewing a huge mouthful of the sandwich and gulping down the scalding tea, all at the same time.

"How can you be sure?"

"I've a lot of experience in this sort of thing, Miss Madison," he said. "I'll have to ask you folks to continue to stay out of that building for a while, until I get a full investigation going. But right now I'd swear that fire was set deliberately."

Elaine looked at the startled faces around the table. With the exception of Hal Weiss', every cup of tea sat abandoned. Alison held a sugar cookie half way to her mouth.

Ever practical, Alan asked, "We can't leave the roof with a gaping hole in it. What if it rains?"

"Well, the upper level is pretty well soaked as it is, from our hoses, but if you want you can get temporary protection up. Work on the roof but don't go inside."

"Oh, dear. Oh, dear." Megan fluttered her hands in front of her chest. "Who ever would do such a thing?" Under the thick makeup she was as pale as the proverbial ghost.

"Perhaps you should lie down, my dear," Charles said to his wife.

"No. I'd rather not. I want to hear what Mr. Weiss has to say." Lizzie added a few heaping spoonfuls of sugar to a teacup and guided it into Megan's shaking hand.

"Surely it must have been an accident," Elliot said.

"I don't think so. It was set on purpose, and a darned clumsy effort it was too. You folks are lucky for that, anyway. I'd say the fire was set with the help of a fire starter. The type people use on barbecues."

"We have plenty of those around," Alan said. "I use them all the time, to start fires in the fireplaces in winter, the grill in the summer." He had taken a sandwich off the platter, but it sat untouched on the table before him.

"Do you keep them all in a safe place?"

Alan sighed and grimaced, his face showing his thoughts. "No, they're where anyone can find them. In boxes by all the fireplaces, out in the hut where I keep the firewood."

"Not your fault, young man," Charles said. "No one wants to have to go running to you if they want to get a fire going."

"A stack of loose papers was placed on top of one of those old boxes you keep up there, with a piece of fire starter underneath. And then lit."

The family gasped.

"Fortunately, packed paper burns badly, very badly. A smoldering toilet roll will make a nice cooker, but it needs attention. No air circulation, you see. Fire would have gone out as soon as the loose papers were all burned up. Lots of smoke, a bad smell and that's all. Excepting that one of the papers must have blown off the stack. I suspect it landed by the window; some old draperies stored there are pretty well destroyed. And once they caught you had enough heat to start on the walls and reach the roof."

"Surely, you can't be serious, Mr. —" Alison said. She pushed her chair back and paced the room. Her normally faultless blond hair was flattened down one side, presumably the side she slept on, and sticking up in all directions at the back, where she had earlier been scratching at her scalp with vigor. Her tailored shirt was wrinkled and awkwardly stuffed into cream wool slacks, and the belt around her thin waist had failed to thread through several of the loops at the back of the pants. Her nail polish was chipped. "Someone left an electric heater burning and it over heated, that's all there is to it."

"I didn't leave the heater on. Why do people keep saying that?" In contrast to Alison, Phoebe was back to her normal self. When upstairs with Moira she had taken the opportunity to reapply her Count Dracula makeup, drench her hair in lacquer, and slip on an outfit of unadulterated black. But under the shock of Weiss' revelations her complexion had turned paler still.

"I believe you, Miss," Weiss said. "'Cause the heater is badly scorched, for sure, but it wasn't the center of the blaze by any means. In fact, it isn't even plugged in."

Phoebe tossed a triumphant smile around the table.

"All right, something else then," Elliot said. "Have you been smoking, Phoebe?"

"No, I have not been smoking." The girl rose to her feet. "And don't you dare accuse me. I didn't start it." She stared at Elliot until her uncle looked away.

It seemed to Elaine that all the hows didn't matter one whit. It was the whys that they should be concerned about. She had questions of her own to ask, but hesitated, unsure if it would be wiser to remain unobtrusive. This wasn't her family, or her home.

The moment to speak passed as Weiss dug appreciatively into his sandwich. They pretended not to notice as droplets of olive oil dripped down his numerous chins.

In retrospect, Elaine's silence was a mistake of enormous proportions. She would spend many sleepless nights wondering if a life could have been saved if she had spoken up.

Chapter Twenty-five

Lunch over, the family scattered. Moira pronounced herself ready for a nap. It was obvious to all that she was about to drop on the spot, and Alison and Phoebe hustled her upstairs. Megan announced with some degree of drama that she was quite exhausted and also in need of sleep. Elliot said that he would be in the library watching the game. Alan went to see to the dogs while Charles escorted Mr. Weiss back to his truck.

Elaine wanted only to get away for a while. This would be a good time to get her car out of hibernation. She'd driven into Bracebridge once, to buy tapes for the recorder, but otherwise hadn't taken out the car for the nearly three weeks that she'd been here.

She followed Charles and Weiss to the back door. Pulling on her hiking boots and taking her coat down from the hook by the door, she could hear them outside, talking in low voices.

So much for keeping everyone informed.

Dave and Amber were crossing the yard. They walked close together, almost touching, but pulled apart as soon as they saw that they were being watched. Amber's pretty face was flushed, making her look all of about twelve years old, and Dave had an expression that would be a perfect match to that of a cat who had swallowed a whole bottle of cream.

"I suggest you have a talk with that young man over there." Charles pointed directly at Dave. "He's been hanging around here a good deal more than one would expect. He and his friends. Ask them where they were last night."

Dave smiled; to Elaine it looked like the smile of a crocodile. His body was appeared relaxed, but his hands were clenched into fists at his side. "If you have something to say to me, sir, I'd prefer if you'd say it to my face."

Amber reached for Dave's arm. He shrugged her off.

"What's this about?" she asked, her voice trembling. "Surely, you can't think that Dave had anything to do with what happened last night!"

Weiss appeared to be a country hick, fat and slow on the uptake, but he knew his job, and his ears pricked to attention. "Do you know something about the fire here last night?" he asked Dave.

"No, I don't. Sorry. If you'll excuse us, Amber has offered me some lunch."

"You started that fire, you ignorant son-of-a-bitch!" Charles roared and stumbled down the steps, scarcely able to stand straight in his rage. "You could have killed us all." He grabbed Dave by the front of his T-shirt and shook the boy like an aging fox with a rabbit in his jaws.

Lizzie ran out of the house to stand on the steps behind Elaine. Alan tore around the corner of the cottage, the dogs at his heels. Hamlet and Ophelia took one look at the scene and, not knowing who was the invader, barked at everyone.

"No," Elaine screamed at the look of red rage that crossed behind Dave's small black eyes. If there hadn't been an audience, she was sure that Dave would have struck out. However, rather than deliver the strong punch that the look seemed to be forecasting, he simply raised both his hands, palms out, and pushed Charles away with about as much force as swatting at a mosquito. The old man staggered backwards, tripped over a stone, and fell heavily.

Even over the racket of the dogs, the yelling of the men, the frightened gasps of the onlookers, Elaine could hear the sickening sound of a brittle, osteoporosis-riddled bone cracking as Charles' arm collapsed under his inconsiderable weight.

He made not a sound, but the color drained out of his face like water being emptied from a bathtub. Weiss, Elaine, Lizzie, and Alan rushed to help the old man up. Amber lifted one hand to her mouth and chewed on her knuckles. Dave grinned, looking as if he had survived a round with a world-class prizefighter instead of pushing an octogenarian to the ground.

"We'd better get you to the hospital, Mr. Stoughton," Alan said.

Charles gasped for breath. "Okay." Some of the color returned to his face, not much, but enough to bring it back to a semblance of life. "But first, I insist that you arrest that man. You saw him attack me, Weiss. You saw it all. You have powers of arrest, don't you? Use them. Imagine, attacking an old man. That punk attacked me."

"What," Dave yelled. "You started it. I barely touched you. Isn't that right, Amber?"

Amber looked from her great-uncle to Dave and burst into tears.

"An old man," Alan shouted, "you have to fight an old man. I'd like to see you try it on me."

Dave assumed a fighter's stance, dancing on his toes, his fists up. "I'm ready. Come on then."

Now Ophelia and Hamlet had a target. They followed Alan's lead, pulled back their teeth and growled deep in their throats as they moved on lowered haunches.

"Only kidding," Dave shouted, folding his hands across his chest and opening his fingers in submission. "I barely touched the old man. It was an accident. I'm a guest of Amber. Tell them, Amber."

"Arrest him," Charles repeated. He leaned against Elaine. He was tall, but bent with old age and new pain, he matched Elaine's height. She slipped her arm tightly around his body. There was no layer of fat to cushion the old bones.

Weiss shuffled his feet. "I'm afraid, Mr. Stoughton, that what I saw was an unfortunate accident."

Dave might try to appear all friendly and innocent, Elaine thought, but a slow fire burned deep inside him and she didn't trust him one inch.

"I'll take Mr. Stoughton to the hospital," she said.

"I couldn't impose," Charles whispered, the pain superseding his anger. "Alan will take me."

"Look." She forced a smile and held up one hand, in which she still clutched her car keys. "I was going for a drive anyway. No imposition."

"I'll help you." Lizzie plucked the keys from Elaine's hand and led the way up the hill to the cars. "I'll tell Alison and Elliot what's happened and I'm sure they'll follow you."

Now that the dogs actually had someone in their sights, Alan had his hands full, dragging them away from their intended prey.

Fortunately it was Charles' arm that was broken, not a leg, otherwise he never would have managed to squeeze into Elaine's BMW. His face had again turned a ghastly white and his lips contorted with pain as he settled into the leather seat. He reached out the hand of his good left arm to stop Elaine as she put the key into the ignition. "Call Weiss over."

She obeyed and Weiss lowered his bulk as much as he was able to squat beside the car window.

"I want you back here tonight, after I get home from the hospital. We still have business to discuss. I want that scum and his no-good friends off my property, today!"

"I don't...."

"They started that fire, and I expect you to prove it." With a sigh that spoke volumes, Charles collapsed back against the soft brown leather of the seat and closed his eyes.

Elaine turned the key, remembering as she did so that the car hadn't been on the road for a week or more. The surface was covered in a fine miasma of dust, but the engine caught the first time and roared into life, glad to be back to work. She soaked the windows with anti-freeze and switched on the wipers to scrape them clean.

She let the engine go and roared down the country lanes at a speed that would have had the late Augustus screaming for mercy. Feeling a bit guilty at enjoying the moment, she peeked out of the corner of her eye at her passenger. Charles' eyes were closed and he was a horrid color but his breathing remained steady. Perhaps she would drop him at the entrance to Emergency and continue on her way. Leaving the Madisons and all their hang-ups to themselves.

But she thought of Moira: her wonderful letters and her dominating family and her fierce determination to be her own woman. And a story she, Elaine, wanted—now needed—to tell.

The hospital wasn't busy, and they attended to Charles immediately. While Elaine waited, she flicked through piles of ancient copies of *Reader's Digests* and *National Geographics*. Almost as good as traveling through a time machine. She didn't have to read for long before a nurse clutching a packet of x-rays escorted Charles back to the waiting room. At that moment, Alison and Brad burst through the swinging door.

"For heaven's sake," Alison exclaimed. She was as disheveled as she had been at lunch. Worse because she had rubbed at her face, leaving black mascara smudged into dark bruises under her eyes.

"You okay, Uncle Charles?" asked Brad.

"Just a fall, young man, can't get this old chap down yet," Charles chucked with bonhomie so false Elaine expected the hovering nurse to boo. "I stood up to Hitler, I can stand up to some young punk, eh?"

"Uh, right." Brad obviously couldn't quite see what Hitler had to do with all this.

"God, this is all getting too much," Alison said. "A nice, pleasant family Thanksgiving this has turned out to be."

"I need to take Mr. Stoughton through to see the doctor now," the nurse said. "Are you the family?"

"We are," Alison said, lifting her chin proudly.

"Then you can come with me."

"Brad, go and get your grandma, then meet us back here. We had a call from the hospital as we were leaving," Alison explained to Charles and Elaine. "Mom is ready to come home, so we thought that we could pick you both up at the same time. Isn't that nice?" Her expression indicated that it was anything but. "We came in two cars, so you can leave, Elaine. The family will manage from here."

Properly dismissed, and not sorry about it, Elaine abandoned her copy of *National Geographic* (January 1980: a cover photograph of Jupiter, taken by Voyager, but looking much more like a Georges Seurat pointillist painting) and returned to her car.

She needed a short walk to clear her head, full as it was of half formed ideas and images, all swirling around, caught in a hurricane, everything moving but nothing settling. Weiss seemed to know his job. If he said the fire had been started deliberately, then arson it surely was. The question then: who would have reason to burn down the storage building? And potentially the cottage as well. Left unattended for a few more minutes the fire might easily have made the jump from one building to the other. To where the family were sound asleep in their beds. Charles suspected Dave and his friends camping out on the island. Dave, she could happily imagine being responsible, but he appeared to have no reason. As for Rachel and Kyle and the others, the idea was preposterous. They cared for Moira, and no one was more vulnerable in a house fire than the elderly and infirm.

There was no sign that anyone had broken into the old guesthouse, or so Alan had reported. But that didn't mean much—Alan locked the building every night, but the keys were kept on a hook in the kitchen, available to anyone in the house.

Not set intentionally perhaps? Phoebe had not been smoking up in the loft; of that Elaine was certain. She'd never seen the black-clad, black-makeup drenched girl smoke. But there was no need for anyone else to go up there after she and Phoebe had finished for the day.

Or maybe there was?

Who knew what reasons people had in a family as complex as the Madisons.

The hospital was close to the center of the small resort town of Bracebridge. She wandered through the streets without noticing her surroundings. A weekday in autumn, the tourists were few on the ground, and most locals were still resting up from the delights of their own Thanksgiving repast.

She stopped at a convenience store to stock up on bags of chips and chocolate bars. Lizzie's cooking was nothing short of amazing but Elaine felt herself to be in desperate need of a jolt of something perfectly junky and overloaded with fat and sugar.

When she got back to her car, several of the local teenagers were hanging about, all baggy pants, enormous running shoes and flannel shirts, sparse beards and numerous, imaginative piercings. They leaned on the hood, smoking cigarettes, and stared openly at Elaine as she pulled her keys out of her jacket pocket.

"Good day, gentlemen. If you'll step aside, I can be on my way." She grinned. "You like my car, eh?"

"Yea, real nice." One of the boys, cigarette drooping out of the corner of his mouth, gaped in unadulterated envy. On cue, they stepped back to allow Elaine to unlock the door and slip smoothly behind the wheel. The engine started with the most delicate of touches to the ignition and purred like a kitten being scratched under its chin. Waving gaily to her circle of admirers she pulled out into the non-existent traffic.

Deciding not to run away after all, Elaine headed back to the cottage. The road wound between patches of open lakes, large and small, and rushing rivers. Flashes of sun-reflecting blue flashed through the green and brown of the woods.

When she got back, Elliot told her that Moira would be indisposed for the rest of the day. Gratefully Elaine informed Lizzie that she would not be down for dinner and crawled upstairs to her welcome bed. It had been one really long day.

Chapter Twenty-six

"Killed who?" Moira asked.

"Amy Murphy. I killed her."

"Moira, it's time to go." A group of her fellow sisters stood on the top of the cliffs that towered over the stretch of rocky beach and the sea beyond. Hard to know how long they had been calling, waving, and generally making a fuss trying to catch her attention.

Jean started down the steps towards them. Moira pushed Ralph out of her lap and jumped to her feet. "I'll come later," she shouted, waving for them to leave.

Jean hesitated. She yelled something unintelligible.

"Ralph will see me home. I'll be all right," Moira called, trying to smile.

For God's sake go away.

Jean shrugged and made her way back up the stairs.

Moira dragged Ralph to his feet. "That's not funny."

"I killed her, M. I killed her."

Tumbling memories. A pretty, cheerful maid. Wild red curls barely contained under a stiff cap, belt pulled in a bit too tight, dancing freckles and a wide smile. Mother complaining that she was "most unhappy with Amy. The girl has airs above her station."

Summer 1939. The last good summer. A sleepless Moira looking for a book, finding instead—Ralph, hair tussled and face scratched, shirt hanging out of his pants, creeping up the staircase without turning on any lights. A sly wink and a finger to the lips as he passed. In those days the upper servants had rooms on the third floor and the lower servants, like Amy Murphy, slept in separate cabins on the grounds.

"I killed her, M. She came to me one night. The night after Paul splashed his brains all over me. And she told me that it's my turn to die. She said I'm a coward, and I deserve to die. Because she died."

"Ralph. Listen to me. You had a dream. One of Mother's maids isn't going to visit you in Italy in the middle of the night to make threats. It was a dream. That's all."

"Not a dream. Not. She was there." He gripped her arms and shook her with sufficient force that her teeth rattled. When she undressed for the night Moira would see a line of finger-size bruises marching across her upper arms, in proper military formation.

"Stop it, Ralph. Listen to me. They're doing some wonderful work in the psychiatric units these days."

"I'm not crazy, Moira. I killed her."

"Then tell me about it." She didn't want to hear. Wanted to run with her hands over her ears and her head down. Run back to the hospital and the crowded wards, the exhausted sisters and broken men. But Ralph needed to talk, and only she was there to listen.

They sat back down. The sun close to a memory, a blaze of orange and crimson lighting up the gentle sea, a cool breeze blowing inland. They were the only people left on the beach.

"Do you remember, her? Amy?" Ralph asked.

"Yes, I do. She was very pretty. I remember that you were mean to her sometimes, although you probably thought that you were only teasing. She ran away one day. We were all at the cottage, except for Father of course. Even Grandfather was there; I remember he came up a great deal more that summer than was his custom. As if he knew that 1939 was going to be the last peaceful summer for a long time. Perhaps forever.

"She took her few things and left without telling Mrs. Czarnecki or anyone. Mother was most upset. Amy never even sent for her clothes back at the Toronto house."

"She never left, Moira. Never. She's still there." His breath caught in his throat. "Except when she's here. In Italy. With me."

Moira's chest clenched. She remembered well the day Amy had disappeared: Mrs. Brooks, the cook, rushing in full of apologies to serve the breakfast herself; Grandfather complaining that the toast was cold, and where was his marmalade—he *always* had marmalade; a sour faced Mrs. Czarnecki carrying clean towels up the stairs, grumbling at every step.

But what Moira remembered most of all was that Ralph had gone. Lazy, indolent Ralph had gotten up before the rest of the family and returned to Toronto. He left a scribbled note on his mother's writing desk explaining that he had forgotten an appointment. She remembered Megan and Maeve, wide eyed, speculating out on the dock that their brother had run off with the maid. Of course, no such thing had happened. Mother phoned home to be told by Father's valet that Ralph had arrived at the house early in the afternoon.

In her mind, whenever Moira thought about the disappearing Amy (which wasn't often, she realized with a pang of guilt) she assumed that the fool girl had run off after a brief affair with Ralph. No one mentioned the matter again. Amy's few possessions were packed up in a box and shipped to her only surviving relative, a sister in New York.

Only a few days later war broke out in Europe, so who had time to think about the strange disappearance of a servant girl?

But someone, obviously, had.

"Did you kill Amy, Ralph?" Moira asked, her voice level and calm.

"I might as well have."

"Good. That means that you didn't. Do you want to tell me about it? I suspect that we've missed the ferry to the mainland. So we have all the time in the world."

"She was in love with me. I never told her she should be. I never lied."

"Did you sleep with her?"

Ralph looked at her over his shoulder.

"Oh, for heaven's sake, you idiot. I'm an Army Nurse. I do know what sexual intercourse is."

He blushed. It gave him an innocent, little boy look that she had never seen before. "Yes, I slept with her, most of that summer. It was a nice summer, wasn't it M?"

"Remind me about her. Did you love her?"

The little boy disappeared. "Of course not. You want to talk like a soldier? She was a common slut. Of course I wasn't in love with her."

If she was in love with you, and because she was just the maid, maybe she wasn't such a slut after all, Moira thought. But she kept her thoughts to herself.

"She told me she was pregnant. That she expected me to marry her."

"And you wouldn't."

"Of course I wouldn't, are you a complete fool?" Ralph was on his feet again, pacing up and down in front of her. "I told her I'd give her some money and she could go to Toronto. Have the baby there. I said I'd talk Mother into giving her a good reference. What else did she expect?"

He actually sounded pleased with himself, looming above her, large and aggressive, outlined against the setting sun.

A few dollars and a good reference. What else could a poor young maid expect? Moira opened her mouth to scream at him, her handsome, privileged, arrogant, self-centered brother. To release all her rage at the unfairness of the world.

But she remembered him weeping only minutes ago on her shoulder and his confession that Amy haunted his dreams.

"Stop pacing, Ralph. My neck is hurting. Amy didn't take your money or your reference, I assume. So what did she do?"

"She killed herself."

"Oh, Ralph." As angry as she was for his callous treatment of a woman who had so much less power and position than he, Moira's heart melted at the cry of pure pain in his voice.

"Did you...find her?"

"Yes. I went to her room. You remember? She slept in that cabin in the woods? The one furthest from the cottage? It was late, I'd told her I was going into town and that I'd come later. I knocked on the door. She didn't answer. I thought she fell asleep, so I walked in. She was lying on the floor, dead. Both her wrists slit from one side to the other. The back of her head was soft where she had fallen and hit her head."

"Oh, Ralph."

"She used a kitchen knife. A big sharp one."

"I remember Mrs. Brooks making a fuss about missing it. But why didn't you call the police? Or the doctor? Or at least wake up Mother?"

"Wake up Mother?" Ralph laughed. It was a harsh, bitter sound, more of a bark than a laugh. "What good would she have been? Grandma perhaps, but she was visiting Aunt Laura after her miscarriage."

"What about me? I was there. Why didn't you come to me? I'd seen dead bodies by then. I was qualified."

"Oh, M. Do you think I could go to my little sister and say 'Come and see my mistress. She killed herself because she was pregnant and I wouldn't marry her'?"

"No. Probably not."

The sun had disappeared and the temperature was dropping fast. Moira's hair was still wet from her last swim and the cold pricked her scalp. The drone of an aircraft sounded high over-head. Instinctively they both looked up.

"American," Ralph said. "A bomber. Strange for it to be all on its own. They make good pilots, Americans."

"What did you do?"

"I got Grandfather. He wasn't happy at being woken up, but came down with me right away. He told me we couldn't afford the scandal. Not now, he said, with war brewing in Europe. Father had some big contracts coming up that might be threat-ened by a scandal."

Moira sucked in her breath. "And you agreed with that!"

"Oh, M. I wasn't thinking straight. I'd had a lot to drink earlier that night. Of course I didn't want Father to find out. You know what he was like."

As straight and hard as a steel rod and just as unbending. Moira knew.

"Grandfather said that if they did an autopsy they'd find out she was pregnant. We had to get rid of her. So we buried her behind the cabin with some of her clothes and things to make it look like she ran away."

He shuddered, whether from the cold wind blowing off the dark sea or the memory Moira didn't know. "His dog followed us into the woods, kept scratching at the ground. Grandfather locked him in the garden shed and then I took him to Toronto. We were terrified the stupid creature would dig something up. What was that dog's name?"

"Horatio."

"That's right. 'I knew him, Horatio.' Then we cleaned up her room."

Moira's mind reeled. Amy Murphy buried in the beautiful woods behind her family's summer home. She remembered the last leave before she left for England. Walking through her beloved woods, ripe with the promise of summer. How she stopped to admire a patch of white trilliums, particularly thick and lovely that year, growing behind the vacant servant's cottage.

She would never walk there again.

"You were foolish, Ralph. Very foolish. You treated a woman like a possession. A possession you could use and then discard. I hate you for that." Moira rose to her feet, and placed her hands on her brother's face, forcing his dark, tortured eyes to look at her. "But you didn't kill her. If she chose to do away with herself, then the deed lies only with her. She was wronged, and you have to live with that. But she was weak. And you have no need to atone for her weakness."

He smiled. It was a feeble smile, but a smile none the less.

She released him and bent to gather up the picnic things. "The ferry must have left simply ages ago and Matron will have my hide on a plate if I'm locked out. So I hope you have money in that pocket of yours."

He laughed. "I'm sure we can find a grateful boat owner happy to transport two valiant Canadian soldiers to the mainland. Provided I offer to pay enough, of course."

The steep stairs up the side of the cliffs numbered in the hundreds. But they were both young and fit and strong and they walked comfortably in each other's company.

"But the cabin," Moira said, as they approached the top. "I can't imagine Grandfather helping you clean up the cabin. It must have been a mess."

"Not too bad." Ralph stepped over the rim of the cliff and reached back to help his sister up the last step. "There wasn't much blood at all. I would have thought there would have been more."

Not much blood.

As a student Moira had done a rotation in the psychiatric ward. She would never forget the young woman the doctors had pronounced cured and ready to return home. The morning she was to be discharged, she had barricaded herself in her private room behind a table and heavy chair and slit her wrists with a smuggled razor blade.

Once the orderlies had broken down the door, Moira was the first into her room. To this day, outside of the operating theatre, she had never seen so much blood.

Yet Amy Murphy had slit her wrists badly enough to die without leaving much blood.

Impossible.

Chapter Twenty-seven

The sun itself wasn't up before Elaine. She opened one eye and peeked at her bedside clock. Five a.m. With a groan she rolled over and pulled the covers into a tight ball under her chin.

It was no use; she'd gone to bed so early that her body refused to settle back to sleep. She lay awake thinking about everything that had occurred since Thanksgiving. When a weak sun finally rose high enough to lighten the sky outside her window, she gave in to the inevitable and crawled out of bed and into the en-suite shower.

Tiptoeing down the stairs, she could hear the dogs in the kitchen and the sound of pots and pans rattling. She left the house through the front doors.

Phoebe sat on the blond wood rail that enclosed the deck, dressed in her usual colors, a dark sweater over black, skin-tight jeans. She was abnormally thin, in the fashion of the day, but her breasts were surprisingly full, the sweater straining at the seams. This morning she was without her bride-of-Dracula makeup.

"Off for a run?" she asked, rhetorically.

"Want to join me?" Elaine glanced at the girl's thin sandals. "I'll wait if you want to put on running shoes."

"Thanks, but no thanks. Not quite the running type."

"You're up early."

"Actually, I haven't been to bed. I keep thinking about the fire. So horrible. And how horrible it must be to get old. The way Auntie Moira looked when Brad carried her out to the fire truck. So without dignity. She must hate losing her dignity."

"I get the impression that sort of thing doesn't matter to her much. Think of the things she saw and did in the war, and then again in Africa. Not much dignity in holding half a man's head in your arms while he pukes out the last meal he'll ever eat. But to be helpless, yes, she probably minds that, a great deal."

The sun was rising in a clear sky behind the cottage, and the lake in front of them resembled a sheet of clear blue glass, laid out neatly, waiting to be placed into a gigantic stained-glass window.

Elaine walked down the steps and Phoebe followed. The two women strolled down the flagstone path to the water's edge. A family of ducks sailed majestically off the dock. The young ones were almost full grown, anxious to test out their independence. Two broke away from the family and waddled up onto the shore looking for handouts.

"I would sit down here on a summer's day when I was a child," Phoebe said watching them, her voice distant. "Feeding the ducks bread and crackers. Grandpa would get mad at me. He says that feeding them encourages them to come around. That was rather the point, Auntie Moira told him. She always came to my defense. She particularly loved the babies when they were all fluffy and tiny."

Elaine laughed. Getting nothing, despite looking cute and deserving, the ducks trundled back to the water in a rush to catch up to their family.

"I think you love your great-aunt Moira very much," Elaine said, not looking at the girl.

"I do indeed. I hate to see her getting so old, so frail. She was terrified the other night, with the fire. She yelled at everyone that she didn't want to be packed off to the hospital." A large tear leaked out of the corner of one eye and Phoebe wiped at it angrily. "Why do we have to get old?"

If Elaine could answer that she could tell Phoebe the meaning of life as well. She kicked at pebbles under her feet.

"She told me some of her adventures. It was me who suggested that she should write it all down. I was so pleased when she said that she would. She's a remarkable woman. I'm glad she's part of my family."

"She's not dead yet, Phoebe. You talk almost as if she is. She has a few more strong years left in her."

"Oh, I know. I guess this is all just so much, all happening at once. Do you know that Grandpa wasn't released from the hospital yesterday?"

"No, I didn't. I went to bed as soon as I got home and slept right through. I hadn't had any sleep the night before. Come to think of it, neither did you. But what's the problem with Charles?"

"They found something funny with his heart. Said he had to stay in until the cardiologist could check him over today. Christ, they'll be giving us a family suite at the hospital soon enough."

"People get old, Phoebe. Death is a part of life. My parents are both gone. And I miss them all the time. Like they must have missed their parents, and they missed theirs and so on down the line."

"I know. But, Elaine, we're the *Madisons*. We're rich. We're important. So why on earth, in the end, are we the same as everyone else?"

Elaine took Phoebe's arm. "That's life, kid. But look at it this way: Moira will live long after her body is gone, if we do a good job on her memoirs."

Phoebe grinned with all the intensity of the sun coming out of nowhere on a dark, storm-threatened day. "You are so right, Elaine. I'm getting dreadfully morbid. Look at those silly ducks, they're following us again."

"A lesson in optimism."

"I hope that you'll let me stay on and help more with the memoirs."

"I'd love it." Elaine meant it. But even if she didn't, she was hardly in the position to tell a member of the family to go away. "Don't you have somewhere to be? School, a job?"

Phoebe shrugged. "School is okay. But I'm getting awfully bored with it. Maybe I could finish out the term and then come back. I love reading Aunt Moira's letters, don't you? I've always loved her the best of all the family, and the letters make me appreciate her more. She's such a contrast to my own mother. And my grandmother. What a loser she is. I don't think I've ever heard her say anything intelligent in my entire life. The way she defers to my grandfather is sick."

"Don't be too hard on her," Elaine said. The sun rising behind them warmed their backs with the promise of a precious Indian-summer day. A motorboat sped past, far out in the middle of the lake. Not many boats at this time of year. The water would be full of them, come summer. The boat rounded the peninsula, the dull roar still hanging in the clear air. "Your grandmother is a woman of her times. Moira managed to break out of the mould. But it would have been an exceedingly difficult thing to do, and probably only possible for the eldest daughter. Once they saw that Moira was developing a mind of her own, your great-grandparents would have clamped down on the younger ones with a vengeance."

"I guess," Phoebe mumbled. "But my mom. She doesn't have to be such a wimp. She's never done a day's real work in her life. She flits about from one charitable cause to another like Lady Bountiful. And then you should hear how she talks behind their backs. Like it's people's own fault that they're poor, or sick or disabled or something. Makes me so mad."

Elaine skirted that topic neatly. She had never met Phoebe's mother, and had no desire to get into a discussion of her faults. "What's your father like?"

"Non-existent."

"I'm sorry."

"I mean he's still alive, and still married to my mom. Not that anyone would notice, and certainly not her. But he's never there, physically, emotionally, or mentally. Never really was. He's an Executive Vice President, la di da, with First Bank. Hope you're impressed. He certainly is."

Over on the island, a shape emerged from the thick cluster of tree trunks and brush and walked down to the water, carrying a large cooking pot. It was a woman, dressed in a long, colorful skirt and heavy knitted sweater. She stepped delicately out onto the rocks, trying to keep her feet dry. Rachel lifted her head and caught sight of them. She waved enthusiastically, her face breaking into a huge smile. Phoebe and Elaine waved back, and Rachel bent to fill the pot with water. Her thick red hair fell forward over her face.

"They won't be here for long," Phoebe said. "Now that they've gotten up Grandpa's nose they'll be given their marching orders."

"That's probably not entirely bad. Winter's coming fast. They couldn't stay for much longer anyway."

"I guess."

Elaine and Phoebe walked along the path that ended at the woods. The woods where no one ever ventured. Without thinking, Phoebe stepped off the path and continued. Elaine hesitated. With someone ahead of her, the sun rising in the sky, and the birds greeting it with enthusiasm, the dark path didn't appear the least threatening. She took a deep breath and stepped off the path.

Nothing happened.

So she walked on.

Boarded up, overrun by weeds and moss and dappled by sunlight, the cabin in the woods looked nothing but simple, harmless. Elaine couldn't remember why, on her last visit, she had found this pleasant copse so terrifying.

"Why does your family stay away from this place? If someone fixed it up, it would make a wonderful guest house. You kids would have loved to have your own private quarters when you were younger, wouldn't you?"

Phoebe's dark eyebrows were creased in thought, and she stroked her chin absent-mindedly. "No one talks about it. I guess my parents were afraid of what we'd get up to out here. Suspicious bunch. This was one of the servants' cottages, a long time ago. In the days when the family had so many servants in the summers that they couldn't all be housed in the main building. Can you imagine?"

Elaine couldn't imagine having any servants at all.

Phoebe stepped over the crumbling old steps and stretched on tippie-toes in an attempt to peer through one of the wooden slats that separated from the door in a hairline fracture. The cabin might have been falling apart at the seams but the boards nailed to doors and windows held firm.

"We were absolutely forbidden to come here. No reasons given, but the order stood firm. Auntie Moira was adamant, but she would never say why. My cousin Arthur, officious prick, Aunt Alison's oldest son, ventured in here on a bet once. He's a lot older than the rest of the cousins. I must have been about twelve at the time. I watched while he pulled the boards off the windows and climbed over the ledge. He had to stay inside all night, that was the bet. Our parents had gone to a party. Aunt Moira wasn't here; I remember that, although I don't remember why. Probably the only reason we dared even think about trying it. As children we were terrified of Aunt Moira. We would try all sorts of nonsense on our parents, most children do. But not Aunt Moira."

"Why?"

"Hard to say. My mom would yell and scream if we did anything wrong; my dad, if he was around, would take his belt to us. But Aunt Moira, she had this way of sighing. And she'd get this look, like she was so terribly disappointed in me. I couldn't stand it. Still can't."

"What happened to Arthur?"

"As soon as he disappeared inside, the rest of us ran back to the cottage as fast as we could. He didn't last an hour, came running though the library, where we were watching TV, as white as a sheet, and shaking all over. He never said a word to anyone about what happened. I always thought Brad and some of his friends scared him on purpose; they were gone for rather a long time, making popcorn in the kitchen. Arthur's never been back to the cottage since. Not even once. Always some excuse or another. He's a big shot corporate lawyer now, for the store."

From what Elaine had learned, from a brief glance at the newspapers, about the dwindling profitability of the family's retail business and the dense black cloud of lawsuits brought by suppliers and employees that hung over the company, she guessed that these days Arthur was too busy to be investigating spooky old buildings.

"Something must have happened here, to keep everyone away," Elaine said.

"Can't see a blasted thing," Phoebe said. "Too dark."

A seaplane flew low above the treetops, beginning its landing.

"If they don't want it any more, why not sell it? This piece of land is far enough away from the main building to stand on its own. It would fetch a nice price."

Phoebe shrugged. "No matter. A lovely mystery, that's all."

"Have you ever been inside?" The girl's casual air emboldened Elaine, who had been scared out of her wits the only other time she came here.

"No." Phoebe held her hand in front of her face, trying to peer though the tiny cracks in the wooden planks. "How about we come down one night and break in? That would be fun. I'll get Brad; he'll join us for sure."

Elaine was tempted. She found something truly fascinating about the old shack. There was a story here, waiting to be told. A family like the Madisons didn't leave a building on valuable property to collapse into rubble. The family's ban on the children's exploration was probably based on nothing more than a desire to protect them from rusty nails and rotting timber. But it wouldn't be terribly wise to incur Moira's wrath over a matter so trivial. It seemed to be important to her, that family and staff stayed well away. And Moira was, after all, Elaine's employer. "Count me out. But I promise I won't rat on you if you try it."

Phoebe clambered down from the front step and they turned their backs on the dark clearing.

A finger ran down the length of Elaine's spine, soft, languorous, lingering, like a lover's caress or the final stroke of a good masseuse. But unlike that of the lover, or the masseuse, the touch was as cold as ice.

Chapter Twenty-eight

On May 16th the Canadians were committed to the battle for the road to Rome. Moira was seconded to a Field Surgical Unit. A duty highly prized among the nurses who knew that it was there that their skills and nerves would be stretched to the limit. There were four Canadian FSUs in Italy, moving as the front moved, sometimes only shouting distance from enemy guns. So close that at night they could see the flashes of artillery, and both day and night the noise echoed through their heads. They were highly mobile, compact units, able to move at the shortest of notice. It was to the Field Surgical Units that the most seriously wounded soldiers were first sent. Two units operated in "leapfrog" formation, jumping each other as the army moved. The forward unit would hang back to evacuate their patients to a Casualty Clearing Station, while its partner moved forward, prepared to receive the next batch of wounded. Each FSU consisted of a surgeon, an anesthetist, two nursing sisters, and five or six orderlies, as well as service staff.

Moira and her companions worked constantly, stopping only to sleep when their exhausted bodies demanded it. Many long years later, when she had the time, and the courage, to remember, she would think of May and June 1944 as the hardest months of her life.

The hardest, the saddest, certainly the dirtiest, but in many ways the best. The months when Moira Madison, privileged daughter of a privileged family, had been tested and not been found wanting.

August 1944. The battle for Rome itself was over, the Allied armies moving steadily north. Moira was stationed at the Number 4 Casualty Clearing Station, where the highest priority casualties were sent. The heat of the Italian August was relentless. The doctors and nurses lived in clothes soaked with sweat. Thick layers of dust covered everything: doctors, nurses, patients, equipment. They were constantly on the move, and when not moving, surgical teams could be operating for thirty-six hours straight, at night by the shifting light of flashlights and lanterns. Moira came to think of a good day as a mere twenty-four hours in theatre, leaving her with a precious twelve hours to clean up, prepare supplies for the next shift, eat, and, hopefully, sleep.

Chapter Twenty-nine

Elaine froze in her steps, as unable to move as if the ice were on her feet, not her back. Only when the touch had passed did she gasp a half-scream and whirl around.

Long shadows cast by the encircling trees shrouded the cabin in darkness. Nothing moved.

"You okay?" Phoebe's brows drew together in concern.

Elaine couldn't speak; she only nodded, swallowing her panic. When her voice had crawled back into her throat and they were walking again, she noticed the scent. That cheap perfume. Sharper than the last time she'd been here. The copse was full of it. When she was a teenager, a friend had picked up a sample bottle of toilet water off the store's display case to spray on her arm. Instead the lid came off and drenched not only the outstretched arm, but the counter, the floor, and a good deal of her friend's coat. They escaped from the store, collapsing with laughter, almost gagging under the power of the sickeningly sweet scent, the prune-faced clerks glaring at them with stern disapproval.

This smell was almost as heavy.

Elaine shivered and hurried to catch up with Phoebe.

The place did give her the creeps.

"Do you think someone started the fire on purpose?" Phoebe asked, once they were again on the sunny flagstone path that lined the lakefront. She didn't seem at all affected by anything that had happened behind the cluster of white pines, and Elaine wondered if she were losing her mind.

"Elaine?"

"Sorry, I was daydreaming. No, I do not. It's an old building, things happen." What was more frightening, a midnight arsonist or a family cottage that turned on its owners for no apparent reason?

"That's what Mr. What's-his-name, the fat fire investigator said. We all heard him." Phoebe grimaced and kicked at a stone with her foot. They followed its progress as it bounced down the hill and hit the lake with a tiny splash.

"I don't know, Phoebe. I still want to go for my run. Then I'd like to get back to the papers and continue where we left off. And I'd like you to help me, if you have the time, that is."

"I told you, I want to help."

"Then why don't we meet in the kitchen in exactly one hour. I'm sure Lizzie's chomping at the bit for us to get those boxes out of her way. Okay with you?"

"Okay," Phoebe grinned, cheerful again, another sudden shift in disposition. Elaine's eldest brother had two teenagers, a boy and a girl, and he was always complaining that he couldn't keep up with their moods, which shifted like fluff blowing in the wind.

"They were saying last night that it looks like we'll have to stay on for the rest of the week, at least," Phoebe said. "What with the fire inspector poking around and Grandpa still in the hospital and all."

"One hour then."

Phoebe traced her steps back to the cottage, and Elaine sprinted up the hill towards the driveway and the road beyond. Before she hit her stride, Hamlet and Ophelia were after her, barking and snapping at her heels. Hamlet circled around the front and stood blocking the way; one side of his lip curled up, his no-nonsense teeth bared.

Elaine jogged on the spot, in no mood to be cowed by this animal. "Get out of my way, you stupid thing," she bellowed. "Bite me and I'll have you put down, see if I don't."

"I don't think he understands." Alan stepped out of the woods carrying a wicked sharp-toothed saw. His curly hair was damp with sweat and drops of moisture dripped down the side of his face. He wiped at them with the arm of his shirt. Keeping their eyes on her, the dogs walked over to stand beside him.

"Cutting wood?" she asked inanely.

"Clearing some brush."

"Nice day for it."

"Cut Hamlet a bit of slack, please, Elaine. He's a real pain in the posterior, but he doesn't mean any harm. He's confused, they both are. All the fuss around here. People coming and going in the middle of the night, fire trucks, smoke. People yelling. Moira too upset to even play with them. They don't know what's happening."

She forced a smile at the dog. He growled deep in his throat. "I'm going for my run, see you later." Three pairs of eyes followed her as she trotted down the driveway.

Spurred on by the madness of the last couple of days, Phoebe's dark musings, the terror of the icy caress, a jolt of adrenaline courtesy of Hamlet—and most of all the sort of highly confusing thoughts that seemed to come over her whenever she found herself in Alan's company—Elaine chewed up the miles of country road.

She was on her way back, the hour almost over when, rounding a corner at full speed, so deep in thought that she scarcely noticed where she was going, she drifted over to the left side of the road and almost ploughed straight into Greg Josepheson. He was also out running, headed in the opposite direction.

"Whoa," he cried, "slow down there. Where's the fire? Oops, bad choice of words. Sorry."

Elaine skittered to a halt. Bending over she rested her forearms on her thighs, trying to catch her breath. "Sorry," she panted, "I was lost in thought. Didn't see you there."

"No harm done. But you're lucky I'm not a garbage truck."

Not sure if she was being mocked, she looked at him. "I do think I would have heard a garbage truck coming."

He smiled, showing a line of white teeth and dancing gray eyes. His Nike tracksuit was new, but fresh sweat soaked the underarms and chest, and his first-class running shoes were scuffed, caked with dirt, heavily worn. "I meant no offence, I assure you." He laughed. "The running up here is perfect at this time of year. Not too hot, not too cold, and not too many people and cars to spoil the solitude. I've been known to get into a bit of a trance myself, on occasion."

His relaxed charm was so natural that Elaine lowered her defenses, swallowed a mouthful of indignation, and found herself grinning back. "My fault entirely. I'm sorry if I've ruined your run."

"Not at all. Too bad I didn't know you were a jogger, I would have suggested we run together. Never mind. I know now. And there was nothing to be ruined, I've about finished. Our place is right over there." He nodded to a discreet paved driveway cutting off from the road and disappearing into the dense bush. There was no handmade wooden sign engraved with the cottage owner's name, nailed to a tree, as there was on practically every other piece of property in the area. No doubt those who came to visit the Josephesons were expected to know the way.

"Would you like to come up and see the place?" Greg asked. "With your interest in the history of the old cottages, you'll like it." He laughed again, a deep laugh, like his voice, full of warmth and good humour. "Or maybe not. Unlike the Madisons' cottage, which I much prefer, my mother wanted everything to be modern. So she ripped out all the charm and character and stuffed in what she saw in magazines. But perhaps I'm prejudicing you. Why don't you come and see for yourself?"

"Thank you, I'd like that."

They walked up the driveway, enjoying the opportunity to cool down from the exercise. The wind felt wonderful nipping at Elaine's overheated face. She unzipped her tracksuit top to let in the fresh air, and simply enjoyed the peace of the woods and the beauty of the day.

The first sight of the Josepheson cottage brought her to an abrupt halt. Huge and multi-faceted, it had been built directly into the rocky hillside in layers of fine old timber and beautifully carved stone, faded dark with time.

"The view first," Greg said, leading her around to the front. It stood high up over the lake, and offered a breathtaking panorama of blue water, brown and green islands, and the vista of the last of the autumn hues dotting the forest beyond. A large boathouse, identical in materials, design, and color to the main building, squatted at the water's edge.

"Beautiful," Elaine said.

He escorted her inside, and the contrast was breathtaking.

Not good, but breathtaking none the less.

"Uh," she said. A writer, she wasn't often at a loss for words. "It's very…interesting."

"Interesting is what Canadians say when they can't think of anything polite to say. You can use the word 'awful' if you like. I hate it. I've seen pictures of how it looked when my father first bought it. Ancient wood paneling, stone and wood floors, classic colors, white wicker table and chairs in the sun room."

"What happened?"

"My mother started by making a few changes. And every year there were a few more. Until we ended up with this. But she's proud of it. Fancies herself as quite the decorator."

"A small price to pay, if it makes her happy."

Greg smiled. "It's nice of you to say so. My sister and I agree. I need a drink after that run. Let's go to the kitchen. It's perhaps the least offensive room in the cottage."

"Do you come up here often?" Elaine asked a few minutes later as she sipped at a welcome bottle of icy Gatorade.

"Not much. When we were children we spent all of our summers and most holidays here. But my sister lives in Texas, her husband's job transferred them there, and I don't seem to find the time. I miss it." His voice dropped to a whisper and he leaned across the Formica table. "I'll tell you a deep dark secret, if you promise to keep it to yourself."

Instinctively, or maybe it was the twinkle in his eyes that gave it away, Elaine knew this was a game. "Cross my heart and hope to die," she breathed, matching his solemnity.

"I've always envied the Madisons. When we were kids, there was only Rosemary and me up here for the summer; we weren't often allowed to invite friends. Bad for Mother's nerves," he drew quotation marks in the air with his fingers, "we were told. So we'd go over to the Madisons' and there would be all these children. A pack of cousins and their friends, in the water and out on the boats, having such a grand time. Both of my parents are only children, so there were no cousins, just me and Rosemary. When they, the Madison children, grew up there were piles of nieces and nephews, and assorted relatives and who-knows-who-else, parties and picnics and fun. While over here we sat around the big formal dining room table, suitably dressed for dinner, the four of us lost in that huge room with nothing to say to each other."

Elaine threw back her head and laughed. "Are you expecting me to be sorry for you, Greg Josepheson? Poor lonely little rich boy. Well, when I was a kid there were a few—and highly obnoxious they were, let me tell you—cousins, but there sure weren't any parties or boating or swimming in the lake. We lived in an apartment in Mimico and in the summer we went to the community pool, along with nine hundred other kids, for our regular dose of chlorine. And a picnic was a broken table in the city park on a lawn covered with goose droppings."

"Well you have me there, Ms. Benson. My childhood wasn't quite the disaster I've always wanted to believe."

They smiled at each other over the Gatorade.

"I thought I heard voices." Olive Josepheson bustled into the kitchen, all flowing silk, fluttering hands, and vacant, welcoming smile. "Dear me, Gregory. We have a guest. Why didn't you call me?"

"I didn't want to disturb you, Mom," he said, his face folding into a gentle smile. "You remember Elaine. Who's helping Moira Madison with her memoirs. I ran into her out jogging and knew she'd like to see what you have done with the cottage."

Mrs. Josepheson patted her short, steel hair. "Welcome, welcome," she simpered. "Would you like me to give you a tour?

Our cottage is quite unusual in the Muskokas, dear. Nothing like it, I have been told."

How could Elaine refuse? "I'd love to. I was admiring the décor as we came in. Greg tells me you did most of the decorating yourself." She handed her glass to Greg and smiled at his mother. She could tell by the gentle look on his face that she'd said the right thing. Her own late mother had advised her: You can always tell the quality of a true gentleman by the manner in which he treats his mother. Unfortunately for her, her own two sons had moved to the opposite ends of the country almost the minute they were of age. At the end there was only Elaine to care for the ailing woman.

As the tour progressed, Elaine didn't know whether to laugh or cry. The cottage was a monstrosity of overlapping styles and hideous taste. Beneath thick coats of paint, shag carpeting and highly polished veneer she caught the odd glimpse of quality woodwork and well-laid brick. It was like peering into a pop rock video to make out the soft, fading light of a daguerreotype behind. But Mrs. Josepheson beamed in delight as she showed Elaine everything, from the Art Deco bathroom to the French Provincial master bedroom and imitation Louis XIV guest bedroom. Not to mention the Italian restaurant front room.

"Thanks so much for amusing Mom," Greg said as they made their way back up to the road. "She's not quite there some of the time."

"You don't have to apologize," Elaine interrupted. "My grandmother suffered from Alzheimer's. Old age isn't fun. When are you going back to the city?"

"At the end of the week. I intended to go down on Tuesday, but the fire upset my parents badly. So I'll stay for a few more days. I won't be missed."

"Nice to be able to do that. What do you do?"

"I own an Internet company. We help major corporations interface between each other in the way that they do business. B2B, it's called. I'm not missing all that much by not being at the office—most of what they need me for can be done on the phone or over the Net."

They walked up the road, enjoying the warmth of the morning sunlight, until they reached the hand-painted sign announcing the entrance to the Madison property. "I'll leave you here," Greg said. "I'm sure you can find the rest of the way back."

"Thank you for showing me your home." She could stand in this road, in the warm dappled sunlight, on this autumn day, forever. The fire, the deserted and foreboding servants' cabin, even the black dog of depression that followed her on silent paws over the Thanksgiving weekend—all was forgotten, soaked up by the peace surrounding her.

"It was my pleasure, entirely," Greg said. "And thank you for being so considerate to my mother." He also didn't quite seem to know how to leave.

Hamlet and Ophelia decided for them. They burst out of the undergrowth with a chorus of barking, display of teeth, and ominously twitching tails.

"Oh, for God's sake," Elaine shouted to the winds as the brief moment of serenity cracked apart like the ice-bound lake at spring break-up. "Can't those dammed dogs keep quiet for ten seconds?"

"Josepheson." A cool voice sounded from behind an old maple and Alan stepped out, still carrying his saw. He snapped his fingers and growled deep in his throat. The dogs retreated to his side.

"Morning, Manners. Your dogs have frightened Elaine. Can't you keep them under a bit of control?"

Elaine's hackles rose as high as the dogs'. "I'm hardly frightened by those two," she said. "All bark and no bite."

"Not everyone knows that," Greg said, his eyes on Alan.

"Better that they don't," Alan replied. He turned his attention. "I found a nice bunch of oyster mushrooms, back through the woods a bit. Lizzie does a great job with them. Would you like to help me collect some, Elaine?"

"Sounds nice. Thanks for the drink, Greg," she said. "I'll see you soon."

"If not before. Enjoy your mushrooms." He turned and before Elaine could reply, disappeared behind a stand of pines to be swallowed up by the bush.

"Charming fellow," Alan said, dryly.

"I like him."

"I'm sure you do." He plunged into the woods, Hamlet and Ophelia at his heels, leaving a perplexed Elaine to follow.

She had forgotten her promise to meet Phoebe. What with Gatorade in the Josepheson kitchen, the lengthy cottage tour followed by mushroom picking in the woods with a brittle Alan, Elaine was more than a bit late.

But Phoebe didn't seem to mind. She sat happily amongst the papers while Lizzie huffed and puffed in an effort to pick her way around the obstacles scattered around her kitchen.

Phoebe sat cross-legged on the floor beside one of the salvaged boxes reading a yellowing letter. The box was scorched on the outside and warped from sudden drying out by the kitchen fire, but fortunately still sound, contents safe. "Scandal, scandal," she screamed as Elaine crouched down beside her. "Listen to this. The gardener, William, and the maid, Sheila, were dismissed on the same day for 'immoral behavior.' What do you think of that?"

Elaine settled into her place on the floor. "I think that either Will and Sheila missed church one Sunday, probably having been kept up until all hours by family demands, or they were having a bit of hanky panky on the side, and good for them. It would be fun to find out whatever happened to then. Perhaps they founded a dynasty of mining magnates or some such. Any last names?"

"Nope."

"Then scant hope, I'm afraid. Whose letter is that, anyway?"

"It is to none other than Mrs. Elizabeth Madison herself, wife of Augustus, mother of Mary Margaret, and thus grandmother of Moira, from her sister in England. The sister is referring to something that Elizabeth told her about."

Elaine's heart almost stopped in delight. "A letter to Elizabeth. How many are there?"

Phoebe shuffled through a pile of papers. "This looks like the only one in this box. It's completely out of date from the rest, maybe got mixed in by mistake. Most of this lot are from Moira to her own mother, when she was in Africa, dated many, many years after Elizabeth's sister's letter."

"We can only hope there'll be more. What's the date?"

"November 1939." Phoebe looked up. "The war had started."

"Still early for them to be too worried, in England. I wonder what Elizabeth's sister did during the war. She would have been quite elderly. Let's keep looking. I'd love to have more letters to Elizabeth and Augustus. Some letters from her would be even better, but that's unlikely."

They worked for the rest of the morning, checking each piece of paper for damp. Fortunately most of the papers dried out nicely. Moira arrived, Ruth pushing her wheelchair, and instructed them to put the boxes into the library, in order to at least get them out of poor Lizzie's way. Alan and Brad were conscripted to help with carrying the precious documents from one room to another.

One box of papers, mostly household accounts by the look of them, but intermixed with a few letters, had been almost completely ruined by smoke and water. Elaine sighed in disappointment. "I'll try to get these cleaned up a bit," she said. "But it'll be hard. We're lucky they were all stored so well. Surprising, considering the way they're stuffed up in that old loft."

"That would be Aunt Maeve, I suspect," Phoebe said. "She did give the old things care and attention at one time, although not much lately."

"Bit hard for her to clamber up the stairs, I expect."

Once the task was accomplished and all the boxes relocated to the so-called library, the room was bursting at the seams.

Their work was interrupted by Lizzie arriving at the door bearing an antique silver tray with turkey sandwiches, tea, and thick slices of carrot cake.

"Thought you'd be hungry about now," she said. "Megan is asking what all the racket is down here." She glanced about for a suitable spot and settled the tray on a fragile, antique side table, out of place in this modern room of Stephen King paperbacks and large screen TV. "Ghosts, I told her, but she went running to complain to Elliot that I'm being cheeky. You'll no doubt be seeing them shortly."

After lunch, Moira summoned Elaine to her study, and she left Phoebe immersed in old letters and household accounts.

"Time to get back to work, Elaine," Moira announced cheerfully. Some of the color had returned to her face and the lines of strain had receded, just a bit. "Can't keep having this much fun forever, now can we?"

Elaine smiled at her employer's enthusiasm and pulled a chair up to the beautiful desk. "Any news of Charles? I was sorry to hear that he had to stay in the hospital."

"He called earlier. The cardiologist has given him the all clear and he can come home as long as he takes it easy for a while. Brad has gone to pick him up. So it looks as if the rest of my family will be staying the week. Blasted nuisance, but I can't demand that they all leave. Charles has a broken arm, Maeve is shaken up about the fire, and the people from the fire department are still poking their inquisitive heads in and out. And to top it all off, we're expecting a visit from the police this afternoon."

"They're convinced it's arson then?"

"Absolute rubbish, as I told Charles on the phone. Complete waste of everyone's time. Although I suppose if there was an electrical fault or something we would want to know about it. So we could ensure that it doesn't happen again."

"Well, I don't think it's rubbish, Miss Madison," Ruth said from her place in the corner. "If the fire inspector suspects someone set that fire, then we had better be careful. It's only wise."

Moira opened her mouth to make a smart retort, caught Elaine trying not to look at her and closed it again. "Perhaps you're right, Ruth."

Elaine busied herself with her tape recorder and notebook.

"Hard on Lizzie," Moira said. "She's called Patty back to help out and sent Alan and Amber into town for enough food to feed an army." Today she wore a deep green T-shirt from the University of British Columbia and a well-used pair of sweatpants in an ugly shade of brown. Two enormous diamonds set into drops of white gold glistened at her ears. "Like my shirt?" The old woman smiled brightly, displaying the aged and crooked teeth. "A birthday gift from my great-niece, Andrea. She's in medical school. I considered studying for a doctor. In my family it was shocking enough to want to be a nurse. But at least that was a woman's profession. Can't imagine what Grandfather would have said, had I become a doctor."

"Do you mean your grandfather, Augustus Madison?" Elaine checked that the recorder had sufficient tape and pressed record. "I'd like to hear more about him."

"Why?" Moira's tone was suddenly sharp.

"For background. He did make your family's money, didn't he? So he's important to your story."

"I suppose he is. Complex man. A domestic tyrant, you could say. He treated his wife and children with less consideration than his pets. But in business, people respected him. I was surprised, when I started to travel, how well people would treat me, simply because I was Augustus' granddaughter."

"Maybe they wanted you to influence him on their behalf."

"When he was alive, perhaps. Yet even after he died, both men and women would seek me out to tell me how much they admired him and that he had helped them or given them a chance. I remember one incident in particular. It was after the war, when I was back nursing in Toronto for a short while, before going to the Territories. I had a patient with a broken leg; she was absolutely delighted to find out who I was. She told me that Grandfather had helped her mother after her father died. He'd been an employee at the store and was killed during some sort of accident in the loading docks. When he died her mother, my patient's mother that is, was left destitute and Grandfather saw to it that she got a bit of money, and found her a place in secretarial school. When she graduated he hired her at the store. She told me that her mother adored him."

Elaine tried not to snort in derision.

Moira read her mind. "Of course I thought the same as you. But she assured me that she was old enough to know that Grandfather asked for nothing in return. He came to their apartment one time only, after the funeral. Had a weak cup of tea out of a chipped cup and a stale cookie, and left an envelope with money and the address of the secretarial college."

"Quite a story."

"I was afraid of him when I was young. He didn't have much to do with us, but he was so cold and distant when he was around. He was quite terrifying."

Elaine could believe it: she had spent long enough staring at that portrait at the bottom of the stairs.

"He loved Ralph. Much more than he did any of the rest of us. But he could be so terribly hard on him. Fredrick, my father, was his only child, so all of his other grandchildren were merely girls."

"Did he think of you that way—merely girls?"

"Yes, he did. He simply ignored us girls. But Ralph, he did love Ralph."

When she spoke of her childhood, Moira's voice was thick with wounds never healed, remembered pain, and pent up anger. But it always softened when she mentioned her brother. Elaine wanted to explore that more, but knew that this was not the time to interrupt the flow of narrative. Instead she scribbled wildly, thinking all the time that Moira had an amazing grasp of human nature. She hoped she could bring that out, in the writing of Moira's life.

"But he was hard on Ralph. Difficult for anyone to live up to such expectations. I sometimes think that is why...."

Elaine looked up. Moira was sitting still, her chair half turned, staring out the window at the naked trees beyond. A red squirrel perched on a branch, looking in, the little face scrunched up inquisitively.

"You think…?" Elaine prodded.

"Nothing. He died in 1944. Grandfather did. The day after they got the news about Ralph. I wasn't there, of course, but they told me that he was walking in the woods, overwhelmed with grief, and his heart simply stopped. He was dead when they found him."

A knock at the door, and Lizzie's frazzled head appeared around the frame. "The police are here, Moira. They'd like to talk to us all. I've put them in the front room. They're asking for Elaine first."

"Very well." Moira sighed theatrically. "And we were getting so much accomplished. Is Charles back yet?"

"Led the police up the drive."

"Nothing for it, but we'll have to continue later, my dear."

Chapter Thirty

September 1944. An exceptionally hot day in a summer of hot days. Moira was writing up her notes on the day's shift, but her mind was in Muskoka. Where her mother and sisters would be trying to find someone to pull up the dock, bring in the boats, and shut the boathouse for the winter. Her mother tried (and failed, but she did try) to be cheerful. But her sisters' letters were full of complaints; the best of the servants had left—the men for the army, the women for factory jobs, only the old and unwanted remaining—the shortage of nice clothes and men under fifty at dances or boating parties, always ending with "but we mustn't complain." Rather than being offended by their petty concerns, their letters amused Moira enormously. Nothing like having one's opinions of others so completely verified. She wiped sweat from the back of her neck and dreamt longingly of gigantic plates of ice, water frozen solid, shifting and heaving with enough force to twist and tear rock: never mind a puny rowboat or manmade dock.

Jean burst into the tent. She had long ago lost the devil-may-care persona of the crafty businesswoman and party girl. Like the rest of them, the new Jean was all work.

"Put that book down, Moira. You have to come with me."

Moira looked at her friend stupidly. Her eyes were so tired the lids felt like industrial strength sandpaper rubbing against her eyeballs. She had worked for thirty-six hours straight, standing beside Dr. Reynolds until the surgeon could scarcely hold his scalpel straight. They tended to one critically wounded soldier at a time. Some had been awake and aware, crying for their mother or cursing God. Most were, fortunately, unconscious. Many died without seeing light again, and a few would wish that they had. They were all young and brave and they all loved mothers and fathers or children and wives or girlfriends, some of whom remained faithful and some of whom did not. Moira closed her heart and tried not to love them all.

Jean plucked the notebook from Moira's fingers and lifted her friend to her feet. "Moira. Ralph is here."

"Ralph, my brother? How nice," Moira said, failing to understand. "But this isn't a good time for a visit."

"I think it's your brother. His tags have that name. You have to come with me."

Understanding at last, Moira ran out of the tent. Jean followed.

He lay in the pre-operative tent. The orderlies had scrubbed the dirt from his face and wiped up most the blood. He was as pale as a Muskoka moon shining on the lake when it was covered with fresh snow, his eyes mere dark hollows in the achingly familiar face.

"Oh, Ralph. God, no." Moira fell to her knees beside the cot. He was conscious, pumped full of morphine, thank goodness. Her expert eyes ran over his body, seeing the uniform shirt soaked red, ripped open, the stomach wound roughly bandaged, still leaking blood.

The orderlies arrived. "Stand back, Sister. We'll take him in now. Doctor's waiting."

"M." He reached out one hand. The first few gentle drops of rain fell on the roof of the hospital tent. The officers were worried about the rains. These flat plains and reclaimed swampland would turn quickly into seas of living mud.

"She's gone, M. Amy's gone. She's left me. Thank you."

Moira leaned over the stretcher to catch his words. "I'm glad, dearest. They're going to take you to surgery. We'll talk when you get out."

"I'm sorry she died, M. I should have helped her."

"Yes. You should have. But it's all over. You stay strong and get better, and we'll talk about her then."

"Sister," the orderly said, his voice breaking with kindness, "we have to go."

Ralph smiled a dreamy morphine smile as his stretcher was hoisted high. "Tell Charlie I don't blame...."

An ambulance pulled up; the back doors flew open, orderlies rushed to unload more wounded. Ralph's words were lost.

He died on the operating table while Moira paced outside in the driving rain. Someone had told Dr. Reynolds of their relationship and he came himself out to tell her. He was a kind man, who hated every minute of this war.

Warm comforting arms enveloped Moira and led her back to the nurses' tent. The staff of Number Four Casualty Clearing Station stood silently as they passed.

Jean held the flap of the tent back and Moira bent automatically to enter.

"Oh, Moira. What can I say?"

She straightened. It was Charlie Stoughton. His uniform was torn and filthy, and a cut over his right eye had dried into a caked mess. His face twisted with the strength of his emotions, and he gathered her up into his arms. They clung to each other for a long time, while Jean fluttered about, patting backs and whispering platitudes, and the rain fell, and the war raged all around them.

Charles Stoughton received the George Cross for his actions that day. Ralph Madison received a grave in Europe, one in a row upon row.

Moira Madison refused to take leave and worked herself around the clock.

The family was at the cottage when the news arrived. Old Augustus Madison died the next day, his heart just giving up. Ralph's mother collapsed and never quite recovered. His two sisters in Canada mourned, but did appreciate the gestures of sympathy from all their friends. His father went to Ottawa and negotiated a new contract for the output of his munitions factories. Mrs. Brooks, mother of no children of her own, who had warmed Ralph's milk when he was a baby, and tested its temperature on her bare arm, draped black crepe over the pictures in the house as had her grandmothers for generations uncounted, then walked out to the precipice overlooking the lake, for once forgetting to prepare afternoon tea, and howled into the wind.

The family, gathered in the drawing room, heard her, and tried not to look at each other in embarrassment.

Only Ralph's grandmother, Elizabeth, received the news without shock. Days earlier, while she was working in her patch of garden, a piercing cry rose from the woods behind the servants' cottages, abandoned since the beginning of the war. A single cry, so loud, so full of pain, it had the birds flying out of the trees, the squirrels scattering for shelter, the boat bobbing on waves on a lake that moments before had been as still as glass. The old woman remembered her own mother's tales of the banshee, gathered up her gardening tools into her neat basket and returned to the cottage. She was dressed in full mourning and waiting for the telegram when it arrived.

Chapter Thirty-one

The police inspector sat in the fine old leather chair, sipping at a bone china teacup. A plate of tiny sandwiches, cookies, and thin slices of seed cake sat on a side table placed within easy reach. Lizzie held the door open for Elaine and pulled it shut silently behind her. She felt like a character in a second rate English country house murder-mystery.

He stood up. "Have a seat, please, Ms. Benson. I'm Inspector Watson." He was coming out the wrong side of middle age, heavily beer-bellied, with a bulbous and brilliantly red nose that would put Rudolph to shame. What hair remained was thin, gray, and greasy. His cheap brown suit was worn shiny in spots, the belt hitched so tightly underneath the eight-month pregnant stomach it looked as if the container of fat would collapse to the man's knees without support. It looked painful.

"This is Constable D'Mosca." He nodded to a much younger man, standing in the shadows beside the cold, dead fireplace. The Constable wore the standard winter uniform of the Ontario Provincial Police. His shoulders were broad and his hips narrow. He watched Elaine with a rather ugly face that completely lacked expression, and nodded once. He also had a teacup and a plate of sandwiches, resting beside him on the mantle. His hands looked as if they would crush the fine china into dust if he dared to raise the cup for a sip.

Elaine wiped her palms on the seat of her jeans and slipped into the offered chair.

Watson sat back down. "I hope you don't mind if I eat my sandwiches while we talk, Ms. Benson. I didn't have the opportunity to have lunch."

"Please, continue," she croaked, wondering what he would say if she did object. Better not to find out.

The interview was crisp and formal. D'Mosca didn't speak, but Elaine could feel his eyes boring into her back. She related the events of the night before last, as best she could remember them. Watson took her step by step though her nocturnal wanderings. She had seen no one, heard the dogs, thought that perhaps someone was in the kitchen but didn't go to investigate.

"You saw no one in the storage building?"

"Not a soul. Until I called the alarm and Alan arrived."

"What do you know about the people who are camping out over on the island?"

Elaine's nerve endings twitched. "Almost nothing. They've been invited to stay by Miss Moira Madison, who is the permanent resident here. They're not trespassers."

"I never said they were."

"Good. They're nice people." Well, most of them, anyway. She kept the last thought to herself.

"I understand that you were witness to an incident yesterday between Charles Stoughton and Dave Thomas. Can you tell me about it."

"Nothing to tell. If you know about it, then you know as much as me. Charles was angry. He accused Dave of starting the fire. He did attack Dave first, although it was all bombast and bluster. He's an old man, for goodness sake. Dave pushed him away and he fell. That's it."

"Why do you think Mr. Stoughton accused Mr. Thomas of starting the fire?"

"Because he doesn't like him. In my humble opinion that's the only reason."

"Did you see Mr. Thomas the night of the fire?"

Elaine thought. "I think so. Some of them rowed over from the island. I would say that's completely natural: you see a fire, you investigate. I think Dave was with them. Yes, I'm sure he was."

"What's the relationship between the people staying on the island and the Madison family?"

"There is no relationship. They are all fond of Miss Madison. She seems fond of them. They keep to themselves."

"Would you say they are fond of Mr. Stoughton, Mrs. Stoughton, or Mrs. Blake?"

"I have no idea."

"But you know they are friends with Miss Moira Madison?"

"Look, Charles doesn't want them there. We all know that. But Moira has invited them. So there you are. As for Megan and Maeve, Mrs. Stoughton and Mrs. Blake, I don't know what they think about anything, and they are highly unlikely to tell me."

"No need to be so prickly, Ms. Benson." Cake finished, Watson wiped his fingers on the colorful paper napkin provided.

"I am not being prickly. Merely helpful."

Behind her, D'Mosca shuffled from one foot to the other. Elaine did not turn around to look.

"Had you met Dave Thomas before you came here?"

"Never seen the fellow before. Why do you ask?"

"Just curious. An occupational hazard. Did you know Donna Smithton?"

Elaine's head spun at the abrupt change of topic. "No."

"You never met her?"

"No. Never."

"But you know who she is?"

"I was told when I arrived, that she was my predecessor. She'd been hired to work on Miss Madison's memoirs first."

"In preference to you?"

"Yes, in preference to me. I guess that means I was second choice. No one wants to think of themselves as second choice. But I didn't sneak up here in the middle of the night, to a place I'd never been, to push a woman I'd never met into the lake, on the off chance that she couldn't swim, so that I could get a job."

"I never suggested that you did anything of the sort, Ms. Benson."

Elaine almost swallowed her tongue. Could she be any stupider? Why not clap herself in irons while she was at it?

"Thank you for your time, Ms. Benson."

Dismissed, Elaine stood up. "You must have a reason for asking me about Donna Smithton. Does that mean that you suspect foul play?"

Watson looked at her.

"It's just that, what with the fire and all, I'd like to know if something suspicious is happening around here."

"Thank you for your time, Ms. Benson."

Suitably put in her place, Elaine made her way out of the room. As she pulled the door behind her, she heard Watson's low voice. "Alan Manners...."

She returned to the study, hoping that they could pick up where they left off. But Moira was distracted and anxious. She chattered on for a while, about friends she had known in the war and lost touch with after. But soon Moira sighed and dismissed Elaine in much the same tone as that used by Inspector Watson. Elaine pretended not to notice the supercilious smile Ruth threw at her as she slipped away.

She wandered into the kitchen in search of a mid afternoon snack and a bit of gossip. But Lizzie also was uncustomarily abrupt. She thrust a tin of cookies at Elaine and turned back to the cookbook. She was studying a full page color picture of a whole fish, salmon probably, covered in a smooth yellow sauce and sprigs of a fresh herb. Elaine hoped that was going to be dinner.

She could get used to having a cook.

Elaine wandered through the house, munching on cookies, and ended up outside, on the deck. The sun was falling fast, casting long shadows through the woods and a band of orange flame across the waters of the lake.

What would it have been like to grow up in this wonderful place? Whole summers filled with nothing but swimming, boating, parties, and playing in the woods and on the rocks along the shoreline. Despite what her speech to Greg may have hinted, Elaine hadn't had a deprived childhood. There was no apartment in Mimico—rather they lived in a three-bedroom detached house in a nice suburb—and most years her parents rented a cottage on Lake Erie or Wasaga Beach for two weeks. But, still, the pokey summer rentals, crammed onto a busy road of identical buildings, were light-years away from this.

Alan emerged from the boathouse pulling a small rowboat at the end of a rope. Watson and D'Mosca clambered aboard; Alan tossed them the rope and they pulled away, heading for the island a few hard strokes off shore.

The younger generation, Phoebe and Amber and Brad and their assorted brothers and sisters, were children any one would envy. But Moira, Megan, and Maeve? No way, Elaine thought. Luxurious surroundings were great, but a loving family was a whole lot better. She didn't know what she felt about the Madisons of her own generation, of whom Alison was the only one she'd met. They were right in the middle, most likely. Short of the freedom their own children knew, but not as trapped in convention, rigid class and gender roles as their mothers.

A loon called out from the far side of the lake; a soft breeze carried the fragrance of the decomposing forest floor and the sound of waves lapping at the shore.

Money can't buy happiness, but it sure can make being miserable a whole lot more pleasant.

Willow danced down to the waterline to greet the rowboat, followed immediately by Rachel, who pulled on the child's arm and pushed her back into the woods. Arms akimbo, feet apart, red hair blazing in the long rays of the afternoon sun, Rachel faced the intruders like a Saxon warrior watching the approach of the Vikings. All she lacked was a double-headed axe.

"They have their bureaucratic hearts set on our Dave as the villain of the piece." Alan climbed up from the waterfront to stand beside Elaine.

"Do you think he started the fire? They seem to think someone did."

"Dave? In a heartbeat, if it suited him. He's a right prick, that one, although he's managed to charm Moira, who's usually a lot more sensitive to people. But I can't see that it would suit him to torch Moira's home. No motive. Quite the opposite. If the house falls down, the occupants leave. The property comes under the surveillance of the insurance company. Never good for squatters. Surveillance, I mean."

"He seems to have a bit of an influence over Amber."

"More the fool her. They've set up quarters over the boathouse. A nice, cozy little love nest. They think no one notices. He rows over when it's dark and goes upstairs, then she sneaks out after dinner and they spend the night in conjugal bliss."

"Are you going to say anything?"

"Me? Of course not. She's of age. She's not being coerced. Stupidity and willful blindness aren't crimes, not yet anyway."

His jaw was tight and his face set into hard lines. The wind caught his hair and fluffed it into gentle curls around his face.

"Do you know anything about the old cabin back in the woods a bit?" Elaine pointed as she talked, speaking without thinking. It was always lying under the surface of her thoughts. She had to talk to someone about it.

"I know that it's there. That no one's supposed to go near it. Have you?"

"Come on, Alan. Tell me you're not curious. That's an incredibly valuable piece of property. Frontage on Lake Muskoka, road access but secluded. Yet it's been abandoned to grow a healthy crop of moss and saplings. The children weren't allowed near it. They teased each other with challenges of who could spend the night in the cabin. And no one managed it. Did you know that?"

"Doesn't surprise me. I've been told to keep it boarded up, but otherwise there's no need to clear the vegetation or trim the trees or to touch up the paint."

"You've never felt anything…strange out there?"

"Of course not. Are you sure that Phoebe's childhood stories aren't playing on your imagination, Elaine? I've never had reason to go inside and that suits me fine. Less work."

"You don't strike me as the sort of man who avoids work, Alan."

He was staring out over the lake, watching the island, as was she. Rachel and the police had moved back into the trees, towards the campsite itself, and there was no further sign of movement. Alan turned his head and looked at Elaine. "I don't avoid work. But I do avoid that which I've been told not to interfere with, and so should you."

"I've never been any good at doing as I've been told."

He laughed, genuine laughter full of mirth and amusement. "Then you shouldn't be working for Moira, babe." His looks were quite unremarkable most of the time, but when he laughed....

A bustle of activity over at the island and a small crowd burst out of the trees at the water's edge. Willow danced ahead to pick up stones and fling them enthusiastically into the lake in order to hear the satisfying sounds they made as they splashed. The adults, however, didn't look quite so happy. It was hard to make out the expressions on individual faces, but body language said enough. The islanders were angry and hostile; arms crossed, legs planted firmly on the gray rock of the shore as they watched Watson and D'Mosca scamper back into their rowboat. For a moment it looked as if the bulky constable would tip the wobbly craft. But incident was avoided, dignity retained, the boat righted, and the forces of law and order rowed back across the narrow strait.

"Stay out of things that don't concern you, Elaine. Please." Alan didn't look at her as he hurried down to the dock to help the police pull aside.

Elaine found herself thinking about that conversation a good deal of the time. If not always in the foreground of her mind, it was now, more than ever, usually resting in the back.

She walked down the flagstone path to stand under the old white pines that marked the entrance to the secluded copse where the servants had spent their summers long ago. But her feet would take her no further. There had to be a reason the family ignored this piece of property so completely.

Elaine set her mind to finding out what it could be.

Chapter Thirty-two

At last it was over. This stage of it anyway. The war in Italy wound down. The wounded were evacuated back to England, the healthy deployed elsewhere. Moira returned to No. 15 General Hospital and in March of 1944 they were sent back to England.

The heart is a creature unto itself. Moira mourned her brother, and all the men she had watched over while they died, but nothing could dampen her excitement at the idea of England. For England meant Grant. And she knew he was as excited to see her as she was to see him.

They were able to plan leave together. A whole week. They would meet in London, visit the jazz clubs they had talked and written about so much.

Moira blushed as she bought a satin nightgown from a tiny London shop. Her mother sent her money regularly, but she had nothing to spend it on. And even if she did, she had no wish to set herself apart from her fellow nursing sisters. She had bought victory bonds with most of the money, and carelessly tossed the rest into a bank account. The negligee was a rare treat.

Moira Madison was an Army Nurse. She knew all there was to know about the facts of life. In theory. She fingered the peach satin and delicate lace while the sales clerk, an older woman encased under a much too heavily made up face and false smile, watched her customer through knowing eyes, and, with a shiver of apprehension, realized that, in reality, she knew nothing at all.

Chapter Thirty-three

By the end of the week, tempers were fraying. Alison and Elliot escaped back to the city, dragging a reluctant Brad with them. They had jobs to return to and Brad, who was in his first year at University, had missed quite enough school. Amber somehow managed to convince her parents over the phone that she was desperately needed to help her grandma. Fortunately for her, they didn't try to verify that fact with Maeve, who had scarcely seen the girl since she returned from the hospital, and so Amber remained free to sneak out to the boathouse in the evenings. Maeve had fallen into a black hole of depression and spent most of the day in her room, only coming down for dinner at Moira's insistence, and then to sit morosely at the table staring at her plate and saying nothing. Charles' arm was wrapped in a cast, and he had assumed the temperament of a bear that couldn't find anything to eat upon emerging from hibernation. Megan bustled about him constantly, trying to be useful, but managing only to annoy both Charles and anyone who really tried to help. Lizzie was run off her feet, taking trays up and down the stairs to Maeve and feeding the unexpected crowd. Only Alan carried on in his normal fashion as he continued moving about the property, doing whatever he did with quiet efficiency. Moira shut herself up in the study for most of the day, reminiscing about her life to Elaine and the eager tape recorder, complaining about the influx of visitors, and trying to alternately coax and bully her sister, Maeve, out of her depression. Ruth brooded with a quiet anger, accentuated by the fact that she was now expected to fetch and carry for Charles, Megan, and Maeve as well as attend to Moira. Elaine and Phoebe continued to plough through the boxes and papers. The girl's dark eyes reflected her own enthusiasm, and Elaine loved educating the eager student in matters of research and biography.

It was a surprise one day when she found herself thinking that she hadn't been so happy for a long time. She'd scarcely thought of her ex-husband, Ian, since Thanksgiving. And now that she was thinking of him, it was to realize that she really didn't care any longer.

By Friday night tension crackled throughout the venerable old cottage. Charles had invited the Josephesons to dinner, throwing Lizzie and Moira into a fit. Lizzie grumbled under her breath about the workload, and Moira seethed over being forced into yet another formal dinner.

Greg arrived bearing a huge bouquet of yellow roses mixed with babies' breath for Moira and a single red rose for Elaine. Both women almost melted under the force of his charm.

He bent over Moira's chair and whispered, "This must be a huge inconvenience for you. You have your work to do. But I thank you for making my parents so welcome."

Moira melted some more.

The only person truly happy about the extended stay of the Madison family was Patty, the woman who came in to help. She was making so much extra money, she confided to Elaine, that she hoped she and her husband would at last be able to afford their longed for dream—a Caribbean cruise, perhaps in the new year.

Alan served drinks in his customary formal manner, and Patty brought in the canapés. Slivers of smoked salmon dotted with capers served on thin slices of toast, prosciutto wrapped around slices of fresh Parmesan, tiny hot pastries. Elaine popped a slice of warm Brie into her mouth and took a sip of Pinot Noir from Oregon and reminded herself once again that this life did have something going for it.

"How are the memoirs coming along, Moira?" Mr. Josepheson asked politely, declining a canapé.

"Extremely well, Desmond. Thank you for asking. Elaine is a dream of a biographer. If you ever hear of anyone looking for a writer I can't recommend her highly enough."

Elaine blushed. But she was hastily brought back to earth.

"Humph," Megan snorted. "Like anyone else would be foolish enough to waste their time and money on such a vain effort."

"Can I get you another drink, Mrs. Stoughton?" Alan asked. He looked rather handsome in a black tuxedo, his freshly washed hair a tumble of black and gray waves.

Megan lifted her glass. "No one's interested in your memoirs, Moira. If I've told you once, I've told you a hundred times...."

"And so you have, dear."

"The long distance forecast is for a mild winter," Charles said, anxious to change the subject before the two elderly sisters came to blows.

It was a semi-formal dinner party. Even Moira had, bullied by Megan, put on a dress and a long string of pearls for the occasion. But Olive Josepheson was attired as for a pre-revolutionary soiree at Versailles. The rich burgundy taffeta dress crackled every time it moved. Which was often considering that the skirt billowed around her legs like a cloud. The bodice was low and tight, revealing yards of wrinkled skin and sagging bosom. She ignored attempts to change the subject. "I've said for a long time that we should tell the story of the Josepheson family. Haven't I always said so, Desmond?" She pulled a slice of smoked salmon off a cracker, deposited the fish on her napkin and demolished the cracker in one gulp.

"I don't think so," Desmond muttered.

"Of course we should. I'm sure that Mrs. Benson would be absolutely delighted to hear all about your adventures in England during the war." She smiled at Elaine. "He was such a hero. Decorated many times over. But he's terribly modest, aren't you, dear? Why don't you come for lunch tomorrow and we can discuss a contract."

"Uh," was all Elaine managed to say.

Megan saved her. "The idea. Waste of time anyway. If I've told Moira once I've told her a thousand times, but will she listen? No, not at all. And it's hardly as if you have anything worthwhile to say. The Josepheson family. Nouveau riche. Ha." She laughed.

The shocking breach of good manners struck Charles and Moira dumb.

"I'm sure Ms. Benson is more than occupied helping Miss Madison, Mother," Greg interjected. He stood beside the fireplace, which was alive with blazing logs and glowing embers, one arm resting on the mantle, a scotch and soda loosely held in the other hand. "But perhaps when she's finished here, she can come over and get a feel for our story."

Olive Josepheson grinned. Elaine nodded stupidly, Megan took a healthy slug of her drink, and the tension broke.

Patty arrived to announce dinner, and everyone departed for the dining room.

As was her custom, Moira excused herself shortly after dessert. Ruth took her upstairs, and the rest of the party returned to the front room. Someone had stoked the fire back to life and lit an arrangement of tea candles that were scattered throughout the room.

"Anyone mind if I smoke?" Desmond Josepheson asked. Not waiting for a reply, he pulled out one of his enormous stogies and touched his silver lighter to the tip. Just as well he didn't wait for permission, no one would have granted it. Alan poured liquors, and the older people settled around a card table. Amber stretched nonchalantly and looked at her watch. She had paid an inordinate amount of attention to the timepiece as the evening progressed. It was still early by her timeframe, one of the advantages of having older relatives and guests.

"It's a beautiful evening, Elaine. I feel like a bit of fresh air, would you care to join me?" Greg stood over her chair, smiling brightly.

"That would be lovely, thank you."

He held out one hand and she took it, allowing him to guide her to her feet. She caught a glimpse of Alan, still serving after dinner drinks; catching her eye, he looked away.

Greg was right: it was a stunning evening. They stood on the deck together, watching the last rays of the sun disappear over the lake, while behind them the stars rose thick and fast in a sky turning the color of an old bruise.

"Beautiful," Elaine murmured.

The soft light of a campfire broke through the trees on the island, and the harsh cry of a loon echoed across the lake. "They always sound so sad, so lonely."

"The loons? They do," Greg said. "They are lonely, but they like it that way. They're not at all hospitable. A nesting pair wants to have a lake all to themselves. I agree with them on that point. But because their numbers are so few, they're particularly susceptible to pollution and human interference."

In the darkness Elaine smiled to herself. Normally so polite and composed, Greg babbled: always a good sign.

"Let's walk a bit," she suggested.

They descended the steps and strolled along the flagstone path. There was a touch of wind, enough to stir the lake waters. Gentle waves lapped against the shoreline.

"Have you ever been to the deserted cabin through there?" Elaine pointed, once they had reached the end of the path.

Greg narrowed his eyes and tried to peer though the trees. It was fully dark now, the stars brilliant overhead. The forest loomed before them, gloomy and foreboding. "No, I don't think I ever have. Is there anything back there? When we were kids we played down here, by the dock and the water, or further up, behind the guesthouse and into the woods. I don't think I ever continued past this path. What is it?" He caught a trace of something in her voice. "Are you okay, Elaine?"

"Yes." She forced herself to sound bright and cheerful. "Let's explore, shall we? The Madison grandchildren love to tell stories of dark happenings and strange noises under these trees." She stepped off the edge of the flagstone path and into the dark embrace of the woods.

Chapter Thirty-four

Moira tossed a pair of dog cookies into the air, one each for Hamlet and Ophelia. The dogs' long nails scratched at the hardwood floor as they scrambled for the treats.

"Thank you, Ruth," she said, settling into the soft downy pillow and pulling up the comforter. "Thank you for everything."

Her words hung, unacknowledged, in the air. Ruth snorted. "It'll be a wonderful to have this place back to ourselves, won't it?"

"It will," Moira sighed. "Then Elaine and I can continue with our work."

That wasn't exactly what Ruth meant. But she busied herself putting pill bottles away and placing a water glass on the night table, within reach. She checked the baby monitor. Everything normal. Switching out the light she pushed Hamlet and Ophelia out the door ahead of her.

"Good night, Miss Madison."

"Good night."

Ruth closed the door firmly.

Moira didn't sleep well any more. She hadn't for a long, long time. Most nights passed at a snail's pace, while she watched the moon rise outside her window, and the bare branches of the trees beat against the glass. But she was always so very tired, that she dared to hope as she excused herself from a dinner party or a gathering in the kitchen, that this one night she would be able to sleep long and deep and serene.

She missed casual dinners around the kitchen table terribly. Hopefully this dreadful business could all be sorted out soon, and Charles and Megan and Maeve and all their hangers-on would depart for the city, leaving Moira and her household at peace.

Moira's bedroom occupied pride of place, overlooking the expanse of lake, the dock and the beautifully crafted boathouse. It had been her parents' room, and before that her grandparents', and now it was hers. Many nights she'd struggled over to the big bay window and settled into the soft cushions to watch the play of light on water and the gentle movement of wind through the trees. She had seen that obnoxious young man, Dave (if not for Rachel and Kyle and little Willow, whom she loved dearly, she would have sent their miserable friend packing long ago), creep into the boathouse. And later, all mysterious as if she were a heroine in a Hitchcock film, that brainless idiot Amber would tip-toe down the steps carrying plastic containers of food, a bottle of good wine, and crystal stemware. Amber wasn't her granddaughter. Moira knew that she really shouldn't interfere, but she'd considered hinting to Maeve that she should keep an eye on the girl.

It wasn't the first time Moira had seen young women slinking around the boathouse at first dark. At least Amber was in the position of power, although Dave might not care to think so. She belonged to the owners' family, a woman with money and a mind of her own, unlike the others Moira had watched, late at night, following no will of their own. She hoped Amber was using good protection and kept her mouth shut. If Charles found out he would feel obliged to attempt to do something about it. Although the girl wasn't his granddaughter, either.

The wind was high tonight. She could hear branches striking the bedroom window, the lapping of waves against the dock, and the soft rustle of the few leaves that still clung desperately to the trees. She drifted off, remembering as if it were yesterday the dear young airman with whom she had spent one heavenly week in the hell of wartime London. Sometimes she struggled to remember his face. For that week, and the months before, he had been the center of her universe. He had been exceedingly fair, his blond hair more white than yellow, blue eyes the palest she had ever seen. He was tall, and heavily built to match, yet he moved with a gentleness that hinted at the fairy ancestor who had given him his coloring. Shot over France, he had forced his smoking plane back over the English Channel, rather than risk crashing it into a French village or farmer's cottage. Spiraling out of control, the fragile craft hit the water and dissolved into flotsam and jetsam. There were no survivors.

For weeks Moira alternately raged and sorrowed when she didn't hear from him, terrified that he had abandoned her, sated with his conquest. Her mother's bitter words mocked her at every turn. "Why buy the cow when you can have the milk for free?"

When they first cleaned out his possessions, they'd missed an unposted letter, addressed to Nursing Sister Moira Madison, Bramshott. His mother found it, the first time she'd had the strength to go through his few things, and sent it to Moira, unopened, with a note of explanation. The letter was short, a few lines of script in an awkward hand, written by a man in a hurry. He told her how much he loved her, he asked her to marry him, and he vowed that in his next leave, if she were willing, they would be married in the chapel near her hospital and his mother's home. Time to go: they were knocking at his door. An easy flight, nothing at all. He would mail the letter when he got back. I love you, he scribbled.

She had read the letter, wept, and gone on duty.

The soft sound of a door opening, a dark shape moving against the background light of the hall before it was extinguished. "Grant, is that you?" Moira sighed, not awake, not asleep.

The shape moved to her bedside. It clutched a pillow to its chest.

"You silly, silly boy," Moira giggled. "This is a good hotel, they provide the pillows. We don't have to bring our own." She had bought a precious bottle of perfume, along with the silk and lace negligee, in an attempt to make herself desirable. The smell drifted through the room. She stroked her chest lightly, feeling her breasts tingle under her fingers, strong and firm. She lifted her arms, ignoring the high-pitched drone of the Spitfires as they headed out towards the Channel.

The pillow fell across her face.

Chapter Thirty-five

"It's cold back here," Greg said. "Must have dropped ten degrees in the last two minutes."

His voice was as insignificant as a fly buzzing around Elaine's head. She pushed dead brush to one side and stepped further into the circle of trees.

"Dark, too. The stars have gone out all of a sudden. We should turn back, Elaine. At least to get a flashlight. I can't see my hand in front of my face."

A chill wind curled around the foot of the boarded-up cabin, lifting decaying leaves off the forest floor and tossing them in the cold air to rise above the ground in a dance gone mad. Old planks and aging shutters groaned as they shifted under the force of the wind. The scent of cheap toilet water was all around her, filling her nostrils, soaking her clothes.

Elaine swallowed repeatedly, trying not to gag.

The air and the dancing leaves swirled, struggling to form substance out of nothing, to pull light out of black darkness.

"Shit," Greg swore furiously as a dead branch struck him full in the chest. Rotten wood cracked, breaking against his weight.

Elaine stopped and stood still, rooted to the ground as thoroughly as one of the old white pines, transfixed by the sight before her. The darkness shifted form and consistency under the force of the cold wind, but slowly it assumed a shape, transparent and illusive but still a force present and visible. It didn't utter a sound and made no further attempt to move, except to undulate rhythmically where it had stopped. Elaine stood and faced it. In the far recesses of her mind she was aware of Greg all around her, banging into stumps and tripping over logs, swearing a blue streak and calling out her name, in tones of rising, but still contained panic. Like one would hear the inconsequential noise of a TV in the other room, while preparing dinner or washing up the dishes. Her eyes fixed on the shape moving before her. It was there, but yet not. She could look right through it, see the outline of the dark cabin and the row of trees behind it. A mouse dashed across the forest floor, straight through the bottom of the shape to disappear into a minuscule crack under the cabin steps.

Elaine watched, saying nothing, not moving, as ethereal fingers reached into her mind. She was not afraid, but a black cloud settled over her heart. She was not afraid, but suddenly she knew that she had to move.

Moira!

She whirled around. Knowing now that she had nothing to fear, she turned her back on it, whatever it might be. "Moira. Something's wrong." She thought she called to Greg, but couldn't be sure if the words were actually passing her caked, dry lips, or echoing around and around inside her head.

"Elaine, stop! I can't see a blasted thing. You're going to fall. Wait for me."

They crashed through the trees, breaking out onto the remains of the wildflower bed that curved along the waterfront. The bare, broken stems and crushed leaves, dying in the cold of autumn nights, were gone, replaced by a riot of color, movement, light, and scent. A Monarch butterfly settled softly on one perfect purple petal. Girlish giggles broke out from the dock, and a motorboat roared as it went past. The boys piloting it were dressed in white flannels. They waved enthusiastically. A maid, managing to look beautiful in a severe black dress that must be almost unbearable in the heat, cap and apron starched until they could stand up on their own, passed in front of Elaine. She carried a silver tray, polished until it reflected sunlight, bearing a glass pitcher filled to the brim with lemonade and dancing ice cubes. There were also neatly cut sandwiches and slices of pale sponge cake. Elaine jogged in place. It was so hot. The lemonade looked so refreshing. The cubes of clear ice melted as she watched. One glass and she would continue on her way.

"Not for you, not for you," the maid hissed. Her tongue darted out of a generous red mouth. It was pink and forked, like a snake. "Not for the help. Not for the likes of you. Don't you have something better to do?" Her voice was soft, tinged with the faintest touch of distant Ireland. A second-hand accent perhaps, learned from a mother or father with a thick brogue.

Don't want lemonade anyway. Sweet and watery. Hideous stuff. Ug.

Moira. Moira.

Elaine snapped back to the present. The maid was gone, the young men in flannels, the sunlight and the butterfly. All gone.

Only the urgent whispering in her mind remained.

Moira. Moira.

She ran blindly, heedless of the ornamental rocks, empty flowerpots, and autumn debris. Greg followed, but she didn't know if she ran from him or if she led him. While they were in the copse a bright moon had risen and illuminated the path in front of them as if Alan had turned on floodlights.

She took the stairs to the deck three at a time and crashed into the door as it failed to open. Locked. She pounded on the door with her fists, screaming for someone to let her in. The dogs had been put outside. Their ferocious senses caught the strong waves of her terror, and they pounded up the stairs to join her.

Elaine fell into the hallway as Alan jerked the door open. Over his shoulder she could see a blur of startled white faces. She pushed him out of the way and ran up the steps.

"Hurry, lass." It was as if Augustus himself whispered to her as she fled up the staircase, Hamlet and Ophelia hard on her heels.

The door to Moira's bedroom, always firmly shut to keep the wandering dogs out, stood wide open. Moonlight flooded the room through the floor-to-ceiling windows and sheer curtains. The shape in the middle of the huge bed was so thin and tiny that for a moment Elaine thought there was nothing there. Maybe this was only the traditional movie trick—pillows piled up to represent the sleeping form as the hero (or villain) crept out of bed under cover of the night. She couldn't see Moira, could see naught but bedclothes. Then the duvet twitched. A low moan as Elaine crossed the room in a rush and pulled the pillow from Moira's face. The old woman looked up at her, brown eyes blinking with confusion. She gasped for air. Elaine helped her to a sitting position.

"What on Earth is going on in here?" Alan was the first into the room. The family followed, speaking at once. It was a large room, but it filled up very quickly. Greg pushed his way through. The right knee was torn out of his trousers, an ugly scratch was beginning to rise immediately above his left eyebrow, and he'd managed to lose one shoe. He looked at Elaine, then at Moira, and sank wordlessly into a chair.

Once Moira had taken in enough air, she settled back against Elaine's arms with a sigh. Ruth burst into the room, clad in her nightclothes. She pushed Elaine aside and tenderly persuaded Moira to collapse back against the pillows.

"A dream, a terrible dream," Moira moaned. Her face was as white as death, the bones beneath the pale skin as sharp as those of a skeleton.

"There, there," Ruth murmured. "Everything's all right. No need to fuss."

"Much ado about nothing," Megan huffed. "The household all in an uproar over a bad dream." Her words were harsh, but her face was almost as pale as her sister's, and she twisted her hands together, over and over.

"Too much wine again, eh, Moira?" Charles interjected a note of false joviality. "Better we all get off and let you get back to sleep. Come along everyone, let Moira have her rest." He herded the family and visitors out of the room. Greg took his mother's arm. Soon only Moira, Megan, Ruth, and Elaine remained.

Lizzie arrived bearing a silver tray with one bone china cup and a practical sturdy brown teapot.

"Terrible dream." Moira's hand shook as she touched the cup that Ruth, one arm supporting her back, held carefully under her chin.

"I'll see to Miss Madison," Ruth said. She fixed them all with an iron stare. "Thank you for your concern." She picked a pillow up off the floor and tucked it under Moira's gray head.

They tiptoed out of the room, Lizzie bringing the tea tray.

An old deacon's bench faced the bottom of the main staircase. Years of damp swimming towels and sodden bathing-suited bottoms, of dogs' excited claws and recklessly tossed skates had marked the dark wood unmercifully. Greg sat there, waiting for Elaine. The cut on his forehead leaked bright red blood: he'd not bothered to attend to it.

She sat down heavily beside him.

"What was all that about?"

"Guess I got a fright," she said, forcing a laugh. "It's spooky in those woods."

"Damn dangerous, if you ask me."

"Did you, uh, see anything—unusual—out there?" She found an unused tissue in her pocket and handed it to him, pointing at the cut over his eye.

"See what?" He dabbed at the cut. "There's nothing to see. It's so damned dark out there, I couldn't see my hand in front of my face, much less anything else."

His voice rose in anger. "What were you playing at anyway, Elaine? I called you, why didn't you answer? And why the frantic rush back to the cottage? I thought you'd lost your mind. Going to tell everyone I attacked you, or some stupid thing."

She rubbed her eyes deeply—God, they hurt—and rose to her feet. It was such an effort. She couldn't remember when she had ever been so tired. "Hardly. But thanks for your concern, anyway."

"Elaine, wait. That didn't sound so good. I'm sorry." He reached out one hand to stop her, but she slipped aside.

"Gregory, there you are. We're ready to go." Desmond and Olive Josepheson had their coats and hats on.

"Coming," Greg said, not looking at Elaine.

She watched them leave. Megan went upstairs to bed, Charles returned to the drawing room. Only then did Elaine give in to her exhaustion and drag her aching body up the stairs, her hands gripping the banister to pull her weight up.

Alan came out of the drawing room. He carried a tray heavy with dirty ashtrays, used glasses, and an empty brandy bottle. His face creased into lines of worry as he watched every tired step.

Chapter Thirty-six

"Do you ever go out to the old boarded up cabin in the woods?" Elaine asked Lizzie, trying to keep her voice light and casual as she sipped her coffee.

"What cabin?"

"Through the woods, past the end of the trail, behind the boathouses?"

"Nope. Never been off the path. The day she hired me, Moira said that it wasn't safe out there, and even if she hadn't, I'm not one for wandering around in the woods." Lizzie's attention returned to her work and she poured thick, creamy batter into muffin tins.

A quick knock and the kitchen door swung open. Without invitation Rachel, Kyle, and Willow burst in. Kyle carried a plastic bucket full of water and they were all grinning broadly.

"We got fish." Willow was almost bursting with excitement. "Lots and lots of fish. So we brought some for you, Lizzie. And for Moira, too."

"How nice."

"Kyle and I caught so many fish this morning," Rachel said, as Lizzie peered into the bucket. "More than we could eat and we didn't want them to go to waste."

"So we thought that Moira'd like them for her breakfast," Willow said.

"What a nice thought," Lizzie said. "I'm sure she will. If you prepare them for me, Kyle, I'll cook them up right now."

"There's enough for you and Moira," Rachel said, pouring a cup of coffee. "And some for Elaine too, of course." She held the cup up to Kyle. He nodded; she passed it over, and poured another.

Kyle knew his way around a kitchen. He collected a cutting board and a sharp knife and carried everything out of Lizzie's way. Willow followed eagerly, one stubby finger rubbing the sticky insides of the muffin bowl, which the cook had handed her.

Rachel settled herself at the table. "Fish for breakfast, Elaine?"

"Not for me, thank you."

"Your loss," Kyle chucked.

"You seem disturbed this morning," Rachel said. "May I ask why?"

"Nothing." Elaine tried to force a grin.

"The forest was unstable last night. Something was seriously wrong. You can tell me about it, if you want to."

Elaine looked up from the depths of her coffee mug for the first time. Rachel's beautiful green eyes were watching her, oceans of calm and understanding.

Another rattle of the wooden door, and Alan came in. For once Hamlet and Ophelia were not at his heels. His cheeks were flushed from the morning chill, the curls damp with dew. "Morning all. Nice fish you got there, young Willow. Catch them all by yourself did you?" he said to appreciative giggles.

"Elaine was upset about some nonsense to do with an old cabin in the woods," Lizzie said, adding a smidgen of oil to a cast iron frying pan and placing it onto the stove. "It's all supposedly terribly mysterious. No one goes there, under pain of death; the children like to pretend that it's haunted. I rather think someone was telling Elaine wild stories in the night. And I can guess who." She winked at Rachel. "An after dinner stroll in the evening woods with a certain attractive neighbor."

"What are you talking about?" The smile disappeared from Alan's face.

"Elaine was out walking with a certain someone and came running in all flushed and breathing heavily," Lizzie giggled. The oil in the pan spat and hissed.

"Christ, have you got nothing better to do than gossip all day?" Alan headed back out the door. "Well, I do. I'll be back when breakfast is ready."

A bewildered Lizzie looked at the door, shuddering in its old frame where it had slammed shut.

"Why's Alan mad?" Willow asked.

"Because men are strange, that's why. Is that fish ready yet, Kyle? The pan is. As soon as the muffins are out of the oven, I'll be taking Moira her breakfast."

Rachel and Elaine sat in their own world, paying no attention to the hubbub around them. So preoccupied was Elaine that she had scarcely even noticed Alan leaving.

She forced a laugh. "I saw a deer, or a bear or something and it scared me. I guess I'm not quite the toughie I pretend to be, eh?"

"Don't disparage yourself, Elaine. Many people think that they have to do that. Whenever anything meaningful, spiritual, beyond their understanding happens to them, they are compelled to demean the experience, and themselves along with it. I hate that." Rachel's soft voice had fallen to a near whisper. She leaned across the table. The hot fat hissed as the filleted fish hit the pan. "If you want to tell me what happened, I want to listen."

"Nothing happened," Elaine said, her voice equally low and intense. "I had a fright, some silly premonition. I thought Moira was in danger. She wasn't."

The green eyes opened wide. "Moira was involved? What happened?"

"Nothing, I told you. I made a fool of myself in front of the family and I wish you'd drop it."

"But something did happen in the woods last night. I could feel it. I was reading to Willow, around the fire, before she went to bed. Then we walked down to the lake. To say goodnight to the stars. She likes to look out at the stars last thing before bed and you can see them best from the beach. And over here, by the cottage, the forest was alive with emotions."

"Emotions aren't living beings, Rachel." Elaine laughed. "I guess I'm not the only one imagining things."

"The woods behind the boathouse have an aura. I saw it the day we arrived. I didn't want to stay, tried to talk the others into leaving. But they didn't understand. Moira was so kind to us, the island so perfect, I couldn't convince them to leave. And maybe I was wrong, because I've felt no anger, or intended harm, from those woods. Only a calm benevolence. Until you came." She reached out and grabbed Elaine's hand in one of her own.

Rachel's hand was tiny but her grip so strong. Elaine wanted to pull away. Wanted to, but couldn't. "Then it changed," Rachel continued. "Talk to me, Elaine. Something is moving out there, I know it is. And you know it too."

"Shit. Oh, that hurts." Lizzie leapt back from the frying pan and ran to the sink. She held her hand under the tap and ran cold water over it. "Hot fat. What a bugger. Grab that pan, Kyle and pull it off the heat. Not you, Willow! Stay away."

The spell broken, Elaine rushed to Lizzie's side, guiltily grateful for the accident.

"Are you okay?"

"A splash of oil. Occupational hazard." Lizzie shrugged, inspecting the damage. The skin on her hands looked clear excepting one small spot, less than the size of a dime, already turning red.

"You should put something on that."

"Later." The cook turned off the water and dried her hands on a tea towel. "Breakfast first. I'm going to take Moira her meal now. Willow, why don't you come with me? She loves to see you. You can put an extra muffin on that plate, in case Moira offers you one."

The girl rushed to obey.

"No breakfast for me, thanks, Lizzie," said Elaine. "I'd better get back to work. Phoebe's no doubt already head first into the boxes."

Rachel's deep green eyes followed her as she fled.

Phoebe, of course, was nowhere to be seen. She was keen but she was also young and indulged and her day didn't start this early. Elaine gathered up the pile of letters she'd left yesterday and flicked through them. Her eyes moved rapidly but her mind registered not a word. She'd slept badly the night before, hardly at all. Tormented by thoughts of how totally she had disgraced herself. Running full tilt out of the woods and away from the extremely pleasant company of an eligible man (handsome, rich, so kind to his dotty mother, and an Internet guru to boot) only to wake up the family matriarch, who needed what bit of sleep she could still snatch out of the long night.

She'd risen early and gone for an intense run. It was always so much easier to make decisions when she was running. What's done is done, she decided, sweat streaming from her brow and down the back of her neck. She would put the hideous night behind and not think of it again (at least not too much).

And she would stay out of the woods, above all else.

Then along comes Rachel with the green eyes, the fabulous lashes, the earth-mother persona, and her new-age senses.

Elaine tossed the unread letter aside with a groan and struggled to her feet. Moira's study was next door to the library. Elaine rapped at the closed door and pushed it open without waiting to be admitted.

Moira was alone and reading, her glasses pushed up high on her nose. Breakfast dishes were cleared away, only a single coffee cup left behind.

"Elaine, welcome." Moira lowered her book and beamed at the sight of her. "I have enjoyed the most wonderful breakfast. Fresh fish caught straight out of the lake this morning. Perfectly delightful. I thought you were going to go through Mother's papers this morning. Have you changed your mind?"

"In a way. Moira, what do you know about the boarded-up cabin in the woods? Behind the boathouse. It used to be servants' accommodation, I understand."

Moira peered over the rim of her glasses. "Why do you ask, dear?"

Elaine set herself in a chair, recently upholstered in soft damask with light shades of alternating gray. She caressed the beautiful fabric, hoping to gather strength. "I was told when I first arrived here that no one ever talked about it. So I decided not to talk about it either. There is more than enough in this fabulous home and the beauty of its surroundings to occupy my spare time."

"Obviously something changed your mind."

"Something did." She stopped stroking the fabric and leapt to her feet. "For heaven's sake, Moira. Everyone talks about mysterious goings-on in the woods, children are frightened, visitors see strange auras, but no one will address the matter."

"All true, my dear. There are some things best not spoken of." The old woman smiled, a huge, genuine smile full of warmth and affection and stained teeth. "When you get to be my age, should you be so lucky, you will no doubt agree."

Elaine walked to the big bay window and pushed the curtains aside. She could see Amber returning to the boathouse, dressed only in a pair of cut-off denims and a T-shirt, carefully carrying a tray with two cups of coffee, two glasses of orange juice, and two plates of muffins and fruit. A bit excessive for one thin young woman.

"I'm well aware that Amber is sleeping with the unpleasant Dave, if you're thinking of telling me something shocking," Moira said.

Elaine looked at her. "Do you think I would try?"

"No."

"Alan thinks that Dave has charmed you into ignoring his faults. Apparently not."

Moira shrugged. "For Rachel and Willow and the others, I keep my opinions of Dave to myself."

"You're changing the subject, Moira. You're very good at that."

"But not good enough, it would seem."

"This goes beyond your memoirs, Moira. If you don't want to talk about certain things, that's fine. I won't try to force it out of you. But I'm wondering if you always sleep with a pillow over your face?"

When Elaine had first walked into the study, Moira had a flush of red in her creased cheeks and lips, enough to break the dreadful pallor of the night before. At Elaine's words, every hint of color fled, leaving the old face pale, shrunken in upon itself.

"What are you saying?"

"Figure it out, Moira. You're bright. I suspect that you're a great deal smarter than I am."

"I had a dream, a dream of my past. Something both wonderful and dreadful all mixed up in one, as it was in life. I'll probably tell you about it one day, if I am ever strong enough. As to how the pillow came to be over my face, I don't know. But thank you for removing it." Moira picked up her book and flicked to the page saved with an old-fashioned, elaborately embroidered bookmark. She was reading P.D. James.

Elaine sighed. Nothing more to be gained here. "I'll come back after lunch. Perhaps we can pick up where we left off."

"Sit down, dear." Once a decision was reached, the old voice was strong and firm. "I know a story, a very sad story, and one that is, unfortunately, probably not at all unique. But it is not my story to tell. Sadly, there is no one left alive to whom the tale belongs. Megan and Maeve were here, of course, fluttering around like the mindless butterflies they so resembled. But in those days little penetrated their veil of self-absorption." She snorted. "Of course, now that I come to think of it, little penetrates their veil of self-absorption these days either. Although Maeve is no longer entirely at fault. Poor dear."

She settled back into her chair and closed her eyes. "I will not betray a confidence told to me by someone in his darkest hour. Of the person who, if the story is true, I would not hesitate to expose to the world, I know only hearsay. I cannot present hearsay as fact. Merely to tell it would be to give it validity."

She focused her sharp brown eyes on Elaine. "Do you recall what Hamlet said to Horatio?"

"Hamlet said a great many things to Horatio."

"That he did. But most memorably: 'I knew him, Horatio.' And then: 'There are stranger things in heaven and earth than are dreamt of in your philosophy.' So let us leave stranger things to greater minds than ours, Elaine. I'm tired. Can you call Ruth, please?"

"Of course."

◇◇◇

Elaine found Ruth in the kitchen, cradling a cup of tea and staring off into space, lost in memories. "Any more tea in that pot?"

"Make your own."

"Well, pardon me! I just asked."

"I just told you."

"Is anything wrong?"

Ruth turned on her, her face twisting out of shape. "Is anything wrong? You interfering fool. Rather you should ask, is anything right?"

Elaine recoiled, feeling as if she had been struck. "I'm only looking for a cup of tea. I don't mean you any harm, Ruth."

"Oh, I'm so sure you don't. Miss Biographer. Precious Miss Historian. Leave me alone."

Elaine considered turning on her heels and leaving the bitter woman to stew in her hostility. Instead she asked, "Can we talk, Ruth? I don't know why you…dislike me so much."

Ruth's eyes narrowed into dark slits. "You dance in here with your PhD and your old books. I tried to read them. Too boring to finish. They're rubbish. But you know that, don't you? If anyone wanted to read anything you wrote, you wouldn't be here, would you?"

The barb was a wild shot, but it hit home with vicious accuracy. Elaine collapsed into a chair. Ruth was right: Elaine was a failure. A washed up biographer with her best work so far behind her it was disappearing over the horizon. An abandoned wife, discarded for the younger woman with good contacts and a cuter butt. "I'm only here to help Moira."

"Fuck you." By the look of surprise on Ruth's angry, pinched face she'd probably never said those words out loud before. "My mother worked here all of her life. She was trusted—loved—by the family. And when she retired, I took her place, the place saved for me. I won't give it up to you."

"I don't want to take your place," Elaine said. "I'm helping with the biography, that's all."

"No, that's not all," Ruth yelled. She slammed her hand down on the wooden table. She was still holding the mug of tea. The mug shattered and tea splashed onto the table and floor, and shards of pottery sliced into Ruth's hand.

"Oh." She watched as a thin stream of bright red blood flowed out of her clenched palm and ran down her wrist. "Oh, dear." All of the rage drained out of Ruth along with the blood. Her shoulders slumped and her face crinkled as the tears began to flow.

"Let me get a bandage. Is there a first aid kit anywhere?"

"Just a tea towel will do. Please. How silly of me. Lizzie will be furious."

"I'm sure she won't even notice it's missing."

"Mrs. Bridges would have noticed."

"Who's Mrs. Bridges?" Elaine pulled a tea towel from the drying rack and ran it under the tap.

"The old cook. She served the family for a long time. She was here when my mother was first hired as a maid. My mother began working for the family when she was a teenager, as a scullery maid, and she rose all the way to housekeeper. And family friend."

"I'd like to learn more about Mrs. Bridges," Elaine said as she applied a light touch of pressure to the wound. "And much, much more about your mother. Will you talk to me about your mother one day? Moira, Miss Madison, has mentioned her many times. She cared for your mother a great deal."

A rush of warm blood flooded Ruth's face and chest. She looked at her hand. Elaine had wrapped it well. "Has she? Talked about my mother? Really?"

"Oh, yes. Why don't you tell me where I can find a bandage? You can't walk around with that towel around your hand. Moira sent me to ask for you."

"Why didn't you say so?" Ruth threw off the towel and ran to the sink. She held her hand directly under the cold-water tap.

Because you were too busy calling me a washed up hack, Elaine thought.

"I'm sorry, if I was…rude." Ruth almost choked on the words. The water ran clear into the drain.

"Once Moira has told her story, and I've read the letters, then it'll be time for me to be on my way. I'll write it all up, but I probably won't be back. I'll miss this place."

"I missed it, all the years I was away."

Ruth fled.

◇◇◇

Elaine dressed for dinner, forcing herself to forget about Moira's mysterious words, the confrontation with Ruth, and concentrate on choosing something decent to wear. A loud knock as knuckles hit the door. She pulled it open, just a crack.

Alan stood there, his rough face like a thundercloud, incongruously peeking out from behind a bouquet of luxuriant yellow roses: tiny, perfect buds hesitating on the verge of bursting open. Elaine's heart leapt at the sight. For a brief moment she lost track of the place and the season and delighted in Alan's gardening skills and his consideration.

"For me," she breathed, pulling the door open wide. "How absolutely beautiful. Come in, please."

"Imported nonsense," Alan growled as he thrust the bouquet into her startled arms. "These came for you. Thought I should bring them up. They won't last long."

And he was gone.

She pulled out the white card attached. "We got off to a rough start last night," it said. "Let me make it up to you. Soon. Greg."

Elaine sighed and slammed the door shut with a flick of her hip. Her delight in the gift faded somewhat once she realized they were not from Alan. Alan was certainly pleasant enough, but he was one cold fish. She pushed the thought aside and decided she would be better spending her time enjoying Greg's kindness than worrying about the possibility of Alan thawing out some day.

There was no need to search for a vase and water. The flowers came in an expensive cut-glass bowl. Thoughtful of the sender to realize that she wasn't living in her own home and wouldn't have such things readily to hand.

The gift was exquisite, but it only managed to distract her for a brief moment. Moira's soupçon of musings and dark hints were more disturbing than a straightforward telling of the story would have been. Elaine had never believed in the supernatural, and she refused to believe in it now. Stuff and nonsense, her mother would have snorted. Moira had kept the story (whatever it was) to herself all these years, and behind it lay the truth about what she believed regarding the deserted cabin in the woods. No doubt the story had built and built upon itself in her mind as time passed, and the aura of the abandoned servants' cabin even more so. That would explain why the Madison children found the place so fascinating. What children wouldn't?

Thoughts may not be voiced, but children pick up nuances extremely well. Great-Aunt Moira thought the place to be haunted. Ergo, it was haunted. And Moira had a strong enough personality to insist that her family leave the place alone, to allow it to fall into ruin and decay. Thus adding to the legend.

As for Elaine herself? The competent, independent, modern, city-dwelling woman of the new millennium? Even she could be influenced by mysterious hints, brought to believe that she saw something which was, in fact, not there. Wildflowers in October? Maids in starched aprons? Stuff and nonsense.

And she, Elaine, who prided herself on being a practical modern woman, PhD in history, biographer, collector of the facts: it was embarrassing to find that her subconscious could be so influenced by an old woman's suggestions. No doubt the same thing had happened to Rachel. The only difference being that the red-haired new age hippie would have been more than happy to listen to Moira's fantasies and then interpret them as the responses of her own senses.

She sniffed at the beautiful flowers. No scent. She started to think of Greg and found her mind shifting to Moira instead. In all her contemplations about the power of suggestion and the nature of long remembered stories, Elaine had pushed (perhaps purposely) to the back of her mind the few facts that were incontrovertible.

She did arrive at the top of the staircase to find Moira's bedroom door standing wide open. Unthinkable that with a houseful of guests, roaming dogs, and a party underway downstairs it would be left that way. And Moira did have a pillow over her face. No one slept like that.

Elaine walked to the window and looked out.

Someone had been in Moira's room.

No problem with that—it was a busy household, a connected family, an elderly woman requiring care. But whoever had opened the door had left in one heck of a hurry, without bothering to wake the occupant of the room. And leaving a pillow as a calling card?

Days ago, Elaine had decided to treat the fire as an accident—caused by someone's carelessness. And to assume that that someone was afraid to step forward and take responsibility. Her money was on Dave and Amber, how like those two to be sneaking around the unoccupied guesthouse at night. Maybe carrying a candle—that was sure to be Amber's idea of romantic.

She pulled the two separate thoughts together in her mind—the fire and the pillow over Moira's face—and they coalesced into a frightening whole. To the mix she tossed in the death of Donna Smithton. Yet Elaine had not the slightest idea of what to do with her suppositions.

For a moment, she considered confiding her fears to the old woman. But Moira was having trouble enough coping with the influx of visitors who didn't appear to be ready to leave anytime soon. Best not to worry her further.

Elaine decided to keep a watch on Moira.

Chapter Thirty-seven

Moira had not gone with the army to France, although she desperately wanted to. Jean and Susan left, overflowing with tearful goodbyes and promises to stay in contact. Moira remained behind in England, tending to the streams of critically wounded men sent back from the battles in France, Belgium, and Holland. She had been in Europe for five years, and could scarcely remember her mother's face, her grandmother's gentle smile, the colors of the sugar maple trees surrounding their house in autumn or the shade of blue that Lake Muskoka would turn under the brilliant summer sun. The only colors in Moira's world were the sharp new red of blood in the theatre and on the wards, the duller, angrier red of wounds failing to heal, the black of burned flesh, the endless sea of soldiers' stained khaki, and nurses' starched, blood-soaked white.

Rose wrote to Moira regularly, as she had ever since the magical weekend in London with Ralph. Apparently Rose had continued to see Charlie Stoughton long after. Her letters were full of her expectation of a fairy-tale marriage and then being whisked off to the imagined luxuries of Canada. Moira wrote back, when she had the chance, her letters whispering caution.

How could she say that just because Ralph Madison had money, his friend might not? How could she tell an English factory girl with stars in her eyes that there were poor people in Canada too? Lots of them. And drought-plagued farms and an expanse of bug-infested wilderness. Endless beyond the imaginings of a girl brought up amongst the neat hedgerows and tidy villages of rural England.

Spring of 1945. Moira was ordered to take leave. She had lost all interest in parties or vacations or in seeing the sights, but Matron realized the girl was getting far too thin, and working far too hard. She called Moira into her office and simply ordered her to go on leave.

There was nowhere she wanted to go. Her grandmother's sister, Moira's Great Aunt Florence, had died the year Moira arrived in England, before she had the chance to pay a visit. And Florence had left no descendants. But as fortune would have it, the day Moira was ordered to take leave a letter arrived from Rose, ending, as her letters always did, with an invitation for Moira to visit her in London.

Before she had time to think it through, Moira wrote back to accept.

Once again, she took the train up to London. It was no longer so crowded and the platform at Waterloo station was largely empty. The focus of the war had moved to Europe.

Rose waited for her at the appointed place, her face lit up by a brilliant smile. She had lost her pudginess in the intervening years, gained a good deal of confidence, and was looking quite pretty. Her dress was new and fashionable, a cheerful yellow with a white belt. A small girl of about two years of age held Rose's hand tightly.

They hugged and kissed and exclaimed over each other's appearance. Then Moira crouched down to greet the girl. "Hello there," she said. "I'm Miss Madison. Who might you be?"

The wide-eyed girl stuck her thumb into her mouth and sucked with enthusiasm.

"This is Pamela. My daughter," Rose said.

"Pleased to meet you, Pamela." Moira thought she took the shock well. She rose to her feet. "You didn't say anything in your letters."

"No."

"She's beautiful."

"Yes, she is. Charlie Stoughton is her father."

"Oh, Rose. No."

Rose pulled herself to her full height and jerked her daughter's arm. "We're going to be married. Once he gets back from France."

Moira struggled to recover. "When did you see him last?"

"Early 1943," Rose admitted. Two years ago. "Then he was sent to Italy and after that to France. But we write, all the time."

You write, Moira thought, her heart heavy.

"He won the George Cross, did you know?" Rose said, her eyes shining with pride. "Oh, I wish this horrid war would end."

"Does Charlie, uh, know about Pamela?"

"Of course he knows. What a thing to say. We'll be married, Moira, as soon as he has leave."

"Of course. Not much longer, they say. Germany has to give in soon." Moira counted in her head. September 1944 when Ralph died. Charlie was a hero. The campaign in Italy was winding to a close. He had leave then. Charlie came to Moira to say goodbye. They cried together, remembering Ralph, and Charlie promised to visit when the war finally was over and they were back in Canada. She could tell that something was bothering him. But for once she allowed herself to indulge her own feelings, sunk into her grief, and ignored the signals Charlie was sending.

Moira burst into tears. "Oh, Rose. Will it ever end?"

The child looked up at this weeping stranger. She reached out a tiny hand and patted Moira's thigh. "'right. 'right," she said. Moira wept all the harder.

Rose gathered up Moira's suitcase and led her out of the station. One hand clinging to her daughter's, the other holding Moira's bag, and still she managed to comfort and guide her friend.

They only had three days, but made the most of it. Rose and Moira took Pamela to the park, or to feed the swans on the pond. Rose explained that she still had her job in the munitions factory and Pamela was in a day-care center the factory operated, so she wanted to spend all her free time with her daughter. Moira had never thought of herself as a mother, a woman with children. Her time with Grant had been so short. But she loved Pamela instantly, and a tiny part of her wondered...what if?

It was a lovely leave. Moira pushed her worries about Charlie Stoughton to the back of her mind and concentrated on treating Rose and Pamela. They went to the pictures and played in the park. Moira insisted on buying Pamela some new clothes and even a few toys from the almost empty shops. The last day of her leave, Moira surprised Rose and Pamela with tea at the Savoy.

The girl sat up in her chair, so straight and proud in her new frock, white socks, and brown shoes. Curly black hair burst out of the new blue ribbons and Moira was happy, for the first time in a very long time.

Arm in arm the three of them walked back to Rose's flat. Moira only had time to pick up her suitcase before she had to set off to catch her train back to the hospital. She kissed Rose and swung Pamela in a high arc. "If Charlie...I mean, if something...anything...should happen to Charlie...I'll help you. Always."

Rose laughed. "You are a dear, but it's time to be on your way." She shooed Moira out the door.

Moira walked down the street. A house at the corner was bombed out, now just a pile of rubble with only one wall remaining. Children clambered happily through the wreckage and made their own playground. Children could always be counted on to make the best of any situation. Charlie Stoughton wouldn't be back. She knew that with as much certainty as she knew that the sun would rise tomorrow in the east (although being in England, no one might actually see it). He was a fortune hunter, that one. A factory girl like sweet Rose had nothing he wanted. Well, something maybe, but that was not enough.

Deep in thought, Moira watched the pavement pass under her feet. She reached the corner and lifted her head to check she was going in the right direction.

People all around her were breaking into a run.

An explosion, and the growl and groan of buildings collapsing.

Before her disbelieving eyes, the block of flats where Moira had spent three delightful days crumbled into dust. Alarms sounded and people ran. She dropped her suitcase and ran also. The flats, homes where families lived and children played, were no longer. As if a spoiled giant child had tired of his toys and trampled them underfoot in a burst of evil temper. A rocket: the new weapon a vengeful Hitler was unleashing on the people of England as his vision of Empire collapsed all around him.

The street came alive with activity in an instant. Moira fell to her knees and scratched her way through timber and rubble. Around her men and women in wardens' uniforms joined her, beating out fire, clambering across the rubble, heaving aside bricks and blocks of concrete, searching for survivors.

With a shout, they pulled out an old woman, her gray hair streaked with even grayer dust. "My husband," she gasped, and the searchers dug deeper.

By nightfall, Moira's hands were a bloody wreck: she had scarcely a nail left on her fingers. She had inhaled so much dust that she was reminded of the Algerian desert when the hot winds blew.

Lights were brought to illuminate the destruction and the searchers carried on. Moira's probing hands found a beautiful silver teapot, shining brightly in the light of the emergency lanterns, and numerous remnants of shattered china ornaments, rough kitchenware, children's toys and scraps of cheap cloth.

They pulled Pamela out around midnight. Her hair was still shiny, the black curls jaunty around their blue ribbons. Her face was pale and untouched, a bit dusty, her legs scratched and bleeding. Moira scrambled through the dust and over the rubble, arriving as Pamela opened her mouth and let out a lusty scream. Moira fell to her knees. She poked and prodded Pamela as the girl screamed all the louder. Miraculously, she didn't seem to have come to any harm.

Moira wrapped the child in her arms and buried her face into her chest as the searchers brought up Rose's lifeless body.

Refusing any help from the ambulance crew, Moira carried Pamela away from the remains of her home and her mother.

She collected her suitcase from the gutter, hailed a taxi, took a room at the Savoy, and settled a shocked Pamela into bed. The next morning, after making arrangements for Rose's body, she set about locating Rose's parents. Fortunately Rose came from a farming village so it wasn't difficult to find them.

Two days later, Moira and Pamela took the train to meet Pamela's grandparents. As Moira extracted herself from Pamela's frightened grip and tucked the little hand into her weeping grandmother's, she remembered that she hadn't contacted the hospital to tell them she would be delayed.

She hoped that Matron would understand.

Chapter Thirty-eight

Moira's mood deteriorated steadily as the weekend progressed. She confessed to Elaine that she wanted only to have her house to herself. To be rid of all these tiring relatives and to enjoy a nice casual dinner (something with lentils would be nice—the very idea of feeding Charles a lentil!) around the kitchen table once again, with scented wood burning in the hearth, and the dogs dozing under the table. But Charles had a bee in his bonnet about the fire and refused to leave. He insisted on calling the police regularly to check on developments. Of which there were precious few. Frustrated with the progress of the arson investigation, he then demanded that the police charge Dave with assault over the incident that resulted in his broken arm, but as Charles had moved first, and Dave really hadn't done anything, there was nothing the police could do.

On Sunday morning, Moira announced that she simply had to get out into the fresh air. Temperatures were well above average for mid-October, and it might be six months before they had this opportunity again. Ruth pushed the wheelchair out to the deck, Alan fetched a table from the storage building, ignoring the "do not cross" tape fluttering, forgotten, in the wind, and Elaine followed with a chair for herself and one for Ruth.

They settled Moira's chair up to the table, and Ruth tucked a thick blanket around the old woman's scrawny legs. Last, but certainly not least, Lizzie appeared with the laden tea tray.

It was so hot that Elaine eyed the clear blue water like a wide-eyed inner-city child arriving at summer camp for the first time. It looked perfect for a quick dip, or a long slow luxurious swim. Too bad about the near freezing nights and what effect that has on lake water.

They spent a productive morning. Moira chatted freely, mainly about the war in Italy and the hardships of operating out of a Field Surgical Unit or Casualty Clearing Station. She could have been a writer, Elaine mused, not for the first time. Moira's command of the language was beyond compare; she had Elaine ready to jump into that lake, not to play, but to soak off the thick, choking dust of the Italian summer of 1944 and the blood of dying Allied and German soldiers.

Moira recalled the crushing disappointment of being left behind in England while the rest of her hospital went to France and on to Holland, the result of the most embarrassing of minor illnesses—an infected bladder. Between the rich words and vivid sentences Moira breathed the light and dark of the war years, the smell and feel and touch of everyday hardships and delights. The blood-rushing tingle of life lived at its peak. The contrast of things that became everyday occurrences: death and destruction and suffering beyond reason all around today; dances and giggling friends and a treat of Mrs. Peeks pudding tomorrow.

Moira was leaving something out; Elaine knew it. She wasn't satisfied that she had heard all there was to learn about the years after the Italian campaign.

On a personal level she was thrilled to realize that her instincts, long dormant while she struggled on one tedious movie script after another (sure to be the next BIG thing, always-one-eye-on-Hollywood-Ian had assured her), were waking up, like a huge old grizzly recovering from a long hibernation. She had the instinctive feeling (this bear knew that delights beyond compare were waiting out there) that something intensely personal, fundamentally important in Moira's life had happened. Something that turned the competent, severe, self-assured yet joyous young Canadian Nursing Sister into a far more cynical woman. Something that turned her into the woman who sat on this beautiful deck on this beautiful day in Ontario in an autumn at the beginning of the new millennium. Elaine would wait until Moira was ready to tell.

And if that didn't happen: Elaine would steer her back at a later time.

A boat pushed off from the island. Kyle and Dave were rowing over to the mainland to help Alan with odd jobs around the property. Charles must have been watching from the windows; he came out onto the deck and stood at the top of the stairs, glowering. He looked very much the landed gentleman in pressed white trousers and an English cricket sweater with colored stripes around the V-neck. Only the cast encasing his arm detracted from the landed-gentry effect.

They watched the rowboat pull up alongside the dock and its occupants clamber out. Moira and the women around her fell silent, waiting for a tornado to touch down. Kyle fastened the rope to the dock while Dave sauntered casually up the lawn.

"Morning, ladies." He doffed a pretend cap; a sneer lurking under the salutation.

"There's no work here for you today," Charles said. He was not shouting; he simply spoke loudly enough to be heard by them all. "So you might as well go back."

Kyle finished tying the boat in a rush and ran up. "Good morning, Moira. Mr. Stoughton. Nice day, isn't it?"

"It is," Moira said.

But Charles was not to be distracted. "I said that there's no work here today. Please be on your way."

Attracted by the voices, Alan rounded the far corner of the cottage. As usual Hamlet and Ophelia were right behind him. They were unsure whether to bark at the invaders or rush to Moira as she had food. They did both.

"Really, Charles," Moira said, breaking a cookie in half and tossing the pieces to her dogs. "These young people are welcome here. I'm sure that Alan has chores he needs help with. Don't you, Alan?"

"Well, uh...."

"Moira, dearest, you need to know a bit more about these people whom you have so kindly invited into your home. It seems that our friend, Dave, has a history with the police."

Dave took a step forward. Kyle grabbed his arm, but he shook it off.

Amber sauntered out onto the deck as if she were on a catwalk in Milan, luxuriating in the feel of everyone's eyes on her. She was dressed as if it were mid-summer rather than a week past Canadian Thanksgiving in high-heeled sandals, a pair of pink short shorts and matching midriff-exposing crop top, informing all the world that she was a boy's toy. She flashed a brilliant smile at Dave.

"This has gone far enough, Moira." Charles didn't even glance at his great-niece. His voice was calm. Calm, under control, and determined. The voice of a man used to being in command, now reaching the end of his patience. "This young man has a police record as long as your arm. Minor stuff to be sure, bar brawls, reckless driving. But we all know that it isn't much of a leap from the small stuff to major crimes."

"Actually, we don't know anything of the sort. Sir," Kyle said.

Charles was not impressed. "I haven't yet looked into your background, young man. Perhaps I should do that next."

"Oh, Charles, do please be quiet. This is getting quite tedious."

"Moira, don't you understand? This young thug and his friends are a danger to you. To us all."

Alan ran up the steps. "Careful, please, Charles. If Dave has a record, that's his business. As long as he's not wanted for anything, and I assume he isn't. The police have had plenty of contact with him. Regardless, it has nothing to do with the others over on the island."

The patrician face turned red with indignation, and Charles turned the force of his wrath onto Alan. "This is family business. I suggest you return to your chores, Manners."

"Charles, stop."

"I will not stop, Moira. You and your lame ducks. Manners here is as bad as the rest of them. As long as he keeps up the pretence of pottering around in the garden and charming you silly, he has free room and board and all the time he needs to devote to his useless attempts at art. For heaven's sake, he must be almost forty. It's past time he made his own way in the world like any respectable man."

Free from the force of Charles' anger, Dave and Kyle wisely decided that discretion was the better part of valor and edged out of the circle of attention. Before leaving, Dave cocked his forefinger at Amber and the girl skipped lightly down the steps.

"That is quite enough, Charles," Maeve said from the doorway. It was the first time Elaine had heard the timid old woman raise her voice. Megan and Lizzie stood behind her. The rising sounds of argument had attracted everyone. Only Phoebe—the dedicated assistant—was missing. A good researcher, caught up in the intensity of her work, wouldn't look up if Napoleon's army were marching across the property (unless it were to take note of the details of the general's uniform, and the types of weapons the men carried), never mind a family squabble.

"If we have issues to discuss," Maeve said, "I suggest we do it in privacy, as a family."

"Well, of course your sympathies are with Moira's lame ducks," Megan huffed, her face twisted and her voice ugly with spite. Elaine's ears pricked up. Family strife always made good copy. Time to find out the whole story of these sisters. But rather than returning the attack, Maeve's eyes filled with tears and she lowered her head.

"Stop this!" Moira's voice was calm, but her hands gripped the edges of her chair like liver-spotted and wrinkled talons. "This is my home and I am sick and tired of you bunch squabbling and yelling. Why don't you go home?"

"I agree," Maeve whispered. "I insist that you take us home, Charles."

Good for her, Elaine thought. Timid Maeve had probably never used the word *insist* in her entire life.

Megan slapped her sister across the face, the sound so shockingly loud it might have echoed across the lake. "How dare you talk to my husband in that tone of voice, how dare you. You vicious old cow." Megan was as well dressed and made up as always, but even the heavy makeup couldn't hide the ugly red blotches that covered her cheeks and neck or the hatred that twisted her painted mouth and narrowed the sculpted eyes.

No one moved. Dave, Kyle, and Amber missed their chance for escape, so caught up were they in the family drama.

"You sit here with me, Maeve." Moira's voice turned to steel, and she patted the vacant chair beside her. "Megan is in need of a nap. Before she starts packing, that is."

Maeve wiped her eyes on the back of her hand. Lizzie handed her an unused paper napkin.

"Megan, go inside!" Charles shouted, his icy control finally breaking. Here he was about to confront Moira about the inhabitants of the island and by implication her supposed leadership of the family, when his fool of a wife turned his issues into a sideshow. "Lizzie, please help my wife upstairs. She needs to rest."

Megan deflated visibly and accepted the cook's arm. Lizzie pulled the French doors shut after them.

"I'm not finished with you two, yet." Charles remembered Kyle and Dave.

Ignoring him, they, along with Amber, disappeared around the cottage, forcing Charles to accept his defeat.

"Why is Amber always hanging around that young man?" he said, to no one in particular. "I would have thought she would have more sense. You have to talk to her, Maeve. Not that you have a grain of sense yourself. Maybe I'll call her father." He walked into the cottage, a tired old man, shaking his head.

"Alan," Moira said, watching her brother-in-law leave. "Would you please go to the island and invite Rachel, Jessica, and Karen to lunch. And Willow, of course. Ruth, we will be having guests for lunch. Please ask Lizzie to prepare something hot and nourishing.

"The time has come to ask them about their plans for the winter," Moira continued. "As much as I hate to say it, they can't spend the winter out there. I'll be sad to see them go."

Alan rowed Rachel, Karen, and Jessica over with a scarcely contained Willow bouncing up and down in the front of the boat. Moira asked Lizzie to be sure the men were called in for soup and sandwiches in the kitchen. Elaine went with Alan to fetch more seating. The storage building still smelt strongly of smoke. She gathered an armful of cushions. They were untouched by the fire, but if they couldn't get the smell out, Moira would surely be wanting to replace them, come spring. As if they knew the reason for the invitation, Rachel introduced the subject as soon as they were all served with glasses of iced tea, a sliver of fresh lemon floating in each. Time to move on, she told Moira. It had been an exceptionally warm autumn but it would be getting cold soon.

"Where will you go?" Moira asked.

"We're going to split up. Me and Jessica are heading back to Toronto," Karen said with a mighty sigh. "There are jobs in restaurants, temp positions in offices."

"I'm off to my mother in Victoria," Rachel said, smiling at the child. "You'll like Victoria, Willow. Lots of water and flowers that last all through the winter."

"No snow?" Willow asked sadly.

"I'm sure we can find some."

"What about Kyle and Dave?" Elaine said.

"Kyle will be coming with Willow and me. We're together now," Rachel said with a touch of a highly flattering blush. "Though I don't know how my mother's friends will react to that."

"And as for Dave, who the hell cares," Karen said. "Sorry, Moira."

"Never heard that expression before," Moira said, making them all burst into gales of warm female laughter.

Lunch was served al fresco. A beautiful meal of thick corn chowder and make-your-own sandwiches. Followed by a warm chocolaty cake-pudding with a rich chocolate sauce and gallons of hot coffee. Perfect for an autumn afternoon. Once again, Elaine marveled at Lizzie's capability to pull a meal for a crowd together out of practically nowhere. She would have been worth her weight in gold back in the gold rush.

"Isn't Dave your friend?" Elaine asked once they were all served soup and were passing around platters of huge buns, cold meat, cheese, and roasted vegetables.

"Not at all. He kinda latched on to us, and we didn't quite know how to get rid of him. We're too polite, I guess. So he tagged along. I'm sorry if he caused some trouble. We all are. Great soup this."

"Thanks." Lizzie had pulled up a chair for herself and was helping Willow choose her sandwich ingredients.

"Not your fault," Moira said.

"He didn't start the fire," Karen said. "I'm sure of that."

"Of course, dear." Moira mumbled the expected platitudes.

"No, really. I know it."

"How can you be so positive?" Elaine asked, debating between ham and roasted red peppers. Unable to decide, she helped herself to both. "He wasn't with the rest of you that night. He didn't come over in the boat, to see what was happening. He was already here."

"He wasn't in camp when the fire started, that's true. But his father died in a house fire when he was a child. Dave was burned, quite badly. I don't know much of the story. His mother wasn't home when it happened, but Dave and his father and sister were in the house. The father died, the sister escaped unharmed. 'Cause it hasn't been hot, you probably haven't noticed that he never takes his shirt off. He never does, no matter how hot it gets. His chest is terribly scarred. He's terrified of fire, won't go near it. Isn't that right, Rachel, Jessica?"

"It's true," Jessica said, shivering despite the sun's warm, caressing rays.

"He won't help make our fire," Willow piped up. "Sits way back. Where it's cold. When we roasted marshmallows I had to cook his for him. And he waited till they were all cold and yucky before he would take them. Ug."

"Doesn't fit my image of him," Elaine said.

"It wouldn't, would it?" Rachel shrugged. "He's got a nasty streak, that boy. And I'm sorry for him because of what happened when he was small, but I won't make excuses for his behavior as an adult." She ripped a hunk off her sandwich and chewed viciously. "He's made things difficult for the rest of the group because he refuses to throw off that chip on his shoulder. I won't be sorry to cast him adrift. Lots of people have had a tough life, but they don't try to make everyone around them suffer because of it."

"Dave doesn't have a chip on his shoulder, Rachel," Willow said from behind a mouthful of milk. "I would have seen it."

The women all laughed, and Moira rubbed the girl's head. "I'm sure you would have, sweetheart. You're welcome to come back next year, you know."

"Thank you, dear Moira." Rachel's green eyes swelled with unshed tears. "But we'll simply have to see where we all are. Will that be all right?"

"Of course."

"Look, Rachel, look." Willow bounced up and down in her seat. "There are ducks, coming to see us. Can I take them some bread, please? I've finished my lunch." She remembered her manners. "It was very nice, thank you, Lizzie."

"You can take the rest of your bread down to them," Lizzie said. "Break it up into tiny pieces, but remember to throw the bread, don't let them eat out of your hand or they might bite you. Without meaning to hurt you."

"I won't." And the girl took off, braids and bright yellow ribbons streaming out behind her.

"She's a lovely girl," Maeve said with a smile. She had stopped crying long ago and was enjoying her lunch, the conversation, and the company.

"That she is," Rachel said. "But she isn't my daughter. I'm guessing you think so."

"I did make that assumption," Elaine said. "But it's none of my business."

"Her mother was my late sister. Danielle was murdered by her ex-husband last winter. Willow saw the whole thing."

"How awful for her." Elaine placed her fork on the side of her plate. The chocolate cake had lost all appeal. "And for you."

Moira's face was tight with anger: she'd heard the story before.

"I took Willow and I love having her. She's recovering, but it's a long, slow process. We were doing all right, living in Toronto. But in the spring Jim, that's my sister's husband, God rot his soul, finally went to trial."

"He didn't get off?" Elaine gasped, horrified at the thought.

"Oh no. I don't think I could have lived with that. He got life. But his new girlfriend, Irene, started calling me up, wanting to see Willow, wanting to take her to Kingston to visit Jim in the pen. Then it got worse; she demanded weekends and visitations, saying she was Willow's stepmother and had rights."

"And does she?" Maeve asked.

"None at all. Irene isn't married to Jim and even if they had been married it probably wouldn't have mattered. Jim hasn't asked to see Willow. Thank God for that, at least. He swears that all this harassment has nothing to do with him.

"She was crazy, started making threats against me. Said if I was dead then Willow would have to come live with her." Tears dripped down Rachel's cheeks. Jessica leaned over and put a comforting arm around her shoulders.

"So I decided we had to get away. Jess and Karen were leaving, off on a road trip they said. They asked us to come along." She smiled at them through her tears. They were crying also. Karen rose to her feet and settled her thick Irish cream knit sweater over her friend's bony shoulders.

"Will you be safe in Victoria?" Moira asked.

"I hope so. My mother married again after our dad died, so her last name is different from mine. Irene has a pretty short attention span. I suspect she's forgotten all about us by now and gone on to torment someone else. What a poisonous couple they were, Jim and Irene. Truly a match made in hell."

"I'll take the plates in. You sit still, Lizzie. You deserve a bit of a break." Elaine scrambled to her feet to gather up crockery and glassware. She always was so helpless when tossed in a sea of emotion. What a nice normal family she came from. How boring she had always thought they were. One brother was a doctor, a common and garden variety family practitioner in Vancouver. The other some sort of a banker, a financial planner he called himself, in a small Nova Scotia town. Her parents had retired early, financially secure.

Phoebe and Alan were in the kitchen, finishing up their own lunch, when Elaine walked in and started loading the dishwasher. As much as Elaine had insisted that she could manage, Lizzie had equally insisted that she would help, and followed her in.

"That's more drama in one morning than I've had in my whole life up until now," the cook said.

"What's happened?" Alan asked.

"Nothing. Someone's life story."

"Makes me realize how lucky I've been," Elaine said.

"It's good to remember that, now and again."

"So what's your deep, dark secret, Alan?" Elaine teased, pouring herself a cup of coffee.

"I don't have one. I'm what you see."

"What's this about art? Charles made it sound awfully insulting this morning. Like in your private life you run a child labor sweatshop or something."

"Nothing. He was ticked off and had to attack someone. And there I stood. The bull's-eye proudly painted on the front of my shirt."

"Don't you know?" Phoebe said brightly. "Alan's a painter, a really good one. He does landscapes, mostly. Moira lets him live here and have a studio and everything if he helps out."

"I see. I had wondered about the reference to smoke damage the morning after the fire. Then I forgot about it. Can I see some of your work?"

"No."

"You already have," Lizzie offered. "In the hall, near the staircase. One of Alan's is hanging there. A woman's hat in a field of flowers? Beside a dark, tired painting by some old guy? Alan's is much better."

"You did that?" Elaine remembered the perfection of the light and the depth of emotion the work had elicited in her.

Alan shifted in his seat. "Not a particularly good piece."

"It's wonderful. I'd love to see the rest of your portfolio. May I?"

"No."

"Of course you can," Lizzie said. "Alan's a bit shy, that's all. I'll take you up there."

"Lizzie." The word was a low warning.

"Oh, all right. I won't. But you should let Elaine see. Alan never shows his unfinished work to anyone," Lizzie explained. "But right now he has a lot of finished pieces he's getting ready for a gallery showing over Christmas."

"A gallery! How wonderful."

"That fire really would have been a disaster, in more ways than one, if it had gotten out of control and passed into the cottage," Lizzie said, tucking the remains of cheese and cold meat into plastic wrap. "Thanks for the help, Elaine. But there's no rest for the wicked. His lordship will be finishing his lunch and wondering why the dirty dishes haven't magically disappeared."

"And I also have enormous tasks ahead of me," said Phoebe, preparing to take her leave with a martyred sigh. "What with the stern taskmaster watching my every move."

Alan shifted uncomfortably and watched his fork with rapt attention as it finished off what remained of his dessert.

"If you don't want to show me, that's all right," Elaine said. "But can I come to the gallery?"

"Can't stop you. It's a public place."

"I love the painting in the hall. It's quite wonderful. Kyle admires it too. He told me so. Does he know you painted it?"

"No."

"Oh, have it your way. I've had enough of pulling teeth." Out of nowhere, Elaine was suddenly angry. "I'll be in the library for the afternoon, if you need anyone to chop wood or lug water."

"Elaine, I…" Alan mumbled, but the end of his sentence was swallowed up in a loud knock on the kitchen door.

Elaine admitted a smiling Greg, arms laden with a potted cyclamen in full glorious pink bloom. "Beautiful flowers for a beautiful lady," he said sweeping into the room.

"Christ, Josepheson. Thinking of taking up residence? Why don't you move right in?" Alan stood up so fast his chair crashed to the floor behind him. "I'll go and see how Kyle and Dave are getting on."

"Bit testy today," Greg said, watching the door slam shut.

"It's been a hard day. For everyone," Elaine said.

"Well, I'm here to make it better." Greg passed her the plant pot. "And to ask if you would like to have dinner with me tonight."

Lizzie and Phoebe skittered out of the kitchen.

"I…."

"You need to get out of here. Have a bit of fun. Say yes." He opened his eyes wide and cocked his head to one side, blinking furiously in the manner of a toddler trying to look loveable.

It worked.

Elaine laughed.

The tiny network of laugh lines around his eyes crinkled with amusement and the edges of his moustache twitched.

"Yes. That would be nice."

"I know you're here to work, so I'll leave you to carry on. But I'll be back, say around seven?"

"Seven would be good."

Elaine returned to the computer in her room. She had some research notes she wanted to check out, details of the Canadian

Army in Italy during World War Two. She logged on to her Internet account and waited for her day's batch of e-mail to download, thinking more of the painting in the hall by the staircase than the prospects of a dinner date.

Chapter Thirty-nine

May 1945. VE day. Throughout England and around the world joyous men, women, and children massed in the streets in celebration. At the hospital, the nurses and orderlies had been given time off duty to join the party. But someone had to keep on working and Moira volunteered to remain on duty. The skeletal hospital staff went to a good deal of trouble to make things nice for the patients. A party was set up in the gymnasium. The nurses had decorated the hall with a bit of bunting and crepe paper, dragged out of who-knows-where. Someone brought in a phonograph and piles of records. There was plenty of food, carefully stored over the last few months in expectation of the oh-so-very-long-awaited day. And beer for everyone, unlimited free beer, flowing in a steady stream like nectar from heaven. All the ambulatory patients gathered eagerly, and everyone who could be wheeled in, came—bed and all, if necessary.

Moira had never in all her life had a drink of beer. Her mother had taught her and her sisters that it was not a suitable beverage for ladies. But she was swept up in the festivities and accepted a drink from a soldier with a laughing face that was no more than a mass of scars and raw tissue. The man was blind, but he was already beginning to recognize people by their step or their voice and had volunteered to help distribute the beer.

"Don't have to walk through the crowds then," he explained with a twisted smile, handing over the bottle. "Stepping on toes and such. Better they all come to me."

The drink tasted strong and bitter. She didn't like it, but drank it down, wanting to be part of the party.

At midnight, Moira stepped outside for some air. The sky was bright from bonfires all over the town and she could hear singing and laughter. She had been told that they were burning blackout curtains as well as Hitler in effigy.

Inside the gym a soldier cried out in pain, too much partying for a broken body, and Moira turned to go back in.

She would remain in Europe for two more years, working with the lost, the dispossessed, the dying.

Chapter Forty

The evening started off well.

Greg escorted Elaine to the dining room of one of the many exclusive resorts that dot the Muskoka lakes. He was charming and witty, the food excellent, the wine plentiful. Their table looked out over the golf course, beautiful in its stark simplicity—the greens brown and silent, lined with naked trees outlined by the white light of a full rising moon.

"I wanted to see you tonight, Elaine," he said over coffee and liqueurs. A cognac for him, a Drambuie for her. "Because I'm going back to the city tomorrow."

"Work?"

"A group of prospective clients are arriving for a long-scheduled visit Monday morning, and we have a lot to do to get ready for them. Things that can't be done long distance."

"Your parents must have been happy that you were able to spend the time that you could."

"My parents weren't the only reason I've been hanging around."

"That moon is beautiful, isn't it," she said, not wanting to hear why he had stayed up north.

"Yes it is. But…."

She hailed a passing waiter. "More coffee please."

"As I was saying…."

"Do you have any idea who might have caused the fire?"

"What? No, of course not. Why do you ask?"

"It's just that I've been wondering. No one's talking about it. The police seem to think that it was arson. They have their eye on Dave, over at the island, but I think that's only because Charles so much wants it to be him."

"The police have been wrong before, Elaine. It's an old building. Bad wiring, no doubt. Nothing much in the way of fire codes when it was built."

"But the Madisons have looked after the property so well." Everything except the servants' cabin in the woods. She didn't mention that.

"But it's still an old place, old wood."

"That's true. Did you meet Donna Smithton?"

"Who?"

"Donna Smithton, the woman who drowned Labor Day weekend off the Madison dock."

"I don't remember if I spoke to her or not. I was at the party, so were a lot of people." At the table next to them, a man threw back his head and roared with laughter. Greg scowled at him. One of the man's companions saw Greg looking at them and hissed at the man to be quiet. He ignored her.

"Why do you keep asking these questions, Elaine?"

"Something's going on there, and I want to understand."

"You're upsetting yourself over nothing. No one has any reason to harm the Madison family. You've been chasing ghosts again." He laughed in an attempt to take some of the sting out of the words.

"I don't chase ghosts."

"Of course you don't. But maybe you let your imagination get away from you, a tiny bit."

"I don't imagine things, either, Greg. And no one imagined the fire, or Donna's death."

"I just think you're reading too much into a couple of unrelated, tragic events. Care for another Drambuie?"

"No. Thank you. It's time for me to get back."

On the drive home, Greg chattered amiably about his company, the hopes he had for this new client. One with deep pockets. Elaine watched the dark trees speed by. She remembered the fire, and later the incessant voice inside her head telling—ordering, demanding—her to see to Moira.

She was not imagining things!

The cottage was dark and quiet as she let herself in. She waved to Greg as he sped up the driveway, the wheels of his car spinning. She had ignored his hints that he be invited in for a nightcap.

The comforting quiet of the old home didn't last long. True to form, Hamlet and Ophelia dashed down the hallway, barking and snarling.

"Oh, for heaven's sake. Don't you two ever shut up?" she said.

"Not when people are mean to them," came a voice from the darkness.

Alan stepped forward and switched on the hall light. He whistled once and the dogs returned to his side.

"I'm not mean. I have a problem with being barked at every time I show my face, as if I were here to steal the family silver or something."

"They don't know that. But if you'd make an effort to get on with them, then they would."

"So all a burglar has to do is treat them nice and he can help himself to the aforementioned silver?"

"They're not watchdogs, Elaine. They're not trained that way. They're Moira's pets. And she's indulged them a bit too much."

"Sorry. Nice doggies?" She held out one hand.

Ophelia sniffed the air, but didn't move. Hamlet growled.

"Have a nice night?" Alan asked.

"Not particularly."

"Why not? Fire in the kitchen? Flat tire? Run out of gas?"

"Boring company." And she drifted up the stairs, leaving an incredulous Alan, a shocked Augustus, and an amused Elizabeth staring at her wake.

Chapter Forty-one

It had become too easy of late, what with midnight fires and
ghostly suggestions, to slip out of the running habit. Elaine didn't
like running—hated it actually. Aerobics classes were much to
be preferred. A nice comfy gym, regular schedule, lively music
to keep the mind occupied while the body did what it had to
do. But while she was living here she wouldn't get to a gym, and
she was all too aware of an aging waistline to give up exercise
for the duration. She forced herself out of bed early and set off
down the long driveway for her run.

Deep in thought, Elaine scarcely noticed the miles passing
underneath her running shoes. Greg would be leaving soon; he
was planning on driving to Toronto with the first light. He had
wanted her to give him some indication that his return would be
eagerly anticipated. But she'd offered nothing. Was she making
a mistake? Rich, handsome, interested in her. What else could a
woman want?

Some degree of reciprocal emotion. Funny thing, love, it doesn't
arrive on demand. Wouldn't life be so much easier if it did? And
Greg could be awfully condescending. For a moment at the restaurant, she almost expected him to pat her on the hand and say
"Don't worry your pretty little head about it."

A definite chill hung in the air. The wind whipped up dead
leaves and stirred thin branches. Winter on its way.

Before leaving, she'd stopped in the kitchen for a glass of
orange juice and idly read a note left under a fridge magnet for

Lizzie from Charles. He and Megan would be leaving after breakfast. He wanted to see his doctor in Toronto about the broken arm, he explained. They'd take Maeve home with them.

The note marked a clear victory for Moira, in the battle if not necessarily the war. Elaine would also be glad to see the household fall back into its routine. They were simply not getting the amount of work done that she had hoped. Phoebe was a great help, and she fairly chewed through the boxes of letters, sorting out the minutia, freeing Elaine to concentrate on the more important ones. But Moira was constantly distracted, bad tempered, and on edge.

And Elaine was not convinced that someone wasn't up to mischief. Wrong word. A fire in an aged, wooden building situated right next to a home occupied by several elderly individuals was by no stretch of the imagination to be considered mischief. She didn't believe that either Lizzie or Alan bore a grudge against Moira or the family. Ruth, however, had a chip on her shoulder the size and weight of a hunk of the Canadian Shield. She did seem to be genuinely fond of Moira, but there was no telling what lay under people's carefully laid facades. Since their talk, when Ruth had cut her hand on the mug, she had been marginally warmer towards Elaine. But appearances, as always, could be deceiving. Who knew where Ruth's misplaced jealousy might lead?

And that left the islanders, Moira's two sisters, Charles, Amber, and Phoebe. Alison, Elliot, and Brad were here at the time of the fire, but they had left before the incident with Moira's pillow.

Phoebe Elaine needed, so she was irrationally taken out of contention for the role of villain. With the imminent departure of the islanders, Amber would soon make her farewells also.

It was dimly possible that the trouble wasn't someone associated with the family at all. Elaine focused her eyes and looked at the forest around her for clues. She approached the Madisons' driveway; if someone were hiding out in the woods, it should be obvious.

She stopped running and snorted at herself. What pretensions of grandeur. It might be obvious to Sherlock Holmes, and even apparent to a *Courier du Bois*, but Elaine Benson wouldn't recognize a misstep in the woods if it rose up and bit her. It was theoretically possible that she would be suspicious of a signpost announcing *Terrorist Camp Here*, but not much less than that.

She jogged back down the driveway and rounded the cottage to walk up the steps to the deck. Yesterday's impromptu picnic had long since been cleared away, and the deck once again stood bare. Abandoned for the winter. She hoped that she would get the opportunity to see this magnificent old cottage in the hot summer weather it had been built for. Her work should be done by then, but maybe Moira would invite her back for a weekend. Mentally, she slapped herself across the face for dreaming. No point in speculating where she would be nine long months from now.

Stopping at the top of the stairs, Elaine settled into her regular routine of stretches and cool down. The dogs barked. Nothing in the least unusual about that. But this was a frenzied pitch unlike the tones she'd heard from them before. Granted she'd only been here a couple of weeks, and granted she disliked those dogs with a passion, but some primitive instinct twitched.

Elaine looked up.

In the woods and along the road the air had been clear, full of the fresh, new light of the rising sun, but down here a soft morning haze drifted in off the water. Elaine stepped off the deck, her nerves standing to attention.

Moira, Moira, the words echoed inside her head, around and around.

She glanced down the flagstone path, to the point where it ended and the dark, forbidden woods closed in. The rolling morning mist stopped exactly at that point, and sunlight tentatively touched the tops of the ancient trees. Below all was darkness. But against the gloom moved a shape even darker still. It was the black of night and of nightmares and it undulated under the first of the old white pines. It could venture no further, confined by an invisible barrier as strong as the Gates of Hades. Not to venture down the flagstone path, out into the sunlight. Never again.

Fingers of thought reached across the gulf of time and space between them and touched Elaine's mind.

Invasive, threatening.

She struggled to push them away.

The scent of cheap dime-store cologne filled the air. Too much, much too much, splashed on in anticipation of a lover's arrival.

Moira, Moira.

A loon cried out through the mist, the sound, as always, heartbreakingly lovely. The dogs continued to bark.

The mist shifted, just a fraction. More a thinning, a pruning of the haze than a clearing. Elaine's heart pounded—she feared that her chest might burst open—and her breathing came short and sharp. But the instinctive reaction to danger was coming from without, not from the depths of her own mind or body.

Moira, Moira.

The shape moved beneath the wide arms of the old white pine. Elaine could see right through it to a squirrel sitting on the branches of a tree, clutching a nut to store over the long, harsh winter.

I cannot go there. So you must. The colors of autumn disappeared. Brilliant, soft green spread out on the long branches of maples and oaks. Flowers burst from the cold soil to form a mass of color in the beds at the edges of the flagstone path. The gardener whistled as he worked. He carried a sharp spade, and dug vigorously into the rich brown topsoil, brought in by the truckload to give a touch of gentility to this land of unyielding rocks, at the few weeds that dared to pop their heads above his immaculate flowerbeds. He was young, smiling and enjoying the day. Elaine could see his body, broken and torn, his eyes wide and surprised; the rich, red Canadian blood leaking into the dark soil of the fertile, abandoned fields of Normandy.

He smiled and touched his cap as a maid passed by. She tossed her black head in indignation, offended by the familiarity.

He laughed and winked at her stiff, retreating back. She carried a tray, laden with glasses of fresh lemonade and crunchy oatmeal cookies, Cook's specialty, and she was hot, very hot, in the black wool uniform, heavy stockings, and crisp white cap. The younger children laughed and played in the water; the dog barked from the shore. The older children, almost adults now, had company, young men and women from school or the city. They lay on striped deck chairs placed along the dock. Watching each other with bold glances or shy smiles. One of the young women, in—to Elaine's critical, modern eyes—a hideously ugly high necked and skirted black bathing suit, held out her right hand lazily, her pink body drinking up the sun's rays. The woman with the tray placed a glass into the open hand. One of the other women rose to her feet and relieved the maid of her heavy burden. Her mouth moved, but Elaine could not hear the words. The maid smiled. It was just a twitch of the edges of her generous red mouth, but the gratitude was palatable.

A man half-rose from his lounge chair and patted the generous swell of buttocks beneath the stiff black maid's dress. The girl jumped. She fled down the narrow path to the kitchen door, cheeks flushed, dark eyes burning with shame. They laughed, the sound following her as she walked, head held high, trying not to run, but the face of the woman who had taken the tray was set into an angry line, and she turned on the young man with the wandering hand. He laughed and pretended to be apologetic, an act that had the other girls giggling behind their upheld hands.

The squirrel dashed down the tree trunk and disappeared into a pile of decomposing vegetation.

Moira, Moira.

The voice was in her head, but softer, further away than before. It was disappearing, drifting back into the cool depths of the forest. Time for Elaine to pull open the French doors and head to the kitchen for a drink.

Or she could follow the beating of her heart and the frantic thoughts of a diaphanous, shifting apparition.

They were on the dock; it was hard to see, through the mist. She walked down the steps. She heard voices raised in anger. Soft voices, muffled by the fog. They cracked with age and were so overflowing with lifetimes of pent-up emotion that Elaine almost retreated in embarrassment.

"You have to stop this. I've told you and told you. But will you listen? No. Like you never listened to a lick of common sense in your life." Megan.

"You are out of your mind, my poor dear, if you think I'm going to abandon the ambition of my old age to satisfy your strange sense of propriety. It's the twenty-first century. No one cares anymore." Moira.

"Well, I care. I care." Voice rising to a shriek. Megan.

As Elaine moved closer they took form through the mist. The two sisters were at the edge of the dock. Moira in her chair, Megan standing in front of her. Cold gray water lapped at the pilings and disappeared into the mists beyond. A seamless blend of land and air and water, all of it mixing into pewter. The loon cried again.

The elevated ramp that carried Moira's chair up and down the hillside rested at the bottom of its route, at the head of the wide wooden dock. The chair was at the other end of the dock, close to the water. Moira had a thick shawl wrapped around her thin shoulders. A beautiful scarf, an inferno of red and orange, shot through with turquoise thread, fluttered around her neck.

Her sister stood over her, dressed more sensibly in a dark blue Burberry raincoat but with incongruous white bedroom slippers, the kind Elaine's mother called mules.

What was real and what was imagination? Memories of the sun-drenched party were fading already, leaving nothing but a dreamy impression in Elaine's mind. But the sisters were here and now. Weren't they? She hesitated, trapped with no idea of what she should do. She didn't want to interfere in a family quarrel, but something was truly amiss here. She opened her mouth to call out, to ask if everything was all right, when Moira struggled half to her feet, anger giving her arms the strength.

"What would you do to stop me, Megan? How far would you go? How far have you gone?"

"You were always the favorite." Megan's shriek had Hamlet barking in accompaniment. The dogs were as undecided as Elaine. They weren't guard dogs, but they knew that their beloved owner was disturbed.

"Mother loved you the most. Always. And you went away to war like you were so special. While I had to stay at home and look after Mother and run the house."

Moira laughed. A sound so strained with emotion and the simple physical effort of rising from her chair that it hardly seemed like a proper human laugh. "As if you had an ounce of energy or ambition in your useless life, Megan Madison Stoughton. It suited you perfectly well to sit at home and wait for the suitors to line up at the door. But I don't want to dredge up the past. What I want to know now is what you had to do with Donna? Or the fire?"

"She wasn't a nice person, that Donna."

"You killed her because she wasn't a nice person?"

"It was an accident."

"An accident you caused, Megan."

"She was as common as dirt. I offered her money to just go away and leave us alone. But she said that if I was willing to pay, she'd hang around to find out just how high I would go. She was going to blackmail me."

"So you killed her."

"Not at all. She suggested that we talk down here, away from the party, where we wouldn't be overheard. She stepped backwards and fell off the edge of the dock. I didn't know she couldn't swim. Anyone who can't swim shouldn't be spending time around the water."

"You didn't call for help?"

"The party was winding down, people were leaving. By the time I found someone it would have been too late."

"So when you realized that you couldn't stop me by killing my biographer, and then trying to destroy the papers, you attacked me." Moira's voice was calm and steady. Strong, now, with no trace of old age or infirmity.

"What attack? Your self-centered imagination is playing up again. Poor Moira. Everything has to be about you. Like when we were children. How you manipulated Grandmother into doting on you."

"You came into my room and put a pillow over my face. For some reason Elaine barged in at the right moment and scared you away."

"What nonsense. You do have to be the center of attention, one last time, don't you?"

"Not nonsense at all. I didn't know what was happening, not then. But now that you're standing upwind of me, I remember your scent. Chanel No. 5, isn't it? You always wear No. 5. Before the pillow pressed down on me I smelt No. 5."

Megan screamed and lashed out. She was tiny and frail, but her rage gave her the strength she needed. Moira half stood at the edge of the dock, the one she had dived off as a child, posed flirtatiously on as a young woman, and watched nieces and nephews swim from as an indulgent elderly aunt. To Moira Madison it was truly a place of safety and comfort, if there were such a thing still to be found in the world.

For one horrible second, shock and disbelief crawled over the tired old face. The diminutive body quivered. And then it was gone. Over the edge with a splash and a thin incredulous cry.

Hamlet lifted his massive head and howled to the sky.

Chapter Forty-two

"What on earth is that noise?" Ruth asked, taking a sip of her tea.

"Those blasted dogs, they don't shut up for a single minute." Lizzie bent into the fridge to select a variety of cold meat and cheeses. Her back turned, Alan slipped through her defenses and grabbed a hunk of bread.

Lizzie whirled around and slapped his hand with a damp dishcloth. "Enough of that, my boy," she said, sternly. "These sandwiches are for his Lordship 'imself. Fer the carriage ride back to London. 'Cause there ain't no good inns on the way, you understand."

Alan and Kyle chuckled and pretended to dive at the slices of meat and cheese. Lizzie swatted at their darting fingers like the pests they were.

"The grub's plenty good here," said Kyle, so well fed before and after a day's work, he had no interest in the sandwich preparations, he only wanted to play the game. "But I don't know if I could stand those damned dogs long enough to get through a meal."

Ruth picked up her teacup. "I hear something else. It sounds like someone's crying."

Kyle laughed. "Oh, yes. It's the ghost of Madison cottage. Crying 'cause she hasn't got the prettiest gown at the ball."

Ruth ignored the comment and pricked up her ears. No one would be crying out loud in this house: terrible breach of good manners. It wasn't crying, she heard. But screaming. An animal caught in a trap? Kyle was making the woo woo sound that represents ghostly moaning to doe-eyed children.

"Shut up, you fool," Lizzie said, her plump arms laden with sandwich fillings. "I hear something too."

Alan leapt to his feet. Kyle followed. Lizzie threw aside the packages of food, and Ruth gently put down her china teacup to bring up the rear.

"Can't you do something about those dogs, Manners?" Charles was on his way down the stairs, still fastening his tie. "Never heard such a blasted racket in all my life."

"On my way now, sir," Alan said.

"Let Alan handle it, Charles." Maeve stood at the top of the stairs, still in her frothy nightgown. "We may not like them, but they are my sister's dogs. Alan will calm them. I'm sure he's extremely capable." She offered what she thought of as her flirtiest smile, the one that had made her so popular in her youth.

Alan burst through the French doors to the deck, his entourage following close behind.

Once they were outside, no one could mistake the human screams for those of an animal. Falling over themselves, they tumbled down the steps and rushed along the flagstone path to the water's edge. Ruth's heart almost stopped when she saw Miss Madison's wheelchair, toppled over, at the end of the dock. No sign of the elderly woman, but something thrashed in the water.

Hamlet perched at the edge of the dock, his toenails hanging over, barking as if his life depended on it. Ophelia, who hated the water, swam in circles around Elaine, bobbing in the gentle waves.

Fully dressed, Alan hit the water with a wave-creating splash, Kyle following almost on the instant.

Ruth stood on the dock, wrung her hands, and watched.

Chapter Forty-three

The water was dark, the consistency of thick tea or ink, caused, Elaine had read, by a high quantity of lead. Difficult to see much of anything, down there. The black water, the mist burning off under the growing strength of the sun, a splash of sunlight on a rogue wave, tiny silver fish scattering in their multitudes, a few larger ones gathering, sensing a feast.

A startled white face and a flash of red and turquoise scarf and churning pale limbs.

Elaine stared into the water for a few precious seconds. Gathering her wits at last she screamed as loud as she could and dove. The shock of her body hitting the cold was almost enough to knock the senses out of her, but she pulled her head back to the surface and screamed again. She struck out in long, powerful strokes to the spot where she'd seen Moira slipping under the waves. Elaine screamed with all the force she could muster as she grabbed the old woman and cradled the thin form to her chest. It was light, ethereal almost, despite being clothed in water-sodden wool and heavy running shoes. Moira said nothing, but she stared at Elaine with wide frightened eyes.

Hamlet and Ophelia set up a tragic chorus of barking that would surely alert the entire county. Ophelia hit the water like a participant in a game of cannon bomb, so beloved of children around any sort of water. There was nothing she could do, and she knew it, but she would try. Hamlet rushed to the dock's edge in a frantic attempt to keep an eye on both his mistress and his mate.

The dog scarcely registered the impact as the force of his formidable bulk hit the fragile old woman who stood calmly at the edge of the dock, watching her sister struggle to live.

Megan gasped. Her thin arms churned as she tried to keep her balance. But she failed, and toppled over into the water.

Elaine feared the worst the moment she reached Moira, now silently slipping underneath the waves. An old woman, a fragile heart. But she grabbed and pulled and screamed nonetheless, hoping that by force of will, if nothing else, she could pour life back into the limp old body.

She kicked out, talking to Moira, telling her to stay strong, moving towards the shore. Slow but steady. She didn't have a hope of lifting her burden onto the rocks.

As if in a dream, strong arms took the weight from her, and gentle strokes guided Elaine back to shore, where she was pulled up and out of the lake.

She shook water out of her eyes and saw Lizzie on the rocks, bent over the barely twitching figure that had been passed up to her, her head moving rhythmically over the tiny body, the fair ponytail bobbing up and down with a life of its own.

Onlookers gathered around, watching, stunned into immobility. Kyle and Alan clambered out of the water, pushing a sodden Ophelia ahead of them.

Moira coughed and spat and vomited a stomach full of Lake Muskoka onto Lizzie's ample lap. Lizzie grinned in delight. "Welcome back to the land of the living, Moira."

Hamlet and Ophelia crawled to either side of their mistress and licked her face in joy.

Ruth burst into tears.

A cheer died in Elaine's throat. Megan! She grabbed Alan's dripping sleeve. "Megan went in as well."

Charles, Maeve, Amber, and Phoebe came stumbling down the flagstone walk, dressed in a wild assortment of traveling clothes and nightwear.

Charles heard his wife's name. "Megan. What do you mean, she went in? Went in where? Where is Megan?"

This time Kyle hit the water first, closely followed by Alan. They floundered around, unable to see anything. Visibility in this lake ended a few inches down.

Amber turned on her heels and fled back into the cottage. Phoebe dove into the lake, her bright yellow flannel Winnie-the-Pooh shortie pajamas flaring out around her as they greedily soaked up the water. She touched Kyle's shoulder, pointed down, and dove.

On the shore, Moira vomited up another stomach full of lake. "What, what?" She was confused but struggled to sit up, pushing ineffectively at the arms around her, not sure if they were restraining her or comforting her.

"There, there. It's all right," Ruth said. "Let Lizzie and me help you up to the house. Please...Moira. You need to be warmed, to rest."

Loving arms lifted Moira to her feet and settled her into her chair.

"Megan. Where is Megan?" She grabbed Ruth's arm, as she felt herself being pushed up the path to the cottage.

"Don't worry about that now, dear. Just rest."

It was a long time before Phoebe, Kyle, and Alan found Megan floating under the dark waters. They knew it was useless, she had been down too long, but once they had her, Phoebe began CPR immediately. Kyle guiding, Phoebe breathing in a steady rhythm, they reached the shore as the piercing siren of an ambulance echoed over the calm lakes.

Capable arms pulled Megan out of the water. The cold body was laid on the rocks and the mechanical process of CPR continued, without response. Paramedics and a stretcher arrived. A paramedic took over CPR, as they wrapped Megan in thick blankets and carried her to the ambulance. Charles, his thin face etched with shock and despair, looking every day, and more, of his age, stumbled to keep up.

Phoebe, Elaine, Kyle, and Alan huddled together by the waterside, listening to the sound of the ambulance as it began the long return journey to the hospital in Bracebridge, the siren screaming. The earlier mist had burned off completely and a weak, but valiant, autumn sun shone in a cloudless azure sky heralding one of the last of the pleasant fall days before winter once again had this land in her unforgiving grip.

They staggered up the hill to the cottage. Dripping wet, shivering with cold, overwhelmed by shock.

Without a word, Alan reached out and gathered Elaine into his arms. She collapsed wordlessly into his embrace. Their bodies melded into a chill, damp blob, which still managed to be so wonderfully comfortable.

Cold, wet, but secure, Elaine mechanically put one foot in front of the other and allowed Alan to lead her up the path. She hadn't known it was possible to be so cold. If her teeth kept on chattering like this they would surely drill a hole right through her skull.

Amber and Lizzie met them at the door, armed with thick blankets. Alan kissed Elaine's hair and held her close before allowing Lizzie to guide Kyle and him upstairs. Amber took charge of Elaine and Phoebe.

Amber pushed the two women into Elaine's room, the closest, and ran to start the shower. When the water was hot and steam filled the bathroom, she helped them strip off the outer layer of their miserable clothes and guided them into the spray, like helpless infants. They stood under the jet of hot water, Elaine clad in bra and panties, Phoebe in her pajamas, soaking up the warmth.

"Aren't you quite the extra from *Night of the Living Dead*," Phoebe said, at long last. "Hope I don't look half as bad."

Elaine laughed, a laugh owing more to hysteria than mirth. But soon they were hugging each other and alternately laughing and sobbing.

Amber pulled back the shower door. "Undies off. No time for false modesty here. Take it all off, ladies."

They complied.

When Elaine and Phoebe emerged, feeling almost like human beings once again, Amber was standing in the steam, thick yellow towels held out in front of her. Elaine remembered when she was ten years old, and being cared for by her mother during a mild bout of the flu. All that attention, and a day off school, too. Wonderful.

Amber had searched under Elaine's pillow and found a neatly folded set of pink flannel pajamas, teddy bears cavorting on fluffy white clouds. Meekly following instructions, Elaine dried herself off and pulled on the pajamas. Slippers and a terrycloth robe followed. Amber then went through a similar ritual with Phoebe. As Phoebe's pajamas were lying in a sodden heap on the floor of Elaine's bathroom, Amber produced a maroon sweat suit.

Dry and warm at last, they were anxious to get downstairs.

The stunned survivors had gathered in the kitchen. Lizzie had the fireplace roaring and coffee and hot cocoa brewing by the time Amber, Phoebe, and Elaine arrived.

Kyle and Alan, showered and dressed in an assortment of warm clothes, gripped mugs of steaming coffee. Alan's woolen sweater and sweat pants were so small on the tall black man that Kyle resembled a boy who had grown out of his wardrobe overnight.

Maeve sat in the scarred old rocking chair by the hearth. As she rocked she hummed a song lightly under her breath. Her cloudy eyes looked at a horizon very far away.

A timid knock on the kitchen door, and Lizzie rushed to admit Rachel and Karen.

"We heard a siren," Rachel said. "What's happened?"

Kyle reached her in one step and gathered her to his chest. "There's been an accident," he said.

She pulled back. "What kind of an accident? Why are you dressed in that ridiculous getup? And your hair is all wet."

"Is it Moira? Has something happened?" Karen asked.

"Moira's all right," Lizzie said. "Ruth is with her. She was in the lake. Elaine pulled her out. I'd better get a pot of tea upstairs. Make sure they're all right. Will you help me, Karen?"

"Of course."

Elaine looked around the room. The kitchen, large as it was, was packed to overflowing. Family, friends, neighbors, and staff were either sitting stoically at the great oak table or milling aimlessly about. Ophelia had been toweled off and she and Hamlet were lying on blankets under the table. For once, they lay quietly.

Alan threw a smile at Elaine that had her still-chilled heart warming rapidly in her chest. She thought of her teddy-bear dotted pajama legs sticking out from under her shabby robe, and her unbrushed hair standing up in frizzy curls.

"They took Grandma to the hospital," Phoebe said. "Granddad has gone with her. We haven't heard anything yet."

"What in heaven's name was Moira doing going for a swim, anyway?" Maeve said from her chair in the corner. She rocked so rhythmically, it was almost hypnotizing. "She hasn't been in the lake for near on twenty years or more. Nor have I. Not quite suitable for a respectable woman's dignity, I have always maintained. The swimming costumes they have these days. How strange that she'd decide to go for a swim today of all days."

They stared at her in disbelief.

"But my sister did always tend to be a mite unconventional."

The sharp ring of the phone cut through the tension in the room. Everyone jumped. They looked at each other, no one wanting to pick up the instrument and hear what they all knew would be terrible news. On the fourth ring, Alan grabbed it. He faced the wall, his back to the room; shoulders hunched, head down, making a cave of his body. He said nothing but "Hello" followed by a few murmurs. He placed the phone back in the cradle, straightened his shoulders and turned to face them.

"That was Charles. Megan was pronounced dead on arrival at the hospital."

"Oh, God," Kyle exclaimed.

Rachel fell into a chair. "How terrible."

Alan threw another log onto the fire, which didn't need one. Expressionless, Phoebe opened the cookie tin and arranged treats onto a tray. Maeve hummed quietly to herself as she continued to rock.

Watching them reminded Elaine of one of Moira's stories. A trip to London spent mostly in the tunnels under the city, while wave after wave of German bombers pounded the city above. She had talked about the expressionless features on people's faces, women trying to be brave, holding back the tears, their children gripped tightly in their arms, forced laughter, and unconscious generosity as bits of food and drink and comfort passed between strangers thrown together.

"Charles wants me to bring the car." Alan looked at Elaine. "Will you be all right?"

She smiled, feeling all warm and cozy inside, and not from her proximity to the fireplace. "I'm fine. Thank you. You go and help Charles. I'm sure he needs you."

"If you're sure, Elaine?"

"I'll walk out with you."

They reached the kitchen door as Lizzie and Karen returned. "Moira's sleeping," Lizzie told them. "But Ruth's sitting with her. We've called her doctor and he's on his way. She wants to see you, Elaine. She asked Ruth to fetch you. But she's asleep now. Ruth'll let you know when she's awake."

"I'll be waiting."

"What happened, Elaine?" Alan took her hand as they walked down the long, dark corridor. They passed his painting, secure in its place amongst the Canadian masters. Elaine smiled at it fondly. It looked even more beautiful than the first time she'd seen it, if that were possible. She would ask him, someday, what lay behind it. The painting was so emotional, there had to be a story there. As they passed the staircase, she could feel the force of Augustus' disapproval digging into her back. She suspected that he was scandalized that a woman of such a lowly position would have the audacity to pass up the son of a prominent Muskoka family. She couldn't see them, the portraits were behind her, but she imagined that if she turned around Elizabeth would have winked.

She pulled her mind back to the question. "They were arguing. Moira accused Megan of killing Donna Smithton, setting the fire, and trying to kill her by smothering her as she slept. Megan didn't deny it. Oh, God, Alan, she pushed Moira into the lake. Her own sister. I saw it. It wasn't an accident, although Megan claimed that Donna's death was an accident. One she didn't do anything to prevent. But I don't understand. Why would she do that? They're sisters. And they're so old." Huge, warm teardrops fell silently down her cheeks. Her chest heaved and her body felt as if it would break in two.

Alan gathered her into his arms and stroked her back. She buried her wet face into his chest. "I don't understand, either," he said. "We probably never will. But it's over. You're all right. Moira's all right."

"But Megan's dead."

"So she is. But from what you've said, I think she brought it on herself. Don't you?" He reached under her chin and tilted her head back. With his forefinger, he wiped a single tear from her face. "Let it all sort itself out, Elaine. You did what you had to do and you did it well. That's all that counts."

She tried to smile, to regain that brief moment of feeling loved and cared for. "Do you think so?"

"I do. But now I have to go. As Lizzie would say, 'is lordship awaits 'is carriage. If it was only his lordship, I'd say forget him, I want to be here—with you, Elaine. But it isn't. It's a tired old man who has just lost his wife of fifty or more years."

Elaine finished the smile. "You're right. But come back."

"I will."

Alan pressed his lips to the top of her curly blond head.

For the rest of the day the household moved through a Jules Verne underwater world, floating beneath the surface, without focus. Lizzie prepared colossal quantities of sandwiches and gallons of tea for which only Dave seemed to have sufficient appetite. Elaine and Phoebe slept most of the day away, their dreams drenched in cold lake water, viewed through sightless, staring old eyes. Charles returned from the hospital and shut himself in the library. The TV blared at full volume from behind the closed door. After depositing Charles at the front door, into Phoebe's competent hands, Alan went straight to the woodpile and spent the day chopping more wood than they would need for the rest of the winter. He told no one of what they had said to each other on the trip home.

Early in the evening, while Elaine was sitting at her computer struggling to type up a cheerful e-mail to her brothers, one full of platitudes about the progress she was making on the memoirs and the beauties of a Muskoka autumn, Phoebe hammered on the door.

"Charles wants to talk to us all. The drawing room in fifteen minutes."

"He won't want me there. I'm not family."

"He told me specifically to ask you."

They were all gathered in the drawing room by the time Elaine arrived. Alan wasn't wearing his smart black suit with the red cummerbund, only a tired pair of jeans and a flannel shirt. He sat in the brown leather chair in pride of place in front of the fire, next to Moira in her wheelchair. The elderly Miss Madison's face was drawn with grief; she had aged ten years since the morning. But she forced a smile for Elaine and patted the couch on the other side of her, inviting Elaine to sit.

Ruth, standing behind Moira's chair, nodded at Elaine, and the edges of her mouth turned up a fraction.

"Please, help yourself, Elaine." Ever the host, no matter the circumstances, Charles gestured to the line of open bottles on the small table.

She poured a glass of red wine. Not really wanting it, but suspecting that she might shortly be looking for an artificial source of strength.

Alan stood as she approached the offered seat and kissed her lightly on the cheek. They gripped hands, for just a moment.

Moira gave them a soft smile, a smile so wise and knowing it brought her aged face back to life.

"Where's Maeve?" Elaine asked, simply for something to say. Reluctantly, she let go of Alan's hand and settled into the chair.

"Resting," Moira said. "We've obtained a private nurse for her. She'll be going home tomorrow."

Charles cleared his throat. "Not to sound too much like a cliché, but you are probably all wondering why I have gathered you here." His thin face was tightly drawn, the skin so diaphanous the bones were nearly visible. The strain showed in every line of his face. Seeking some degree of courage in the traditions of his youth, he had dressed to the nines—gray trousers ironed to a knifepoint, crisp white shirt, navy blue blazer, and smart gray tie.

"When I returned from the hospital this afternoon—" he stopped to take a long sip of water— "I spoke to Moira." He nodded at his sister-in-law. "For a long time. A conversation we should have had many, many years ago. She—we—decided that you all deserve to hear the story."

"Megan." His voice broke on the name, but he swallowed heavily and continued. He remained dry-eyed. "Megan was acting only in my interests, as she saw them. However mistaken she might have been, she was determined to protect my reputation until the last." Again he raised the glass to his mouth. It was empty. Lizzie rushed for a jug of water.

Charles gave her a slight smile as she poured. "I told Moira this afternoon about my great shame, the burden I have lived with my entire life. I'm going to tell it to you now. Megan wanted to protect my story at all costs. If she'd confided in me, I would've told her that it no longer matters. Most of my contemporaries are long dead, my life coming to a comfortable end. But the truth will out, as indeed it must."

"Ironically," Moira interrupted, "I knew nothing about this. 'The guilty run where no one pursuith.' What an apt phrase. All these long years Megan thought I knew Charles' heavy secret, and she lived in fear that I'd reveal it. When I announced my intention of writing my memoirs, and then hired Donna Smithton to assist me, she feared that the time had come. Had I but known how frightened she was, I would have assured her that I have no interest in dredging up the riddles of the past, and certainly not in spreading muck and gossip. After all, my memoirs are about me. Not the doings of my family."

She took a deep breath. "This all came to pass because I simply didn't know, although I do now. Even as she…confronted me…down on the dock, I thought she was referring to something else. How terribly sad. As Charles has said, who would care, so many years later?"

Charles took a deep breath, and a swallow of brandy, which sat in a beautiful cut-glass snifter on the table beside him, for an ounce of courage. Then he spoke.

Chapter Forty-four

It was an incredibly hot day in early September 1944. The Italian campaign was vitally important in keeping German divisions occupied that otherwise would be in France, where the battle towards Germany itself was underway. "The soft underbelly of Europe," Winston Churchill called Italy. The Canadians were part of Operation Olive, whether after the trees or the woman's name I never did find out. I remember the dust most of all. It was soft and white, like fresh powdered snow, and could lie three to four inches deep on the ground. Some of the men from the Northern climes would try to fool themselves that it was snow, for a few seconds at any rate. The morale in our sector was high that day; we all hoped that the Italian campaign was almost over. And surely Germany would then fall quickly.

It didn't work out that way. The Germans fought for every inch of territory and reinforcements were arriving constantly.

I don't remember the name of the town; you'd think that it would be burned into my brain, but I've forgotten, totally. A number of years ago my unit went on a reunion trip to Italy. Do you remember, Moira? The family encouraged me to go. But I had no wish to see it all again. I see it often enough, in my dreams.

It was just a dusty Italian village, one like so many others. Practically destroyed by the time we arrived. You couldn't walk down the main street without picking your way through piles of rubble—all that remained of people's homes and lives. The Germans were scarcely out of earshot before the civilians crept back. That was what upset me most of all. Watching those old women in their black shawls, dragging dirty-faced toddlers behind them. The entire population of Italy seemed to consist of nothing but bent old women and eerily quiet children. The women picked through the remains of their homes and businesses, sobbing and crying, and occasionally exploding with joy if they came across some remembered object still reasonably whole.

A few buildings were intact, not many, and a number were still standing despite missing a wall or two, a roof perhaps.

We thought the town was secure, the enemy long gone. We were over-confident and that error will follow me to my grave. And one far worse. Because it was my responsibility, and mine alone. I was in charge of a small platoon. We'd fought bitterly to get to this miserable village, almost certainly no more interesting alive than it was dead. I had lost three men. One dead, another wounded—he'd stepped on a landmine and lost most of his foot—the third assigned to take the wounded fellow back to the Field Surgical Unit we'd passed a few hours previously. Out of the dust and the rubble we saw the reflection of ourselves, another Canadian unit, also short-manned, also parched, frightened, and yet much too cocky.

We met in the town square with a good deal of backslapping and handshakes. The old women didn't even look up although the children danced around, some trying to speak English, thanking us for saving them from the Germans and begging for candy and cigarettes at the same time.

The first bullet caught Corporal MacGregor right between the eyes. None of us knew what had happened for a few seconds. MacGregor's face burst into a red fountain and he sort of crumpled to the ground. A German sniper, of course. We couldn't see him, but another bullet hit the ground right behind Ralph, Lieutenant Madison, Moira's brother, my friend, and the leader of the platoon we'd met in the ruined palazzo. The women were screaming and the children crying. I remember wanting to yell at them all to shut up. To give me peace and quiet in which to think.

But Ralph shouted that everyone was to go into the big house across the square. He called to the old women and the children and urged them to follow us. He yelled at them in French, which of course they didn't understand. He grabbed at a little girl and dragged her by one skinny arm. Her grandmother followed. Maybe it was her mother, who could tell, the way the war had aged these women? And her companions followed her.

The house had once belonged to an influential family. The back wall was blown out and the interior stuffed with rubble, but there were still some fine pieces of furniture more or less intact and a couple of nice paintings on the remaining walls. I remember looking at those paintings. They might have been old masters, but what did I know? I was surprised that the Germans had left them behind. They took everything else that wasn't nailed down. As well as a great deal that was, the bastards. There was an enormous black grand piano in the room, placed against the back wall that was no more. It looked to be in such perfect condition that it could have been placed directly onto the stage at Carnegie Hall or some such place. A light coating of dust, but otherwise the piano wasn't touched. Not a scratch on it. Sunlight flooded in through the non-existent wall, and threw a beam of light against that damned piano, catching every particle of dust in a golden halo.

My wife loves piano music. I won't allow one into our house. She begs me to take her to a concert, but I won't go with her. So she goes with one of her sisters or a friend and they all laugh at what an uncultured boor I am. But I've never been able to look at a piano again, after that day.

Once we made it inside, the sniper stopped shooting. No need to waste bullets. We ran though the house to the back. There was a large garden, with a beautiful statue in the center of what had once been a fountain, now full of rubble instead of water. The rest of the garden was nothing but weeds, although I could make out the neatly laid rows of the formal flowerbeds, choked with more rubble. The garden was contained by high wall: a thick stone wall, six feet high or more, running completely around the back yard. Unbelievably, amongst all this destruction, that dammed wall didn't have a mark on it. Private Turnbull laughed and said that if Hitler could get hold of that wall we would never get to Berlin. He was a good man, Turnbull. He would laugh at anything. He cheered the other men up no end.

Ralph Madison made an attempt to get to the wall. He stepped out into the garden. Nothing. He went a bit further, and then dashed across the ruined garden. A line of bullets followed him and the snipers forced him back into the house. There was more than one of them, and at least one was high up in the tower in the center of the town. The Italians have a name for that type of tower, but I don't remember it now.

So there we were, two platoons, undermanned by a large margin, two old hags in black rags, moaning and making the sign of the cross over their chests, one younger woman we had at first taken to be older because she was dressed the same as the grandmas, and three filthy, frightened children.

Ralph sent a couple of his men upstairs to see what was there. Nothing, they reported back. Not even a roof.

So there we sat. In a luxurious Italian home that was only missing a roof, a back wall, and furniture to be a proper delight. With six Italian civilians who, judging by the look on their faces, regarded us as the source of all their problems.

Ralph assigned men to the windows, to make sure the Germans didn't try to sneak up on us. "We'll be out of here at nightfall," he said. His voice was full of confidence. It always was. The women didn't understand what he said, but his tone settled some of their anxiety.

One of the little street urchins in particular seemed to like Ralph. It was a girl, of course, and she climbed onto his lap and fingered his tunic buttons. He patted her dirty dark head and whispered soft words into her ear and after an initial objection her grandmother, if that was who one of the older women was, relaxed.

I've promised that I'll give you an honest account of what happened that hot, dusty day in Italy. And so I will. You may have noticed that I have talked about what Ralph said, and

Ralph did, but nothing of myself. And that is, simply, because I did nothing. I did nothing but sit in the corner, with my rifle clutched to my knees. I would let Ralph take care of everything. My men watched me out of the corner of their eyes, but I knew that everything would be all right. Because Ralph Madison was there. The men soon turned to him and started taking their orders from him, even my men, and I was glad to be left alone, in my corner. I found a cushion, soft, the color of fresh cream, and amazingly enough somewhat clean. A cushion that must have sat on a settee at one time, probably graced by the thin bottoms of beautiful Italian noble women. I clutched it to my chest, on top of my rifle, and let Ralph decide what we were to do.

We waited until nightfall. No one said much. One of the old women started to wail until the younger one snapped at her. Ralph let the child with the huge dark eyes play with his buttons and when she tired of that game he turned out his pockets and let her go through what she found there. The other children were two boys, a bit older than the girl. They were getting restless, wanting to explore the house, but held back by the sharp hiss of mother and grandmothers. We'd been told that the Germans left mines behind. Everywhere they'd been.

"Do you like my sister, Stoughton?" Ralph said. It was early dusk, the shadows lengthening outside the (empty) windows. Almost time to go.

"Miss Madison seems like a lovely young lady," I replied. What else to say?

"She won't have you, you know. She's got you pegged for a gold digger. She's very perceptive that way."

I flushed and cuddled my pillow closer. The rifle was in the way and I pushed it aside. "I certainly don't know what you mean." The men were listening and not even pretending not to.

"I have two other sisters. Not as feisty as Moira, by any means. But one of them is somewhat pretty, they tell me. And a good deal more malleable."

Private Turnbull laughed and nudged the man beside him. He was one of Ralph's men, so I never did learn his name.

"I like 'em feisty, Lieutenant," Turnbull said. "How's about I meet your sister?"

Ralph laughed and the girl on his lap laughed also. She didn't know what was funny, but if her hero laughed, so would she. "If you can charm her, you can have her, soldier. But she'll take no nonsense. So you'll have your work cut out for you."

The younger woman swore at us in a stream of Italian. What brought that on, I didn't know. Perhaps she understood a bit of English and didn't like the way Ralph and the soldiers were talking. She sat down at the piano and fingered the keys. To the surprise of everyone the notes rang pure and clear. Her long, thin fingers danced expertly over a light scale. I closed my eyes and cuddled my pillow. My mother had played the piano. It reminded me so much of home. The sound echoed around the standing walls and flew through the open roof.

The black piano, so perfect it could have played at Carnegie Hall, exploded like the opening of the jaws of hell. Black and white keys flew everywhere, tiny bits of shrapnel in their own right. The woman didn't move. She looked at her hands. Only they weren't there.

She screamed, long and loud and piercing. The old women screamed, and the boys ran in circles screaming, and the girl screamed as she was bounced out of Ralph's lap as he leapt to his feet and rushed to the woman's side.

Mercifully, she took one look at her bloody stumps and fainted dead away.

As if they'd heard the booby trap going off, the Germans launched an artillery barrage moments after. The town was exploding all around us, and the remains of the back wall of the house burst into flames. Unfortunately there were still remnants of fine curtains handing in shreds over the garden windows. They caught fire in an instant.

Private Turnbull was the first out the door. He was struck down with one shot and collapsed on top of the rubble at the front door, the side of his head missing. He wouldn't be courting Nursing Sister Moira Madison after all.

I have very little recall of what happened then. Ralph ripped scraps of fabric off a decaying tablecloth and wrapped the woman's hands, the ones that were there no longer. Men ran for the back garden, but they were cut down quickly. The house was burning; the ancient timber and precious carpets left behind by the Nazis welcomed the greedy fire with enthusiasm.

The old women were still screaming, but trying to hide the children in their voluminous black dresses. Ralph's little girl-friend clung to his leg, sobbing hysterically as he tried to gently pry her fingers off his pants and tend to the wounded woman at the same time.

That's the one thing I remember well about that horrible few minutes. How calm Ralph Madison was. He didn't upset the child any further by yelling at her, or pushing her away. An incredibly perfunctory job of bandaging done, he ran to the window, dragging the sobbing child behind.

He issued orders quickly. Two men took up positions at the window and tried to get the German snipers in their sights. The others were sent to fight the fire, one to continue tending the injured woman and drag her away from the approaching inferno. The back half of the house, as well as the staircase, was in flames. One of the Italian boys grabbed my pillow and used it to beat at the fire. Little fool. Couldn't he see that we were all doomed?

They were making some progress. The fire was retreating against the combined onslaught of our men and the old women and children. One of the men yelled in victory as he hit a sniper concealed in the remains of an upper floor of the building across the town square at the moment the German settled for a direct shot.

We would have made it. Ralph Madison and the remains of his (and my) platoon, two elderly black-clad Italian women with all the energy and hatred of demons direct from hell, a group of children, and a woman out cold. We would have made it to safety, had the Germans not decided this would be a good time to recapture the town.

One of my men, I don't remember his name now, pulled me to my feet. "For God's sake," he hissed, his eyes as dark and thin as those of a serpent. "Be a man, Lieutenant. Hell's waiting for us all, but there's a special level reserved down there for cowards."

I looked at him. He was a huge, ugly farm boy. Tiny black eyes, nose as long as a carrot, arms and legs that wandered all over the place when he walked. He never could stay in formation on parade.

He spat in my face.

He picked up my rifle from where it had fallen and shoved it into my arms. I wiped the spit off my cheek and straightened up, trying to pretend I had some measure of dignity. "No need to be insulting, soldier. Time to teach these Jerries a lesson, eh?"

He spat again, fortunately this time aiming at my feet.

One of the Italian boys, Christ, he couldn't have been more than ten, had skipped out into the enemy fire and scooped up Turnbull's rifle. He lugged it back into the building and smiled at me, muttering incomprehensible words as he brandished the weapon, trying—and failing—to look fierce.

Oh, God, I thought. The damned fool of a boy expects me to do something.

The fire was gaining on us. The back way was impassable. The roar of the flames and stifling smoke filled our world. The old women alternately prayed and howled in terror, the injured woman moaned softly as she struggled towards consciousness, the boys screamed their defiance, and the girl looked at Ralph with wide-eyed awe. Our men were ready, balancing their rifles, waiting for Ralph to give the word. No one paid any attention to me.

"We have to go," Ralph said, his voice low and steady. He spoke in French to the boy with the rifle. Of course he didn't understand the words, but the child knew their intent. "Keep firing as we move," Ralph said. "Make them keep their heads, and their guns, down. You there, what's your name?"

"Jones, sir.

"I want you to carry the injured woman, Jones. Can you do that?"

"Yes, sir."

"If you can, try to keep something covering her wounds. But don't stop to do it."

"Yes, sir."

"McNeill, Watson, and Kowalski. Surround the women and kids. Drag them out of here if you have to. And protect Jones. I'll be in front. The rest of you spread out behind us. Are we ready?" He looked at each one of us in turn, as if the strength of his will alone was enough to carry us through the gates of hell.

The old women clutched their shawls and murmured prayers under their breath, but they knew what was happening and by the tilt of their heads and thrust of their chins I knew they'd follow Ralph Madison right past those gates.

He pried the girl's fingers off his pants and passed her hand to one of the women. A real man doesn't go into battle with an undernourished five-year-old female clinging to his leg.

The heat from the fire was all around us. Another portion of the ceiling collapsed in an inferno of screaming wood and howling flames. We had to leave by the front door, and leave now, if we were to leave at all.

Ralph and some of the unassigned soldiers went first, followed by his phalanx: three solders surrounding the women and children, Private Jones carrying the woman with no hands as if she were a huge rag doll, and the boy, gripping the unfamiliar rifle, about to be inaugurated as a man. Last, and most certainly least—me.

There were more of them than we'd expected. Many more, coming at us from all sides. As well as the snipers we knew about, a new group had burrowed into the rubble across the street.

A bullet caught Ralph full in the chest. He went down. His girlfriend wrenched herself out of her grandmother's grip and collapsed to her knees at his side, keening like generations uncounted of women before her.

I screamed in terror. If Ralph was dead, what hope remained for the rest of us? I fell, collapsing onto the two black-shrouded women as I went down. One of them was stretching out her hand towards the girl.

The men stood their ground, some through sheer bravery, some because what else could they do—the building behind them was completely enveloped in flames. They might have made it, had they not gone back for the old women and the children, overcome by paralyzing terror. The boy had thrown away his rifle, and like the child he was he cried his fear into his grandmother's chest.

The girl caught a bullet in her arm. Open mouthed, she stared at the blossoming red stain. Watson scooped her up. But he stood immobile, the sobbing body gasping in his arms. He didn't know where to go.

Jones made a break for the right, still carrying the wounded woman. The Germans let them go.

I heard the rapid rattle of gunfire and then I saw the blessed sight of a group of Canadians advancing towards us. Moving cautiously, they crouched in the shelter of blasted buildings and mountains of rubble, but kept up a continual stream of fire against the German in the tower.

The sniper must have been leaning over, trying to get a good shot—heroic idiot—when the bullet found him. He drifted to the ground, turning over and over as he passed through the air, only to hit the ground with a dull, boring thud. The life force exited his broken body with a sigh and a whoosh.

The older Italian boy cheered.

Then our soldiers were all around us, bending over the dead, comforting the women, praising the children for their courage. Other than Jones, who staggered back to us under the weight of his now conscious, screaming burden, I was the only man left standing.

I don't really remember what I thought when I realized that. Ralph was trying to breathe through a wound in his chest, black blood soaking the front of his shirt.

Watson lay over the girl. Dead. He'd provided a shield for her body with his own. She struggled up from underneath him and fell to Ralph's side sobbing her heart out, until someone pulled her away and gathered her up. The men were all dead or dying, except for Jones, who watched me with angry eyes as the medics crouched over the woman with no hands.

Ralph was still alive. Gasping pain with every breath, his life-blood soaking the ground around him. Our army had retaken the town; the enemy was well out of the way. An ambulance made it into town, the bright Red Cross a beacon of hope against the dark masses of rubble. Quickly they bundled Ralph into it. His admirer tried to follow, but strong arms held her back until a medic reached her side.

The ambulance pulled away. One of the old women grabbed me by my arm and broke into a stream of Italian.

One of our rescuers spoke a fragment of broken Italian. In later years, when I had the presence of mind to wonder why I was never exposed, I realized that the boy thought his command of the language was much better than it actually was. Otherwise, surely he would have asked for help with the translating. Instead he communicated with the two old women by himself, nodding furiously as they waved their arms and babbled into the wind.

"She thanks you," the would-be interpreter told me. "She praises the greatness of the Canadian army and all the men who have come over the seas to fight for freedom against the forces of tyranny."

I had my doubts that the old woman said any such thing. They would have been better off left to escape from the rubble of their homes by themselves, rather than dragged into a death trap by the heroic Ralph Madison.

Had I not been standing quite so incredulous at that moment, the bright light of a camera bulb going off would have had me diving for cover.

The man behind the camera stepped forward. He was dressed in army fatigues, but with no emblem or rank or division. He gripped my hand tightly.

"It's a wonderful thing you've done here, Lieutenant." His uniform was Canadian but his accent pure Dublin. He turned and nodded to the group of civilians, sitting on a hill of rubble. A Canadian medic was wrapping the girl's arm in lengths of bandages. Jones followed wordlessly as the woman with no hands was carried into a second ambulance. Neither of the old women or the children seemed much concerned about her. Perhaps they didn't know her.

The two old women sat on either side of the little girl. They were quiet now. Stoic almost. Passing their strength through to her. The older boy sulked at having had his rifle taken away.

"Canada won't forget what happened here today." The newspaperman grinned at me, and scribbled in his notebook.

I hitched a ride with the next ambulance leaving for the FSU where they'd taken Ralph. By the time I got there he was dead.

For some reason they decided I was a hero. The fool of an interpreter had misunderstood the old women's mutterings, and then the newspaperman's photo and story got into print, and from then on events had a life of their own.

There was certainly a hero that day, but it was Ralph Madison, not me. All of them, in fact, were heroes. I'll never forget Jones, carrying that woman as tenderly if she were his own sister or mother. Watson, falling on the little girl. All of them were heroes.

But not me.

I took their George Cross, not knowing how to say no.

I wondered why I never heard from Jones, the only other Canadian survivor, about what had happened. Found out a long time later that he'd been killed a few days after. The younger woman lived, at least to get past the casualty clearing station. Though what kind of a life she would have—an Italian peasant woman who could play the piano but had no hands—I never wanted to consider.

When the war ended I wrote to Ralph's parents in Toronto. They were delighted to hear from me. They invited me up to their family cottage on Lake Muskoka and even sent me a train ticket.

I swear to God, I actually expected that the sister I'd met in England and then again in Italy, Moira, the Nursing Sister, would be there. I planned to tell her what had really happened. I rehearsed my words all the way up north on the train. She would understand. How fear can turn a man's bowels to ice water so that he can't move. And then how humiliation makes him stand silent and ashamed when he should speak out. I wanted only to pour myself on her good graces and tell her that her brother was the hero, not I.

But Moira wasn't there. Still in Europe, her mother told me with a sigh. No time for her family any more. Always such a selfish girl.

Perhaps even more than that day in Italy, I'm ashamed that I allowed Mrs. Madison's bitter words to pass without comment.

I had never in all my life been to a place as beautiful as the Madison summer home. After the unspeakable horrors of Italy, and then France, I truly had found peace.

Moira wasn't there, but Ralph's other sisters were. Maeve and Megan.

I loved Megan from the moment I saw her, and I don't want you to think otherwise.

She was all that I had longed for, in England, in Italy, and later in France: pure and lovely and untouched by human tragedy. She would never become, I swore right there by the side of that sparkling blue lake, an old woman covered in a black shawl scratching through rubble in search of the remnants of her life.

I loved Megan, and I love her still. And she has always loved me. Her family welcomed me because they thought me to be someone I was not.

But not my Megan.

Chapter Forty-five

The coroner's inquest was quick and decisive. Accidental death, she pronounced, and that was the end of it. Megan's body was released for burial, and the family prepared to gather at their home in Toronto.

Once again Lizzie pulled out bread and sandwich ingredients and set about preparing lunch for the journey. Moira would travel to the city, but she insisted that she could stand to be away from her own home for two nights only. She would attend the funeral, but then return north the next day. Megan's son, Charles, was dispatched to fetch Moira along with Ruth and Amber. Phoebe had already left with Charles, her grandfather. Her parents had cut short their Hawaiian vacation to get back for Megan's funeral.

Charles the younger was practically the image of his father and namesake. The same emaciated body, long gangly limbs, face bones so prominent that the flesh appeared to have been slapped on as an afterthought. But he had none of his father's reserve, and he greeted Lizzie and Alan like old friends, and shook Elaine's hand with warm enthusiasm.

"I'm sorry for your loss, Mr. Stoughton." Elaine said the time-honored words.

"Thank you. But Mr. Stoughton's my father. I'm Charlie."

It was early afternoon when he arrived, and he accepted a beer in the kitchen before packing the car up and heading back to Toronto. Lizzie's sandwiches were piled in the center of the old oak table, and the big teapot was full. Hamlet and Ophelia lay on the floor, edging forward just in case someone dropped a scrap or two. Moira and Ruth joined Lizzie, Alan, Amber, Elaine, and Charlie at the table. From next door they could hear the sounds of hammering as a work crew finished replacing the fire-damaged roof of the old guesthouse, now storage shed.

Footsteps on the stone path, the excited babble of a child, and the kitchen door flew open to admit Willow and the rest of the islanders.

Lizzie got up to make another round of sandwiches and more places were made at the table.

"Well, we're off, Moira," Kyle said. "I'm glad we caught you. We can't thank you enough for your hospitality."

"My pleasure."

"If not Lizzie's," Rachel said.

"I live only to serve," Lizzie answered, placing a glass of milk in Willow's hands.

Charlie was introduced and heart-felt sympathies expressed all around.

"Where's Dave?" Elaine asked.

"Said he's not coming with us," Kyle said.

Amber looked up, sharply. "What do you mean, he's not going with you? Where's he going?"

Kyle mumbled into his sandwich and the women fussed over their own food.

Charlie drained his glass, refused a refill, and pushed his chair back. "Time to be on the road. I'll go and pack the van. I brought the van. Better to get the wheelchair in, Aunt Moira."

"I'll give you a hand." Alan tossed a crust of bread to Ophelia, earning him a dark look from Lizzie and an equally fierce one from Hamlet.

"Have you got your bags ready, Ruth?" Elaine asked. "I'll help you bring them down."

"Thank you." Ruth treated Elaine with brittle reserve; Elaine sensed that jealousy still tugged at her, but the open hostility had faded.

Moira's chair was bundled into the back of the van, and she was settled stiffly in the front, seatbelt tucked firmly across her concave chest. Ruth sat in the back. Alan, Lizzie, and Elaine stood in the doorway, preparing to wave goodbye. The dogs had been locked in the kitchen for fear they would try to follow Moira all the way to Toronto. The islanders had their own transportation packed up and ready. To no one's surprise, it was an old Volkswagen Kombi. The type that had taken many hippies down the road to Woodstock.

Alan had run his hands lovingly over the surface. "You keep this in good shape, buddy."

"It's my baby," Kyle said, proudly. "It's got to see Rachel and Willow to the West Coast. We'll drop Karen and Jessica in Toronto first."

"Good luck."

They gripped hands tightly.

"Where the heck is Amber?" Charlie leaned on the horn.

"I'll see if I can find her," Elaine said.

She heard voices in the kitchen. Sure enough, Dave had appeared. He gripped Amber's arm and both their faces were tense and red. A duffel bag lay at his feet.

"Everything okay here?" Elaine asked, smiling brightly as people usually do when coming across an uncomfortable situation.

"Fine," Dave said. "This is a private conversation."

"Actually, Elaine." Amber pulled her arm away. Finger marks were outlined against the pale skin. "Dave was just on his way."

"Fuck off, lady."

"Pardon me," Elaine said, "I didn't quite get that."

"Please, Dave. Don't make this too difficult. I'm telling you to leave," Amber said. "I'm going to my great aunt's funeral and I'm not coming back."

"If you don't want to walk to Toronto, Dave, you'd best be moving. The van is about to leave," Elaine said.

His look was so full of venom she almost took a step back.

"Amber, do you want me to call Alan and your uncle Charlie?"

"No need. I'm sure Dave understands me. Don't you, Dave? I didn't intend for you to think that I was inviting you to live here. I'm sorry if you did. I'm going home."

"All right. Give me your number, and I'll call you."

"No, Dave, I don't want you to contact me, please. Can we just go now?"

"You bitch, you said...."

"I wanted to like you, really I did." The tears streamed down her face.

Dave's hands were clenched into fists at his side and the blood vessels in his face were about to pop. Elaine flexed her fingers and prepared for a confrontation. Like she could do anything.

"But I can't deal with all the anger you have inside. Against my family. Even against me. You've had a hard life. But I can't excuse it any more."

Amber turned to Elaine, her chest heaving with great sobs. Her pretty face had turned ugly, soaked with tears and mucus. "He called Great-Aunt Megan 'a crazy old bitch who deserved to die because she was a waste of space.' And then he said my grandma would be next. Go away, go away." Amber ran out of the room.

"Time to be on your way, Dave. If you're lucky, your friends will offer you a ride. Though why they bother is beyond me."

"Bus is leaving, man." Kyle crossed the room and picked up Dave's duffel bag. "If you want a lift I can take you as far as T.O. But then I got places to go." He held out his spare hand. "Come on, man. You don't want to walk."

Dave threw Elaine a venomous look, shoved Kyle's hand out of the way, and stalked out of the kitchen.

She smiled at Kyle. "Thanks."

"Our problem. We brought him."

By the time they were back outside, Amber had settled in the back seat of the van beside Ruth. She had stopped crying and stared into her lap. Dave climbed into the Kombi, his face like a thundercloud.

The engines started almost at the same time and with much waving and tooting of horns they drove down the long driveway. Willow's little face was pushed up against the back window. She waved almost as enthusiastically as did Moira in return.

Chapter Forty-six

At long last Elaine had been invited up to the artist's studio on the third floor. A recent renovation, the windows stretched from floor to ceiling, pure glass panes filling most of one side of the building. The soft northern light streamed in. Far below, specks of sunlight sparkled gold on the blue lake. The forest stretched to the horizon, brown and naked, its brief splendor spent for another year. Lizzie sat on the dock, her bare feet dangling in the cold water while Ophelia snoozed at her side.

The studio was large and airy, not much in the way of furniture but crammed with blank canvas, finished paintings, sealed crates, and shelves of paint tubes, brushes, and turpentine. A single sink and drying rack lined the back wall.

"Moira gave you all this?" Elaine said, when she finally found her voice.

"She did indeed. She's a wonderful woman. She knew my grandparents in the war. Over in England. Burt and Betty Jones, my mother's parents. They owned a shop in the town near where she was stationed."

"Bramshott."

"That's right. My mother was in an accident one day, so the family story goes, in the early days of the war. She was hit by a Canadian soldier driving his motorcycle too fast down the country lanes. Apparently Moira happened on the scene and kept Mom from bleeding to death until they got her to the hospital."

"What a great story." A painting off in the corner caught Elaine's eye. It was a silhouette of a wheelchair from the back, the artist watching the occupant as she watched a group of children and dogs clambering on the rocks.

"My parents immigrated to Canada after the war. My mother was a nurse, and many years later she ran into Moira at a convention of some sort. They recognized each other and there you have it."

"Where are your parents now?"

Alan smiled. "Still going strong. They were invited for Thanksgiving, but they don't travel much any more. They're saving their strength for the weekend of the gallery opening. You'll meet them then."

She bent her head to examine the room. This was where Alan had assembled all his work, in preparation for the gallery showing. Most of the paintings were packed into crates, awaiting transport, but a few still lined the walls. As Elaine picked her way among the canvases she realized that the painting in the dark hall represented but a sample of what this man had to offer.

"You love it up here, don't you?" she said, bending close to examine a watercolor of a young woman caught in the act of diving off a wooden dock, into a lake turned orange by the setting summer sun.

"What was your first clue?" Alan's deep voice was filled with a smile.

"I'm psychic that way."

He stepped behind her and wrapped one arm around her waist. He kissed the side of her neck and allowed the other hand to dance down her spine.

She shivered and settled back into the embrace. He turned her around and kissed her deeply. Elaine lifted her arms and wrapped them around his neck.

Far across the lake a loon sounded. Hamlet and Ophelia ran through the woods, barking and scattering wildlife before them, and Lizzie pushed herself to her feet, knowing that it was time to go in and start dinner.

◇◇◇

Moira returned from the funeral spent and drawn. But she got up early the next morning and was immediately on the phone in her study. When placing the call, she shooed them all, even Ruth, outside.

Shortly before lunch Moira called Alan in and told him to prepare for visitors.

Lizzie was stacking the lunch dishes in the dishwasher, while Elaine sipped the last of her tea as she jotted thoughts down in her notebook, when they heard cars pulling into the driveway. The two women wandered out to see what was happening. Moira sat on the back step, Ruth standing stoically behind her chair.

Constable D'Mosca clambered out of the leading truck. His companions were dressed in heavy work wear. They had a dog with them, a huge, drooling German shepherd pulling eagerly at his leash. The men donned plastic gloves, hoisted shovels, and followed Alan down the path to the boathouse and past the end of the flagstone path into the woods. Hamlet and Ophelia were confined to the kitchen, protesting the invasion of their territory, by canine and human, for all they were worth.

Elaine accompanied the men as far as the first white pine, but then she turned and fled back up the path to the house. Ruth was settling Moira into her study. The book of choice today was a Stephen King. An odd choice for the English-police-procedural-loving Moira.

Moira turned to the bookmarked page and didn't look up. "I think you should be there, Elaine. For your own peace of mind, if nothing else."

"Is your mind so settled, Moira?"

A bony finger marked the place and the brown eyes stared at her. "Oh, yes, my dear. It certainly is. And I'd like it very much, if you would represent me."

"Then I'll go."

"I should have done this many years ago. I suppose I simply wanted to pretend that there was nothing there. That nothing had ever happened."

When Elaine arrived at the clearing in the woods, two men were digging as several others stood by in silence, watching. Alan's face was drawn and tense. He tried to smile at Elaine but the smile failed. The day was cold, it was almost winter after all, but D'Mosca had taken off his jacket and sweated profusely into his uniform shirt.

The men stopped digging. They looked at Alan and shrugged. They watched the dog scratching through the piles of newly decaying leaves and long-resting soil.

Elaine dropped to the ground and snuggled up against the old building, digging her butt into a patch of soft green moss. She felt nothing threatening, and her back needed the support. A hint of cologne lingered on the air, but it wasn't fresh, not overwhelming. Rather like a distant memory, the way a room would hold the scent of a woman's perfume or a man's cigar long after the party was over, and everyone had gone up to bed.

"Not there." She pointed. "Over there. Alan, the dog is in the wrong spot. Under that jack pine, the big one. Tell them to dig there."

He directed the skeptical men and crouched down in front of her, taking her face between his hands. "What do you know, Elaine?"

"Nothing. But they're in the wrong place. I don't want them wasting their time."

They had dug down about a foot when every hair along the cadaver dog's back shot upright. He ran to the excavation, dodging between the shovels, and scratched at the dirt.

"This is it. I think we have something here." The men bent their backs into the effort.

Minutes passed. The dog alternately dug and paced, caught up in the excitement. Locked in the house, Hamlet and Ophelia howled their frustration. Alan glanced over his shoulder at Elaine. She nodded and he grabbed a spare shovel.

She never saw what they found. But the digging stopped as if by a signal and the men stepped back. Those who had been standing silent, watching, stepped forward. They carried a heavy bag. A body bag. Elaine had heard that horrible expression during a news commentary on the First Gulf War, many years ago.

Alan stood in front of her, blocking her view. "Can I take you back to the house, Elaine?"

She raised one hand and allowed herself to be pulled to her feet. "Yes, please. I think we should tell Moira, don't you?"

Alan touched Elaine's forehead with his. "Yes, we should."

Moira Madison looked out the study window at the view she loved most in all the world, but for once she scarcely noticed it. She'd never sensed anything unusual near the old servants' cabin, but she knew that some did. On the day after the family received the news of Ralph's death, the day her husband, Augustus, died, Moira's grandmother, Elizabeth, had issued firm orders that the cabin was to be permanently sealed and the building and grounds left unattended. Rumor and superstition grew in the family, as they were sure to, and almost sixty years after Elizabeth's death, her instructions remained enforced.

Until today. When the men had finished their work, Moira would have the old building torn down and the woods cleared. And in the spring they'd build a new cabin on the spot, something welcoming and cheerful, with wide windows and a wraparound porch and a nice woodland garden. A guest house for the next generation of Madisons. Or maybe a summer place for Alan and Elaine.

Moira thought about her grandmother, and wondered what the old woman knew. Or what perhaps she merely suspected in the dark recesses of her mind.

For Moira was sure that Augustus Madison had killed Amy Murphy, and used the guilt-stricken Ralph to help him cover up the crime. Before the war, when they all learned far too much about death and dying, Ralph would have been unlikely to be aware that when the heart isn't pumping blood, a body doesn't bleed very much. Whether Augustus knew anything about medicine or not, he would never have trusted his fate and his reputation to a country coroner or village family doctor.

Moira's grandfather was a tough old man, none tougher. Ralph's death would have been a blow, but how much of a shock could it have been: all over Canada, all over the world, for many long years families were constantly braced for tragic news. Moira wondered why Augustus' heart, as unbending as the rest of him, had given way so quickly.

When he was walking in the woods.

Alone.

Perhaps Amy Murphy wrote the end of Augustus Madison's story after all.

From the hallway she heard Alan's voice, followed by Elaine's light murmur. They had come to tell her what the men had found.

Moira bent her head over her book and prepared to look surprised.

To receive a free catalog of Poisoned Pen Press titles, please contact us in one of the following ways:

Phone: 1-800-421-3976
Facsimile: 1-480-949-1707
Email: info@poisonedpenpress.com
Website: www.poisonedpenpress.com

Poisoned Pen Press
6962 E. First Ave. Ste. 103
Scottsdale, AZ 85251